THE
ALEXANDRIA
CONNECTION

Adrian d'Hagé was educated at North Sydney Boys High School and the Royal Military College Duntroon (Applied Science). Graduating into the Intelligence Corps, he served as a platoon commander in Vietnam, where he was awarded the Military Cross. His military service included command of an infantry battalion, director of joint operations and head of defence public relations. In 1994 Adrian was made a Member of the Order of Australia. In his last appointment, he headed defence planning for counter-terrorism security for the Sydney Olympics, including security against chemical, biological and nuclear threats.

Adrian holds an honours degree in theology, entering as a committed Christian but graduating 'with no fixed religion'. In 2009 he completed a Bachelor of Applied Science (Dean's Award) in oenology or wine chemistry at Charles Sturt University, and he has successfully sat the Austrian Government exams for ski instructor, 'Schilehrer Anwärter'. He is presently a research scholar, tutor and part-time lecturer at the Centre for Arab and Islamic Studies (Middle East and Central Asia) at ANU. His doctorate is entitled 'The Influence of Religion on US Foreign Policy in the Middle East'.

ALSO BY ADRIAN d'HAGÉ

The Omega Scroll
The Beijing Conspiracy
The Maya Codex
The Inca Prophecy

ADRIAN d'HAGÉ

THE ALEXANDRIA CONNECTION

MICHAEL JOSEPH
an imprint of
PENGUIN BOOKS

MICHAEL JOSEPH

Published by the Penguin Group
Penguin Group (Australia)
707 Collins Street, Melbourne, Victoria 3008, Australia
(a division of Penguin Australia Pty Ltd)
Penguin Group (USA) Inc.
375 Hudson Street, New York, New York 10014, USA
Penguin Group (Canada)
90 Eglinton Avenue East, Suite 700, Toronto, Canada ON M4P 2Y3
(a division of Penguin Canada Books Inc.)
Penguin Books Ltd
80 Strand, London WC2R 0RL England
Penguin Ireland
25 St Stephen's Green, Dublin 2, Ireland
(a division of Penguin Books Ltd)
Penguin Books India Pvt Ltd
11 Community Centre, Panchsheel Park, New Delhi 110 017, India
Penguin Group (NZ)
67 Apollo Drive, Rosedale, Auckland 0632, New Zealand
(a division of Penguin New Zealand Pty Ltd)
Penguin Books (South Africa) (Pty) Ltd
Rosebank Office Park, Block D, 181 Jan Smuts Avenue, Parktown North, Johannesburg 2196, South Africa
Penguin (Beijing) Ltd
7F, Tower B, Jiaming Center, 27 East Third Ring Road North, Chaoyang District, Beijing 100020, China

Penguin Books Ltd, Registered Offices: 80 Strand, London WC2R 0RL, England

First published by Penguin Group (Australia), 2014

1 3 5 7 9 10 8 6 4 2

Text copyright © Adrian d'Hagé 2014

The moral right of the author has been asserted

All rights reserved. Without limiting the rights under copyright reserved above, no part of this publication
may be reproduced, stored in or introduced into a retrieval system, or transmitted, in any form or by any
means (electronic, mechanical, photocopying, recording or otherwise), without the prior written permission
of both the copyright owner and the above publisher of this book.

Cover and text design by Adam Laszczuk © Penguin Group (Australia)
Cover photograph: running man © Mark Owen/Trevillion Images;
statue image: Jean-Pierre Lescourret/Getty images; temple image: Michael Snell/Getty Images
Typeset in 12.5/18.5 Granjon
Printed and bound in Australia by Griffin Press,
an accredited ISO AS/NZS 14001 Environmental Management Systems printer.

National Library of Australia
Cataloguing-in-Publication data:

d'Hagé, Adrian, author
The Alexandria connection / Adrian d'Hagé
9780143799504 (paperback)
Art thefts – Investigatio – Fiction
Manuscripts (Papyri) – Fiction
Nature – Effect of human beings on – Fiction

A823.4

penguin.com.au

For Jacqueline

PROLOGUE

Flying near its ceiling, the CH-47 Chinook was touching 140 knots. Captain Brett Bestic had positioned himself just forward of the starboard door gunner. He leaned on the backs of the seats of the pilot and co-pilot, and scanned the dark valleys below through his night-vision goggles. A member of the famed SEAL team six, the dual Navy Cross winner was on his fifth tour of duty in Afghanistan, but he had promised his wife, Sally, this would be his last. His son Ryan would turn four next month, and Sally was right. Ryan hardly knew he had a father. It was time to pursue a new career and leave the fighting to the young ones coming on. He had done his bit. Far below, the distinctive beat of the Chinook was faint, but it still carried clearly to the mountains above the Korengal River.

'The Infidel! He is coming!' The young al-Qaeda commander quickly extracted from its box the Scorpion surface-to-air missile that had been delivered by mule, only that morning, and he moved to a position behind a pile of rocks. Both he and his number two were already proficient on the Stinger, which the United States had provided when Russia had invaded Afghanistan, and although the Scorpion was a next-generation missile, it had taken less than two hours to master the new technology. The commander locked the battery coolant unit, or BCU, into the grip stock, to provide power for the missile's pre-flight systems and argon gas to cool the infrared seeker system. He locked the sight assembly into position and pointed the launcher toward the sound of the approaching helicopter.

'He is flying very high,' the commander observed, engaging the safety and actuator switch, which in turn activated the BCU. He could hear the missile gyro systems spooling up, and he searched the sky with the system's thermal-imaging night sight. The Scorpion system was capable of detecting both fixed and rotary-winged aircraft well beyond the missile range of 14 000 feet.

'I have him!' The infrared acquisition signal beeped and the secondary signal vibrated against the young man's cheekbone. He un-caged the seeker, holding the switch down, and the signal was stronger still. The commander smiled grimly. The argon-cooled detector in the missile's seeker system had focused on the infrared energy of the Chinook. The young man held his breath to avoid the toxic fumes of the missile's rocket motor, and slowly squeezed the trigger.

The Scorpion launch rocket ignited in a blaze of fire and smoke, shooting the missile out of the launcher. Clear of the firing system, the dual thrust rocket motor lit and within seconds, the long, thin missile reached its cruising speed of over 2400 kilometres an hour. The passive infrared and ultraviolet sensor arrays in the missile nose cone tracked the Chinook, the computers continually anticipating the target's course and changing the missile's trajectory as it closed in on the aircraft at over Mach 2.

'Incoming!' the co-pilot called, but they were the last words the pilot and Captain Bestic heard. The highly classified Scorpion missile not only had a much longer range than the Stinger, its systems had been specifically designed to defeat the CMWS, or common missile warning system, fitted to Chinooks operating in Afghanistan. It was even capable of defeating the new advanced laser-jamming systems.

The Chinook from the 160th Special Operations Aviation Regiment exploded in a fireball of fuel, propelling aircraft, engine and body parts into the fiery night. They fell in a surreally gentle series of blazing arcs toward the dark mountains below.

1

ALEXANDRIA, EGYPT

Curtis O'Connor casually turned and searched both sides of Alexandria's Sidi al Mitwalli Street. Old habits died hard, even for CIA agents taking a break. The pedestrians were mainly Egyptian men and women, some wearing the hijab, others more Western in their dress. Since the street protests over the military's overthrow of Mohammed Morsi and the Muslim Brotherhood, hundreds of Egyptians had been killed by the military, and tourism was almost non-existent.

Tall, fit and solidly built, O'Connor's thick dark hair fell roughly into place. His face was tanned, and his blue eyes held an air of mischief, but that could be deceptive. Curtis O'Connor had one of the sharpest minds in the CIA.

'I love this place!' Aleta exclaimed, her long black hair shining in the sun and her dark eyes dancing with a sense of discovery. The renowned archaeologist had gained international acclaim when she, together with O'Connor, had unearthed the Maya Codex and the Inca's lost city of Paititi. Aleta and O'Connor wandered past Alexandria's wedge-shaped Attarine Mosque, its ornate minaret soaring above the bustling intersection of Sidi al-Mitwalli and Mesgued el Attarine streets. 'Did you know that mosque was once a Christian church dedicated to Saint Athanasius?'

'The fourth-century patriarch of Alexandria,' said O'Connor with a grin. It was a game they played, challenging one another's knowledge. 'Wasn't he the guy who got cross with people who denied the Trinity and the Christians' claim that Christ was God incarnate?'

'*Cross* doesn't quite cut it,' said Aleta. 'But religion can be such a crock ... Christ never uttered a word about the Trinity ... that "God the Father, God the Son, God the Holy Ghost" dogma. That was *our* invention.'

'Council of Nicaea, 325 AD,' O'Connor agreed, 'the three-in-one proposition.'

'We're a strange species,' Aleta mused, a thoughtful look on her oval face. They turned south, headed toward Souk el-Attarine, one of Alexandria's most famous markets where the stalls were filled with ornate brassware, carpets, antique furniture, *galabiyas* – the long traditional dress of the Nile Valley, spices, perfumes, gold, leather goods and *sheeshas* – the charcoal-burning devices characterised by a long hose through which flavoured tobacco smoke was drawn through a water jar. But for Aleta, this was no ordinary shopping expedition. Ever the archaeologist, she was on the lookout for documents and anything else that might shed light on the ancient Egyptian civilisation.

'One of my contacts put me on to an old stall in the market where they make papyrus,' she said. Made from the pith of a tall grass-like plant that grew in abundance in the Nile Delta, papyrus was a paper-like substance that had been used by the ancient Egyptians for centuries, dating back to around 3000 BC. 'A colleague of mine made a brief visit years ago, and he thought they might have some older documents,' Aleta added excitedly. A short while later they reached the souk, where the goods overflowed onto the narrow streets and alleys.

'In here,' said Aleta, disappearing into a narrow doorway. O'Connor checked the alley and followed her into the shop, the walls of which were festooned with hand-painted papyrus. The intricate designs included scarabs, the beetle-shaped amulets that were said to protect the ancient Egyptians from danger; Horus, the falcon-headed god of kings with his sacred eye; ankhs, the key of life; the funerary mask of Tutankhamun; the tree of life; and myriad other Egyptian motifs painted in bright blues, yellows, golds and blacks. Inside, a young girl wearing a dark blue hijab was making papyrus, an art as old as the pharaohs themselves. The girl flashed them a beckoning smile, and Aleta and O'Connor went over to her heavy wooden workbench.

'Your first time in Egypt?' the young girl asked, flashing them a warm smile.

'No, but it's good to be back,' said Aleta.

'Have you seen the papyrus-making?'

'No, I haven't actually,' Aleta lied easily, sensing the disappointment in the girl's voice. 'What's your name?'

'My name is Aliaa.' Her dark eyes mirrored the warmth of her smile, and she picked up a long, thin-stemmed papyrus reed.

'This is the papyrus plant that grows along the banks of the Nile,' she said. 'It was holy to the ancient Egyptians, firstly because of the flower on the top, which looks like the rays of the sun and is used for making perfume; and secondly, because the triangular stem is the same shape as the Pyramids.'

Aliaa picked up a knife, cut the stem into 20-centimetre lengths and deftly sliced the pith of the reed into thin slivers. 'Once we've cut the plant, we need to squeeze out the excess water and sugar,' she said, rolling the slivers with a well-worn rolling pin, 'and then we soak the strips in water.'

'How long do you soak them?' asked Aleta.

'That depends on what colour we want the papyrus paper. For a light colour, we soak them for three days, and for the darker colours, for six,' she said, extracting a sliver that had already been soaking in a plastic tub of water.

'Once we've soaked them, we can start to lay them crisscross on top of each other, to make the paper.' Aliaa laid one strip at a time on top of a small piece of carpet, alternating between horizontal and perpendicular.

'When we've formed the paper, we cover it with another piece of carpet and put it under this press for three days,' said Aliaa, sliding the carpets under the old machine and spinning the handle to apply the pressure.

'And *voilà*!' Aliaa picked up an already formed papyrus. 'If you hold it up to the light you can see the lattice-like patterns.'

O'Connor reached into his wallet and extracted fifty Egyptian pounds.

'Oh . . . that's very kind, sir, but not necessary . . . not necessary at all,' said Aliaa, waving O'Connor away. Since the trouble on the streets, the exchange rate had fallen to the point where an Egyptian pound was only worth fourteen cents, but Aliaa was having none of it. 'This is my job . . . it's enough if you feel you would like to buy one of our papyri.'

'Do you have any older papyri?' Aleta asked.

'We do . . . but they're kept in the storeroom and my father has gone to the mosque for midday prayers,' said Aliaa, a note of uncertainty in her voice. 'He won't be back for an hour or so . . .'

'That's such a pity. Do you think he'd mind if we had a look?'

'I guess not . . . the storeroom's in the cellar,' she said, leading the way toward a heavy wooden door. Aliaa switched on the lights, which were encased in rusted iron grilles, and she led the way down stone steps to a narrow passage where storage shelves had been hewn out of the rock.

'The papyri have been here for a very long time . . . the shop was started by my great grandfather,' Aliaa explained. 'I'm not sure what you'll find . . . my father's getting on and he doesn't come down here any more, but you're welcome to have a look around. I'll be upstairs if you need me.'

Aleta opened the first of the cardboard cylinders and translated the hieroglyphics. 'Wow. This one's a medical treatise . . . I'd say around fourth-century BC,' she added. She opened a second, and then a third. 'What an extraordinary collection,' she said finally. 'Surely the old man must know how valuable these are?'

'Who knows?' O'Connor replied, keeping an eye on the stone steps, 'but since my ability to read Egyptian hieroglyphics is on a par with my prowess at quilting and knitting, I'm not going to be much use to you here, so I might wait for you upstairs.'

Aleta smiled. 'Never comfortable when there's only one exit, are we,' she said, reading his mind. 'We're on a diving holiday . . . who's going to be looking for us in Alexandria?'

'Call it a sixth sense, but I'll remind you of the holiday status when we get back to the hotel room.' Curtis let his hand wander down Aleta's back.

It had only been a few hours, but that didn't prevent Aleta wanting him. 'Stop it . . . we'll get arrested . . . although I won't need reminding,' she added, and she kissed him softly.

Almost an hour passed before Aleta emerged from the cellar carrying two cardboard tubes. 'Is your father back yet, Aliaa?' she asked.

Aliaa smiled and shook her head. '*Salat al-Jummah* . . . Friday prayers. He'll probably be having tea with the Imam and the other elders. Did you find anything that interested you?'

'Just these two . . . although they don't have prices on them.'

'I'm not even sure I should be selling them, but my father won't miss them. Would a hundred pounds be okay?'

'Very reasonable, and buy yourself a little something,' Aleta said, handing over three Egyptian fifty-pound notes.

'Oh . . .'

'I insist,' Aleta said, 'and there's no need to wrap them.' She gave Aliaa a warm smile.

'So what have we found?' O'Connor asked as they emerged into the alley.

'We need to get back to the hotel, because if these are what I think they are, your amorous thoughts might have to wait until we examine them more closely.'

'No more shopping . . . they're *that* good?

'That good,' said Aleta, linking her arm through his. She could barely contain her excitement.

Built in 1929, the elegant white colonial Hotel Cecil overlooked Alexandria's eastern harbour and Saad Zaghloul Square. Winston Churchill had stayed here, as had Somerset Maugham and Al Capone; during the Second World War, the British Secret Service had maintained a suite here as a base for their operations in Alexandria. The walls held many secrets and they were about to stand witness to the uncovering of another.

O'Connor and Aleta walked into the lobby, into the charm of a bygone era of marble floors, brass lamps, and old-world furniture. Huge white stone columns decorated with ornamental gold figures supported the high ceiling. The bellboy opened the lift cage's ornate wrought-iron door and O'Connor and Aleta rode the old wooden lift to the top floor.

'So . . . what have you found to excite your archaeological senses?' O'Connor asked, when they had gained the privacy of their suite. He pulled the curtains to the balcony, revealing stunning views across the eastern harbour to Fort Qaytbey on the far western breakwater.

'Let's keep the best till last,' said Aleta, putting on a white pair of gloves and extracting the first papyrus with all the care one might employ to handle a delicate piece of Murano Venetian glassware, 'but this is still going to send a shiver down the spine of all those evangelicals in the Bible Belt, not to mention the Vatican,' Aleta said, laying the ancient papyrus out and translating the beautifully inscribed pintail ducks, reeds, eyes, flamingos and a host of other symbols the Egyptians used to record their ancient messages. 'Over the years, archaeologists have found fleeting evidence that Christianity might be based on the religion of the ancient Egyptians, but until now, we've had to glean pieces here and there from the Book of the Dead, the Coffin Texts, the Pyramid Texts . . .'

'Until now?'

'This is the fabled Horus Papyrus,' she said excitedly. 'The Egyptian equivalent of the Christian Bible . . . and possibly the only time the complete Egyptian religion was recorded in a single document.'

'So what's the threat to Christianity?' O'Connor asked, a bemused look on his face.

'Look . . . this is Horus, the 5000-year-old sun god of Egypt,' Aleta said, pointing to the hieroglyphic symbol of a falcon-headed man with a red and white *pschent*, or crown. 'His mother, Isis was often depicted as the "Mother of God" and "the Great Virgin" or *hwnt*. The Egyptians afforded her the same reverence as Christians give to Mary.'

'So this virgin birth idea is not unique to Christianity?'

'Far from it. There are any number of ancient gods with a virgin birth attributed to them . . . the Indian god Krishna was born of the virgin Devaki with a "star in the east" heralding his arrival; Dionysus of Greece had the virgin mother Semele, and performed miracles like turning water into wine; Mithra of Persia . . . the list is extensive, but the parallels depicted on this papyrus get even more intriguing,' Aleta said, pointing to another series of brightly coloured hieroglyphics. 'Horus was born just after the winter solstice, on 25 December, the same date the Christians chose. His birth was heralded by a star in the east: Sirius, the brightest star in the night sky. Christ's birth was accompanied by three wise men or what the Christians called magi, but in Egyptian mythology, the wise men are represented by the stars Mintaka, Anilam and Alnitak from Orion's belt.'

'So you think the early Christian writers drew on all of this?'

Aleta smiled. 'The parallels are far too close to be a coincidence, although the Vatican and the evangelicals in America – those who believe Christianity alone provides salvation – they will dispute this vehemently because the Egyptian religion threatens the very uniqueness of Christ. At age twelve, Horus was a prodigal child teacher. At thirty, he began his ministry after being baptised by Anup,' she said, continuing to translate from the priceless document. 'Horus had twelve disciples, and he performed the same miracles as Christ was said to have performed, healing the sick and walking on water.'

'Raising the dead? That's my favourite,' said O'Connor with a wicked grin.

'For a Catholic boy you haven't retained too much reverence, have you . . . but yes,' Aleta said, pointing to a depiction of Horus resurrecting Osiris using the Egyptian cross of eternal life. 'Like Christ, Horus was said to raise the dead, but the next part of this papyrus would be enough for the Vatican to bury it in the deepest recesses of their Secret Archives . . . but let's leave that for the moment, because the other papyrus is even more explosive.' Aleta laid out the second papyrus with even more care than the first.

'This is a map of the old city, and this papyrus dates back to not long after the city was founded by Alexander the Great.'

'You paid twenty bucks for a document that's over 2300 years old . . . shame on you,' O'Connor said with a smile, sitting down on one of the gold-backed chairs beside the coffee table where Aleta had laid the papyrus.

'God knows how long this papyrus has been in that basement. Archaeologists can work for a lifetime without making a single significant discovery, but if this is genuine,' Aleta said, her voice filled with excitement, 'it will attract worldwide interest, because according to this map, the lost Library of Alexandria would have been located in this region here.' Aleta pointed to an area near the harbour's eastern shoreline that was now under water.

'I seem to remember they've done quite a bit of exploration already. Wouldn't they have found this?'

'Those expeditions are all relatively recent, and you're right, they've done a fantastic job. They've uncovered a large number of artifacts, but they've never found the library. Come and stand on the balcony and I'll give you an idea of what we're going to see when we dive this harbour.

'Imagine a straight line between us and Fort Qaytbey on the far side,' said Aleta. She extended her arm toward the ancient stone fort built in the fifteenth century by the Muslim Mamluke Sultan al-Ashraf Qaitbay as a defence against a threat from the Ottoman Turks. 'A few hundred metres out from the current shoreline they found the submerged island of Antirhodos. That island was the private property of the Ptolemaic kings and some scholars think the palace of the last pharaoh of ancient Egypt, Cleopatra was built there.'

'And that line of pharaohs started with Ptolemy I?'

Aleta nodded. 'After he conquered Egypt in 332 BC, Alexander the Great was installed as pharaoh, but after his death, a long line of Ptolemys followed him. The island was completely paved, and divers have discovered the remains of a palace, along with a Sphinx bearing the image of King Ptolemy XII.'

'Ah . . . Cleopatra's father.'

'Probably the only bit of Egyptology you remember, and I'm not talking about her father!'

'Hurtful and unnecessary,' O'Connor said, grinning broadly.

'But true.'

O'Connor had long ago conceded Aleta's encyclopaedic knowledge of ancient civilisations, and he listened intently while she indicated the places where the harbour had already given up some of its secrets.

'Over there, divers have found the remains of a port which in ancient times, was reserved for the king's galleys,' said Aleta, pointing toward the eastern breakwater, 'and closer in, not far from this hotel, they've discovered another palace. Many scholars, myself included, think this was Mark Antony's final retreat before he committed suicide.'

'Cleopatra must have been a remarkable lady,' O'Connor said, a wistful tone in his voice. 'Just think: she's the last pharaoh of Egypt, and to shore up her power, she gets into bed with Caesar, and then when he's murdered, she hops into the cot with Mark Antony.'

'Has it occurred to you that it might not have been just about power? She might have been attracted to them!'

'I thought that might get a rise out of you – never fails.' O'Connor let his hand slide down Aleta's thigh.

'When the teacher has finished her history lesson you might . . . *might* be able to entice her into bed, but until then, pay attention!' Aleta's dark eyes danced mischievously and she made no attempt to brush O'Connor's hand away.

'If you look beyond the palm trees down there to the far corner of Saad Zaghloul Square, that's where the two obelisks that became known as Cleopatra's needles were built to guide ships into the harbour. One obelisk now stands on the Thames Embankment in London, and the other's in Central Park in New York. And this hotel was built on the place where Cleopatra likely committed suicide . . . This city has so much history.'

'And the Pharos?'

'Along with the Great Pyramid of Giza and the Hanging Gardens of Babylon, one of the seven wonders of the ancient world.'

'High?'

'Massive. The bottom storey of the lighthouse had over three hundred rooms, just for the mechanics and labourers. There was a second, octagonal storey and then a third, and on top of that a lantern with a seven-metre statue of Poseidon on top of it. The Pharos lighthouse was three times higher than the Statue of Liberty in New York harbour.'

'Too big then to be powered by olive oil?'

'Way too big . . . this one was wood-fired. The wood was stored in the bottom storey and hydraulic lifts were used to raise it to the fire at the top.'

'And the mirror reflected the light from the fire?'

'I'm not so sure,' said Aleta. 'There's a lot about the ancients we don't understand, and it's quite possible that the Alexandrian mathematicians discovered the optical lens, although we'll probably never know, because their discovery was lost to science when the lighthouse was destroyed by an earthquake in the fourteenth century.'

'How do you know this papyrus goes back to Alexander's time?'

O'Connor asked as they came in from the balcony. 'How do you know it's not a copy or a forgery?'

'I've worked with ancient papyri before, and this one has all the look and feel of one that is centuries old, but I agree, we need to make sure. I have a colleague at the Alexandria University, and he can carbon-date this from a fragment, but if it's genuine, it gives us a very accurate indication of all the areas of the ancient city that are now under water.'

'Built by Alexander?'

Aleta shook her head. 'Alexander the Great might have founded this city when he invaded and kicked the Persians out of Egypt, but he left for campaigns in Iraq and areas around the Khyber Pass before the first brick was laid. The city was built by Ptolemy I and his successors. In fact, Ptolemy and you might have had a lot in common.'

'Ruggedly handsome, witty conversationalist, and exceptionally good in bed.'

'I doubt historians have the slightest idea of Ptolemy's expertise in bed,' said Aleta, rolling her eyes, 'but they do know that when Alexander died in Babylon in 323 BC, Ptolemy was not unlike an agent of the CIA. He stole the body before it reached Alexander's birthplace of Macedonia and brought it back here where he built an opulent tomb for his former Pharaoh. Ptolemy I and his successors then set about building one of the greatest cities of the ancient world . . . temples, royal palaces, wide colonnaded streets and public baths. As you can see from this papyrus, much of the old city has slipped beneath the waves, but we know Ptolemy I founded a *mouseion*, what we might call it a museum. It housed laboratories and a medical school where they conducted dissections, which Greek culture outlawed in

Athens, as well as lecture halls and rooms for visiting scholars like Archimedes and Euclid, and of course the library.'

'And how do you know this map is accurate? I'm not doubting you,' O'Connor added, sensing Aleta bristling at her academic professionalism being challenged. 'I'm just playing Devil's advocate.'

'You're right to question. As a scientist yourself, you will know that every good academic and scientist does, so perhaps we should get a second opinion from another of my colleagues, Professor Hassan Badawi, the director of the Cairo Museum.'

'Didn't they have a break-in there recently? He may not have time to see you.'

'Yes, but that was during the riots in Tahrir Square. A bunch of amateurs looking for gold got in through a skylight, but it's calm for the moment. I'm sure he'll spare us half an hour.'

'Well even if he can see you, showing him the papyrus with the map will start the hares and hounds running in all directions . . . buggering up a perfectly good diving holiday. Why don't we take a photograph of the papyrus and show him that. That way no one will actually know we have the map, and we can be vague about where we discovered the photo – somewhere he can't immediately check.'

'Let's split the difference. We can donate the Horus Papyrus to his museum, which will give him kudos – although once that becomes public, it will also spark furious debate, so we can ask that no announcement be made just yet.'

'And you can tell him you discovered the photograph in a second-hand book . . . one you picked up in an obscure book fair.'

'No wonder you're back in the CIA, although I'm not sure I'm in favour of that,' Aleta added, getting up and moving around behind

O'Connor's chair. 'But I guess you'd never settle for a nine-to-five existence, would you,' she said, moving her hands down O'Connor's shirt front and stroking his hairy chest. He turned to look up at her and she bent down and kissed him, gently at first, and then more hungrily. 'Take me to bed,' she whispered.

2

VILLA JANNAT, ISLAMABAD, PAKISTAN

The sun rose over the Margella Mountains, bathing the garden capital of Pakistan that was nestled in the foothills. In the 1950s, the government had decided to relocate the capital from Karachi to a more central location. The name 'Jannat' in Urdu meant 'Paradise', and Khan's large patio, lined with potted palms, cacti and marijuana plants, overlooked the distant, well-planned capital with its wide streets and myriad parks and gardens.

Lieutenant General Farid Khan, the sacked head of the ISI, Pakistan's Inter-Service Intelligence agency, adopted the prostrate position facing Mecca as he neared the end of his *Fajr,* the dawn prayer, the first of the five prayers for the day. He touched the old wooden patio floor with his forehead: *'Allahu Akbar . . . Subbana rabbiyal-a'la . . . Ash-hadu alla ilaha illallahu . . .* Allah is great; oh Allah, glory be to you, the most high; I bear witness that there is none worthy of worship but Allah.'

His prayers completed, Khan stood and remained facing the

direction of Mecca, seething. He had no doubt Washington was behind his sacking, and one day, the West would be brought to account. The world, he had vowed, would be brought under Islamic control, and subject to the only law Khan recognised, the Sharia.

Khan descended to the locked and alarmed gallery beneath his spacious study. The short, swarthy, thickset general had spent thirty years getting to the top of Pakistani military intelligence. Along the way, he had not only mastered the corrupt corridors of power in Islamabad, but courtesy of his membership of Pharos – an ultra powerful and highly secretive group that met once a year in Alexandria – he had also acquired an intimate knowledge of financial markets. Khan was now the wealthiest man in Pakistan. His sprawling villa, protected by a large contingent of privately funded armed guards, was located in the steep, picturesque hills to the north of Pakistan's capital Islamabad.

Khan deactivated the alarm, and stepped into his gallery, where the temperature and humidity were strictly controlled. He ran his hand through his thick, black hair and stopped to admire Van Gogh's *Congregation Leaving the Reformed Church in Nuenen, 1884.* The small oil on canvas, which the master had painted for his mother when she had broken her thighbone, was one of General Khan's favourites.

Khan moved on to the *Congregation*'s companion, the *View of the Sea at Scheveningen,* which Van Gogh painted at the beach near The Hague, in 1882. Khan stepped back and admired the artist's rough brush strokes and his bold use of thick daubs of colour: the dark clouds, the greys and whites of the thundering, foaming waves, and the flag on the solitary boat, whipping in the wind. Both

the *Congregation* and the *View of the Sea at Scheveningen* had been
stolen from the Van Gogh Museum in Amsterdam in 2002, and
now, courtesy of a wizened art dealer in Venice, Zachary Rubinstein, they were Khan's.

The exclusive ownership of the world's greatest masters gave
the Pakistani general a great deal of pleasure. He had even pondered the possibility of acquiring the *Mona Lisa*. It had been stolen
before in 1911. Vincenzo Peruggia, an Italian Louvre employee
who wanted the painting hung in Italy, had hidden in a broom
closet and simply walked out after the museum had closed, with
the priceless masterpiece hidden under his overcoat. Security had
improved since then, but nothing was impossible. The painting
went missing for two years before it was recovered in Florence,
and since then, it had been subject to an acid attack in 1956, had
a rock thrown at it the same year, and had red paint sprayed at it,
prompting the Louvre to protect it with bullet proof glass. On rare
occasions, Khan mused, the painting was entrusted to other museums, but he'd concluded that the security surrounding the world's
best-known painting meant it was now out of reach.

Despite his extensive collection, there were three additions he
desperately wanted to own: Van Gogh's *Poppy Flowers*; Tutankhamun's falcon pendant; and the greatest Egyptian artifact of them
all, Tutankhamun's gold mask.

Van Gogh's *Poppy Flowers* had been painted three years before
the artist's suicide and it had disappeared from the Mohammed
Mahmoud Khalil Museum in Cairo in 2010. In an unguarded
moment, Rubinstein had alluded to knowing where it was, and
General Khan would have given a great deal to know who had it.

Khan's other passion was the ancient artifacts of the Pharaohs.

His collection was growing, and the recent unrest in Egypt had provided more than one windfall. Rubinstein had secured for Khan the exquisite statuette of Tutankhamun's sister, *A Daughter of the Pharaoh Akhenaten*. With it had come the possibility of the two additions he wanted most of all. Both were housed in the famed Egyptian Museum of Antiquities on the banks of the Nile in Cairo. The first, Tutankhamun's funerary falcon pendant, superbly fashioned from solid gold, lapis lazuli, carnelian and turquoise, had been discovered by Howard Carter in a wooden casket in the treasury of Tutankhamun's tomb. The falcon's wings of red, blue and black semi-precious stones were spread, as if to protect the dead pharaoh. In its solid-gold talons, the falcon grasped the *shen* rings of eternity and the *ankh* keys to life, showing the 'boy king' was promised an eternal afterlife. Curiously, Rubinstein had indicated that for a price, the pendant might be acquired. And then there was the mask, the greatest prize in all of Egyptology.

Khan looked at his watch. It was time to leave for the lawless border town of Peshawar. From there, he would make the crossing through the Khyber Pass into Afghanistan, and on into the soaring mountains of the Hindu Kush. It was one of the most dangerous crossings in the world, and he had only agreed to meet with the Afghan Taliban and al Qaeda after persistent requests from the Pharos group, and an inducement that had been too tempting to refuse. If he was successful in integrating the Taliban and al Qaeda into the Pharos plans, the elusive Sheldon Crowley had agreed to attempt to obtain for Khan the funerary mask of the boy King Tutankhamun.

Khan paused briefly to admire Jean-Baptiste Oudry's 1753 painting *The White Duck*, stolen from the Marquess of Cholmondeley's collection at Houghton Hall in Norfolk, in the United Kingdom. Khan smiled. The textures of the duck feathers were extraordinary, and he was now the only one who could appreciate them.

3

CAIRO

The Egyptian Museum of Antiquities was just across the street from where O'Connor and Aleta were staying at the Ramses Hilton on the eastern bank of the Nile.

'My contact's just texted me the carbon dating of the papyrus,' Aleta said, as they crossed the road. 'Matches Alexander the Great and Ptolemy I's time . . . around 330 to 300 BC. It's genuine!' she whispered excitedly. When they arrived at the museum entrance, the director, Professor Hassan Badawi, his dark skin baked from countless hours exploring in the desert, was waiting to whisk them through security.

'*Ahlan wa sahlan* . . . welcome, welcome,' Badawi said, kissing Aleta on both cheeks. 'It's been far too long, but I see from the papers you've been very busy . . . first the Maya Codex and now the lost city of Paititi. Magnificent achievements!'

'You're too kind, but I couldn't have done any of it without this man, Hassan. Let me introduce you to my colleague, Doctor Curtis O'Connor.'

'I've read so much about you, I feel I already know you, Doctor O'Connor,' said Badawi, gripping O'Connor's hand. 'Come . . . follow me.'

'What's with the "Doctor"?' O'Connor whispered as they followed Professor Badawi into the museum.

'Credibility. You won't get any points here for your assassination skills, but around archaeologists of Professor Badawi's standing, even a doctorate on lethal viruses carries *some* weight.'

O'Connor gently dug her in the ribs.

'So . . . what brings you to Cairo?' Badawi asked, after tea had been served in his hundred-year-old office. Lined with books on Egyptology and archaeology, the office had housed directors since the museum was built in 1902. Behind Badawi's desk there were photographs of him briefing various world leaders in front of the Great Pyramid of Giza, as well as one of him meeting the Pope in the Vatican.

Just down the corridor, the deputy director of the museum, Doctor Omar Aboud, adjusted the headphones connected to the listening device he'd installed in the director's office.

'We're here on holidays. I was browsing in a papyrus factory in Alexandria, and I found this,' said Aleta, opening the protective folder and extracting the papyrus that had been inscribed at least 3000 years before the birth of Christ, yet paralleled both the Christian doctrine and the life of the Christian saviour himself. She laid it out on Badawi's desk.

Badawi picked up a magnifying glass, and it was some time before he spoke. 'The Horus Papyrus . . . you've found the Horus Papyrus! The first time we've had a conclusive record of the extraordinary similarities between the religion of the ancients, and the stories in the Bible . . . it will cause an absolute furore among the Christians.'

O'Connor, who had long ago ditched organised religion, looked on with bemused interest at the excitement an archaeological religious discovery could ignite.

'We'd like to donate it to your museum, Hassan, but on condition that you keep it quiet for the moment, because there's something even more important we have to show you, and the last thing we want is media interest in what we're after.'

'That's very kind of you. I'll make sure it's secured in the vault until we make the announcement . . . but you have something more important than the Horus Papyrus?' said Badawi, a look of both surprise and excitement on his face.

Aleta extracted the photo of the papyrus map she and O'Connor had taken. 'Just before we left Peru, I came across an original edition of Howard Carter's book on the tomb of Tutankhamun, so I bought it . . . and this was being used as a bookmark.' Aleta handed a photo of the papyrus map to Professor Badawi.

The professor studied it in silence. 'Where did you say you bought this?' he asked finally, 'because this may be a very important find.'

'So you think what's in that photograph might be a genuine map?' Aleta asked.

'The layout and the Greek language all point to that,' Professor Badawi replied, 'and if this is a photograph of it, it means the original document has been found. Where did you say you bought the book?'

'Unfortunately, it was from a roadside stall in Lima, and that's going to be difficult to trace, but I'll do what I can.'

'As Aleta will attest,' said O'Connor, 'ancient civilisations are not my long suit. I have to confess I don't know a lot about the Library of Alexandria, but as well as giving us a location, might this throw some light on what happened to it?'

Professor Badawi smiled. 'It's entirely possible. Alexander didn't get to see his own library – it was left to one of his generals, Ptolemy I, and subsequent pharaohs to build and stock it – but we do know that Alexander wanted all the works of the nations he conquered to be translated into Greek and housed under the one roof.'

'When Alexander conquered Egypt,' Aleta added, 'Alexandria was a logical choice for a new centre of both Hellenism and world trade. It had a natural harbour, a good supply of water, and an existing colony of Greek-speaking Macedonians.'

'Precisely,' Badawi agreed, 'and Ptolemy I and those pharaohs that followed in the Ptolemaic dynasty were determined to make Alexandria *the* centre of learning and culture in a panhellenic world.' Badawi's dark eyes twinkled with enthusiasm for one of his favourite subjects. 'So we're not only concerned with what might have happened to the library,' Badawi continued, 'but also with what was in it . . . possibly as many as 700 000 papyrus scrolls, including the personal library of Aristotle which found its way to Alexandria from Athens.'

'And some very famous scholars studied there,' said Aleta, turning toward O'Connor. 'Archimedes, Herophilus, Saint Catherine – who was beheaded for her Christian beliefs by the Roman Emperor Maxentius – and Euclid.'

Badawi nodded. 'Intriguingly, some of Euclid's original papyri have since been found at a place called Oxyrhynchus or modern day al Bahnasa, which is about 150 kilometres to the south of here on the west bank of the Nile,' he explained, 'so it's more than possible that documents from the Great Library found their way into the desert, and were not lost at all.'

'I thought Julius Caesar burned it?' said O'Connor, smiling disarmingly.

'My colleague is a great fan of Elizabeth Taylor, Hassan,' said Aleta apologetically.

Badawi rolled his eyes. 'Hollywood has a lot to answer for,' he said. 'Ever since *Cleopatra* hit the screen, Caesar – who was it that played him?

'Rex Harrison,' O'Connor offered.

'Thank you – Rex Harrison. Ever since Rex Harrison and Elizabeth Taylor tangled lips on the big screen, Caesar's been blamed for not putting out the fire he started when he wanted to wipe out the Egyptian fleet in the harbour. I suspect that far from being destroyed on the night of the harbour fire, the destruction of the library occurred over many centuries, and that much of its content is still to be discovered. And we have to remember that there was more than one library. The library everyone talks about was part of the *musaeum* complex of the city, but there was also a daughter library in the Serapeum Temple, which was built by Ptolemy III as a dedication to the god Serapis – a Greek and Egyptian god who was the protector of Alexandria. The daughter library held hundreds of thousands of papyri as well.'

'I plan to show him the ruins while we're in Alexandria,' Aleta affirmed.

Badawi nodded approvingly. 'There's nothing left above the ground, of course, other than the column of Diocletian which stands on top of the original site, but archaeologists have excavated the area and you will see the recesses in the walls where the papyrus books were stored.'

'So what happened to that library?' asked O'Connor.

'Pope Theophilus ordered it destroyed in around 391 AD . . . not the first time the church has burned books that threaten its rigid dogma,' Badawi added ruefully.

'Would papyrus survive this long?' asked O'Connor.

'Depends where and how it's kept. The whole area of Alexandria was subject to repeated earthquakes and tidal waves, which is why so much of the ancient city is now beneath the sea, and papyrus, of course, would not survive in water unless it was in a very tightly sealed container. But out in the desert . . . that's another matter,' Badawi said. 'The dry climate out there helps to preserve ancient papyri, and we only have to look at what's been found at al Bahnasa to confirm that. After the British took over Egypt in 1883, two young British archaeologists, Bernard Grenfell and Arthur Hunt, started to excavate around al Bahnasa and they discovered layers of papyri beneath the rubbish of the more recent occupants: thousands of priceless documents written by Euripides, Sophocles and other authors of the Greek tragedies, along with the most complete set of Euclid's mathematical diagrams yet found. It's one of the most important archaeological sites in the whole of Egypt and some archaeologists were hopeful it might even turn up the Euclid Papyrus.'

Aleta nodded. The average guy in the street would not likely have heard of the papyrus, but like the Ark of the Covenant, it was one of those prizes archaeologists could only dream of finding. 'I've been on the lookout for that for years.'

'The Euclid Papyrus?' O'Connor asked.

'Said to have been written by the father of geometry about the same time he wrote *The Elements* in 300 BC – a treatise on the real reason the pyramids were built,' Badawi replied. 'There's fierce debate in academic circles as to whether that's a myth, or whether the Papyrus actually exists, although if it did, there would almost certainly have been a copy in the Great Library. For some years, there's been a rumour around the souks about a fragment that was supposedly sold on the black market, but we've never had any proof of that.' Badawi smiled. 'As Aleta knows only too well, Egyptology is full of intrigue. The Horus Papyrus might be a threat to Christianity, but if what's rumoured to be in the Euclid Papyrus is true, it may turn academic scholarship on the Pyramids of Giza on its head.'

As Badawi escorted them out of his office, his deputy was walking toward them.

'My deputy, Doctor Omar Aboud,' said Badawi, introducing them. O'Connor was immediately on alert. The gangly Aboud had avoided eye contact, and although not definitive, it could mean Aboud had something to hide.

4

VENICE

'The Tutankhamun mask would be very difficult to steal, signore.'

'But not impossible.'

'Nothing is impossible, signore . . . for a price.' Zachary Rubinstein's dark eyes glinted in the half-light of the cluttered back room of his art gallery.

Galleria d'Arte Rubinstein was located off the open square of the Campo del Ghetto Nuovo, the Jewish quarter of the Cannaregio region of northern Venice, not far from Venice's railway terminal and the Canal Grande. The quarter had a rich, but tragic history. In 1516, under the Venetian Republic, Jews had been compelled to live in what was now the oldest Jewish ghetto in the world.

The old art dealer scrutinised his wealthy visitor. His client's thinning silver hair was combed straight back without a part, curling over the collar of a Borrelli shirt. He had an aquiline nose, distinguished sideburns, and a neatly trimmed silver beard and moustache. His round, red face and double chin were indicators of an extravagant life, which made age difficult to judge, but Rubinstein thought his client to be around sixty and he knew well that he was dealing with Sheldon Crowley, the chairman of EVRAN, the largest energy and arms conglomerate on the planet.

'Shall we say ten million euros on account, and one hundred million on delivery?'

It was a standard arrangement for every illicit artifact Crowley had purchased from Rubinstein, and Crowley pushed a briefcase across the gnarled wooden table. Rubinstein opened it to find one hundred packets, each containing two hundred used €500 notes. In 2010, British banks had banned the high-value euro notes after finding that nine out of ten were linked to organised crime and terrorism, but Rubinstein's client favoured them for the same reason as his colleagues in organised crime: they took up far less space than US $100 bills.

'You can count it if you wish. It's all there.'

'That won't be necessary,' said Rubinstein, smiling thinly as he closed the briefcase. He would count it later. In the past, it had always been there, right down to the last euro. 'In the meantime, I have some information that may interest you. You have heard of the Rhind Papyrus?'

'Of course. I've not only heard of it, I've seen it, although like a lot of priceless Egyptian artifacts, it's not located in Egypt but in a museum with high-grade security, which makes artifacts like that much harder to get hold of,' the client added pointedly. 'Apart from a few fragments held by the Brooklyn Museum in New York, most of the Rhind Papyrus is held by the British Museum in London. If I recall correctly, it was looted from Pharaoh Ramesses II's temple, and it's still the best example of Egyptian mathematics found to date.'

Rubinstein nodded. 'It's the earliest record in the history of mathematics, and it contains the means of inquiring into the world's secrets, but . . .'

The old Jewish art dealer paused, choosing his words carefully. 'You may not be aware there is a companion, the whereabouts of which have remained a mystery.' Rubinstein watched the colour drain from the client's face.

'The Euclid Papyrus?' Like his co-conspirator in Pakistan, Crowley was not only an avid collector of stolen masters,but he too had a passion for Egyptology and Egyptian artifacts, and he was instantly on alert. If what was alleged to be in it turned out to be true, for Crowley, that spelled extraordinary danger.

'I thought the Euclid Papyrus vanished with the Library of Alexandria?'

'The media and most Egyptologists think so too,' Rubinstein replied, his lined and weathered face devoid of emotion, 'but I have a contact in the Egyptian Museum in Cairo.' Rubinstein trusted no one, and he stopped short of naming the museum's shadowy deputy director. 'The director has had a visit from two people, one of whom has been on the lookout for it for years. They've apparently discovered a map of the ancient city of Alexandria, or at least a photograph of one.'

'And who are these two people?' Crowley demanded.

'Curtis O'Connor and a Doctor Aleta Weizman. You may have heard of them?'

'I seem to remember reading something about them,' Crowley lied. Weizman and O'Connor's search for artifacts in the jungles of Guatemala and the Amazon had already attracted his attention, and he had noted Weizman's interest in the Maya, the Inca and the

Egyptians. 'Are they the ones who unearthed the Maya Codex in Guatemala?'

Rubinstein nodded. 'Weizman is a world-renowned archaeologist – originally from Guatemala, with an extensive knowledge of ancient cultures.'

'And O'Connor?' Crowley probed, keen to know how much Rubinstein knew.

'He's a CIA agent.'

'I can understand an archaeologist having an interest in the Library of Alexandria . . . but a CIA agent? What's the connection?'

'We're not sure. They've operated together before, although this time they may be just holidaying. O'Connor – how shall I put it – has a fair bit of form in the bedroom, and Weizman's pretty easy on the eye, so taking some time off in Alexandria might not be significant. And they're both keen divers, so their choice of country may reflect the proximity of the Mediterranean. On the other hand . . .' Rubinstein's voice trailed off.

Crowley made a mental note to direct his executive assistant, Rachel Bannister, to compile dossiers on the pair.

'Strange they've chosen to holiday in Egypt . . . the place is going up in smoke,' Crowley said, more intrigued than ever.

Rubinstein shrugged. 'I don't think a few protests in Tahrir Square or on the streets of Alexandria would worry those two. They seem to know how to handle themselves.'

'Is it possible they have a lead, not only on the Library of Alexandria, but the Euclid Papyrus as well?'

'I'm not absolutely sure,' said Rubinstein, 'but if they unearth the old library, it's possible it contains a copy of the Euclid Papyrus, and that would rival the discovery of Tutankhamun's tomb.' Given his client's request, Rubinstein's comment held more than a touch of irony, but if Crowley recognised it, he showed no sign.

'Where's the map now? Did anyone make a copy?' Crowley demanded.

'Not as far as we know. The director of the Cairo Museum, Professor Hassan Badawi, and Doctor Weizman are old friends, so in the event that she and O'Connor do uncover the fate of the library, and perhaps even more importantly, the Euclid Papyrus, Weizman would undoubtedly have assured Badawi that he would be the first to know.'

Crowley fell silent, his mind racing. 'Keep me informed, both on the Tutankhamun mask and the Euclid Papyrus,' he said finally, getting to his feet.

'Of course,' Rubinstein replied, and he accompanied his client to the gallery door, which opened on to a narrow cobblestone alley.

Crowley crossed the Campo del Ghetto Nuovo square to the Calle Ghetto Vecchio bridge, one of many hundreds enabling Venetians to cross the myriad small canals that defined the city. A long, narrow barge approached, loaded with mineral water and other staples, and the helmsman manoeuvred it under the bridge and on past two shiny black and gold gondolas. Irritated by the throngs of tourists, Crowley pushed his way along the narrow bridge, past kosher restaurants, and bakeries advertising Jewish cakes, *Specialita: Dolci Ebraici della tradizione Veneziana.* Aromas of baked bread mixed with freshly ground coffee permeated the air but Crowley was never in a mood to dally. He reached the wider Fondamenta Pescaria, crossed another canal and headed toward the Canal Grande where his Super Aquarama speedboat was waiting, polished mahogany glinting in the afternoon sun.

As soon as Crowley was seated, his boatman, black cap at a rakish angle, released the painter from the red and white striped mooring pole beside the jetty. Centuries before, the colours had represented the families who owned them, but now, the 'barber poles' simply added another colourful backdrop to the ancient maritime city.

The twin V8 Chrysler engines throbbed into life and the boatman eased into the seemingly impossible traffic that plied Venice's canals. Cream and green *vaporetti,* the ferries that formed the mainstay of the Venetian transport system, fought for right of way among water taxis and lighters, barges and gondolas, and the boatman throttled back to allow a vaporetto dell'arte to pass. More comfortable than the normal vaporetti, the vaporetto dell'arte carried tourists from Ferrovia at the Santa Lucia train station, down the grand canal to San Marco Piazza and the Giardini jetty, allowing them to visit the Peggy Guggenheim Collection, La Fenice Opera Theatre, the Doge's Palace and a host of other museums and galleries.

The speedboat surged toward the western industrial end of the canal, leaving behind centuries-old buildings that boasted a rich compendium of Byzantine, Ottoman, Phoenician, Renaissance and Baroque architecture, alongside the Venetian Gothic style and the ubiquitous lancet arch of the elegant *palazzi* lining the canal. The boat passed under the rail bridge and the Ponte Della Libertà, the bridge opened by Benito Mussolini in 1933 to provide road access from the mainland, but that traffic was restricted to the western edge of the city. No cars were allowed in the centre of Venice itself. The boatman glanced around. The familiar blue and white *polizia* boats of the Venice water police were nowhere in sight. He ignored the 20 km/h limits for the *Leguna Veneta,* and opened the throttles. The superbly maintained engines roared into life and Crowley's silvery-grey locks streamed in the wind as the boat planed to 50 knots, powering north toward Venice's Marco Polo airport where Crowley's private jet, a long range Gulfstream G550, was waiting to take him to Corsica.

Crowley stared unseeingly across the lagoon, the boat's deep leather seats cushioning his ride. His thoughts turned to the Rhind Papyrus and its companion, the Euclid Papyrus. Unbeknown to the Jewish art dealer, Crowley had already acquired a priceless fragment of the Euclid Papyrus from an even less reputable dealer in one of the souks in Cairo. A competent Egyptologist in his own right, Crowley had been able to decipher some of the hieroglyphics, and it had been enough to send a chill down his spine.

The Euclid Papyrus purported to contain details of the real reason behind the construction of the pyramids. But Crowley only had a fragment, and some of it had been encoded. The Greeks and the Romans, Crowley knew, were the first to employ encryption aggressively, but the Egyptians and Mesopotamians had also used codes. A Babylonian tablet, dating as far back as 2500 BC, contained words from which the first consonant had been deleted. Most of the ancient codes, by today's standards of encryption, were relatively simple, but the Euclid fragment had stubbornly refused to yield its secret, one that had the potential to threaten Crowley's vast fossil-fuel, forest and arms empire. The need to decrypt the fragment was now urgent, he reflected, and the recovery of the rest of the papyrus even more urgent. But if Rubinstein was right, O'Connor and Weizman might lead him to it.

Crowley extracted a 'clean' mobile phone from his soft leather attaché case. He typed in a short text and sent it to General Khan. Short or not, it was a text he would come to regret.

5

PESHAWAR, PAKISTAN

When General Khan's driver pulled up outside the safe house in Peshawar, the young, slightly built Taliban field commander, Tayeb Jamal, was waiting for him, sitting in the back seat of one of the Taliban's ubiquitous Toyota pick-ups. Two more Taliban warriors sat in the open tray behind, ready to tear the tarpaulin off their heavy anti-aircraft machine gun. Jamal's driver gave the signal for the convoy of six trucks behind to start their engines.

Khan knew well the risks he was about to take. The Taliban and al Qaeda were unlikely bedfellows, but when it suited their purpose, they would work together. Khan fully intended to harness that synergy to attack the West, with the ultimate aim of imposing Sharia law.

Khan had been born in Karachi into one of the wealthiest families in Pakistan, and he could trace his lineage back to the Pashtun tribal areas that straddled the modern border between Pakistan and Afghanistan, marked by the old British colonial Durand Line.

British colonialism was just one of many issues that fuelled Khan's anger. The British, he reflected, with their 'big hands on little maps' approach to the world, had a habit of drawing borders along ridge lines and rivers, because they were easier to identify on the ground, and the Durand Line was no exception. Named after Mortimer Durand, foreign secretary for nineteenth-century British India, well before Pakistan came into existence in 1947, the line had been put in place in 1893. After the British withdrew from Afghanistan after the second Anglo Afghan war, the Durand Line served to define the spheres of influence between the British and the Emir of Afghanistan, Abdur Rahman Khan. But the line ran straight through Pashtun tribal areas, splitting villages and towns. Further south, it split the Baluchistan area, similarly dividing the ethnic Baluch on both sides. What had become the border between Afghanistan and India, and later Pakistan, might appear on international maps, Khan thought, but he and his Pashtun tribesmen would never recognise it.

Where the meddling British had left off, the United States had stepped in. Just after 9/11, the Afghan Taliban had sheltered al Qaeda terrorists in caves in the soaring snow-capped mountains of the Hindu Kush, and the Pakistani Taliban had similarly provided shelter on the Pakistan side of the border, in the notorious Federally Administered Tribal Areas. Washington had pressured the president of Pakistan to either join the US in the hunt for Bin Laden and al Qaeda, or face the consequences. 'You are either with us, or against us,' President Bush had demanded. No one in the world would be allowed to remain neutral.

The United States had also demanded a crack down on the Islamists inside the ISI Agency, insisting that 'the beards' be weeded out. Khan and many other Pakistani generals in both the Army and the powerful ISI had watched aghast as their government had kowtowed to a United States who supported Pakistan's arch-enemy, India. The Pakistani president had started at the top, sacking Khan for 'being too Islamic'. Ever since he'd been awarded the sword of honour for graduating at the top of his class at the Royal Military Academy, Sandhurst, Khan had harboured a burning desire to assume the top job as chief of staff of the Pakistan Army. But with his career now in tatters, and the mask of Tutankhamun on offer, the risks of crossing into Afghanistan to harness the Taliban and al Qaeda would be worth it.

'It's market day here in Peshawar, but we should be across the border in an hour, *insha'Allah*, God willing,' said Jamal, as the driver approached the centre of the city and slowed for a herd of goats blocking the road. Tayeb Jamal was one of a number of rising young Taliban field commanders who had appeared on the scene since 9/11. The US drone strikes over Afghanistan and Pakistan had been increasingly successful, and many of the older Taliban commanders, who might have been willing to negotiate peace, had been killed. Their places had been taken by a new breed of fanatical young Islamists whose only education had been gained at the hands of hardline clerics in the Madrassas, the Islamic religious schools that had proliferated in the border area.

'You have the Khyber covered?' queried Khan. At its narrowest point, still short of the border, the ancient pass was only two hundred metres wide.

Jamal smiled, cradling his AK-47 in his lap. He was wearing the traditional Afghan *shalwar kameez* – loose baggy brown trousers covered by a three-quarter tunic. His face was almost covered by a black *shemagh*, the customary Afghan scarf favoured by Taliban fighters. 'As much as the Infidel likes to think he has subdued this area of Pakistan and Afghanistan, General, nothing moves across the border without my men observing it. We should be in Jalalabad before midday, and once it's dark, we'll turn north toward Asadabad and the Hindu Kush.'

The convoy slowed as it moved down the Grand Trunk Road running through the middle of Peshawar. Young men on motorcycles fought for road space with the tuk-tuks, the three-wheeled motorised rickshaws that were weaving around herds of goats and brightly coloured buses belching thick, black diesel fumes. Pitifully thin donkeys pulled *tongas,* two-wheeled flat bed carts running on rubber car tyres, piled high with carpets, vegetables, freshly baked bread and live chickens. The lanes and alleys running off the trunk road into the old city, with its narrow wooden-shuttered buildings, were even more crowded. In the nineteenth century, the Kissa Khawana bazaar, the 'street of the storytellers', was famous for its *Kawa Khana* – tea shops festooned with tea cups, teapots and brass *samovars* – the big ornate charcoal-burning pots used to heat water. Here, professional storytellers would regale tea drinkers with poetry and prose. Then, as now, Pakistanis mingled with Afghans, Tajiks, Uzbeks and Iraqis, and the Taliban mingled with all of them; moving unnoticed among the barrows piled with pyramids of fruit, and coal braziers where chickens were already roasting, the whole permeated by an aroma of cinnamon, nutmeg, ginger, mango powder, turmeric and myriad other spices. Sounds of gunfire rent the morning as gunsmiths tested their dubious homemade weapons.

'The shura is scheduled for tomorrow night.' The centuries-old assembly of village elders was a Pashtun tribal consultation for settling important village and tribal issues, one that had been in place for as long as the different tribes had been warring among one another in the harsh and unforgiving landscapes of Afghanistan and Pakistan.

'And the Americans?'

Jamal grinned beneath the scarf covering his face. 'The Infidel will never learn . . . he had to pull out of Vietnam in the seventies, he was forced out of Lebanon in the eighties and he had to leave Somalia in the nineties, and before too much longer, he will be out of Afghanistan. Time is on our side, General. In the Korengal Valley, he's in the process of handing over Fire Base Phoenix, which was manned by his airborne 503rd Infantry, and he's long since closed the southern Korengal outpost further down the valley. The only other base in that area is well to the north near the Pakistan border. But you needn't worry, there isn't a unit in the Afghan Army where we don't have informers. Once we get to the Pech River, we'll split the loads onto mules. There are six different destinations, but he may be watching Korengal, so we'll approach through the valleys to the east. Provided the current deployments don't change, we'll be able to avoid his ground forces. The Infidel's drones are another matter though,' Jamal added ruefully.

'There is a safe place to wait in Jalalabad?'

'My cousin's timber yard. We can park the trucks there until nightfall, and then we'll head into the mountains under cover of darkness.'

'What view is the shura likely to take?'

Jamal shrugged. 'Mullah Akbar and some of the other tribal elders are old school. They still think it's possible to reach a peace agreement with Kabul and the Infidel.' Mullah Mohammed Akbar was one of the Taliban's senior leaders, second only to the spiritual leader of the Taliban, Mullah Omar, on US intelligence agencies' 'most wanted' lists. 'But the president and his cronies in Kabul are corrupt, established and propped up by the *Kafirs*, the unbelievers in the West. My generation is gaining the upper hand, and it doesn't matter what the elders think, we will never agree to a government that violates the laws of Islam!' Jamal spat out of the window of the Toyota. 'After the shura, I will introduce you to Omar Yousef. Perhaps you have heard of him?'

General Khan nodded. 'The Americans have a file on him.'

'Then you will know that Yousef is one of al Qaeda's up and coming commanders. He is young, but already a veteran . . . someone in the mould of Osama bin Laden, *Allah Yarhamak,* may Allah have mercy on him. Yousef will not be afraid to strike the West.'

The convoy reached the university campus on the outskirts of the city, where the Grand Trunk Road became Route N5, the dusty highway that led west to Afghanistan. Khan scanned the mountains near the border.

Twenty-five thousand feet above them, a predator drone circled over the convoy. The pilots were flying it from a remote cockpit 11 000 kilometres away at Creech Air Force Base in the Nevada desert, 80 kilometres north of Las Vegas. Hour by hour, the pilots focused the drone's cameras on the Toyota and the trucks.

A short while later, the convoy began its ascent toward the ancient Khyber Pass, for centuries a critical choke point in the Silk Road. The Persians, the Greeks and Alexander the Great, and more recently the British armies had all passed through there from Afghanistan, on their way to the Indus River in what had then been India. The broken, arid foothills of the Safid Kuh mountains rose sharply, and the convoy ground its way up to Ali Masjid Fort, named after the prophet Mohammed's cousin Ali, and built by the British in the nineteenth century atop a rocky outcrop at the narrowest point in the pass. A mirror flashed and Jamal leaned from the cab with his own mirror and returned the signal. 'The Infidel can't intercept these signals,' he said. 'Sometimes the simplest means are the best.'

Khan continued to scan the surrounding hills. Steep precipitous cliffs of shale and limestone soared above the pass. Here it was barely two hundred metres wide. The road, still on the Pakistan side of the border, wound up to Landi Kotal Fort which, at over 3500 feet, was the highest point in the pass. Beyond the pass lay the town of Towr Kham, and the border with Afghanistan.

The pilots and intelligence analysts at Creech Air Force Base watched the convoy's progress with interest.

Darkness cloaked the tall, straight cedars and pine trees on the soaring massifs of the Hindu Kush. Laniyal, a small village of stone huts, sat halfway up a mountain – part of the range overlooking the Korengal Valley. The higher peaks were covered in snow, and the fires from a dozen other villages flickered in the distance on the mountains to the west and south. It was here that the village elders had gathered for the shura. A dozen younger Taliban warriors stood quietly, away from the light of the fire, faces hidden behind their black shemaghs, ubiquitous Soviet Kalashnikov AK-47s and RPG-7 rocket-propelled grenade launchers slung over their shoulders.

On the granite outcrops above the valley, more Taliban fighters protected the approaches through the mountains, and they scanned the dirt road running alongside the river below, their infrared night-vision goggles acquired courtesy of the US Army. It was not the first time US high tech equipment had found its way into the hands of the enemy. Over three hundred Stinger missiles, each capable of bringing down an airliner, had gone missing when the US supplied the freedom fighters, the Mujahideen and Osama bin Laden in their fight against the Soviets in the eighties. Now hundreds of the high-tech goggles originally purchased for the Afghan army and police were in the hands of the Taliban.

Hakim Babar, the village headman, began by acknowledging the presence of Mullah Akbar, the Taliban's powerful shadow governor for Eastern Nangarhar Province, before opening the shura for discussion. 'There is only one item on the agenda tonight, and that's to reach a decision on whether we join the peace talks, or continue the fight. *De Pakhtu lar ba neesa* . . . we will be looking at this from the perspective of the Pashtun. The Americans and President Karzai are proposing talks that will lead to a power-sharing arrangement between the Taliban and the current government in Kabul. The alternative is to continue the fight and widen cooperation with al Qaeda.'

One by one, the village elders put their views.

'The Americans are pulling out,' one ventured, stroking his straggly white beard. 'We can consolidate our gains here in Kunar Province and wait them out.'

'And the same can be said for the south in Helmand and Kandahar,' another agreed.

'But the government in Kabul is not to be trusted,' warned a third. He was one of the few who had been educated past elementary school and capable of reading English. 'We are one of the poorest countries in the world,' he said, 'yet the banks in Kabul lend millions to their cronies so they can invest in expensive villas overseas . . . like the islands off Jumeirah in Dubai.'

'And we are not being true to the Prophet, peace be upon him,' Tayeb Jamal interjected, no longer able to contain his frustration. 'We, the Taliban, have a delegation in Doha in Qatar, waiting to make peace with the Americans and the Kabul government. They've been there for years, and what do we have to show for it? They've done nothing but live in air conditioned villas and drive around in luxury cars, while we're out here on the ground doing the fighting for them,' he continued angrily. 'A peace process has to be on *our* terms . . . and the people in Kabul need reminding of that, and of the Prophet's teaching, peace be upon him. A government in Afghanistan has to be true to Islam and ensure that Sharia is obeyed.'

'And if the Infidel won't recognise our rights, then we should join with our al Qaeda brothers, and start attacking him again on his own soil,' said another.

Sitting in the shadows, General Khan listened intently, quietly nodding in agreement.

Mullah Akbar had remained silent during the fiery speeches, but now he intervened. 'Our delegation in Doha has already agreed not to launch any offensives outside of Afghanistan. We have some things in common with our al Qaeda brothers, but they are focused against the West. Our focus is here, in Afghanistan,' he warned.

'All the more reason we should support them.' Jamal's response was respectful, but his dark eyes were blazing. 'The Infidel continues to kill our women and our children with his drone strikes . . . here and across the border in Pakistan. His soldiers have killed dozens of our villagers in this valley alone, and he thinks nothing of taking our livestock. The drone strikes will not stop until we bring him to his knees with another 9/11.' Jamal's fiery interjection was greeted with a chorus of agreement from the younger fighters.

At the conclusion of the shura, Mullah Akbar and General Khan retired with Hakim Babar to the latter's stone hut on the edge of the village clearing. They sat on the worn carpets, and waited until the women had served them with tea and a platter of raisins and almonds.

'So, Farid. What's the current view in Islamabad?' Mullah Akbar asked, stroking his reddish beard. 'Are you still in touch with those in power?'

'My friends inside the ISI keep me very well briefed, and the major concern is still India,' General Khan replied. 'She already threatens our borders in the north-east of Kashmir, but if New Delhi gains more influence in Afghanistan, then Islamabad fears Pakistan will suddenly have a threat in the west as well. The Taliban can help prevent that so the ISI will continue to support them.'

'And the United States? Still pressuring your president, I see.'

'Our president has made a very big error in cosying up to Washington, and the people won't let him forget it. The Americans like to see themselves as some sort of shining beacon of democracy, but it's a democracy they impose with bombs, bullets and drones, and the Pakistani people have had enough. Over 90 per cent of Pakistanis dislike Americans, so it doesn't matter what our president says or does, the ISI will continue to support you on both sides of the border.'

'That is good to know,' said Mullah Akbar, cradling a chipped china cup. 'This fight has a long way to run yet.'

'Not for the Americans,' replied Khan. 'The American public is very tired of the body bags. Within a year, perhaps two at the most, the Americans will have very few troops left on the ground. Will you make peace with Kabul?'

'That will depend,' said the Taliban governor. 'We are continuing to work to convince the Afghan people that we are a legitimate political force, and the incompetence in Kabul is helping us. A lot of people are turning to us to resolve disputes, because we provide a solution a lot more quickly, and the formal system is corrupt. The government has very little authority outside of Kabul, but if we are to gain legitimate power, it will require patience, which is often in short supply among the younger generation.'

'And al Qaeda?'

'Protecting al Qaeda immediately after 9/11 was very costly to us, so publicly, we will continue to deny any support, but up here . . .' Mullah Akbar opened his palms and smiled enigmatically. It was all the confirmation General Khan needed.

Their weathered, brown faces dimly illuminated by the light of a flickering oil lamp, General Khan, Tayeb Jamal, and Omar Yousef, the young, battle-hardened commander of al Qaeda in Kunar Province, sat around a rough-hewn wooden table. High in the granite mountains, the village was even more remote than Laniyal, and here, the pine, oak and spruce trees reached through the mists toward the night sky. In contrast to the slightly built Jamal, the bulky Yousef worked out in a makeshift gym, with concrete-filled petrol cans at the ends of star pickets substituting for weights. His thick neck was supported by a broad chest and shoulders, his dark hair closely cut, and his brown eyes ever suspicious.

General Khan fired up the satellite connection to his laptop. 'I have a plan to bring the Infidel to his knees,' he began, and he gave the young warriors the bare essentials of his intentions. The scheme had been conceived by Pharos, and once put in place, Khan was due to report back to the shadowy group of international powerbrokers at their annual meeting in Alexandria. The young Taliban and al Qaeda ideologues might have seen themselves as martyrs for Islam, but as far as the Pharos were concerned, the Taliban and al Qaeda were just cannon fodder for their extraordinary agenda.

'The plan will be executed in three stages, and all communications are to be through the chat room on the website stampgeekcol.com. This is the code list,' Khan said, handing over what appeared to be a catalogue of stamps. 'Each of those stamps has a corresponding letter of the alphabet marked beside it, and there is more than one choice for each letter. The additional stamps have phrases attached to them,' he continued, handing over a separate list, 'and you have each been assigned an innocuous login name. To give me forty-eight hours warning of the attacks in Phase One, you simply go to the chat room and put up a notice that you've acquired a US #231 1893 Columbian Commemorative stamp.' Khan pointed to the American Bank Note Company's violet-brown two-cent stamp depicting Christopher Columbus coming ashore at Guanahani in San Salvador, where he had claimed the land in the name of King Ferdinand and Queen Isabella of Spain. 'A stamp collectors' website is the last place the Infidel will look.'

'And the Australian and British stamps?' asked Yousef.

'They refer to our operations against the Infidel's sycophan-
tic allies . . . and the cells we're building to attack those countries,'
explained Khan. 'So to announce that an attack is about to begin
in Australia, you would post that you have acquired the 1963 five-
penny Blue Mountains Crossing stamp,' he said, pointing to the
dark blue stamp that contained images of the explorers Blaxland,
Wentworth and Lawson. In 1813, the three explorers had finally
blazed a route across the previously impenetrable Blue Mountains west of Sydney, and they were pictured looking toward the
as-yet unexplored western plains from the top of Mount York. 'To
let us know an attack has commenced in the United Kingdom, you
simply post an acquisition of a 1941 King George VI two-and-a-
half-pence stamp. None of these stamps are particularly rare, but
they're rare enough to warrant announcing that you've added them
to your collection. Phase One is an attack on this choke point here,
with the best launch sites here, and here,' Khan said, outlining the
details of the first of the attacks on the West. 'Once that attack is
successful, we will wait.'

'Why?' Yousef demanded. 'Why give the Infidel time to recover?'

'There is no point in executing the next two phases while the
Infidel is at a heightened state of alert. To attack then risks failure,'
Khan lied, knowing the delay was essential for the shadowy power-
brokers in the West to take advantage of it.

'Phase Two is to take place when *I* post an acquisition of stamps,'
Khan said, pointing to the 1971 issue of the Republik Österreich
two-schilling stamp featuring the Austrian nitrogen plant at Linz.
Khan smiled at the irony of the code. Linz had featured prominently
in the early life of Adolf Hitler.

'Once Phase Two has been executed, we will wait again, but the final attacks in Phase Three will be the most devastating of all, and they will start when I indicate I have acquired the 1960 American four-cent stamp,' Khan said, pointing to the blue and red stamp inscribed with George Washington's entreaty to 'Observe good faith and justice to all nations'. 'The Infidel has ignored the wishes of his first president, and that will be his downfall. *Insha'Allah*, these final attacks will plunge him into the abyss.'

The conversation was interrupted by the unmistakable sound of a Chinook helicopter. Suddenly the night sky was lit up with a fireball, and the explosion reverberated around the snow-capped mountains.

Yousef and Jamal cheered and General Khan smiled.

'Your fighters have not taken long to get the new missiles into action.'

'No . . . and with your help, we can get many more of them, yes?'

'It will be difficult, but not impossible, my friend. In the meantime, the Infidel will be looking for us, so it's time for me to leave. When next we meet, the plans for the attacks on the choke point and the other two phases will be well advanced.'

Yousef and Jamal chorused in unison. '*Insha'Allah*!'

6

CHÂTEAU CORNUCOPIA, CORSICA

EVRAN, the world's largest energy and arms multinational, dwarfed companies like Chevron, ExxonMobil, Lockheed Martin and BAE Systems. EVRAN's chairman and silver-haired CEO, Sheldon Crowley pushed a button under the desk in the stone-walled study of his château, high in the hills above Sartène on the French island of Corsica, and a huge screen rose silently from the depths of a cedar sideboard. Crowley switched on CNC to find the news was not good. The newsreader was outlining a dramatic shift in White House policy.

'Speaking in Huntsville, Ontario, before a meeting of the leaders of the G7 countries, President McGovern described global warming as our greatest challenge. Here's a little of what he had to say.'

The camera cut to vision of the president. 'The warming of our planet is the greatest crisis facing humankind today.' Standing at the edge of a lake in Ontario's Muskoka Municipality, the tall, distinguished Texan cut a powerful figure. '97 per cent of scientists now agree – this warming is primarily due to human activity, and in particular, our burning of fossil fuels,' the president warned. 'After the failures of the climate change summits, especially in Copenhagen, it will be up to countries like the United States and the other members of the G7 to show leadership. To that end, in the United States, I will shortly be introducing legislation on carbon that will see tough new emissions standards, particularly for coal-fired power stations.'

Crowley watched the broadcast, his anger growing. EVRAN's stakes in the coal industry were massive. The multinational controlled some of the world's largest coal mines, over half of the power stations in the United States, and many more around the globe. Emission controls would slash hundreds of millions from the EVRAN bottom line.

'We need market-based solutions to climate change,' the president continued, 'and for the big polluters, that will mean a charge of around US $10 per tonne of carbon dioxide emitted. It will also mean an increase in the price of fossil fuels. We can't leave it to the fossil-fuel industry, which is driven by huge profits, to regulate itself; we need to level the playing field so that wind, solar, and wave technology can compete. So I'm very pleased to see that China, now the world's second largest and fastest growing economy, has been invited to attend the G7 meeting here in Canada, and I'm very much looking forward to my discussions with the president of the People's Republic.'

'A radical change in policy for President McGovern,' the news anchor intoned, 'and as some analysts have observed, it's doubtful that McGovern would have pushed for a fee on carbon emissions if he were facing re-election, but as a man in his second term, he perhaps sees this as the legacy of his presidency . . . Now to news at home. Convicted murderer Wesley Robinson's last-minute bid for clemency has been rejected by the governor of Oklahoma. Robinson was convicted of the assassination of oil executive Marshall Bradley, and will be executed by lethal injection at ten a.m. tomorrow at Oklahoma's State Penitentiary in McAlester. In other news —'

Crowley angrily flicked the switch and the screen disappeared into its recess. He rose from his desk and stared through the château's large double-glazed windows, toward the distant coast of Corsica thousands of feet below, and the blue Mediterranean beyond. The castle dated back to the fifteenth century, when the viceroy of Corsica built it to control the central area of the island, and its original purpose mirrored Crowley's plans for the wider world. But if Washington was going down the carbon-tax route, the impact on EVRAN would be catastrophic.

Crowley had always been a big donor to both sides of politics, including to McGovern, whom he'd met with several times. He'd urged the president to can any idea of punishing business for emissions, but clearly that influence was waning, and for Crowley, getting his own man elected to the White House – someone he could control – was now the only way forward. If successful it would perfectly complement Pharos's broader strategy. But there was very little time: nominations for many states would be closing soon. It would necessitate either getting one of the declared candidates on side, or a relatively late entry. In the meantime, Crowley needed a replacement for his hit man, Wesley Robinson.

He picked up the phone and punched in a series of digits. Protected by AES 256-bit and Twofish algorithms and ciphers, the EVRAN system was virtually unbreakable.

'Yes, sir?' The phone was answered immediately by Eugene Reid, a convicted felon appointed by Crowley to head EVRAN's Area 15. Located over 8000 kilometres away on the secure top floor of EVRAN's headquarters in Dallas, in one of two glass-fronted twin towers, Area 15 was the code name for EVRAN's top-secret commercial intelligence unit. It had amused Crowley to designate the unit with the reverse code of the notorious Area 51 in Nevada, one of America's most sensitive military bases. But unlike its desert cousin, which focused on military threats, EVRAN's Area 15 was tasked with commercial espionage, targeting other energy giants like British Petroleum, Royal Dutch Shell, Chevron and Exxon-Mobil. And Area 15 had more sinister purposes.

'Elias D. Ruger,' Crowley said. 'He's about to stand trial for murder in Chicago. We need to put in a fix to get him in front of Judge Braydon O'Reilly.'

'I'm on it, sir.'

In the 1980s, the FBI had conducted Operation Greylord, a three-year undercover operation to expose endemic corruption in Chicago's courts, which at the time included a ring of clerks, in effect 'bagmen' tasked with passing bribes to corrupt judges. Judges' chambers had been bugged, and the US Department of Justice had authorised dummy cases for undercover agents and lawyers to 'fix' in front of those judges suspected of taking bribes. The last judge to be caught in the sting was Judge Thomas J. Maloney, convicted of taking over US $100 000 in bribes to acquit hit men and murderers. Crowley smiled to himself. The gap left by Maloney had been more than adequately filled by Judge O'Reilly.

Crowley put down the phone, confident that his man would be acquitted. Unlike other countries, once an accused was acquitted in the United States, the district attorney was prevented by law from appealing, even if new evidence emerged.

Crowley got up from his desk and moved toward a heavy steel door set in the inner stone wall of his office. He punched the fifteen-figure code into the lock. The door swung open noiselessly on its finely engineered bearings, and Crowley switched on the lights to illuminate the subterranean passage. He had been down here countless times, but as always, he felt a surge of adrenalin as he descended the fifty stone steps that led to an underground vault carved out of the rock. At the end of the narrow passage that led from the base of the steps, Crowley punched in a longer code that opened the final steel door. It had taken over two years and some three million dollars to construct, but the state-of-the-art gallery within was equipped with conservation and preservation systems that would not have been out of place in either the Metropolitan Museum of Art in New York City or the Louvre. Computers controlled the temperature and light levels. To guard against mould, sensitive psychrometers provided readouts on the relative humidity, and 20-watt LED lamps minimised infrared and ultraviolet radiation, all enemies of ancient masterpieces.

Crowley threw a switch to override the computers, and soft lights illuminated a dozen priceless paintings. He moved silently across the sprung wooden floor, and stood in front of Rembrandt van Rijn's *Christ in the Storm on the Sea of Galilee,* the Dutch master's only seascape. Crowley had acquired the Rembrandt and many others through Zachary Rubinstein. The Rembrandt was part of the proceeds from the heist of the Isabella Stewart Gardner Museum in Boston. On 18 March 1990, thieves stole thirteen priceless works that had never been recovered. In addition to the *Storm on the Sea of*

Galilee and Vermeer's *The Concert*, they made off with three other Rembrandts, including a self-portrait housed in the Dutch Room on the second floor, as well as Manet's *Chez Tortoni* and five other masters. The FBI, Crowley knew, had spent countless hours on the case, and despite the Gardner Museum offering a reward of US $5 million for information leading to the recovery of the works, their whereabouts remained a mystery.

Crowley smiled to himself. It gave him deep satisfaction that he and he alone was able to view the only seascape Rembrandt had ever painted. Crowley never ceased to be moved by Rembrandt's *chiaroscuro* – the artist's use of both light and dark to create the extraordinary tension in the seventeenth-century oil on canvas. The small sailing boat, with Christ in the stern, was about to be engulfed by a huge wave, and Rembrandt had used the boat's wind-torn mast to effectively divide the painting in two. To the left, he had captured a dramatic yellow light that shafted through the storm clouds, drenching the torn sail; but below the mast, where Christ was admonishing the disciples who were bailing desperately, Rembrandt had rendered the stern in semi-darkness, a darkness that was devoid of hope. Crowley nodded approvingly. Rembrandt had added an extra crew member, with a face bearing a striking resemblance to the artist himself, something Rembrandt occasionally included in his paintings, almost as an additional signature.

He paused at Vermeer's masterpiece, *The Concert,* showing three figures around a piano. Valued at US $300 million, the stolen painting was the most valuable ever to disappear from public view. The paintings of Jan Vermeer, of which there were only thirty-five known to exist in the world, invited interpretation, and Crowley had sometimes wondered whether Vermeer was depicting an illicit love affair between two of the three figures by the piano. Alongside it hung JMW Turner's 1813 work, *Landscape in Devonshire*. Oil sketches on paper by the great artist were very rare, and this was part of the proceeds of a robbery at the Leeds City Art Gallery in 1998. Turner was known as 'the painter of light', and Crowley never tired of studying the wonderful contrasts in the landscape. Climate change researchers from the Academy of Athens had started to examine the old masters to give them clues as to what the skies looked like before records were kept, and Turner's work, with his astounding sunsets and use of natural light, was being used to provide an estimate of aerosol optical depth – the amount of dust, smoke, volcanic ash and sea salts in the atmosphere. This was one Turner that would not be available to them, he mused, as he moved to admire yet another of his stolen acquisitions, Vincent van Gogh's *Poppy Flowers*.

It had been painted in 1897, shortly after Van Gogh had moved to Paris from the Netherlands, and it was in Paris that Van Gogh experimented with Impressionist styles, influenced by the likes of Toulouse-Lautrec, Pissarro and Gauguin. Van Gogh began to introduce vibrant colours into his work, of which *Poppy Flowers* was one of the finest examples. Valued at US $50 million, it had been stolen from the Mohammed Mahmoud Khalil Museum in Cairo in June of 1997. Ten years later, it was recovered in Kuwait, only to be stolen again from the same museum. Now it was Crowley's, and the authorities didn't have a clue. Crowley allowed himself another rare smile. General Khan, he knew, wanted the painting desperately, but when Crowley had discovered it was on the black market, he had immediately offered US $5 million more and gazumped the Pakistani. Rubinstein had always been amenable to the highest bidder, although Crowley had been furious when he discovered the dealer had inadvertently given Khan a clue as to where *Poppy Flowers* might have finished up. Now there was an even bigger prize, and Khan had already put the mask of Tutankhamun on the table as a price for his cooperation in the Hindu Kush. But it was one thing to offer a priceless icon, and quite another to actually hand it over. In Crowley's world, the sly little general had a use-by date. Thoughts of the Jewish dealer turned his attention back to the Euclid Papyrus, and he made his way past the Van Gogh to a glass display case on the far wall. Crowley had brought in a renowned expert from the Egyptian Supreme Council of Antiquities, ostensibly to advise on the preservation of a minor papyrus scroll he had purchased legally some years before. The EVRAN CEO had listened intently while the papyrologist explained that like the masterpieces at the other end of the gallery, papyrus was also vulnerable to oxidation, hydrolysis and acidosis, and to light. The pigments and metallic inks used by the ancient Egyptians often contained arsenic, which was especially sensitive to light and could fade entirely. In the past, the salt content of the Egyptian soil in the Nile Valley had provided a natural defence against microorganisms and fungi, so under the careful guidance of the papyrologist, Crowley had ensured that the environment of the Valley of the Kings had been faithfully replicated.

Crowley stared at the priceless fragment, browned by the centuries and secured between two pieces of three-millimetre glass by Japanese paper tabs and wheat starch paste. The contents of even this small fragment were explosive, and Crowley was in no doubt the scribe had been guided by a very high-ranking Egyptian official, perhaps Ay himself, the grand vizier or prime minister of Egypt when the nine-year-old Tutankhamun had been installed as pharaoh in 1332 BC. Crowley and many professional Egyptologists suspected that Ay might have been responsible for the king's death at the young age of eighteen. Recent X-rays of Tutankhamun's mummified body had revealed that the boy king had suffered a massive blow to the back of the head, and it was Ay who had most to gain from the king's death, succeeding him as the penultimate pharaoh of the eighteenth dynasty of the New Kingdom.

The eons had turned the ancient black ink to grey, but it was still legible, and for the umpteenth time, Crowley wrestled with the translation of the hieroglyphs: pintail ducks and scarab beetles, feathers and claws, interspersed with male and female figures, ropes and bowls, and signs for water. Crowley possessed an intimate knowledge of both the alphabetic elements and the logographic representation of whole words. To the EVRAN CEO, the first words on the Euclid fragment were clear enough.

The ancient text was headed 'Pyramids – Construction'. But under the sub-headings of 'Purpose' and 'Energy', the text made no sense, and the scribe appeared to have coded the contents list of what presumably followed on the missing pages.

As he often did on his way out of the gallery, Crowley opened the small combination safe that was set into the rock wall near the door. It contained just one thick file, and he extracted the beautifully crafted red leather folder that was embossed with gold letters: 'Pharos – A New World Order'. Crowley felt the power coursing through his veins as he thumbed the manifesto. It was all coming together.

Eight thousand kilometres away, at the direction of Crowley's executive assistant, Rachel Bannister, Area 15 was working on a critical task. Crowley had recruited Juan Pablo Hernandez, a brilliant young hacker who had served time for busting into some of the most sensitive areas of the CIA. Hacking personal computers and mobile phones was now part of Area 15's suite of capabilities.

Hernandez's agile fingers flew across the keyboard. The target was an odd one – a Professor Marcus Ahlstrom, a Nobel Prize–winning nuclear scientist – but Hernandez didn't question it. He was now earning more money than he ever dreamed of, for hacking activities that were protected inside the impenetrable firewalls of Area 15. Hernandez ran a series of programs, and although EVRAN's computers were not quite up to the power of America's National Security Agency, they were more than a match for a scientist whose internationally recognised expertise obviously didn't extend to protecting his activities on the internet.

The four groups of numbers on the screen uniquely identified Ahlstrom's laptop. Hernandez looked at his watch – just before ten a.m., which meant it was getting on for five in the afternoon in Stockholm, and Ahlstrom was online. Hernandez pulled up Ahlstrom's browser history and scanned a series of academic journals and technical articles, when suddenly, the professor went totally off tangent with an avalanche of porn sites: *Pretty Hairy GF Sucks Cock and Gets Fucked; Hairy GF With Small Breasts Spreads; Blindfolded Blonde Wife Sucks Cock and Gets a Mouthful*. Ahlstrom had logged on to over fifty sites.

Hernandez shrugged. He would include it in Ahlstrom's dossier, but so what, he thought. The professor's bored in Stockholm and, like hundreds of millions of other human beings on the planet, he'd sought a diversion. Hernandez scanned further to find the professor had gone off on a gambling tangent, which for the mathematically minded hacker was a little more interesting, particularly when he found that Ahlstrom had attempted to log on to one of the world's biggest gambling sites. It was currently under federal investigation.

Hernandez transferred the data into Ahlstrom's dossier. His fingers flew across the keyboard again, excavating Ahlstrom's password for another worldwide betting agency. Ahlstrom must get paid well, he thought, as he noted five bets, each of US $2000 on horse races at Royal Ascot in the United Kingdom; Churchill Downs in Louisville, Kentucky; Royal Randwick in Sydney; Sha Tin in Hong Kong, and Chantilly, at Oise in France. But it was the next series of sites that got Hernandez's attention. Prostitution, he knew, was illegal in Sweden, but it hadn't stopped a bevy of escorts, faces pixelated, advertising their wares. Ahlstrom had clicked on to just one with an invite: *Hi! I'm Frida. I'm so horny, and I'm hot! Big boobs, and a very sexy ass. I'll take you into some very interesting places, where you won't be disappointed, so cum on over!*

Hernandez noted the telephone number, and a short while later, he had the prostitute's address. He turned back to Ahlstrom's emails, and a short while later, he had a smoking gun.

'Paydirt!' he muttered, and this time it had nothing to do with prostitutes. Small amounts of cocaine for personal use were legal in Mexico and Portugal, but Ahlstrom was in Stockholm. And while the death penalty for drug use was generally confined to places like Saudi Arabia and Singapore, if Ahlstrom was caught, neither the Swedish police, nor the Nobel Foundation would likely be amused.

By the time Crowley emerged from his subterranean vault, the sun had already set, and a fiery red glow over the clouds above the Mediterranean had given way to the softness of the night. He made his way onto the stone balcony where Rachel Bannister was standing at the balustrade, staring out to sea. The evening breeze ruffled her long, curly red hair across her bare shoulders. The plunging neckline on her elegant black Dolce and Gabbana gown gave glimpses of her full, creamy breasts. Far below, the lights of Sartène glinted off the cobblestone streets of the medieval mountain commune.

Rachel turned and smiled seductively. She had learned long ago not to probe her boss on what might be behind the steel door in his office. 'It's such a balmy evening, I've told Chef we'll eat out here,' she said, inclining her head toward the table set for two. The sterling silver cutlery and crystal glasses reflected a soft light from the solid silver candelabra.

'Good decision,' Crowley responded, his mood lightening as he contemplated the hand-written menu on the white linen tablecloth.

'Clos des Goisses, 1988.' Rachel passed Crowley a baccarat crystal flute. A fine stream of bubbles from one of the world's truly great champagnes formed off the tiny but deliberate imperfections in the crystal.

'1988 . . . one of his best,' Crowley agreed, savouring the bouquet of yeast and vanillin.

'Did you find out anything on O'Connor and Weizman?'

Rachel nodded. 'Our man inside Langley has given us some useful information on O'Connor.' It was expensive, but Crowley made it a practice to ensure EVRAN maintained contacts in key government departments, and in the White House.

'O'Connor's an interesting one . . . brought up in Ireland in

Ballingarry, a dirt-poor mining town in southern Ireland. His father was a drunk and used to lay into O'Connor at the slightest provocation. When the father died, O'Connor's mother moved to Kilkenny where she supported herself with cleaning jobs and, not to put too fine a point on it, a succession of men friends after hours.'

'Educated?'

'O'Connor? Highly. One of his mother's men friends paid for O'Connor to go to boarding school in Dublin, but when one of the priests tried to abuse him, O'Connor beat up the priest and escaped. He's Mensa material, and he went on to Trinity College where he completed an honours thesis in chemistry, followed by a doctorate on lethal viruses and biological weapons.'

'Is that why he finished up with the CIA?' Crowley's sense of danger was heightened. If O'Connor turned out to be a threat it might take some careful planning to eliminate him.

'Eventually. He started out with Big Pharma, but didn't like what they were doing, so he took a pay cut to join the CIA.'

'A CIA agent with ethics . . . interesting combination.'

'Maybe, but he's arguably one of the best agents they have. O'Connor eventually ran afoul of the CIA's last deputy director, Howard Wiley. Wiley had sent him to Vienna to assassinate Aleta Weizman, who at the time was getting up the nose of the vice president because of her exposure of the CIA's activities with the death squads in Guatemala. When O'Connor tumbled to Wiley's reasons for the contract on her, he jumped ship and protected her. The pair went on the run, and despite several attempts to assassinate them both, they survived . . . right through to the discovery of the Maya Codex and the Inca's lost city of Paititi. Wiley's now behind bars, and likely stay there for the rest of his life.'

'Hmm.' Crowley stroked his ample chin thoughtfully. 'So O'Connor's back with the CIA?'

'They brought O'Connor's old boss – a guy by the name of McNamara – out of retirement to replace Wiley, so O'Connor's back on the payroll.'

'Married?'

'Divorced and no kids. He's had a succession of women in his life, but it doesn't seem like commitment is part of his lexicon. Although he and Weizman are probably entangled,' Rachel said with a touch of wistfulness.

'And what about Weizman?' Crowley asked.

'Like O'Connor, she's divorced and doesn't have any children. She's an internationally renowned archaeologist, with an interest in ancient civilisations . . . taking after her equally famous archaeologist grandfather, Levi Weizman. Weizman senior was employed by Himmler and the Nazis to investigate links between the Maya and the Aryan master race, but he and his wife were murdered at Mauthausen, while Weizman's father escaped to Guatemala as a boy. Weizman herself was brought up by Lake Atitlán, but when she was ten, her parents and siblings were murdered by General Montt's death squads.'

'Who were supported by Washington,' Crowley observed. 'That might explain why she's been outspoken against the CIA.'

'Exactly. Wiley was the CIA's chief of station in Guatemala City, and he was seen in Lake Atitlán's San Pedro square on the day her parents were murdered there. Years later, Weizman recognised him. She'd become a serious threat, and Wiley wanted her out of the way.'

'So you've confirmed they're in Alexandria?'

'Yes . . . apparently on holidays.'

'Is it just coincidence that they're there now?' Crowley asked. In only three days time, the Pharos Group, comprised of the world's most powerful elite, would meet for their annual conference.

'We think so. They have some expensive rebreather diving gear with them, which may or may not be significant . . . because the likes of O'Connor and Weizman are never really on holidays. Both dossiers are in your briefcase.'

'We'll need to keep an eye on these two,' said Crowley.

'Am I permitted to know why?' Rachel asked, raising an eyebrow.

'Let's just say they might be a threat . . . time will tell. And apropos of Alexandria, how are we looking there?' Crowley asked after the chef had brought out the first course of snails in garlic butter.

The secrecy surrounding Pharos was not unlike that associated with the secretive Bilderberg Group, which had been started back in 1954 under the auspices of Prince Bernhard of the Netherlands, taking its name from the first conference held at the Hotel de Bilderberg in the Netherlands village of Oosterbeek. Meeting in secret ever since, the Bilderbergers had included the likes of Queen Beatrix of the Netherlands, Queen Sofia of Spain, members of the Rockefeller and Rothschild families, Gerald Ford, Margaret Thatcher, Henry Kissinger, Tony Blair, and a hundred more of the world's leaders in politics, banking, industry, the media and the military. The conspiracy theories were rife, amid accusations the Bilderbergers were planning a New World Order, facilitated by a shadowy, powerful clique pulling key economic levers, the United States invading Iraq to secure oil and bases in the Middle East, and a plan to reduce the world's population. But whatever the agenda of the Bilderbergers, the Pharos Group was far more powerful, and Pharos *was* planning a New World Order. One in which this small group of already mega-wealthy and immensely powerful individuals would control a hidden one-world government through control of the world's monetary reserves and stock exchanges, and by controlling the world's major political systems.

The plan was ambitious, but provided the Pharos group could engineer crises to strike fear into the hearts of investors on the world stock markets, it was achievable. The world's major political systems would be taken over by Pharos candidates, leading to a non-elected one-world government. A common single currency, controlled by the Pharos merchant banks, would replace all other currencies, and as the stock markets fluctuated wildly, other financial institutions would be crushed and ultimately eliminated.

The plan went beyond mere financial and political control though, to the heart of society and culture itself. The middle class would also be eliminated, leaving only rulers and servants. The number of children in families would be regulated and the world population reduced. National boundaries would be abolished, and a single legal system of world courts would operate under a unified Pharos legal code, upheld by a one-world government police force, a one-world military with standardised equipment, and a single, controlled, multinational media corporation. For Crowley and the other members of Pharos, it was the ultimate power that Hitler, Goebbels and others had only dreamed of: a subservient population under the control of a small Illuminati.

'We're all set for Alexandria,' said Rachel. 'I've put a copy of the latest Oxfam report in your briefcase. The figures indicate that the wealth of the eighty-five richest people in the world is now equal to the entire wealth of the 3.5 billion people in the bottom half.'

Crowley smiled. The plan was on track.

'The pilots will be standing by at Figari Sud-Corse from eight a.m. tomorrow.' An alternative to Aéroport d'Ajaccio Napoléon Bonaparte, the island's major airport, the smaller provincial airfield of Figari Sud-Corse was perfect. It was less than 50 kilometres away, and with an 8000-foot runway, it would easily accommodate the EVRAN Gulfstream G550.

'The background papers for Alexandria are also in your attaché case,' said Rachel, 'but there'll be time enough for that tomorrow.' She leaned forward and stroked Crowley's arm, giving him another glimpse of her breasts, her nipples already hard.

Crowley felt the familiar primeval stirring in his loins. Rachel was not the only woman to turn him on, but her abandonment, both in the bedroom and out of it, gave him a satisfaction that his wife, Lillian, had long since ceased to match.

Chef appeared, pushing a polished wooden flame cart, from which he served the crispy duck. He poured the Château Latour, which had been decanted and left to breathe for an hour, waited while Crowley tasted it, and then retired.

'The attendees have all responded?' Crowley asked.

Rachel nodded. She had already committed it to memory. The list of invitees was never allowed out of Alexandria. 'General Khan will be there . . . you asked about him particularly?'

'Little Pakistani shit,' Crowley swore.

'Then why invite him?'

'He's an Islamic nutter, and no friend of the West. He wants the entire world subject to Sharia law, but the short answer is we need him,' Crowley admitted, savouring his Latour.

Rachel looked at her boss quizzically, but he didn't elaborate.

'Louis Walden will be there,' she said, aware that the media mogul was also critical to Crowley's plans. The tentacles of Omega Centauri Corporation, the world's largest media multinational, reached into every corner of the globe. Walden controlled vast numbers of television and radio stations, newspapers, magazines, and film studios.

'As will René du Bois,' she added. Crédit Group, with assets exceeding a staggering US $20 billion, dwarfed the holdings of HSBC, Deutsche Bank, Barclays, JP Morgan Chase, the Bank of America and the Industrial and Commercial Bank of China combined.

'He's able to travel?' Crowley asked.

'That will depend on the appeal today,' said Rachel, thinking back to the last Alexandria conference where she'd made the mistake of being alone with Du Bois in the lift. The powerful French banker had attempted to grope her, and Rachel had promptly slammed her knee into his groin.

'The charges are serious, but his lawyers are confident his passport will be returned. I had a message to thank you for your testimonial. We'll know by midday tomorrow.'

Crowley nodded. A Filipina kitchen hand had accused Du Bois of sexual assault, but the CCTV footage had mysteriously disappeared, so in the end, it would come down to the word of the hired help against that of the world's most influential financier. Crowley smiled to himself. Not only was the kitchen hand up against one of the most formidable legal teams money could buy, but Louis Walden had seen to it that a photograph of a prostitute outside a brothel in Manila, photoshopped to closely resemble the kitchen hand, was now getting wide coverage in Centauri outlets. The story was getting legs in the rest of the media, which was just as well, Crowley thought.

The Pharos meeting could not be postponed, and like Walden, Du Bois was critical to the objectives of Pharos.

'And the rest?'

'All have accepted,' Rachel confirmed, quietly naming fifteen of the world's most powerful elite: mega-wealthy industrialists, European royalty, politicians and the military, including the former Head of the World Bank, Samuel P. Talbot, former US secretary of state, Bradley 'Jay' Guthrie, and the former chairman of the US Joint Chiefs of Staff, General Blaine T. Bradshaw. The Pharos Group might have been smaller than the Bilderbergers but the power was more concentrated, and every member was of the same mind. It was time to take over the world's political and financial institutions. It was time for a New World Order.

'When do you think Pharos will move?' Rachel asked, leaning forward seductively.

'Soon,' Crowley opined. 'The global financial crisis has put us in a powerful position, and we're well on the way to controlling the world's financial systems, but we need more progress on the political front. I was listening to that dropkick McGovern earlier tonight . . . he's now talking about a carbon tax, something he wouldn't have dared raise in his first term. We're going to need insurance . . . our own man in the White House,' Crowley said. 'But we can talk about that on the way to Alexandria.' He reached across the table and fondled Rachel's breasts.

Rachel rose from the table and slowly led Crowley across to the balustrade. The lights of Sartène and the other villages dotted around the mountains glimmered below. Rachel turned toward her boss and let her hand wander, fondling Crowley's growing erection.

'Unzip me,' she commanded huskily. Crowley obliged and she

let her gown fall to the cobblestoned patio, standing in only her black lace Agent Provocateur knickers. Rachel slowly undid Crowley's belt, knelt in front of his bulge, and released his throbbing cock. She took him in her mouth, and then ran her tongue up and down his shaft. Still taunting him, she slowly and deliberately got to her feet, stepped out of her knickers, turned and leaned on the balustrade, her breasts swinging above the stonework.

'Fuck me,' she whispered, parting her legs and staring at the lights of the villages below. 'Fuck me.' The words caught in her throat as Crowley grasped her hips and plunged into her.

7

NATIONAL SECURITY AGENCY, FORT MEADE, MARYLAND

Five a.m. The dawn was breaking over Fort Meade. Barbara Murray, a senior analyst at the National Security Agency, slowed on Route 295 South and took the exit marked 'NSA Restricted Entrance'. Now in her fifteenth year with the world's largest and most secretive intelligence collection agency, Murray was working on some of the most sensitive material in the world, in the compartmentalised Special Collections section which required a clearance over and above TOP SECRET. The section was tasked with monitoring the phone calls of world leaders, friend or foe.

A short while later, the petite freckle-faced redhead passed through the first security barrier, one of over a hundred watch posts protecting the installation, and she pulled into a space in the car park, one of 18 000 provided for employees. The car park was already close to half full, and despite Murray's director calling her at three a.m. for a task that had the highest priority, neither the time of the request nor the state of the car park was unusual. The NSA operated around the clock, 365 days a year.

'Crypto City', as it was known to the thousands of personnel who worked there, was not unlike West Berlin before the wall came down. The 'city' had every amenity, including its own private bank, shopping centre, movie theatre, sporting facilities, big band jazz group, police force, fire department, eleven cafeterias – the largest capable of serving 6000 personnel – and clubs for everything from battle gaming to ham radio – even a yacht club. Despite being landlocked behind a heavily guarded fence, Room 2S160 of the Ops 1 building had been set aside as a meeting room for members of the Arundel Yacht Club, one of the most exclusive yacht clubs in the world. Only those with an NSA clearance were allowed membership.

Murray locked her car and made her way across to the operations building, a massive complex protected by dark, one-way glass, behind which was an orange copper screen, an air gap, and more glass panelling. Codenamed 'Tempest', the shielding was designed to ensure that no electromagnetic radiation or signal could escape, much less allow would-be eavesdroppers to penetrate the building. The NSA seal, a huge painting of an eagle grasping a key in its talons, dominated the foyer of the pentagonal-shaped entrance. Murray inserted her colour-coded security pass into the access terminal and punched in her personal identification code. The light turned green and she pushed through the turnstile, while deep below the corridor, an officer on the early morning shift in NSA's Security Command Post watched her enter. The command post monitored hundreds of cameras focused on all but the most sensitive areas of the massive complex.

A short distance away, on the second floor of the specially designed NSA computer building, banks of some of the world's most powerful supercomputers hummed quietly as they scanned the electronic spectrum. The supercomputers worked twenty-four hours a day, and would melt if it were not for the massive cooling system one floor below, where 8000 tonnes of chilled water passed through huge pipes, cooling the system's fluorinert, a clear, tasteless, inert fluid used to keep the state-of-the-art machines at an operating temperature. The NSA no longer had the world's fastest computers – that honour now belonged to China and the Chinese National University of Defence Technology's 'Tianhe-2', which was capable of a staggering thirty-three petaflops, or 33 000 billion calculations a second – but the NSA was moving to catch up, and a huge new data supercomputer centre had been completed in Utah. Murray knew it would be needed. Since modern technology had taken over from the telephone and the telegram, the electronic spectrum had become unimaginably crowded. In 1973, when Motorola introduced the first mobile phone, it weighed over a kilogram and was a quarter of a metre long; it wasn't until 1992 that the NSA had seen the first text message. But since the commercialisation of the internet in 1995, the electronic spectrum had reached a point where over 300 billion emails were sent around the world every day; in the United States alone, over six billion texts went through the ether. The NSA's 'Dishfire' program was designed to vacuum a substantial number of those, including the location and numbers of mobile users around the world.

Murray made her way through the labyrinth of corridors until she reached OPS 1, the home of the National Security Operations Centre. She entered a glass booth, swiped her card and waited for a green light which told her to look into an eyepiece for iris-recognition. The booth also calculated her weight, a precaution against two people being in the booth, and once 'CONFIRM' showed on the data screen, she was allowed through.

The essential start to the day achieved – coffee from the section's nonstop percolator – Murray punched another series of codes into her computer, and pulled up the task the director had ordered her to undertake with such urgency:

Target:
Lieutenant General Farid Khan.
Sacked head of Pakistani Inter Service Intelligence Agency.
Broad spectrum.

Murray knew that with over 10 000 employees, both military and civilian, the ISI was one of the biggest intelligence agencies in the world, but more importantly, the ISI had long held links to the Taliban and other terrorist groups who might pose a threat to Western nations.

Murray started to dig, and it wasn't long before she hit one of a series of firewalls around the internal workings of the ISI. Clearly, Khan was not fully 'retired': he had the highest priority for computer access. Murray's fingers flew over the keyboard as the NSA's massive computers went into high gear. Less than ten minutes later, in what would have taken a home desktop thousands of years, billions of possible codes and combinations had been analysed, and she was behind the firewalls and into Khan's ISI accounts. A short while later, Murray had possession of two personal emails, and four mobile phone numbers.

Murray punched in another code and pulled up XKeyscore. It was just one of many NSA top secret spying programs. STELLAR

WIND targeted telephone companies and internet providers to gain access to domestic communications. BLACKPEARL was designed to get inside banking operations like the SWIFT network used for international transfers, as well as well-protected large commercial networks, like Brazil's massive Petrobas energy multinational. Across the Atlantic, Britain's GCHQ was employing an equally top secret TEMPORA program to tap into the fibre-optic transatlantic cables carrying internet traffic between the United States and Europe.

XKeyscore was an extension of the Echelon program, which for years had connected the NSA with listening stations around the world, including Menwith Hill in the United Kingdom; Australian satellite communications stations at Pine Gap, Geraldton and Shoal Bay in the Northern Territory; Waihopai and Tangimoana in New Zealand; Griesheim–Darmstadt in Germany; Gander in Canada; and a host of other top secret collection bases. Far more powerful than Echelon, XKeyscore gave the NSA the capability to tap into any conversation anywhere in the world. It could also tap into any personal computer to discover what websites the user had been visiting, what search engines and criteria a target might be using, the contents of emails and SMS messages, and real-time video conversations. It was a capability only limited by the sheer volume of internet traffic, and the billions of intercepts were held on what was known as a metadatabase – data that gave leads to more detailed data.

Murray again tasked the supercomputers, and an avalanche of Khan's emails and phone intercepts appeared on her screens. She smiled to herself. It was not the first time, nor would it be the last, that XKeyscore would provide a window into embarrassing emails. Just as some senators and representatives in Congress maintained private email addresses, in the mistaken belief they provided protection for their illicit affairs, the Pakistani general not only had a mistress, but in a country where alcohol was not readily available, he had enough influence to ensure his fridge was well stocked.

> Arrive Lahore tomorrow, Pearl Continental, meetings and dinner until 9, but car will pick you up at 8.30 and bring you to the staff entrance - Presidential Suite - keys with driver in envelope. Krug in the fridge. Looking forward to getting together again!
> Farid.

In fact, the general was a very busy boy, Murray mused, as she opened an email for another assignation in Karachi the following evening. Murray probed past the peccadillos, looking for anything that might connect the general and the Pakistani ISI to activities that could threaten the United States. An hour later, Murray had a lead, although it was just a snippet, and it would need further investigation. Khan had received a text from a mobile phone not found anywhere on the NSA's metadatabase, and the text appeared to emanate from somewhere in Venice:

> Scorpions en route. Artifact acquisition in train.

Khan had forwarded the information on the scorpions to a satellite phone in the Hindu Kush.

8

ALEXANDRIA HARBOUR, EGYPT

Dr Omar Aboud had chosen his position well, high on the upper parapet of Fort Qaytbey, hidden at the rear of a deep loophole slit. To those tourists exploring the fort, it appeared that he was just another one of them, albeit equipped with powerful binoculars.

Aboud watched O'Connor and Aleta with interest as they prepared to dive. He noted the location the pair had chosen, a small protected inlet just to the west of the fort, but it had not escaped his notice that his targets were preparing to dive with Dräger LAR V rebreather scuba gear, the same type the US Navy SEALs used. Interesting, Aboud thought. O'Connor, he'd been briefed, had completed the SEAL combat diving course. Was the Dräger equipment just O'Connor's scuba gear of choice, Aboud wondered, or was there a darker motive? Dräger gear was state-of-the-art, and because exhaled air was purified for rebreathing, the system was capable of much longer endurance than a normal set of open-circuit tanks. More importantly, Dräger left no telltale trail of bubbles.

O'Connor scanned the area around the stone base and the ramparts of Fort Qaytbey, but Alexandria was a recognised dive site, and no one appeared to be taking the slightest notice of either him or Aleta. In 1961, an Egyptian diver had stumbled on a collection of statues off Fort Qaytbey, the site of the old Pharos lighthouse, and since then, Jean-Yves Empereur, the diminutive Honor Frost, Franck Goddio and others had explored the archaeological site. Over the years, a picture had begun to emerge of what the old city of Alexandria would have looked like. It was a picture that Aleta was familiar with, but she was keen to explore for herself.

'You're still expecting someone to be tailing us?'

'Hope for the best, plan for the worst . . . it's an old CIA dictum,' O'Connor said. 'Put it down to habit.'

'So what can we expect to find?' O'Connor asked, changing the subject.

'A lot more than archaeologists of the past thought was here,' said Aleta. 'For decades, they concentrated on the Valley of the Kings and the other tombs along the Nile. It wasn't until the 1990s that we realised that the ruins of the old city of Alexandria are not only beneath the footpaths, where you can find part of an ancient water system, but there are extensive ruins beneath the waves. Even though some of the sphinx and columns have been brought to the surface, there are thousands of items still on the sea floor, and some of the huge blocks and columns are undoubtedly part of the Pharos lighthouse.'

'It must have been quite something.'

'It was, and one day, when you're not busy in your black world, I'd like to dive a little further out, because about thirteen kilometres from here we can find the wreck of the SS *Aragon*, which was sunk by a German submarine in 1917 with over 2500 marines on board.'

'I seem to remember there was another British ship close by?'

'HMS *Attack* . . . she came to the rescue of the *Aragon*, but was blown in half. They both lie on the seabed, not far apart . . . but let's see what we can find today,' said Aleta. 'Once we've explored the area beyond the fort, we'll need to get back into the inner harbour, and I'm in your hands. It's over a kilometre to the eastern breakwater, and the visibility won't be great,' she said.

'No problem, I've got the course mapped out,' said O'Connor, checking his wrist compass, 'although you would think if there was anything else to be found on the eastern side, other archaeologists might have discovered it?'

Aleta smiled. 'If we subscribed to that theory, many of the great discoveries would still be waiting to be made. Howard Carter worked for five years in the Valley of the Kings, and he found very little. Lord Carnavon, who was financing him, gave him one last season in 1922, during which one of Carter's workmen stumbled on an ancient set of steps which led to Tutankhamun's tomb.'

'Let's see what we can find,' O'Connor said with a grin, leading the way to the edge of the water. O'Connor and Aleta did a final negative pressure test, opened their cylinder valves and double checked the pressure on them, confirmed their oxygauges, and checked the bailout bottles and the buoyancy compensator low pressure inflators. O'Connor made the 'O' ring signal with his thumb and forefinger, the international diving signal for 'I'm okay'. Aleta responded, and they disappeared beneath the smooth waters of the Mediterranean.

Aleta knew visibility could get down to less than a metre, but the weather had been kind, and although hazy, it was out to 30 metres or so, and O'Connor followed easily in the wake of Aleta's bright yellow fins. They headed out the inlet where ubiquitous bream and other small species flitted past. Almost immediately, the first of thousands of broken pieces of Greek columns came into view, not far from where the massive statue of the Egyptian goddess Isis, the mother of Horus, the hawk-headed Egyptian god of war, had been recovered. It was here that the massive statue of Ptolemy that had once stood at the base of the Pharos lighthouse had also been recovered by marine archaeologists. Aleta changed direction to the north-east, and shortly afterward, a massive headless sphinx appeared, still sitting on the sandy bottom where it had lain for centuries. For the next hour the pair explored the obelisks, stone door posts from the Pharos lighthouse and Ptolemaic statues. Suddenly, Aleta froze, and turned, with one hand making a fin in front of her mask, the international signal for shark. O'Connor moved forward to protect her. A big great white had chosen this moment to put in a rare appearance off Alexandria. The shark started to circle, which was never a good sign, but it was not yet moving in a zigzag pattern, which O'Connor knew was an indication of an immediate attack. O'Connor unhurriedly motioned Aleta back to the sphinx. Both knew that sharks had tiny sensors in their snout and lower jaw that picked up electrical signals in the water that were caused by muscle contraction. To swim quickly at this point would be to mimic the signals of a wounded fish or seal.

The great white was now circling a metre from the bottom. With their backs to the ancient monument, O'Connor had limited the shark's options to a frontal attack.

O'Connor moved his palm up and down, signalling Aleta to remain calm, and they watched the magnificent creature in awe.

Even though it was over four metres long, and would have weighed over a tonne, its movements were unhurried and graceful. The torpedo-shaped shark was a deep grey on top, changing to white on the underbelly. Its huge round eyes were wide open, although just before an attack, the shark would roll them back into their sockets for protection.

The animal disappeared behind the blind side of the sphinx and the pair waited for it to reappear. O'Connor and Aleta had encountered great whites before, and while never a zen moment, both knew the shark's preferred prey consisted of seals, dolphins and rays, which they usually attacked from below. Attacks on humans were almost always a case of mistaken identity – to a shark, a board rider with arms and legs extended could look like an elephant seal from below, but with over 3000 razor-sharp teeth, and a bite that exceeded one tonne of pressure per square inch, that was usually cold comfort to the board rider.

The animal appeared around the sphinx, closer now, and suddenly it charged, pectoral fins down and back arched in classic attack mode.

9

CORSICA

The low hills to the north of Corsica's Figari Sud-Corse airfield flashed past the windows and the EVRAN Gulfstream G550 powered into a clear Mediterranean sky. The aircraft climbed quickly, banking to the left toward the Italian island of Sardinia, before setting a south-easterly course that would take it across the southern tip of Italy and on to Alexandria on Africa's northern coast.

As soon as they reached cruising altitude, the steward appeared with Crowley's customary croissants, percolated coffee and champagne.

'Did you make any progress on getting us a scientist to debunk this climate change crap?' Crowley asked Rachel who was seated in the plush leather chair opposite. 'I've got a feeling this is going to be front and centre at the next presidential election, and we need someone with gravitas who can swing the voters against it.'

Rachel withdrew a folder from her soft leather attaché case. 'Down to three candidates, but before we left, I received a report from Hernandez in Area 15. The most promising is a Professor Ahlstrom.'

'The Swedish Nobel Laureate?'

'One and the same – due to receive his prize in Stockholm next week for his groundbreaking work in nuclear physics.'

'So why would someone like Ahlstrom be a candidate? He's more likely to speaking out *against* fossil fuels?'

'You need to look to the second page,' said Rachel. 'Area 15 has turned up some interesting data on our professor. Ahlstrom's presently at the Massachusetts Institute of Technology, which is about as prestigious as it gets, but as you can see from the report, our man has some interesting habits.'

A slow smile spread across Crowley's face as he scanned Rachel's report and the meticulous research from Area 15. 'So even the Nobel's ten million Swedish krona isn't going to get this guy off the hook?'

Rachel shook her head. 'And it's not quite that much. The prize varies according to how much the committee has in the fund, and given the current sluggishness of world financial markets, it's rumoured that this year it'll be reduced to eight million krona, which is a little over a million dollars. But as you can see from the report, in between frequenting nuclear physics laboratories, our man Ahlstrom has expensive habits . . . mainly cocaine, gambling and high-priced call girls, and his wife's just filed for what's going to be a costly divorce. Vivienne Ahlstrom's a well-regarded scientist in her own right, and until now, she's turned a blind eye to Ahlstrom's dalliances, but now the kids have left, apparently she just wants out.'

'Can she be bought? If we go with this guy, we'll need to settle this quickly.'

'If you mean, "will she remain out of the spotlight?", I think so. She's already got someone else on the scene, so I think she'll be happy to settle. Half the Nobel should do it, but she'll want the house.'

'Make sure she gets it.' Crowley stroked his chin thoughtfully. 'Homeless and up to his armpits in debt...'

Rachel nodded. 'It will be a real coup if we can get Ahlstrom to switch camps. If a scientist of his reputation starts to rubbish climate change science, the rest of the world will listen. And I think it's a better than even chance. The drug thugs and the banks are already circling.'

'And the other two?' Crowley asked, flicking through the remaining dossiers.

'They're possibilities, but they're pretty clean. I've only included them because they're both well known and like Ahlstrom, highly respected in the broader international scientific community, and from our point of view, they'd be pretty credible. But although both have had the odd affair, none of those are ongoing, and their finances are in much better shape, so the leverage for us isn't nearly as strong.'

'How much is it going to cost to bring Ahlstrom on board?'

'One and a half million should get the drug barons, bookmakers and banks off his back, and if we offer him a place to stay – a town house should do it – then it's a matter of how much he'll want to jump off the climate ship.'

'Half a million a year?'

Rachel frowned. 'That might be a little generous. If you want me to negotiate though, I'll keep that one in reserve.'

'Let's do it. As soon as this conference is over, get yourself up to Stockholm. I'll have Prince Johan organise you a ticket for the

Nobel ceremony,' Crowley said, handing back the folder. Half a million a year would be money well spent, he thought. It was only a fraction of what he paid Rachel, but she was as ruthless as she was good in bed, and worth every dime.

'And the security situation in Alexandria?'

'The military are expecting protests, but that shouldn't bother us. They're mainly confined to the harbour foreshores.'

Crowley nodded, a satisfied look on his face. The more unrest there was in this part of the world, the more likely oil prices would rise.

The EVRAN corporate jet rolled to a stop on the south-west side of the runway at Alexandria's Borg el Arab International Airport, away from the main terminal. In a measure of the power of the Pharos group, immigration and customs procedures that might take mere mortals and even government officials an hour or more were handled quickly and discreetly. Three black Mercedes were waiting on the tarmac: one for Crowley and Rachel, and two for Crowley's personal bodyguards, several of whom were moonlighting members of the powerful Egyptian military.

A short distance after leaving the airport, the small convoy swept past the outlying areas of Al Hawwariyyah and Qaryat Shakush, already threatened by the advancing Sahara Desert to the west. The largest desert in the world was expanding at the rate of six kilometres a year, which over the next one hundred years would not only prove a problem for cities like Alexandria on the Nile delta, it would devastate many areas of the African continent itself – but that was not a thought Sheldon Crowley entertained. For the CEO of the world's largest emitter, the chardonnay-swilling, leftie fluffballs who constantly advocated government taxes to eliminate climate change were a far bigger threat. They reached a large roundabout and turned right onto the Cairo–Alexandria Desert Road and the convoy weaved its way past rusted buses belching black smoke, ancient Soviet Lada taxis in their ubiquitous yellow and black livery, camels and rubber-wheeled horse-drawn carts of doubtful origin.

The convoy came to a halt outside the huge wrought-iron gates of the Kashta Palace, in the wealthy Somuha area to the south of the city. The palace, like many that had once belonged to Egypt's King Farouk, had been used as a guesthouse for VIPs. The eighteenth-century building, modelled on the Palace of Versailles, had accommodation for up to forty guests, and for the Pharos Group, it was perfect. Secure and secluded, it was away from the troubles erupting on the Corniche, the waterfront promenade that ran around Alexandria's harbour. And not only was the Kashta Palace removed from any disturbances, the fifty hectares of gardens made it almost impossible for anyone to eavesdrop on conversations as the participants strolled along the paths in breaks between briefings.

Rachel opened the window of the Mercedes and produced two passports. The guard snapped to attention and saluted.

'*Ahlan wa sahlan, Sayad* . . . welcome back, sir.'

Crowley waved dismissively, and the convoy moved up the long, gravel drive lined with palm trees. Between the Pharos meetings the palace was left vacant, guarded by a skeleton security staff; now, every hundred metres or so, the convoy passed detachments of the Pharos guards. Heavily armed with Heckler & Koch MP5 sub-machine guns with laser sights, earpieces in place and dressed in black, they were instantly recognisable. More were stationed around the perimeter of the gardens. The whole area was covered by CCTV, with security controlled from a command centre in the basement beside the extensive wine cellar. The convoy swept under the stone portico supported by magnificent stone pillars, topped with the carved faces of the pharaohs, from Tutankhamun to Ramesses II. Above the portico, on the third floor roof, more armed guards scanned the perimeter from behind the stone balustrades.

To the outside world, the existence of the shadowy, eponymous Pharos group was virtually unknown, and even those who had heard of it had no idea that Pharos himself was Sheldon Crowley. Next morning Pharos surveyed the fourteen men and one woman seated at the polished mahogany table of the conference room. They either controlled a substantial proportion of the world's resources, or were in very strong positions of influence, or in many cases both. But no single member had the power to achieve a New World Order on their own. The membership had been carefully crafted to create a powerful hidden synergy. On the wall behind Pharos were two large, framed quotes:

'Let me issue and control a nation's money and
I care not who writes the laws.'
– Mayer Amschel Rothschild, 1744–1812,
founder of the House of Rothschild

Beside it was another framed quote:

> *'Behind the ostensible government sits enthroned*
> *an Invisible Government owing no allegiance and*
> *acknowledging no responsibility to the people.'*
> *– Theodore Roosevelt, 1858–1919,*
> *twenty-sixth president of the United States*

Together, the quotes encapsulated the ideology of the Pharos Group.

In front of each place at the table was a soft leather folder containing the participant's confidential briefing notes on the current world financial situation and predictions for the movement of stocks and shares. The folders included secret information on the G7 governments of the US, the UK, Germany, France, Italy, Japan and Canada, as well as detailed notes on a rising Russia, China, India and Brazil, and predictions on the likelihood of political change.

'Given the upheavals in the Middle East,' Pharos began, 'the world is more unstable than at any time since 1939, and that is something we intend to turn to our advantage. I am reminded of a statement by the thirty-third president of the United States, Harry S. Truman. In 1941, when he was a little-known senator from Missouri, he said, "If we see that Germany is winning we ought to help Russia, and if Russia is winning, we ought to help Germany, and that way let them kill as many as possible." It is a strategy we can employ throughout the Middle East and beyond, as we move to gain ultimate power. That strategy is at Flag A of your briefing notes. Firstly, we need to take control of the world's finances and stock exchanges; and secondly, we need our people at the top of the major political institutions. Any views?'

'Fortunately for us, not many people know that the US Federal Reserve is owned by the banks and not the government.' René du Bois, the tall, distinguished CEO of the world's largest merchant banking group, spoke with a heavy French accent, and an air of authority. Much to Pharos's displeasure, a small section of the French media was still pursuing the allegations made by the Filipina kitchen hand, but at least Du Bois' lawyers had been successful in getting his passport returned.

'We are already the major player in the Fed,' said Du Bois, 'but we need to increase our own holdings while we weaken the other banks to the point we can wipe them out, one by one. On the wider front, the key to control is *debt*.' Du Bois paused to let his emphasis take hold. 'As you're well aware, when governments need money, they print money, buy their bonds and charge interest. The money goes into circulation via the banks, which create more money through customer loans, which goes into circulation through additional banks, which in turn repeat the process. *Debt* is the key to our control of the world money markets. We're also in positions of influence at the World Bank and the International Monetary Fund, and through those organisations, we can impose much more debt on the developing countries to keep them in a position of subservience.' Du Bois smirked. It was all so easy for those on the inside. Even those in positions of political power rarely understood who was really pulling the levers.

'We, of course, need to continue to improve our position vis-à-vis our stock holdings, by manipulating the world's stock markets. Nowhere have we been more successful in this manipulation than through this mythical war on terror,' Du Bois continued, 'especially in the Middle East. It's this region that offers us the greatest opportunities to create chaos on the stock markets. Once the masses are enslaved through overwhelming debt, we can influence a change from capitalism and democracy to acceptance of our world government.'

'Changing that culture of capitalism will not be easy, especially in emerging consumer economies like China,' observed Samuel P. Talbot, the baby-faced former Head of the World Bank, 'although I agree with the thrust of the argument. We can use the World Bank and the International Monetary Fund to increase control over developing counties, but we need continued control of the majority of the world's media to ensure the real picture is not reported,' he said, looking at Louis Walden, the short, balding media baron.

'Changing the culture is difficult but not impossible,' Pharos observed. 'Our own energy and finance multinationals will continue operations unabated, and once we have more of our people in bodies like the UN, we can start a campaign aimed at getting the masses to agree to a post-capitalist world. Through the media, we create the perception that the capitalist system is riven with corruption, and driven by pursuit of blind profit. We begin to make a very strong case that people will be much better off under the control of a revitalised UN – essentially a world government whose finances we control, and where universal production brigades produce only what is needed on a sustainable basis. The lunatic Left embraces it, and the masses rise up against greed and corruption to embrace a wiser system of ration quotas and an acceptance of duties assigned to them. But first,' he warned, 'we have to gain control of the world's political systems from within.'

Pharos turned to a new section of his folder. 'You will see from your briefing notes at Flag B that the only political systems we can predict with any certainty, at least for now, are those of China and Russia. For China's chairman, Xi Jinping, it will be business as usual, although he will face growing pressure from the hundreds of millions of his countrymen who are not sharing in China's newfound wealth. And therein lies an opportunity to destabilise the regime, although that may be a couple of years off yet . . . Any thoughts?'

Pharos listened intently as the discussion ranged from likely GDP growth rates, to future labour problems under the one-child policy that had produced a birth rate that was the lowest in Chinese history.

'And we should be mindful of another weakness which we can turn to our advantage,' Louis Walden added, 'and that's the internet. Sina Weibo, the Chinese equivalent of Twitter, is starting to give the wider public a voice, and although the government has managed to maintain their censorship controls, they're vulnerable to cyber attacks.'

Pharos made a note as the participants probed the weaknesses of the Chinese regime, before the discussion turned to Russia.

'Vladimir Putin is firmly in control,' said Pharos, 'and the Russians have plans.' Pharos flicked the remote, bringing up a map of what Pharos analysts predicted Europe might look like with a resurgent Russia. 'With the annexation of the Crimea from Ukraine, Russia has gained the rights to huge oil and gas reserves in the Black and Azov Seas off the Crimean coast – ten billion barrels of oil and four trillion cubic metres of natural gas, and that's just the start.'

'Apart from Germany and France, the Eurozone is still a basket case,' Du Bois agreed, 'but there are weaknesses in the long term. Russia badly needs capital investment, and if the oil price drops, we can exploit that, because that will impact on the Kremlin's ability to improve living standards.'

Again, Pharos listened intently before he brought the discussion to a close. 'As long as Vladimir Putin's there, the political systems in Russia are going to be a tough nut to crack, but the situation in the United States is very different,' he said, with a rare smile. The discovery of large-scale shale oil deposits had the potential to finally bring the United States self-sufficiency in energy and free her from the shackles of unfriendly regimes in the Middle East and other tenuous overseas supplies.

'The problems in the United States start with the current administration,' Crowley observed. 'McGovern made a speech in Huntsville the other day – the usual left-wing nonsense about climate change, when half the country's digging themselves out from under snow drifts, for Christ's sake. But McGovern's not taking any notice of that, and now, for the first time, we may see a move toward legislation taxing carbon emissions. One of the greatest threats we face to our operations in coal, oil and gas is a tax on carbon, and it's got to be stopped. We need the Republican Party back in power.'

'And we would need someone in the White House we could control,' the former secretary of state Bradley Guthrie observed. 'Someone we could count on.'

'And to guarantee that, we need someone with skeletons in his closet. I'm working on that,' Crowley said, an air of confidence about him.

10

ALEXANDRIA HARBOUR

The massive great white zigzagged toward O'Connor and Aleta, its lower jaw extended, vicious serrated teeth now horrifyingly visible. O'Connor moved in front of Aleta to protect her. Great whites, he knew, often took a sample bite out of humans, but would mostly let go and move on. But O'Connor wasn't about to become part of the sampling process. He pressed his fins against the submerged sphinx, propelled himself toward the attacking shark and smashed his heavy metal diving light into the animal's sensitive nose.

O'Connor was slammed back by the force of the impact and the torch tumbled out of his outstretched arm, but he had struck the shark at its most vulnerable point. At the top of the food chain, with no predators, great whites were not used to prey that fought back, and the huge animal scraped along the side of the sphinx as it abruptly turned and swam away.

'Okay?' O'Connor signalled with his forefinger and thumb.

Aleta's face was ashen behind her mask, but she managed a smile and returned his signal.

Just to be sure, they waited for five minutes, but when the graceful animal didn't return, O'Connor gave the signal for Aleta to follow him. He set his compass heading at 90 degrees magnetic and they swam due east for 600 metres, with O'Connor constantly checking behind to ensure the great white hadn't returned. Abeam of the western breakwater, O'Connor changed his heading to 142 degrees and they entered the harbour through the main channel, which at its deepest was only nine metres. Its western counterpart was one of the oldest ports in the world, handling over three quarters of Egypt's shipping trade, but the eastern harbour they were entering was not navigable for large vessels and it sloped gently upwards toward the shore. The water was murkier now, although the coarse grey sand of the bottom was still visible. Two reefs lay to the east, and after another thousand metres the submerged island of Antirhodos appeared in the distance.

Aleta took the lead and O'Connor followed her around the royal island, which had once stood two metres above the sea. Aleta swam slowly across the paved white rocks of the Roman roads, across fallen red granite columns to a magnificent statue of a priest of the goddess Isis, and on to a sphinx, the face of which bore the image of Ptolemy XII, Cleopatra's father. A school of double-banded bream drifted among the sunken ruins, oblivious to the two divers.

Aleta turned north, crossing an area that had once been a royal port. Two hundred metres on, she pointed out the ruins of the Timonium, a small, luxurious palace built by the Roman general Marcus Antonius. Antonius had taken refuge there after he and Cleopatra had been defeated by Octavian at the Battle of Actium.

O'Connor and Aleta reached the main peninsula of the Poseidium, and the ruins of the Temple to Poseidon, where mariners once offered prayers for safe voyages. Both divers paused, knowing they were now opposite their hotel. They were getting close to where the old library had been indicated on the papyrus map. O'Connor withdrew the waterproof copy from his belt bag and placed it on the old Roman road, orienting it with his compass.

Aleta, her face animated behind her mask, indicated 'one hundred metres' and gestured toward the north-east. O'Connor nodded in agreement and switched on his underwater GPS. Prior to the dive, he'd hidden the satellite radio antennae beside some rocks just out from the eastern shoreline, enabling communication with the satellite above. The transducer in the water converted the satellite signals to acoustic signals which O'Connor's GPS was now picking up. In the murky conditions, the range of the system between transducer and wrist display was restricted to less than a kilometre, so O'Connor had relied on his compass when they were outside the harbour; now, O'Connor knew it was accurate to within five metres. He indicated with one forefinger behind the other for Aleta to follow, and they set off on a bearing of 63 degrees magnetic.

As best they had been able to calculate from the papyrus map, the ancient library lay submerged at 29° 54' 17" east, 31° 12' 27" north. Minutes later, the GPS flashed a warning they had reached the preset location, and O'Connor turned to indicate to Aleta that the library might lie beneath. He expected a look of disappointment. The sand had built up over the centuries, and there wasn't much to see, but O'Connor didn't have Aleta's archaeologist's eye. Instead of showing disappointment, Aleta swam determinedly toward the sand.

Without the benefit of a precise satellite location, other divers would not have seen it, but Aleta had noticed something. She held her fingers up in a 'v' to one eye, signalling 'look', and then she pointed to the rocks in the sand. Aleta slowly swam along their length, running her hands above those that formed an unnaturally straight line. She stopped suddenly, indicating where the line intersected another at right angles.

O'Connor swam toward her, following the faint outline. When he reached her, he could see the excitement in her eyes. They had found the top of a long, ancient wall. Whether or not it was the library was open to question, but it did not take the pair long to confirm that Aleta's excitement might be justified. O'Connor reached for the small trowel he'd attached to his belt, and the centuries-old sandy silt came away in clouds, revealing the start of what was a series of stone recesses which, in the old library, would have reached almost to the ceiling. For the next hour, the pair dug down at random locations along the buried walls, revealing more storage areas, some large, some small. Both knew that none of the hundreds of thousands of papyri would have survived, but to have located the most famous library in the world . . . it was on a par with the discovery of the tomb of Tutankhamun.

O'Connor checked his wrist display and the oxygen partial pressure. By his calculations they had just over thirty minutes left. He formed his hands into a 'roof', meaning it was time to go home, but Aleta had found something else and she gave the signal for 'wait'. O'Connor watched as Aleta unearthed four tiny canopic jars at the back of a lower recess. The jar covers were shaped to resemble the four sons of Anubis, the god of death and embalming.

Aleta carefully placed the small jars in her carry pouch.

The ancient Egyptians used larger versions to store the organs of the deceased, and the jars would normally have been found in the sarcophagus of a pharaoh's tomb, separate from the mummy lest they cause it to putrefy and decay. Duamutef, the jackal-headed god representing the east, watched over the stomach; Hapi, the baboon-headed god of the north, protected the lungs; Imseti, the human-headed god of the south, cared for the liver; and Qeb-ehsenuef, the god of the west, protected the intestines.

Aleta was about to follow O'Connor when she noticed the round lid of another, much larger jar poking through the sand and silt at the rear of the recess. She checked her wrist display, signalled again to O'Connor to wait, and gently eased the artifact from where it had rested for centuries. Noting the lid was firmly sealed with pitch, Aleta pointed to O'Connor's pouch for a calico carrier and together they cautiously slipped the polished pottery jar into the bag.

From his position on the ramparts of Fort Qaytbey, Omar Aboud watched through his binoculars as the pair emerged on to a small strip of sand, not far from the modern library of Alexandria. What, Aboud wondered, was in the calico bag?

11

KASHTA PALACE, ALEXANDRIA

Rachel Bannister handed Crowley the dossiers on the Republican candidates for the presidential election. 'Pre-dinner drink?' she asked.

Crowley nodded. 'Chablis.'

Rachel selected a Valmur Grand Cru from the well-stocked fridge in Crowley's suite, and settled into a Louis XV chair that was finished in fine red silk.

'Is *this* the best the Republicans can do?' asked Crowley, a quizzical look on his face.

'Well might you look surprised,' said Rachel. In a practised move that accentuated her cleavage, she leaned toward the gold-legged glass coffee table. 'They're not a particularly impressive lot. Of the twenty-one candidates who have declared, there's only three or four of them who are in with any sort of a show.'

'The first four?'

Rachel nodded. 'William J. Stephenson is a two-term senator

and as you'd expect, coming from North Dakota, he's a strong conservative. He supported both the invasion of Afghanistan and Iraq, and he's anti-abortion, a climate change sceptic and anti-federal healthcare.'

'So am I.' Crowley scowled. 'I'm fucked if I'm going to pay for those lazy sons of bitches who don't want to work, and want everything as a fucking entitlement. Any dirt?'

'We're working on it . . . but he's a strong Catholic.'

'So was Kennedy. What about this next guy . . . Weaver?'

'Bennett Weaver, current governor of Idaho, and another strong conservative. Similar views to Stephenson, and vehemently opposes same-sex marriage.'

'Anything on him?'

'He's a Lutheran, but despite his outspoken opposition to gays, there are rumours he may be a closet homosexual.'

'Wouldn't be the first time,' Crowley chuckled. 'Who was that dickhead evangelical pastor who was thumping the pulpit against gay marriage every other week, and then had to own up to paying for gay sex?'

'There's been a barn full of them. The guy you're talking about is the evangelical from Colorado, but I'll let you know about the Idaho governor.'

'And the woman?'

'Martha Wylie, South Carolina. In her third term in the House of Reps. Another strong evangelical Christian, and no skeletons . . . at least none that I can find.'

'Jesus Christ, we're surrounded by God-botherers. Are *any* of these any good to us?'

'It's still early days, but even after you make a sizeable donation, there's no one on that list who's likely to come into our tent.'

'What about Davis?'

Rachel's eyes widened. '*Carter* Davis? The governor of Montana? You've got to be kidding. He's as thick as hog shit.'

'Exactly.'

'Sheldon . . . I've met that moron. It's not common knowledge – yet – but he can't keep his dick in his pants for more than twenty-four hours.'

'We should get some proof of that.'

'That won't be a problem. How many bedrooms do you want bugged?' Rachel replied, rolling her eyes.

'Three should be enough. He wouldn't be the first one in the White House to play around, and he won't be the last. But that's my point; he's got a wife and three young kids, and skeletons in his closet that will give us leverage. Don't forget Woodrow Wilson. The likes of the Rockefellers and Rothschilds needed their man in the White House, and they had Wilson over a barrel.'

'Woodrow Wilson had skeletons in the closet?'

'Oh yeah.' Crowley chortled, relishing the little-known revelation about one of the country's heroes. 'While he was a professor at Princeton, Wilson had a long-standing affair, writing hundreds of passionate letters to a woman he'd met while vacationing in Bermuda. Everyone has a skeleton in the closet. See what you can find out about our friend Davis, and if there's enough there, set up a meeting with him when we get back to the States.' Crowley savoured his wine and picked up the second folder, on the Democrats. 'What are the latest polls?'

'Hailey Campbell's still dominating with a 61 per cent approval rating. That's down from when she was secretary of energy, but she's still way out in front of Vice President Bilson and the rest of the field.'

'But she's vulnerable?'

Rachel nodded. 'Yes . . . and as much as it pisses me off to say so, she's vulnerable because she's a woman.'

Crowley's eyes wandered to Rachel's cleavage. 'But feisty, like you.'

'That's not going to cut any ice with the lunatic Christian Right. What is it? The woman must obey the husband and all the rest of their crap and carry-on. And gender's not the only thing she's got going against her. Campbell is on the record as being pro-choice, pro-universal health care and pro-climate change; but on the plus side, Americans trust her. She will make climate change an issue.'

'Which is why we'll need a scientist of Ahlstrom's calibre on the Davis campaign. He'll need to blow every one of her arguments on climate change out of the water.'

Rachel nodded and made a note. 'And the other issue is terrorism and the war in Iraq. She's been against the war right from the start, but the wacky Christian Right and half the Tea Party see that war as God's war against the Muslims. Campbell's everything the Christian Right loves to hate. As far as the evangelical bloc is concerned, in this election it's going to be ABC.'

'Anybody But Campbell. You're right, and we can turn that to our advantage. There are over forty million of these evangelicals, a sizeable number of whom will turn out for whichever candidate their pastor endorses. In a country where it's not compulsory to vote, that's a very powerful bloc. Bush's campaign manager, Karl Rove, knew it well. Without the God-botherers on side, George W. wouldn't have beaten Kerry in 2004, let alone Gore in 2000. Davis doesn't know it yet, but he's about to have his moment on the road to Damascus.'

'And how do you intend to achieve that? Apart from Christmas, Easter and the Fourth of July, Davis wouldn't be seen dead in a church.'

'Pastor Matthias B. Shipley . . . our new secret weapon.'

Rachel rolled her eyes. Shipley was a favourite of Lillian, Crowley's fervently religious wife. On one occasion, Rachel had had to suffer through one of Shipley's tub-thumping sermons on the evils of homosexuality, followed by tea and scones at Shipley's Hermit Road mega-church.

'What makes you think someone like Shipley is going to support a dirt-bag like Davis? For starters, has it occurred to you Davis has been divorced? The evangelicals are pretty keen on quoting JC on that little number. If I recall my Bible and Matthew, it went "But I say to you that every one who divorces his wife, except on the ground of unchastity, makes her an adulteress; and whoever marries a divorced woman commits adultery." '

'I didn't know you were religious,' Crowley said, a look of astonishment on his face.

'I'm not. It's just that I was brought up in a convent,' Rachel said, shuddering at the memory of it all.

'Well, the evangelicals got behind Reagan in 1980, and we can take a lesson out of that campaign. Reagan was divorced, remarried, and he'd signed a bill on legalising abortion when he was Governor of California – *and* he was running against Jimmy Carter,' Crowley said. 'You couldn't get a more Christian candidate than that guy – he started out teaching Sunday School and took Bible study when he was in the Navy.'

'You seem to be forgetting that Reagan had the likes of Billy Graham behind him, and Reagan had charisma. What was his remark to the evangelicals? "I know you can't endorse me . . . but I want you to know that I endorse you and what you're doing." That brought the house down, with two thousand evangelical pastors all cheering and shouting,' Rachel said. 'I'm willing to bet Shipley won't have a bar of Davis, let alone work to get two thousand pastors in to back him.'

'Two nights in Cannes says we can, so we'll need to persuade him. See what dirt you can dig up on Shipley, because you're going to run the Davis campaign.'

'What! You can't be serious. Who's going to look after you?' Rachel demanded.

'I'll manage. I'll have a word with Louis Walden, and we'll get Omega Centauri behind your campaign. The rest of the media will follow. And if you get our guy up, there'll be a very big bonus,' Crowley added.

In Crowley's world, everyone had their price. But he had misunderstood his assistant's motivations, and it would cost him dearly.

In the first break between discussions the next morning, Crowley sought out General Khan and asked him to take a stroll. He chose a path shaded by palm trees, some distance from the palace. Security guards shadowed the pair at a distance, and the guards on the roof followed their progress through binoculars, reporting their position to the command centre in the basement. Crowley turned the discussion toward the three-phase attack he had charged Khan with executing.

'As a result of the global financial crisis, we're in a very powerful position,' he affirmed, 'but we need those peaks and troughs to continue, Farid, at a much greater intensity. Unlike the other banks and big investors, we'll know when they're coming, so we sell at the top, just before the crashes, and then buy in again when the market hits rock bottom.'

Khan felt a surge of power flow through his very being. It had taken him a while to understand the Pharos strategy, but eventually he'd realised the ruthlessness of the plan. The Pharos Group's massive holdings on the world's stock markets enabled it to sell off huge amounts of equity, which in turn could drop the markets up to two percentage points. But Khan had also come to realise that for the group, this wasn't enough. They were out to crush the other banking groups, one by one, until they had complete supremacy. Pharos needed prior knowledge of events that would cause lemming-like panic on Wall Street and the other bourses, so they could sell before manipulated drops. But to manipulate the market to that extent, Pharos needed Khan's help. Badly.

'The subprime mortgages served us well, but they've run their course,' said Crowley. 'How did your discussions with our friends in the Hindu Kush go?'

'The plans are in place,' Khan replied evenly. 'Where it suits their purpose, the Taliban and al Qaeda will take every chance to hit the West.'

'Good, because it's time to put the Arab Spring to our advantage. Washington's stepping up its drone strikes, and we need to move before they have a greater effect.'

'The drone strikes are actually having the opposite effect to what Washington wants,' Khan ventured, 'and in the long term, they're doing us a favour. Washington's been very successful in killing off the older leaders, but many of those were tired of the constant conflict, and they were prepared to sue for peace. The younger generation who have replaced them is different. Firstly, Washington is now struggling to profile them, and secondly, the younger Taliban and al Qaeda leaders have much more fire in the belly. They're rash, and they'll take some heat over the Chinook they've just downed, but we can harness them.'

'Phase One?'

'In preparation . . . and they have the stamp codes for the website. That will give you forty-eight hours notice.'

'Good.' Crowley savoured the thought of yet another global financial crisis. 'What the markets hate most is uncertainty, and if there's uncertainty with oil supply, oil prices will skyrocket and other stocks will slump.'

'The attacks on the choke point will take place just as soon as my contacts can get in position,' said Khan. 'But if they're successful, the markets could stay down for quite a while.'

'The headlines will be full of doom and gloom,' Crowley agreed. 'But I assure you, it will be short-lived, and that will leave Du Bois free to work on the money supply. Once the markets rise again, we will strike with Phase Two, causing another crash, and then we strike again with Phase Three.'

'The anti-ship missiles – where are we at with them?' asked Khan.

'We've got that covered. They're already en route, and you will get them the same way as the Scorpions.'

'Taipans?'

Crowley nodded. 'And to ensure the Middle East remains

thoroughly destabilised, I'm arranging for a second shipment to follow out of Brazil.' Four years earlier, Crowley had successfully lobbied Congress for a US $200 million EVRAN defence grant to develop variants of an anti-ship missile.

'Taipan is based on Boeing's SLAM-ER, but this one can be launched from a vehicle as well as fighters. It has a range of over 200 kilometres, which is more than adequate for our purposes, and it's more accurate than anything else on the market . . . the trick will be to get the vehicles into position.'

'I'm quite capable of managing all this, but it's very dangerous work, and I'm the one who's running the biggest risk here.'

Crowley glanced at the wily little Pakistani, anticipating what was coming next. 'Meaning?'

'The mask of Tutankhamun is a very attractive inducement, but at the moment, it's just that – an inducement, and there's no guarantee such a well-known icon can be procured. But as an indication of good faith, there *is* an additional article that might be already available. Like you, I am an admirer of the great masters, particularly Vincent van Gogh. There is one painting in particular that I have long sought for my collection: *Poppy Flowers*. I had hoped to acquire it through an art dealer in Venice, but unfortunately, one of his clients beat me to it. Given your interest, and the very high risks you want me to take, I was wondering if you might assist me?'

'That might be possible. The price would be US $60 million, but that's conditional on the success of the attacks on the choke points, and you would have to arrange for the collection of the painting – and the mask – in person.'

'Always assuming the mask can be acquired,' said General Khan, his dark eyes glinting with anticipation.

'But the attacks on the choke point will only be a start,' Crowley warned.

'Oil again?'

Crowley shook his head. 'Cobalt 60. One of the most prolific radioactive substances on the planet, and one of the most dangerous. It might only have a half-life of five years, but Cobalt 60 emits gamma rays so powerful that exposure to even one gram of this stuff is enough to kill you. I'll be able to deliver Cobalt 60 to the three target countries in the next few months. That will be followed by Phase Three, which is designed to achieve something close to a worldwide market panic, where we can gain absolute control.'

12

CECIL HOTEL, ALEXANDRIA

'I am so excited!' Aleta exclaimed, once they had regained their hotel room. 'I can't be certain, but those recesses in the walls are a very positive indicator. They're exactly the same as the recesses you will see in the daughter library.'

She slipped on a pair of white gloves and ran a sharp knife through the thick layers of pitch that sealed the glazed jar. 'Whoever sealed this jar didn't want any air or moisture getting in,' Aleta said, working as a surgeon might to carry out a delicate operation. She slowly eased the tightly fitting lid off the jar and stepped back as the centuries-old foul air was released. Covering her nose, she shone a torch inside.

Aleta extracted an ancient, cracked leather roll from inside the jar. She laid it gently on the coffee table and carefully unrolled it, revealing two yellowed papyri. For a moment or two, she scanned the faded Greek words on the first ancient parchment.

'My God . . . this is part of the library *pinakes* – the catalogue! Out of the hundreds of thousands of papyri in the library, there's only fifty or so listed here, so they're probably some the library's most important documents.'

'Someone's gone to a lot of trouble to record them,' O'Connor observed.

'Yes, it was a bit different back then' Aleta said thoughtfully. 'No electronic copies or storing them in the cloud. We have to remember, we found this only a metre or so from the top of the submerged wall, which would mean it was stored in the highest recesses of the library, near the ceiling.' She scanned the parchment again 'This pinakes lists works by Euclid, and papyri from Aristotle's personal collection,' Aleta said, running her eye down the list. 'Archaeologists have only uncovered fragments, but from this list, it looks as if the library held Berossus' complete history of the world in three volumes, his *Babylonaica*. As well as Sappho's poetry and songs,' Aleta continued, translating the Greek. 'Sappho wrote around 600 BC, and she was probably one of the finest musicians of the ancient world. And look – Hypatia. Her works were stored here as well.'

'And the other papyrus?'

Aleta turned her attention to the second document. Her heart skipped a beat, and it was some time before she spoke.

'This is even more illuminating,' she said finally. 'Euclid worked and studied here around 300 BC, when Ptolemy I was pharaoh, and Alexandria was the capital of Egypt. Euclid wrote here the basis of today's Euclidian geometry, his *Elements,* all thirteen books of it. The primary copy, the Heiberg manuscript, is held by the Vatican in the Secret Archives.'

O'Connor rolled his eyes. 'They would keep something like that to themselves, wouldn't they. A wonder they didn't burn it. So is this the Euclid Papyrus?'

Aleta shook her head, ignoring O'Connor's disdain for all things Catholic. 'It's an engineering treatise . . . a combination of ancient Greek writing and Egyptian hieroglyphics, but the reason I say illuminating,' she said, 'is that this document proves the Euclid Papyrus *does,* or at least *did* exist.' Aleta's dark eyes were flashing with an archaeologist's excitement of discovery.

'And how do we reach that conclusion?' asked O'Connor, peering uncomprehendingly at the ancient letters.

'This is Euclid's notation, which refers to another document he wrote on the ancient pyramids. He says here "I have already dealt with pyramids of a triangular base in Propositions III, IV, V, VI, VII, VIII and IX in Book XII of the *Elements*. But having sighted these calculations of Pharaoh Khufu's engineers, the real purpose of the Great Pyramid is now clear. I have confirmed their calculations and recorded this on a papyrus hidden separately, the answers to the location of which, lie in the heavens." The Euclid Papyrus. We've got to find it!' Aleta exclaimed.

'The answers lie in the heavens? Some sort of cryptic code?' O'Connor wondered, pondering the diagrams on the papyrus.

'I think you may be right,' said Aleta. 'Look . . . do you see this series of circles at the bottom?'

'I've seen that design somewhere before . . . one of the codes used by ancient civilisations, isn't it? The Flower of Life?' O'Connor mused.

'Yes, but it's not so much a code in itself as one that has codes embedded in it. I remember studying this when I was working at the Temple of Osiris at Abydos. One of these days I'll show you over the site, but of all the ancient markings on the temple walls, the most striking is the Flower of Life.'

'Why single that out?'

'Because firstly, it's so different to the usual hieroglyphics, and secondly, it's related to energy. We now know the Egyptians were not the only ancient civilisation for whom the flower was important. You will find the Flower of Life carved into the balls under the feet of the Fu dogs, the guardian lions at the entrance to the Forbidden City in Beijing.'

'But the Imperial Palace postdates the Egyptian civilisation. Does that mean the Chinese got it from the Egyptians?'

'It's hard to tell. When the Ming and Qing dynasties occupied the palace, there's evidence both were aware of the importance of the Flower of Life, but so were the Indians. You can find it on the Harmindir Sahib, the Golden Temple in Amritsar in India, which is one of the Sikh religion's holiest shrines. We think it was passed on from the Egyptians, but we don't have proof.'

'Couldn't they just be coincidental separate discoveries?'

'Perhaps, but I find it interesting that somehow, this Flower of Life has appeared right across the ancient world.'

'So if that's Euclid's notation on the papyrus,' O'Connor said, returning to the priceless artifact, 'what do you think he's getting at?'

'Other than indicating there's another, even more important papyrus, I'm not sure. But I've seen speculation from well-respected scientists and mathematicians about a code hidden within this hexagonal design of the Flower of Life. There's also speculation that the code may hold a link to the earth's natural energy systems, and that's what Euclid could be getting at. Curiously, the Flower of Life design appears frequently in the crop circles in England.'

'Hmm . . .'

'You don't buy these crop circles do you? You've got sceptism written all over your face!'

'No – as a scientist, I have an open mind. The Milky Way galaxy alone contains another thirty billion solar systems like our own, and we now know there are more than one hundred billion galaxies in the universe. That adds up to trillions of planets, so there's a very high probability that some of those planets are going to be in the "Goldilocks zone" where it's not too hot, nor too cold to support life . . . but start subscribing to a theory of aliens making crop circles and the media will accuse you of not being wrapped too tight in the head.'

'And since when has the media been the arbiter of science?' Aleta demanded.

O'Connor grinned. 'The media might not be the arbiter of science, but they do influence public opinion, and the last time I read anything on this, the public firmly believed crop circles are made by untidy patrons who've been thrown out of the Elephant and Castle at midnight.'

'Open mind, my foot! You're on the Elephant and Castle team!' Aleta dug him in the ribs. 'You think they're all a hoax!'

'There are plenty of crop circles that *are* man made. Who was it that started all of this?'

'Bower and Chorley . . . a couple of pranksters who heard about some crop circles that appeared in 1966 at a place called Tully in Australia. A farmer by the name of George Pedley was driving his tractor around nine in the morning, when he heard a hissing sound, and then he saw a flying saucer rising from one of his swamps.'

O'Connor raised his eyes to the ceiling.

'You can laugh all you like, but Australians are pretty down to earth. They like their booze, but I doubt Pedley was blotto at nine o'clock in the morning. He and another farmer discovered that not only were the reeds in the swamp flattened into a circle, but in the process, an unknown force had uprooted all of them from the bottom of the lagoon. The RAAF investigated, with inconclusive results, but it's become the Australian equivalent of Roswell.'

'That may be, but it doesn't alter the fact that it inspired Bower and Chorley, using ropes and planks of wood and garden rollers, to pull the wool over everyone's eyes in the UK for years.'

Aleta took a deep breath, and then exhaled loudly. 'There's no doubt that many of them are man made,' she agreed, 'but some of them are so intricate that it's just not possible to create them in one night. Are you familiar with Carl Sagan's message that was transmitted from the *Arecibo* radio telescope in Puerto Rico in 1974?'

O'Connor nodded. 'Part of the SETI program – the search for extraterrestrial intelligence. I remember that message . . . a pictogram in binary code that detailed the human race, the solar system and our methods of communication.'

'Exactly, and it might interest you to know, Curtis Seamus O'Connor, that in August 2000, an intricate crop circle appeared alongside the Chilbolton radio telescope in Hampshire in England. A year later, the image of a face appeared in the wheat nearby, with the strands so delicately and intricately flattened that they resembled pixels in a photograph – a binary code of zeros and ones, no less. Wheat waving in the breeze is not the easiest medium to work with when you need that sort of precision. And five days later, the strangest pattern of all appeared – one that contained an answer to the SETI message.'

'A clever hoax?'

'Not if you take into account it would have taken more than twenty-four hours to produce, and it was so intricately designed that it would have been impossible to construct it without lights. The field was covered by the Chilbolton security cameras, and they turned up nothing.'

'Leaving aside the fact that you have to suspend belief to buy into Roswell and little green or grey men, where does all this leave *us*?'

'I'm not sure, but unlike you, I *am* keeping an open mind, because the crop glyphs of the Flower of Life and its association with energy have appeared too many times for it to be coincidence. But aside from that, there's something else,' Aleta said, pointing to another diagram at the bottom of the papyrus. 'We've long suspected that the pyramids of Giza have been linked to the structure of our galaxy, and if you look here, you'll see what I mean.'

'That looks like an aerial map of the pyramids?'

'Yes, the Giza Plateau . . . but look at the dots superimposed over the *top* of the pyramids,' Aleta said, her excitement rising again. 'I've seen this theory before where it's postulated that the pyramids were aligned with a constellation in our galaxy, and the dots over the tops represent prominent stars. I think Euclid's trying to tell us something here. The Egyptians, like the Maya and Inca, were great astronomers, and it would be no coincidence that the pyramid layout in Giza matched the night sky, but it's the dot out here that has me intrigued,' she said, pointing to a spot on the papyrus.

'Lines up over a rock formation?'

'Yes, that dot falls over an area known as Gebel Ghibli – Arabic for southern hill. It's a few hundred metres from the Great Sphinx. It has me intrigued, and I may have to go back to Professor Badawi to get his help on this one.'

O'Connor reached to view a text on his encrypted cell phone. 'Shit,' was all he said.

'Don't you dare tell me that's a text from Washington! We're on holidays!'

13

CIA HEADQUARTERS, LANGLEY, VIRGINIA

'**H**e's waiting for you.'

O'Connor flashed a willing smile at Chanelle, the attractive blonde-haired personal assistant to the CIA's Director of the National Clandestine Service.

'And the weather?'

'Stormy – he's just come back from briefing the president.'

O'Connor knocked on the inner door of the seventh floor office.

'Come in.' Previously known as the DDO, or Deputy Director of Operations, the CIA's chief spymaster swivelled away from a computer that was isolated from the world's hackers by a dizzying array of firewalls.

'Ah . . . O'Connor. Have a seat,' Tom McNamara said, gesturing toward one of two cracked and worn, brown leather couches. McNamara had a big, round face, grey hair that he kept very short, and piercing blue eyes. Weighing in at 120 kilograms, the huge barrel-chested ex-Marine regularly pressed 150 kilograms in the gym. He picked up a crimson folder marked 'TOP SECRET – NOFORN', meaning no foreign national would be given access, and he moved from behind his desk to settle in to the other couch. 'Pleasant flight?'

'Cattle class,' O'Connor replied, feigning a hurt look. The flight from Alexandria to Washington had taken a bum-numbing twenty-one hours.

'Remind me to send one of our private jets next time.' Tom McNamara looked at O'Connor over the top of his tortoise-shell glasses, a hint of a smile at the corners of his mouth, but then his lips hardened. 'A few days ago, a Chinook from the 160th Special Operations Aviation Regiment was shot down near the northern border of Afghanistan and Pakistan,' McNamara said. 'It's not yet public – the Pentagon's having difficulty tracking two of the next of kin, but as soon as they're contacted, they'll hold a media conference. It could have been worse, but we've still lost four crew and four SEALs . . . eight of the best.'

O'Connor nodded soberly, waiting for his boss to continue. As tragic as the loss of the chopper and the SEAL team was, he knew McNamara would not have recalled him from leave unless there was more to it. Responsible for running the CIA's international web of agents, along with countless black operations, some of which even the president wasn't briefed on, in many ways McNamara was more powerful than the director himself. O'Connor had no doubt his boss had something else in mind – something that would be very tightly held.

'I called you back here because of some highly sensitive intelligence we've gleaned on the Pakistani Taliban,' McNamara continued. 'The Chinook incident just adds to our fears. In a nutshell, somebody is supplying the Pakistani Taliban with American-made surface-to-air missiles. The chopper was heading toward the Hindu Kush mountains, but it was shot down before it reached them, flying at a height of over 8000 feet.'

'Stinger?' The ubiquitous shoulder-fired surface-to-air missile had been the mainstay of US ground troops for over three decades. In 1979, when the Soviets invaded Afghanistan, the United States decided to send the missiles to Osama bin Laden and the Mujahideen, the Islamic freedom fighters, to help them drive the Soviets out. O'Connor and McNamara both knew that over 500 of the state-of-the-art missiles had been supplied across the border with Pakistan. Travelling at nearly 2500 kilometres an hour, the deadly accurate Stinger used an infrared system to lock on to the heat from an aircraft's exhaust, and it could bring down any aircraft flying below 10 000 feet, including a commercial jetliner. Like so many armies before them, the Soviets had been defeated in the rugged, unforgiving terrain of Afghanistan, and when the Soviet army withdrew, the CIA desperately tried to buy the missiles back, but many of them had found their way into the hands of bin Laden's al Qaeda.

'It could be, but we're not sure. A lot of those Stingers would be unserviceable now. Have a look at this.' McNamara opened a file at a flagged XKeyscore intercept from the NSA, and pushed it across the coffee table. The intercept read 'Scorpions en route. Artifact acquisition in train.'

O'Connor frowned. 'Is that all there is?'

'It's not much,' McNamara agreed, 'and we're still unsure who sent that text, but it was received by the ex-head of the Pakistani ISI, General Farid Khan.' McNamara wasn't the only one who thought the ISI, notorious for their support of the Taliban, were a law unto themselves. 'He forwarded the information on to a satellite phone located in the Hindu Kush, and it wasn't one of ours.'

'Careless of him.'

'He probably thought a short text would go unnoticed.'

'So even though he's been sacked, this General Khan still wields some influence in the ISI?'

'We think he still wields a lot of influence. He was one of the most powerful generals in the Pakistani Army, and he was sacked by the Pakistani president at our behest. I've been talking to our station chief in Islamabad, and he tells me the ISI are furious with their president . . . and ours for that matter.'

'And you think that text's a reference to the Scorpion missile system?' The successor to the General Dynamics Stinger, the Scorpion had been manufactured by EVRAN, and the missile's guidance systems and power plant were so highly classified that Congress and the president had issued an edict preventing EVRAN from making the missile available to any military outside the United States, even to allies like Israel and Australia.

'It's looking that way,' said McNamara, 'although the artifact acquisition reference remains a mystery. Not long after that text was sent we received some satellite imagery on a shipment of timber, ostensibly bound for Kabul,' McNamara continued, pulling out a series of satellite photographs. 'You can see the convoy there quite clearly, moving through the Khyber Pass, and on across the Pakistan–Afghanistan border; but the shipment never made it . . . at least not to Kabul.'

'Attacked by the Taliban?'

'It was made to look that way, but there were no casualties, and when the convoy reached Jalalabad, just across the border, instead of continuing west to Kabul, it turned north along the Kunar Bajaur link road through Asadabad and on to Asmar.' McNamara spread a map of the Pakistan–Afghanistan border area across the coffee table. 'When they got to Hajiabad,' McNamara continued, pointing to a small town north of Asmar in the foothills of the soaring Hindu Kush, 'they transferred the timber to a pack of mules.'

'An awful lot of trouble to get timber into the Hindu Kush. You think there was more than timber on those mules.'

'Exactly, particularly since there's Indian cedar around . . . not a lot of it, but it's a darn sight closer than what they can get from Pakistan. And on the lower slopes of the Hindu Kush, they'd have access to holly oaks. And to add to the puzzle, even though Pakistan has extensive forests, over 75 per cent of their soft wood and a good deal of their hard wood is imported, so Pakistan's a fairly unlikely exporter.'

'If that timber's just a cover, we need to know find out where it came from, because that might lead us to whoever's supplying the missiles,' McNamara concluded, leaning back on the couch.

'And how do you propose we do that?' O'Connor asked, already suspecting the answer.

'Not me . . . you.' McNamara's smile was broader now. 'One of our jets is standing by to take you to Afghanistan, to Bagram Airfield, where a SEAL team is waiting for you to join them. Their dossiers are in this folder, although I suspect you'll know most of them.'

'Have I done something to piss you off lately?'

'No, but you undoubtedly will, so I'll hold this one on account,' said McNamara, looking pleased with himself. 'I've just come from briefing Rebel,' he continued, more seriously, 'and he's pretty pissed.' Ever since Franklin D. Roosevelt, the White House Communications

Agency had assigned code names to presidents, first ladies and other VIPs and installations. Kennedy had been known as Lancer, while Jacqueline had gone by the code word Lace. President McGovern was known as Rebel, while the first lady, very much her own woman, had been assigned Reformer.

'Rebel wants us to confirm whether or not the Taliban have Scorpions, and if they do, who's supplying them. I don't need to tell you, but at the moment, this thing is burning my ass,' McNamara said. 'How's Aleta?' he asked, moving back behind his desk.

'Enjoying Alexandria, or was. So other than not talking to you, she's in good shape.' O'Connor kept to himself his misgivings about leaving her alone in an Egypt still troubled after the military coup.

'Tell her I'll make it up to her,' McNamara responded, his smile returning. Weizman was well known inside the CIA, although not always with affection. The archaeologist's exposure of the CIA's dark involvement in the deaths of 200 000 civilians in the Guatemalan civil war had not gone down well in some quarters. It was an involvement that prompted then president Bill Clinton to apologise to the people of the desperately poor Latin American country during his visit to Guatemala City in 1999. But there was also unflagging respect from the more honourable men and women in 'the Company', as the CIA was known to insiders. Weizman had proven herself more than once under fire, as she and O'Connor had fought their way in and out of ancient tombs in the jungles of Guatemala and Peru.

Deep in thought, O'Connor headed back to collect his bag from the office he'd been temporarily assigned in the old headquarters building. He had a deep foreboding . . . a sixth sense that Aleta was in danger.

14

CREECH AIR FORCE BASE, NEVADA

The lanky crewcut ex-F15 pilot walked toward the unmanned aerial vehicle ground control station. Just eighty kilometres to the south of the base, the staff of some of the world's largest hotels and casinos were coming to the end of another night on the famed Las Vegas strip, but for Captain Trent Rogers, that might as well have been in another world. Once the sun rose out here, the heat haze shimmered off the desert, drifting toward craggy brown mountains almost devoid of vegetation and etched by myriad small ravines. In this godforsaken place, the top secret 432nd Wing of the US Air Force operated MQ-9 Reaper and MQ-1 Predator drones. When terrorists were on the move, no matter where they were in the world, pilots like Captain Rogers supported allied forces by flying remote reconnaissance, surveillance and attack missions. Rogers wasn't sure why, but the commander of the Wing had rung him personally to tell him his leave was cancelled, ordering him to report for the early morning briefing.

Captain Rogers took his place in the briefing room and the nuggety commander of the 432nd, Colonel Joe Stillwell, another ex-fighter pilot, took the podium. A normal shift would have been briefed by one of the duty mission commanders. Something out of the ordinary was clearly afoot.

'We've recently received intelligence of increased terrorist activity to the north-west of the Khyber Pass in the Hindu Kush,' Stillwell began, flashing up a map of the area marked 'TOP SECRET'. 'As part of Operation Sassafras, an element of SEAL team six was sent in to investigate but their aircraft, a Chinook from the 160th Special Operations Aviation Regiment, was shot down here,' he said, indicating with the red dot of his laser pointer, 'twenty kilometres west of the Pakistan–Afghan border, to the north of the town of Asadabad.'

Stillwell flicked up more satellite imagery, which gave a close-up of the foothills of the towering, snow-capped Hindu Kush. 'At the time, the aircraft was flying at altitude, and the wreckage is scattered over a wide area, so we suspect a SAM . . . and a surface-to-air missile has serious implications for our own operations,' he continued.

'Another patrol, call sign Mohegan One Zero, has been inserted into this area here,' Stillwell said, circling with the red dot of his laser an area of steep, almost impassible terrain. 'The CIA is also sending in one of their most experienced field teams, call sign Hopi One Four. They'll be landing at Bagram shortly, where they'll marry up with another fire team from SEAL team six for an insertion to the north of where Mohegan One Zero is searching for the bodies from the downed Chinook, and Hopi One Four will take over the original task of surveillance. You'll be given an update as soon as we have Hopi One Four's flight plan and coordinates for their insertion.' Colonel Stillwell turned away from the map to face his pilots.

'The task list today is like four pounds of sugar into a two-pound bag,' he observed wryly, flashing up a top secret tasking pane. 'There are twice as many missions as we have aircraft, but the top priority goes to Operation Sassafras, and as the most experienced pilot, Trent, you're first cab off the rank.'

Rogers nodded, allowing himself a sardonic grin. Stillwell's compliments were as rare as rocking horse shit.

As the sun was coming up over the Nevada desert, it was setting behind the Hindu Kush and Bagram Airfield, one of the busiest airports in Afghanistan. No fewer than nine different parking areas housed different types of aircraft. The Special Forces ramp housed some of the most highly classified aircraft; the ISR or intelligence, surveillance and reconnaissance ramp contained Beechcraft MC and RC-12s, bristling with surveillance equipment; the big C-130 cargo planes were on the tactical ramp, alongside the transient ramp for aircraft passing through; and further down, scores of Black Hawk helicopters and twin-rotored CH-47 Chinooks were parked on the Army ramp. Across the runway, there were bays for dozens more OH-58 and AH-64 Apache attack helicopters, bays for the squadrons of F-15E and F-16 fighters, and a ramp for the Predator and Reaper drones. The Russians had built the base in 1976 during their invasion, and the base was still littered with the remains of rusted Soviet equipment. A new runway, 21-03, had been added, allowing the original Russian runway to be turned into Taxiway Zulu, but it was so bumpy that the fighters were unable to use it, making things even more complicated for the hard-worked air traffic controllers with fighters needing to taxi on runway 21-03.

The lights around the Bagram hangars were already blazing, and under the watchful eye of a master sergeant, the Predator and Reaper ground crews were scrambling to prepare the drones for night flying. Satellite time delays could pose problems for the flight crews in distant Nevada, particularly where instant responses were required in take-offs and landings, so the ground crews at Bagram would launch and land the unmanned aerial vehicles, or UAVs. Once the UAVs were airborne, the ground crews would alert the crews at Creech. Using internet optical fibre to Europe, the pilot and the sensor operator would grab the required data via a KU-band satellite in geosynchronous orbit, log in to the plane, and assume control.

A crewman finished fuelling the second of two fifty-gallon tanks on the Predator assigned to Captain Rogers. Powered by a four-cylinder, hundred-horsepower engine, the same engine used on snowmobiles, the aircraft could reach speeds of 120 knots, and altitudes of up to 25 000 feet. The Reapers were even more impressive.

Another crewman checked the nose of the aircraft, which contained the Hellfire targeting system, the electro-optical infrared systems, and the laser designators and illuminators. Yet another checked the Hellfire missiles loaded on the pods under the wings. Once the crew chief was satisfied, an umbilical cord from a start cart was plugged into the starter-connector in the aircraft's ground panel. The controller held the aircraft stationary, waiting for the control tower at Bagram to give permission for take-off.

Captain Rogers eased himself into the left-hand seat of the pilot's console at Creech. His weapons controller, Sergeant Michelle Brady, her blonde hair tied back in a bun, was already logging into her systems, and in the third seat behind sat Major Ryan Crowe, a dour, experienced intelligence analyst from Langley who was there to assist with interpreting the images and gaining approval for a strike. The cockpit looked more like something from a financial trading floor than a fighter or 747 cockpit. The joysticks were akin to those found on a video game, and instead of gauges, switches and avionics, the pilot and weapons operator were surrounded by video and computer screens, a keyboard and throttle levers. The view screen, directly in front of Rogers, gave him live video of what the Predator's cameras could see. Unable to see left or right, unless the cameras were panned, it was like flying an aircraft through a straw. The Heads-up Display, or HUD, provided numerical data on airspeed, angle of attack, vertical speed, bank angle and altitude, all of which was superimposed over the camera readout. Above the HUD, the map display gave the aircraft's position, and a digital readout panel on the right showed the heading, wind speed, fuel status and ground elevation, not dissimilar to the information found on GPS units. Yet another monitor screen provided information on communications frequencies. Suddenly, Roger's headphones crackled:

'Night Thruster Two, this is Bagram Lima Romeo, how do you read me, over?'

'Night Thruster Two, fife by fife.'

'Lima Romeo, aircraft is straight and level, holding at six thousand feet, three nautical miles to the north of Bagram field. Traffic includes Nine Three Zero Heavy – a C-5 Galaxy on late finals,

Arson One Seven and One Eight – two F-15s on finals, and Hopi One Four, a Gulfstream IV on approach, flight level 190. Are you ready to assume control, over?'

The CIA weren't stuffing around, Rogers mused. Hopi One Four, he knew, was carrying the CIA ground team, and they were already inbound. The foothills of the Hindu Kush came into focus on the cockpit screens. 'Night Thruster Two, I have control. Thank you and have a nice evening, out.'

O'Connor strapped into the Gulfstream jump seat for the landing and put on a set of headphones. From past experience, he knew the descent would be a wild ride. Bagram Airfield was still subject to both mortar and machine gun attacks, and aircraft on long, low approaches were sitting ducks for a Taliban armed with machine guns mounted in their ubiquitous Toyota pick-up trucks. To avoid this, even the big transport aircraft would dive on the airfield from altitude.

The co-pilot, ex-Marine Corps major Brad Spalding, depressed the transmit button. 'Bagram, good evening, this is Hopi One Four, flight level 190, heading 240, request runway 030, rapid descent.'

'Hopi One Four, runway 030, cleared to six thousand, traffic is two F-15Es on late finals, maintain heading and report when visual.'

'Hopi One Four.'

O'Connor grinned to himself as the pilot, another ex-Marine Corps major Chuck Moran, switched out the cabin lights and threw the Gulfstream jet into a spiralling dive. He'd flown with these guys before. Both ex-fighter pilots, they knew what they were doing.

'Hopi One Four, field in sight, request visual.' Spalding handled the comms while Moran pulled the aircraft out of the dive and levelled out.

'Hopi One Four, you are cleared visual, contact tower on one two zero decimal one.'

'Thank you and good evening.' Even in war-torn Afghanistan, the niceties on an air traffic control net usually prevailed.

'Bagram Tower, good evening, this is Hopi One Four, four miles to run, visual 030.'

'Hopi One Four, altimeter is 30.05, you're cleared to land runway 030, winds three two zero at ten to fifteen knots.'

Moran rolled the Gulfstream into another dive and pulled out at 1200 feet and lined up on the runway lights. Suddenly, the cockpit was hit with a blinding laser light, and the aircraft shook as a burst of heavy machine gun fire raked the fuselage. Moran slumped over the controls while Spalding, blood streaming from bullet wounds to his wrists, battled to get the aircraft back on an even attitude.

O'Connor undid Moran's harness, grabbed him under both armpits and hauled him back into the main cabin, but even as he laid him on the cabin floor, he knew the pilot was dead. The plane shuddered again, and O'Connor deftly vaulted into the bloodied left hand seat, crammed the headset on and pressed the intercom.

'You okay, Brad?' he asked. Spalding's face was ashen. He turned toward O'Connor and then slumped back in his seat.

A fire warning sounded for the port engine. O'Connor struggled to control the stricken aircraft.

15

CAIRO

A short distance from the director's office, Abdul Assaf pretended to be a mature-age student sketching Pharaoh Khafre's statue; a cruel and despotic pharaoh, he had ruled Egypt with an iron fist around 2500 BC. He had built the second largest of the Pyramids at Giza, and some academics credited him with building the Sphinx. Assaf's sketch could have been that of a four-year-old child, and Assaf was neither aware of the history behind the extraordinary statue, nor did he care. His was an entirely different focus. The museum was strangely deserted and the guards, bored with their low-paying jobs, took no notice. The Arab Spring might have rid the Egyptians of the dictatorial President Mubarak, but the violent protests that had erupted after the removal of his successor, President Morsi, had reduced a once vibrant intake of tourists, and lifeblood of the economy, to a trickle.

Assaf turned his attention away from Pharaoh Khafre's statue and the Old Kingdom exhibits, and made his way through the ground floor, noting the locations of the CCTV security cameras, the staircases, and the general layout of the exhibits. He made his way up the north-west staircase toward Room 3, where the funerary mask of Tutankhamun would have normally attracted a large crowd.

'The museum has two main floors and a basement,' the dark-faced Assaf said, laying out the museum floor plan on the dining room table of the apartment he'd rented in a crowded area of Heliopolis, not far from Cairo's international airport. It was very high stakes, but he had broken into other museums before, and US $250 000 was an attractive enticement. Assaf's co-conspirators were eager with anticipation. Athletic and fit, Mahmoud Nassar would be with him on the break-in, and the overweight Abdul Kassab would drive the getaway van.

'The ground floor is arranged in chronological order of the kingdoms. The first floor is arranged thematically, and we'll be focusing on Room 3 at the very northern end of the building.'

'And these are the stairs?' Nassar asked, pointing to the icons on the plan.

Assaf nodded. 'The two closest access stairs are in the north-west and north-east corners of the building. A daytime robbery is out of the question, even if we took a hostage. There are just too many guards, but the night shift's a lot smaller. And if we do it around midnight, there'll be less traffic on the road. We need to be at the Alexandria airport to load the mask by eight a.m.'

'And apart from the guards, what's the rest of the security like?' asked Kassab.

'It's tighter than it was since the museum was broken into by protestors, but they were idiots just looking for gold. They missed priceless artifacts that would have sold for millions of dollars on the black market,' said Assaf, 'but don't get any ideas . . . we'll only have time to go for two artifacts – the mask and Tutankhamun's gold falcon pendant which is in the same location. There are 200 cameras, and they're not all visible, but they certainly cover Room 3 and Tutankhamun's mask. The control room is here,' he said, pointing to where he'd marked it on the plan, 'but my contact tells me the computers are old, and they're not capable of recording twenty-four hours a day.'

'Not automatic?' asked Nassar.

'No. The screens in the control room are connected to cameras in the various rooms and halls, but the system's pretty antiquated and if an incident occurs, a guard has to press a record button on a VCR.'

'There's a big protest scheduled for the day after tomorrow,' said Kassab. 'Can we take advantage of that?'

'That would've been a good idea a year ago, but since the protesters are prone to looting, the military will move in with their armoured personnel carriers, so we need to do this tomorrow night, before the protest in Tahrir Square.'

'So what's the best way in?' Nassar asked.

'From what I've seen, there are any number of skylights with cracked windows that are vulnerable, but once we're in we have to be able to disable the night shift guards. Since the last break-in, they've installed new lasers, especially around Room 3 and the mask, so I've ruled out getting in through the roof. But there is another way.' Assaf got up from the table and disappeared into the main bedroom.

'Courtesy of one of my contacts in the Egyptian Police Force,'

Assaf said, coming back and throwing Nassar and Kassab dark blue, military-style Egyptian police uniforms. 'I think you'll find they're your size, but try them on.'

As his co-conspirators checked the clothes, Assaf continued. 'Once we've got the mask, it will be secured in this box.' He took the lid from a crate lined with polyurethane foam, made to fit the mask precisely.

'What's with the explosives?' asked Nassar, looking at a second box behind Assaf.

'Just in case we have to destroy the van,' said Assaf. 'So watch and learn, both of you. You might have to do this yourselves one day.' Assaf reached into his bomb-making kit and extracted one of several old Nokia cell phones he kept for remote detonation.

'First you dismantle a cell phone – any of the old ones will do – and locate the vibrator,' he said, pointing to the rotating head on a small element about the size of a triple-A battery. 'When the phone receives a text or a call, the head spins. We cut a hole in the side of the phone to expose the rotor and fasten the phone to a wooden base. A chopping board does fine.'

Assaf bolted two screws through the board and attached wires, which led from the screws to the phone. 'We use alligator clips to connect with ordinary torch batteries which will power the detonator for the plastic explosive. When the phone rings, the rotor spins, completing the circuit.'

It was after midnight when Abdul placed a portable flashing blue light on the roof of the van, drove up to the wrought iron gates of the museum, and blew the horn. A guard appeared from the small guardhouse, rubbing his eyes, and Assaf got out of the passenger seat.

'We're responding to an alarm – quickly – open the gate!'

'Alarm? There's been no alarm . . .'

'Not here, you imbecile, at the central security control centre. If you still want to have a job in the morning, open the gate!'

The guard, a confused look on his face, fumbled for his keys and opened the double gates. Assaf got out to help the guard close the gates while Kassab drove on toward the central fountain and the main entrance. With the gates closed, Assaf pulled a CZ 75 semi-automatic nine-millimetre pistol from his holster.

'Inside!' Assaf shoved the guard inside the guardhouse.

'One false move from you and you're very dead,' he hissed, holding the gun to the guard's head. 'But do exactly as I tell you and you'll live to see another day.'

The hapless guard nodded, his face ashen.

'Put a call through to the guards in the museum telling them you have a fault in your alarm system here. Tell them the police have arrived and they're at the front door waiting to check things inside the museum. And remember,' Assaf growled, glancing at a photo of a woman and two small girls, 'one false move and you'll never see your wife or either of your daughters again.'

With shaking hands, the guard picked up the phone and punched in the numbers. 'No . . . I have a fault here, but the police think it's coming from your end. They're at the front door. *Shukran*, thank you.' The guard replaced the dirty bakelite handpiece in its cradle and turned toward his attacker.

'One of the night shift is on his way . . . it will take a couple of minutes for him to come up from the security room.'

'Sit in the chair!' Assaf whipped a length of nylon cord out. The guard winced in pain as Assaf tied his hands behind him.

'How many guards inside?' Assaf demanded, pressing the barrel of the gun against the guard's head.

'Just two,' the guard stammered, 'they've been cutting back lately —'

He didn't finish the sentence. Assaf pistol-whipped him and the guard slumped forward, his head hitting the desk. Assaf took some gaffer tape from his pocket and quickly wound it twice around the guard's head, sealing his mouth. He needn't have bothered. The guard was dead. Assaf recovered the guard's keys, locked the guardhouse door behind him and doubled past the fountain to join Nassar.

The lock on the museum door rattled and one of the night shift police opened it. 'We don't have any alarms going off in here,' he said.

Assaf smiled disarmingly. 'Better to be safe than sorry, with all the protestors on the streets. Do you mind if we check your systems? We'd like to start at the control room.'

'Of course. Follow me.'

Assaf and Nassar followed the policeman down toward the control centre. Before they reached the outer door, Assaf swung his pistol hard, striking his target behind his right ear.

'Bind and gag him,' Assaf hissed. He crept up to the control room and peered over the ledge of the window. The other guard had his back to him, sitting in front of a bank of old computer screens, several of which were blank. Assaf could see the desk was equipped with just the basics: two phones, a control panel, and a microphone. The guard had accessed the internet and was watching porn on the closest screen.

Assaf opened the door and the guard turned, a sheepish look on his face. 'It gets boring in here . . .'

Assaf smiled. 'That's okay,' he said. He took a pace toward the embarrassed guard and smashed him on the side of the skull with his pistol.

The guard slumped onto the control room floor and by the time Nassar had dragged the other guard into the room, Assaf had his target bound and gagged.

'Get their keys. We'll need them for Room 3,' said Assaf, searching the switches on the control desk for the laser system. Thirty seconds later he had it. 'Here!' he said, and he switched the system to daytime operation. 'My contact was right,' Assaf added, pointing to a pile of old security videotapes. 'The Smithsonian this is not. Let's go!'

Assaf led the way to the ground floor, through the exhibits of the Old Kingdom and the Middle Kingdom, and up the stairs to Room 3.

Once inside, both men paused in front of the centuries-old artifact, instantly recognisable around the world.

'I can't believe they don't have this more heavily guarded,' Assaf said, staring at the boy king's funerary mask displayed inside a glass case. Made of solid gold, the mask weighed eleven kilograms and was interspersed with blue glass stripes and precious lapis lazuli. The forehead featured a royal cobra next to a vulture, symbols of the goddesses Wadjyt and Nekhbet, and below the mask the chestpiece was covered with rows of blue lapis lazuli and turquoise, and red carnelian.

'Probably because no one would be able to sell it, at least not on the open market.' Nasser was nervous now.

Assaf took a small hammer from his pocket and smashed the glass on the side of the cabinet. The noise was deafening. He quickly smashed the remaining glass shards away from the wood, grabbed the bottom of the stand and eased the artifact from its enclosure.

'The pendant,' he said, indicating another display case. Nasser smashed the glass, extracted the priceless bejewelled falcon and slipped it into a separate bag. The art dealer in Venice had provided very strict instructions. The mask was to be delivered to a contact at Alexandria's airport. A charter jet would be waiting to take them to a small airport in the south of Italy, and then on to Venice, where Assaf would deliver the pendant personally to Rubinstein's gallery.

'Let's go,' Assaf said. He reached for the Motorola two-way radio handset on his belt. 'Cobra, over.'

'Cobra, on my way, out.' Kassab had kept the van running, and he eased away from the restaurant complex at the side of the museum and drove around to the front.

Assaf walked purposefully down the front steps to the van and placed the priceless mask and pendant in the specially padded crate. He secured the lid and leapt into the front seat

Nassar closed the front door to the museum behind him and jumped into the rear seat of the van, just as a police car, blue and white lights flashing, stopped at the wrought iron gates near the guard house.

'*Xara!* Shit!' Assaf swore. Assaf put the magnetic portable blue light back on top of the van. 'Drive toward them . . . slowly,' he ordered, screwing a silencer on to his pistol.

16

BAGRAM AIR FIELD, AFGHANISTAN

O'Connor struggled with the controls of the stricken Gulfstream. A loud warning tone sounded and both master warning glareshield switches illuminated. The left fire handle also illuminated and the solenoid popped it from its stowed position. O'Connor glanced at the rest of the gauges and swore. The left fuel-control switch was illuminated, and a 'left engine fire' message had appeared on the crew alert display.

O'Connor rotated the left fire handle to the first of the discharge positions and called the tower. 'Bagram Tower, this is Hopi One Four, we're taking ground fire, pilot deceased, co-pilot is lapsing in and out of consciousness. Request emergency fire crews, port engine on fire, over.'

'Bagram Tower, copied, traffic is Night Thruster Two airborne three miles to the north, one one eight decimal fife.'

Sounds like it's all in a day's work for those guys, O'Connor thought ruefully. He glanced at the co-pilot. Spalding was slumped in his seat but he'd regained consciousness, and O'Connor switched to the intercom.

'Talk me down, Brad,' he said calmly. O'Connor had done some flying with the Marines, but he was by no means a pilot. He concentrated on maintaining a glide path. 'We've got a fire in the port engine. I've activated the fire handle, but the warning lights are still on.'

Spalding nodded. The three-beep warning tone was filling the cockpit.

'Hit the discharge two position on the left fire handle.' Spalding was almost as calm as O'Connor, his training kicking in. 'That'll activate the other bottle in the engine nacelle.'

O'Connor reached for the handle on the cockpit centre pedestal, and the warnings ceased, but both men knew they were now flying on one engine and the aircraft had rolled toward the dead one.

'Use the rudder to counter the yaw, and keep it below 200 knots,' Spalding directed, pointing to the airspeed indicator. 'Flaps eight degrees.'

'Eight degrees.' O'Connor reached for the selector and set it.

'We're going to be crabbing sideways on to the runway, so you will have to aim off to the right and straighten at the last moment. Bring the power off a fraction . . . we want 180 knots.' Spalding's voice quavered as he fought to retain consciousness. 'Flaps twenty degrees,' he croaked.

'Flaps twenty.'

'Extend the landing gear.' Three green lights lit up, indicating the landing gear was locked.

'Landing gear down,' O'Connor confirmed. At least that was working, he thought, grimly concentrating on getting the Gulfstream down in one piece.

'Increase power . . . maintain 140 knots, flaps 40 degrees, maintain 700 feet per minute descent.'

O'Connor checked the altimeter, lowered the flaps a further 20 degrees and eased the starboard throttle lever forward. He glanced at Spalding, but the co-pilot had lost consciousness again.

'Guess you're on your own, buddy,' O'Connor muttered. The 'piano keys' on the threshold were fast approaching and O'Connor could see the emergency fire trucks, their lights flashing either side of the runway. He switched focus from the runway to the instruments and back again. The threshold flashed past slightly to port, and at 50 feet he brought the starboard thrust lever to idle, straightened the aircraft and held the nose elevation. The aircraft slammed on to the runway, blowing a tyre, but O'Connor held the nose until it came down as the lift decreased. He immediately pushed the brakes on the rudder pedals, deployed the spoilers, applied reverse thrust and countered with nose wheel steering as the blown tyre and single engine thrust threatened to slew the aircraft. The plane slowed and when it reached 60 knots, O'Connor lowered the spoilers, but as he disengaged reverse thrust a heavy machine gun opened up from beyond the far runway threshold. Two fifty-calibre rounds shattered the cockpit windscreen, missing the co-pilot and O'Connor by centimetres.

O'Connor calmly dialled up the fire control frequency for the drone crew in Nevada. 'Night Thruster Two, this is Hopi One Four, taking fire from beyond the northern threshold, over.'

Captain Rogers banked the Predator drone gently so as to not lose control, mindful of the fractional delay of satellite transmissions between Creech and his aircraft airborne over Afghanistan. He headed south, back toward Bagram, scanning the villages to the north of the airfield.

'Bottom left of screen!' Major Crowe exclaimed. The intelligence analyst, call sign Sentinel, had detected two men firing what looked to be a vehicle-mounted weapon from the cover of a small village.

'Possible new target, designate one zero, white pickup truck beside mud hut.'

'Pilot copied.'

'Sensor copied.' The tight-knit crew calmly and deliberately prepared to attack. 'I've got him.' Sergeant Michelle Brady adjusted the cross hairs onto the target. The two al Qaeda operatives, she knew, would have no idea they were in her infrared and laser sights. The small drones could be neither seen nor heard from the ground. It was the weapon the terrorists feared most.

Major Crowe scanned the village for movement. Satisfied there was none, he gave clearance to lock on to the target. 'You're cleared to lock on to Target One Zero.'

'Pilot, copied.'

'Sensor, copied. Code?'

'Pilot – entered.'

'Sensor, weapon power?'

'Pilot, on.' Together, Rogers and Brady went through their well-worn procedures to ensure the AGM-114 Hellfire air-to-surface missile would lock on to the target and find it.

'Sentinel, confirm your weapon configuration.'

'Pilot, four missiles.'

Major Crowe made a final check of the area for any sign of other movement. Satisfied the area was still clear, he authorised engagement. 'Sentinel, you're clear to engage the pickup, Target One Zero, at your discretion.'

'Pilot, cleared to engage pickup truck. Arm the laser.'

'Sensor, laser armed . . . lasing.'

'Within range . . . three, two, one. Rifle!' Captain Rogers fired one of his Hellfire missiles, and almost immediately, two small boys riding pushbikes came into view, heading toward the pickup.

'Oh no!' Michelle Brady gasped involuntarily. Like Captain Rogers, she had two small boys of her own. The drone crew watched helplessly as the missile of death, travelling at over 400 metres a second, silently approached the target. To try to divert it might cause even more casualties. The control screen pixelated as the missile unerringly found its target and the pickup exploded in a ball of flame and smoke. Brady saw what she thought was a pushbike arc into the night air. Captain Rogers continued to circle over the target, numbed by what he had seen unfold on the screen.

'It's no one's fault,' Major Crowe said finally, breaking the silence that had descended over the control cockpit, 'we did everything we could. It's the ugliness of war,' he added, cursing the terrorists who so often took refuge among innocent villagers, or in mosques, and in the process ignoring the Qu'ran, which forbade fighting in places of worship.

The briefing room at Bagram had been secured, and O'Connor flicked on the classified satellite images.

Neither the commanding general in Afghanistan nor Special Operations Command had been amused, but when the president's chief of staff leant on them, they had no choice but to allow O'Connor overall command of the operation in the notorious Korengal Valley, a valley that had seen more action than any other part of Afghanistan; but at the tactical level on the ground, the four assigned members of SEAL team six were more than happy. O'Connor's reputation preceded him, and they had worked with him before, as had the other four handpicked members of the CIA's Special Activities Division, all veterans of the hunt for Osama bin Laden. They knew the Hindu Kush well.

'When we withdrew from the Korengal Valley, al Qaeda and the Taliban were given free reign,' O'Connor began, letting his laser pointer rest where the Korengal Outpost had once stood in a dusty abandoned timber yard on the side of a steep mountain. 'But not before more than thirty Americans gave their lives, including, as you're only too well aware, many of our own Special Forces. The Chinook from the 160th Special Operations Aviation Regiment was shot down here,' O'Connor said, pointing to an area to the east of the valley. 'But it was flying near its ceiling, so we suspect the Taliban or al Qaeda, or both, have somehow obtained surface-to-air missiles.' O'Connor didn't elaborate. The possible loss of Scorpion missiles was still in a compartment above TOP SECRET.

'The overall mission of Operation Sassafras is twofold,' O'Connor continued. 'First, the 503rd will be operating to the east of us, trying to locate the members of SEAL Team Six and the crew of the Chinook. That's now a recovery mission, not a rescue. The bodies are likely to be scattered over a wide area, with a centre of mass in this area here,' O'Connor said, pointing to an area to the east of the Korengal Valley.

'We'll be looking for any evidence the Taliban or al Qaeda have acquired missiles, and we'll be operating in the Korengal Valley itself.' Several of O'Connor's team exchanged glances. They were being inserted into an area not far from where eleven Navy SEALs and eight pilots and crew had perished in fierce fighting some years earlier, on the slopes of Sawtalo Sar. Operation Red Wings had seen a total of no fewer than three Navy Crosses awarded, two posthumously and the third to the sole survivor of the operation, Marcus Luttrell. The commander, Lieutenant Michael Murphy, had been awarded a posthumous Medal of Honor, the United States' highest military award.

'This mission won't bring back those we've lost,' O'Connor added soberly, 'but if we can confirm the Taliban or al Qaeda have missiles, and determine the source, it might help prevent further casualties.' He turned back to the map. 'We'll come in from the east in two Black Hawks, flying low and fast, north above the Kunar River, and then we'll turn west where the Kunar meets the Pech River. Once we reach this position here, where the Korengal Valley intersects with the Pech, we'll turn south and head down the valley to an area near the old Korengal Outpost, where we'll fast-rope to the ground.' O'Connor pointed to the timber yard. 'Fire support will be provided from two Apache attack helos. As best we can determine from the intelligence available, the Chinook took fire from this general area here,' he said, pointing to an isolated village high on a precipitous ridge line. 'So that will be the first village to get our attention. Any questions?'

'Any fucking *questions*,' Petty Officer Louis Estrada, the short, muscular SEAL team leader muttered. 'What about the villagers . . . any help from them?' he asked.

O'Connor shook his head. 'At best, expect them to be neutral.

At worst, expect them to be reporting our every move to the Taliban. The villages in the Korengal are so remote, the occupants don't take kindly to other Afghans, let alone us. Treat them all as if they're hostile.'

O'Connor glanced over the pilot's shoulder at the instruments glowing softly in the dark. The two Sikorsky Special Operations Black Hawks were touching 120 knots an hour and, in an effort to evade an attack from Taliban surface-to-air missiles, they were flying at just 100 feet above the Kunar River. The possibility of a direct hit from an RPG, the ubiquitous Soviet rocket-propelled grenade, was the lesser of two evils. Either side of the Black Hawks, two Boeing Apache attack helicopters were covering the mission. Armed with massive 30-millimetre cannon, 70-millimetre air-to-surface rockets, and Hellfire air-to-surface missiles, the Apaches not only packed an impressive array of armaments, they were also designed to absorb small arms fire from the ground. To the north, O'Connor could see the lights of Asadabad, the capital of Kunar Province, twinkling in the distance. Over the years, Asadabad had been the scene of more than one major battle between insurgents and Soviet and Western armies, and the tension mounted as they approached. The door gunners used their helmet-mounted night-vision goggles to penetrate the darkness, and they scanned the fields either side of the riverbank.

O'Connor steadied himself against the door pillar as the pilot banked hard where the Pech River met the Kunar, and they headed west above the Pech River road, toward the villages of Andraser and

Watapur. A bare two kilometres further on, O'Connor braced as a line of red tracer pierced the night. He could hear the *crack-thump* of the rounds as they passed perilously close to the rotors.

'Gangster One . . . this is Alley Cat Seven,' O'Connor's pilot radioed the northern Apache. 'I'm taking ground fire, estimated 800 metres ahead near the village of Managai . . . could be coming from the suspension bridge, over!'

'Gangster One, copied, wait out.' The pilot of the Apache on the north side of the river was flying close to the mountains, and he could see the tracer clearly. 'Gangster Two,' he radioed the Apache on the opposite side of the river, 'a pity, but I'm going to have to take this sucker out.' All of the pilots were aware of the enormous effort the Coalition had put into improving the roads and bridges in the Pech River valley, as part of a program to try to win the hearts and minds of the locals, and the Malkana Bridge connecting the village of Managai with the other side of the river was no exception. The heavy oiled timbers had not long been restored.

'Gangster Two, copied.'

The pilot of the northern Apache banked toward the bridge, giving his gunner in the front seat a clear view of the target. The gunner activated the laser rangefinder and locked on to the Taliban insurgent. The terrorist was firing from the middle of the suspension bridge and the gunner's night-vision system picked him out clearly.

'Engaging!' The Hellfire missile left the port stub pylon in a blaze of flame and smoke, its computers reacting to the onboard radar system. Seconds later, the bridge erupted and the firing stopped.

O'Connor looked over the door gunner's shoulder as they tore past. The middle of the bridge had been completely blown away, and the ends were hanging drunkenly into the water on either side of the river. The engineers who had so recently restored it wouldn't thank them, but there had been no choice.

Minutes later, O'Connor's lead Black Hawk banked savagely again, and they headed south into the Korengal Valley, notorious for some of the most ferocious fighting of the war. Here the river was flanked on either side by soaring, forested, snow-capped mountains. The stone huts of remote villages were perched precariously on the ridges.

The pilot of the lead Black Hawk flared the aircraft and brought it to a hover above the old vacated Korengal Outpost. The crew chief flung the thick, coiled rope out the door and watched it tumble to the small clearing ten metres below the chopper. He turned and gave the thumbs up and O'Connor led the way, reaching for the rope with his gloved hands. He flung himself away from the chopper and fast-roped to the ground. The rest of the team followed and they quickly spread out from under the Black Hawk's powerful downdraft and took up defensive positions.

'Incoming!' The call was from the furthest edge of the clearing. A Taliban or al Qaeda machine gun, O'Connor wasn't sure which, opened up from a ridge across the other side of the river. Then a second, and a third. Fiery red tracer arced across the gorge from three different positions. It was going to be an interesting day in the office, O'Connor thought grimly.

17

KASHTA PALACE, ALEXANDRIA

On the last evening of the conference, Sheldon Crowley strolled along a path in the heavily guarded Kashta Palace gardens. Louis Walden, the world's most powerful media mogul, accompanied him.

'It's not a problem to get behind him, Sheldon, but Carter Davis? Is he the best we can do? Somewhere in Montana there's a village looking for its idiot,' Walden grumbled.

'Lobster Davis – million-dollar body, or at least he did have when he was first elected, and a head full of shit,' Crowley agreed, 'but unlike the other candidates, we've got him on toast. He ran for governor on a platform of pro-family, but that doesn't stack up. We've done a bit of digging on our friend Davis, and he's got form in more than one bedroom.'

'I've always taken the view that if you're not in the bed, or under it, you don't really know what's going on. How good are your sources?'

'They've been under the bed, electronically speaking. If we can get Davis into the White House, he's ours.'

'That's a big "if",' said Walden. 'Even if you get him through the primaries, how do you think he's going to stack up in a national debate? The bastard's all tip and no berg.'

'We'll cross that bridge when we come to it. I'm putting my personal assistant, Rachel Bannister, in charge of the Davis campaign. It would be handy if you could assign someone on your side.'

'Hmm . . .' Walden fell silent. 'I'll get one of my editors to call you,' he said finally. 'Joe Humphrey. He's a complete asshole, and he's helped to unseat more than one government overseas, which is why I employ him.' Walden chuckled. Nothing gave him greater pleasure than the power he wielded through his media empire, and given the plans of the Pharos Group, he was about to wield a whole lot more. 'What's the campaign theme?'

'Same theme as he used for the gubernatorial campaign . . . family man, clean living, anti-drugs and the usual guff on jobs and the economy.'

'Christ – does anyone in the media have a whiff of the real Davis? Because if this stuff's already out there, he won't make first base.'

'We've got a list of the women he's screwing, and we'll pay them out. Whatever has to be done, will be done . . .'

On the final day, just before lunch, Crowley sought the company of the chairman of Crédit Group, René du Bois.

'I have it on good authority there will shortly be further instability in the Middle East,' Crowley began.

'What do you mean by "further instability"? The place is already going to hell in a hand basket.'

'Let's just say I have intelligence there are going to be more attacks . . . major ones. They're not likely to have a lasting impact on the stock market, but the initial fluctuations will be very significant. We need to be in a position to take advantage of that. In the short term, the price of oil will go through the roof.'

'If that happens, the market and the super funds will be nervous – there'll be a corresponding fall in the other stocks,' Du Bois observed.

'Precisely, and that will include the banking sector, which is where you and I come in.' Crowley confirmed the list of key banks Pharos was targeting covertly. Both men knew well that if either Crédit Group or EVRAN reached a 30 per cent holding in those registered on the London Stock Exchange, under the British City Code on Takeovers and Mergers, they would be forced to make a cash offer to the remaining shareholders at the highest price of shares in the preceding twelve months. 'As long as neither of us go past the 30 per cent mark, when the time comes to move, between us, we'll have well over fifty per cent of the voting rights.'

Du Bois smiled. UK law had a specific provision to prevent companies 'acting in concert', but given the Pharos code of silence, that would be impossible to prove. 'Pity it wasn't that easy in the US,' he said.

Crowley nodded. Under the US Securities Exchange Act of 1934, an acquirer who purchased more than five per cent of the voting shares of any company registered in the US was required by law to file their intentions with the Securities Exchange Commission. To counter this, the Pharos Group had formed myriad front companies, each holding between four and four and a half per cent of the big Wall Street banks. 'It hasn't been easy,' Crowley agreed, 'but the latest figures are encouraging for us. The big five on Wall Street have had to downgrade their earnings estimates by more than a billion.'

'I saw those figures,' said Du Bois. 'Those bastards are running into some pretty strong headwinds. Some of their legal fees are going through the roof and when the Fed stops printing money, we'll be in a very strong position to achieve control.'

The Pharos conference was drawing to a close, and it was time for Crowley to address what he considered to be the biggest threat. 'The latte-sipping left wingers in governments around the world want to cripple us with a carbon tax,' he said, opening the argument on the last item on the agenda.

'Having served as this president's secretary of state in his first term, I think I know him pretty well,' Bradley Guthrie replied. 'He's failed in the Middle East, and there's precious little to show at home. Healthcare's bogged down on Capitol Hill, he's up to his armpits over WikiLeaks and the NSA spying on Americans, not to mention the French and the Germans. Even the Australians are pissed off with him for allowing contractors access to material that should have been much more tightly held. The economy's still sluggish, and the president will want to take steps on the environment to ensure he leaves a legacy. He'll go hard on this.'

'All the more reason we've got to stop him,' Crowley growled. 'Carbon tax in Europe peaked at US $30 a tonne in 2008, and now it's down to less than US $4, but they're still talking about US $20 a tonne in Washington. It will cost us billions.'

'Part of the problem is one of McGovern's advisors on energy,

Megan Becker,' offered General Bradshaw, the former chairman of the US Joint Chiefs of Staff. 'Degrees in environmental science and international relations. McGovern parachuted her into the god-damn CIA when that lost city of the Inca thing with O'Connor and Weizman blew up a couple of years ago.'

'She did enough damage back then,' Crowley agreed. 'Now she's even more dangerous.'

'Can we get rid of her?' pondered Bradshaw.

'I'm working on that. And don't worry, if I get who I'm thinking of to refute Becker and McGovern's crackpot ideas on global warm-ing, we'll consign climate change to the trashcan. If they can do it in Australia, we can do it in America.'

An hour later, Pharos brought the final session to a close, allow-ing the staff to wheel in a buffet of Maine lobster, beluga caviar, Périgord truffles, and a host of other delicacies.

Once the staff had departed, Pharos addressed his colleagues. 'Ladies and gentlemen,' he said, looking briefly at the framed quotes on the wall behind him. 'President Theodore Roosevelt put it this way. Behind the ostensible government sits enthroned an invisible government owing no allegiance and acknowledging no responsibility to the people. The founder of the House of Roths-child, Mayer Rothschild, was well known for his view that whoever issues and controls a nation's money cares less about who writes the laws. Much of our wealth might come from energy and arms manu-facturing, but with Washington hell bent on bowing to the greenies and the loony Left, and their push for taxes on fossil fuels, it's time for us to put Roosevelt and Rothschild's observations into practice.' Pharos raised his glass of Dom Perignon.

'Join me in a toast. To the New World Order!'

18

EGYPTIAN MUSEUM OF ANTIQUITIES, CAIRO

'Keep driving toward them,' Assaf ordered. He checked the silencer on his Czech CZ 75 and put the nine-millimetre pistol back in the side pocket of his trousers.

'What has happened?' the police sergeant demanded of Assaf when they reached the gates. The sergeant's driver, a young, recently graduated constable, looked nervous.

'Nothing to worry about,' Assaf replied, feigning nonchalance. 'We had an alarm, but everything is secure.'

'What do you mean, nothing to worry about?' the sergeant demanded. 'There's a dead guard in the ticket booth! And which unit are you from? Why are you driving a civilian van?' he asked. Suspicious, he reached for his radio.

Assaf withdrew his CZ 75 and fired twice, hitting the sergeant in the chest. He was dead before he hit the ground. His driver gasped and reached for his weapon, but Assaf fired twice more, and the young policeman collapsed over the wheel. Barely a hundred metres beyond the museum, Cairo's chaotic traffic continued to stream along Meret Basha toward Tahrir Square, the occupants of the cars, trucks and buses oblivious to the muffled gun shots.

'Mahmoud! Abdul! Get the bodies into the van. The museum guard too. Quickly!' Assaf retrieved the sergeant's radio and both policemen's identity cards.

'Mahmoud, get the mask and come with me in the police car. Abdul, you follow in the van. We'll take the desert road to Alexandria.'

'What if we're stopped?' Kassab asked nervously.

'Why would a police patrol be stopped? Leave the blue light on top of the van. But if we are stopped, leave the talking to me.'

Assaf, driving the police car, eased out of Wasim Hasan Street and on to Meret Basha.

'Papa Charlie One Zero, sitrep on the museum, over.'

Assaf reached for the handset. Mindful that the duty officer in the command centre might pick up a change in voice modulation, he kept his response brief. 'Papa Charlie, false alarm, back on patrol, over.'

'Roger, out.'

Assaf breathed a sigh of relief, and headed on to the 6 October Bridge, named in honour of the Egyptian Army's successful crossing of the Suez Canal during the 1973 Yom Kippur War against Israel.

A little over an hour later, he turned off at Wadi Nashat, a small collection of buildings on the desert road to El Alamein. 'Park the van behind that small sand dune,' he ordered Kassab.

Assaf rigged the van with plastic explosive, connected the old Nokia cell phone to the detonators, and poured petrol over the bodies of the policemen and the guard.

'Why don't we blow it now?' Kassab asked. 'What if someone finds it?'

'What if this . . . what if that,' Assaf muttered, getting back into the driver's seat and slamming the police car into gear with a grinding crunch. Kassab was starting to get on his nerves. 'Just get in the car.'

Assaf headed north-east across the desert toward El Hamam on the outskirts of Alexandria. The high beam on the headlights was blown, and Assaf peered into the pre-dawn darkness. 'You're such a worrywart, Abdul,' he said. 'If we blew the van now, you'd see it for miles around. We'll blow it once we've handed the mask over and boarded our own jet. Even if they do find the van quickly, it'll take them days to identify the bodies, and by that time we'll be back in France. Provided we get rid of this heap of shit before it's due back in the yard, they'll never connect us.'

The three black Mercedes were waved straight through the VIP security gates at Alexandria's Borg el Arab International Airport and on to the tarmac where the EVRAN corporate jet was waiting, pilots strapped in, and engines quietly turning. Crowley did not like to be delayed.

Leaving Rachel to organise the bags, Crowley strode up the short set of stairs at the front of the aircraft. 'Cargo on board?' he asked the chief steward.

'Loaded and secured, sir.'

Crowley and Rachel settled into the plush, beige leather seats in the for'ard cabin as the steward appeared with two crystal glasses of

1995 Salon, one of the world's rarest champagnes. It was made from the first pressings of a single variety, chardonnay, from a small vineyard in Le Mesnil-sur-Oger, south of Reims in northern France, but only from the very finest vintages. Such was the quality control of the fruit, the world had only seen this champagne on thirty-eight occasions in the past ninety years.

The Gulfstream tore down the runway, powered into the air, and crossed the desert coast, the dark blue-and-white livery and the stylised volcano logo of the EVRAN Corporation gleaming in the harsh morning sun. Climbing steeply, at over 3000 feet per minute, the Gulfstream quickly reached its cruising altitude and the steward reappeared with hot buttered croissants.

Crowley switched on the live news feed. All of EVRAN's jets were equipped with the latest integrated systems that allowed reception of Ku-Band Direct Broadcast Satellite or DBS television signals and Crowley had access to the whole spectrum of programs available from the DBS satellites. News of the daring robbery was being carried to thousands of stations in nearly 200 countries, and Crowley flicked on the Al Jazeera English channel.

'In what has been described as the most daring robbery this century, thieves broke into the Egyptian Museum of Antiquities in Cairo early this morning and made off with just two artifacts, the funerary mask of Tutankhamun and his priceless falcon pendant,' the newsreader began. 'We're joined now by our political correspondent in Cairo, Muhammad el-Masri. Muhammad, do we know who discovered the theft, and if the police have any leads?'

The picture switched to the stocky, bald-headed el-Masri standing in front of the salmon-coloured museum, now roped off with police tape.

'I think it's fair to say that the Egyptian Tourism and Antiquities Police, who are responsible for the security of hundreds of ancient sites throughout Egypt, are astounded by the brazen nature of the robbery. Just after midnight, the thieves, posing as police responding to an alarm, turned up to the museum and tricked security staff into letting them in. I'm joined now by Colonel Halabi from the Tourism and Antiquities Police. Colonel Halabi, thanks for your time – can you explain what must be one of the biggest lapses in security in modern history?'

The strain was showing on the swarthy face of the deputy commander. 'As a result of the protestors, our security had recently been upgraded, but when thieves are dressed in police uniforms, the lapse, although regrettable, is understandable.'

'You say regrettable, but we're talking about one of the world's best-known icons here, along with a priceless pendant. Who would want to steal them? Either would be almost impossible to sell?'

Colonel Halabi nodded. 'This is not the work of amateurs,' he said. 'Over three billion dollars worth of art and artifacts are stolen every year from collections around the world, and many of those finish up on the black market, or are sold to museums by using false provenance documents. But the Tutankhamun mask and the falcon pendant would be *very* difficult to sell, even on the black market, so we suspect that this has been done to fill a contract for a private buyer.'

'Was anyone injured in the robbery?'

'We are not sure. One of the guards is missing, and two policemen are also missing. We found the police vehicle near the airport at Alexandria, but there is no sign of the officers.'

'Could they be involved?'

Colonel Halabi shrugged, well aware that the bulk of the Egyptian police force was poorly paid, albeit some of the 'lucky' ones. Since the overthrow of the Morsi Government, tourism had all but ceased and over half the population, more than forty million Egyptians, were living on or below the poverty line, many on less than US $2 a day. 'We hope not,' said Halabi, 'but we are not ruling anything out.'

'Do you think the Tutankhamun mask and the pendant could already be out the country?'

'Again, we're not ruling that out, and we've put out an alert to airports around the world.'

'Colonel Halabi, thanks very much for joining us.'

The image faded back to the newsreader in the studio. 'And that was our political correspondent, Muhammad el-Masri, reporting from Cairo. Not only a loss for the Egyptian Museum,' said the newsreader, 'but the world at large. Tutankhamun assumed the throne of ancient Egypt in 1332 BC when he was just ten. He was arguably the best known of the Egyptian pharaohs, largely because his tomb was discovered intact. Hundreds of artifacts remain in the Cairo Museum, but the best known of all, the funerary mask, containing over eleven kilograms of solid gold, is now missing. Heaven forbid that it would ever be melted down,' the newsreader said, turning toward camera two. 'Now to news in the United States. In a surprise move in Chicago, where notorious gangster Elias D. Ruger has been on trial for murder, Judge O'Reilly has dismissed the charges on the basis there was insufficient evidence to convict. And in another surprise move, furious Cook County District Attorney Glenda B. Mitchell has spoken out against what she has termed inequities in the United States justice system.' The vision faded to

Chicago where Attorney Mitchell was addressing a large contingent of media on the courthouse steps: 'We are surprised, and more than a little disappointed with this acquittal. In our view, the case against Ruger was very strong, and in any other country, there would be an immediate appeal, but in the United States, that avenue is denied us.'

'Turning to politics, the Republican Party is deeply split over its nominees for the presidential primaries, with the Tea Party seemingly moving further to the right —'

Crowley flicked off the broadcast.

'Pretty brazen, that theft,' Rachel observed, puzzled by the lack of reaction from her boss.

'It happens. Security at some of these museums in developing countries is pretty minimal,' he said, opening an online copy of the *Daily News Egypt*. The headline 'STOLEN!' took up half the front page.

Beneath it, a huge picture of the Tutankhamun mask, along with the falcon pendant, took up the rest of the page.

Thousands of feet below, near the desert wadi of El Alamein, a mobile phone rang and a battered white van exploded, burning the bodies inside to ash.

19

KORENGAL VALLEY, AFGHANISTAN

O'Connor kept his head down as the Taliban peppered the old Korengal outpost with machine gun fire. Puffs of dirt and rock kicked up as the red tracer rounds ricocheted and arced gracefully into the night. Then came a heavier sound: *crump . . . crump . . . crump*. From an initial impact point further down the ridge, high explosive rounds were creeping toward the Americans' position.

'Mortars!' O'Connor's number two, the lanky chief petty officer Rudy Kennedy, engaged the Taliban with a burst of fire from his MK11 sniper rifle. 'We better get those fucking base plates before they zero in on us!' the CPO yelled to O'Connor.

'I'm on it,' O'Connor acknowledged, reaching for his radio handset. 'Welcome to the Korengal Valley!' he added. The pair grinned at each other as the bullets ricocheted around them. They'd been in tighter spots than this together.

'Gangster One, this is Hopi One Four. We're taking small arms fire from halfway up the ridge to the east of our position. Mortar fire from the same direction, over.'

Black shapes tumbled down the ropes suspended from the second Black Hawk, until the rest of the team had hit the ground. But as Alley Cat Four lifted off sharply, the starboard engine exploded.

'This is Alley Cat Four, we've been hit!' The pilot struggled to control the crippled machine, crash landing heavily on top of a pile of timber further up the mountain.

O'Connor reached for his handset again as he broke cover and sprinted toward the stricken chopper. 'Black Hawk down!'

'Alley Cat Seven, copied.' The lead Black Hawk banked sharply and took up a position behind the ridgeline, ready for a hot extraction.

'Gangster One, copied, out to you. Gangster Two, copy?'

'Roger, infrared has located the mortar base plate, over.'

'Roger, you take the base plate, we'll deal with the small arms . . . I'm starting my run now.' The pilot of the first Apache dived toward the machine gun flashes on the ridge. The gunner in the forward cockpit calmly tracked the Taliban with the night-vision system on his helmet, a forward-looking infrared system that was slaved to the sights on the aircraft's chain gun. Wherever the gunner pointed the crosshairs, the chain gun automatically locked on to the target. The Apache shuddered slightly as the huge thirty-millimetre rounds ripped into the first of the Taliban machine-gun positions. The gunner tracked his sights on to the machine-gun flashes further up the ridge and blasted the Taliban insurgents with another burst. The Apache was barely 300 metres out when he silenced the third position.

'Gangster Two, this is Gangster One, all yours, over,' the pilot radioed, peeling away to give the second attack helicopter a clear run on the mortar base plate.

The gunner in the second Apache was already tracking the muzzle flashes from the Taliban's 81-millimetre mortar tube, a single weapon being fired from a small clearing near some stone huts halfway up the ridge. Seconds later, the Hellfire missile found its mark. The mortar barrel and baseplate, along with the dismembered bodies of two insurgents, arced into the night. The ridge fell silent.

O'Connor and CPO Kennedy reached the burning Black Hawk in time to help the pilot extract the wounded co-pilot from his harness. 'Alley Cat Seven, this is Hopi One Four,' O'Connor radioed, 'we're going to blow this bird.' This was no ordinary Black Hawk. It was one of two used in the raid on Osama bin Laden, and the gear on board was 'above' top secret.

'Alley Cat Seven, roger, standing by for extraction.'

'Hopi One Four . . . co-pilot has serious stomach wounds, out.'

As soon as the Black Hawk crew had cleared the crash site, carrying their wounded brother-in-arms, O'Connor and CPO Kennedy rigged the downed aircraft with explosives and O'Connor set the timer.

'Timer on, let's get out of here.' The pair doubled down the ridge line, and thirty seconds later, Alley Cat Four exploded in a ball of fire. The aircraft burned fiercely and O'Connor gave Kennedy the thumbs up. The highly classified gear would soon be reduced to ash.

'Hopi One Four, this is Gangster One,' the lead Apache radioed. 'We're getting low on fuel. Will you be requiring any further assistance this evening, over?'

O'Connor grinned to himself. 'This is Hopi One Four . . . not unless you can whistle up a regiment of tanks. Have a Budweiser when you get back.'

The three aircraft headed north back down the river, and an eerie silence settled over the valley.

Ten kilometres to the south, Tayeb Jamal and Omar Yousef were high in the mountains, and deep in conversation. Reports of the fiery clash had already reached their remote village.

'We lost another ten men tonight, Tayeb. The Infidel is going to pay for that.' The flickering light from the oil lamp caught the hatred on Yousef's young face. Seated at the rough-hewn table where they had planned so many attacks on the Americans, Yousef turned and spat on the ground. 'Do you think he's back to stay?'

Jamal shook his head. 'No. He'll be trying to recover the bodies of those in the Chinook we shot down, although it's a little odd that he's back in this valley. I've had a report of more of them to the east, which is where the bodies are more likely to be.'

Yousef smiled, a slow, sinister smile. '*Alhamdulillah*, thanks be to Allah, the Infidel's new missiles are being turned against him. When do we get more?' he asked eagerly.

'General Khan is working on it,' Jamal replied. 'In the meantime, while the Infidel is in this valley, we need to make sure the ones we have are well hidden.'

'I've sent messages to the villages. They are all hidden below ground.'

'Good. We need to save them for the big targets, which brings us to tomorrow. Our sentries have the Infidel under observation.

It looks as if there are eight of them, and they're spending the night at their old observation post.'

'Then why not attack them while they're sleeping! We can annihilate them!'

'Patience, Omar. The Infidel has a lot more firepower in the air than we do, and attacking that stronghold at night when each of them has night-vision goggles puts us at a disadvantage, and we can't afford to get into a long firefight. We need to use the one thing we know better than he does . . . we know these mountains like the backs of our hands. The Infidel has to rely on his technology. So we'll observe. He won't move until morning, and we'll be waiting for him.'

The dawn came quickly, far too quickly for O'Connor and his men. To the east, the mists enveloping the peaks of the mountains were tinged with pink. Breakfast was a sparse affair from the 'first strike ration' – a high-energy cereal bar and an instant coffee. For lunch, there was a choice of either a long-life barbecue beef or a bacon-cheddar sandwich, designed to deliver 2900 calories, with a pouch of tuna or chicken chunks for dinner, supplemented by beef jerky and peanut butter and crackers. From the reception the team had received on their arrival, and with secrecy and surprise now lost, O'Connor knew calories would likely be in deficit by the end of the day.

'Okay,' he said, 'listen up. Our job's just got that much harder. Latest intel?' he asked, turning to the team's intelligence operator, Alejandro 'Chico' Ramirez, an oval-faced twenty-six-year-old Latino from Arizona.

'JSOC are reporting more movement to the south,' Chico confirmed, his satellite laptop open on his knees. The Joint Special Operations Centre commanded some of the most sensitive US Special Forces operations. 'They're not sure how many in the group. I'm trying to get some confirmation and I've asked for a drone to be assigned. The enemy seem to be concentrating near the village of Laniyal, a couple of clicks to the south of here.'

'Should make life interesting,' O'Connor observed dryly. 'Air support?' O'Connor had insisted on the inclusion of an air force combat air controller, and not just any combat controller. The lanky Hank Ventura was one of the best. He and his number two, twenty-two-year-old Milton Rayburn, a two-tour veteran from New Jersey, were equipped with satellite radios and a SOFLAM, a Special Operations Forces Laser Acquisition Marker. The classified kit looked like a very large pair of binoculars mounted on a tripod. In what was known as 'painting the target', the number two would fire a laser beam directly at the target. Once the target was located, Ventura would call in whatever air support was available, and with the help of a global positioning system, laser guided bombs would be linked to the SOFLAM from thousands of feet above. The Taliban would have no idea they were being 'painted'.

'Hens' teeth and air support around here have got a lot in common,' Hank replied, in his slow, southern drawl, 'but we should be able to count on a couple of F-16 Vipers and the drone Chico's asked for, and if we're really in the clag, we may be able to prioritise a Ghostrider.' The C-130 Hercules gunships – massive flying weapons--delivery platforms – were armed with the most fearsome array of cannons and missiles known to modern warfare. They had been in use in various forms since the Vietnam War, but the latest C-130H version was equipped with massive 30-millimetre cannons capable of firing at 200 rounds per minute; 140-millimetre rocket-powered Griffin missiles; Hellfire missiles; huge 250-pound GBU-39 bombs; and the smaller Viper laser-guided glide bombs.

'We may need all of that and more. We'll stick to the high ridge-lines above the river until we get near Laniyal. Stay spread out, and cover your arcs of fire.' O'Connor positioned himself just behind the lead scout and the patrol moved out, heading toward the next village, a group of stone huts perched halfway up the steep, rocky mountain slope.

High on the opposite mountainside, Jamal and Yousef watched through their binoculars.

'The Infidel is moving out, my friend,' Jamal observed. 'We'll need to get word to Laniyal. *Insha'Allah*, he will be drawn into the ambush.'

The commander of the 432nd Wing of the United States Air Force at Creech Air Force Base, Colonel Joe Stillwell, brought the briefing to a blunt conclusion. 'Last night, their time, call sign Hopi One Four, the combined CIA-SEAL team in the Korengal Valley, came under intense mortar and machine-gun fire from the Taliban during their insertion into the old Korengal outpost, so it looks as if these bastards are back with a vengeance,' Stillwell warned, turning toward Captain Rogers and his crew

'Dawn is just breaking over there, and given their reception last night, it won't be long before it's on again. Any questions?'

'Predator or Reaper?' Rogers asked.

'This mission's about as tough as they come, so you've been assigned a Reaper . . . brand-new one, I'm told.'

Captain Rogers grinned. He would have given anything to be back in the cockpit of an F-16 Viper, but the Reaper was the next best thing. The latest drone had a speed of over 300 miles per hour, carried a staggering one and a half tonnes of armaments, and even with that load, it could stay up for fourteen hours.

'Bagram are preparing it as we speak – armament configuration is four Hellfire missiles and two 500-pound GBU-38 bombs.'

O'Connor signalled the lead scout to halt. The village of Bibiyal lay directly ahead, and beyond that, further down the valley, was the village of Laniyal. O'Connor indicated for two of his men to move and cover the village from higher up the ridgeline and then he focused his binoculars. The houses, constructed from rock and thick cedar beams overlooked the Korengal River below. Gnarled trees dotted the area, their growth stunted by the rocky soil, but where they could, the villagers had terraced the hillsides, planting wheat, and the foliage on the trees in the citrus orchards was thick. Smoke drifted up from the early morning fires and two of the village elders came out and sat on the roof of the nearest house.

O'Connor moved forward cautiously, using the cover of the trees until he was closer to the elders.

'*Sahr pikheyr*,' O'Connor greeted them in Pashto. 'Good morning,' he repeated, showing himself, his M14 rifle pointed toward the ground. The safety catch was off, ready for instant use. Afghanistan had two official languages that were widely used: Pashto and Dari.

O'Connor was fluent in both, but in the Korengal Valley, the six major tribes were surrounded by the Safi Pashtun tribes, and Pashto was the lingua franca.

'Cover me,' O'Connor ordered, and he moved toward the elders. The rest of the patrol held the village in their sights, the machine gunner on the ridge easing the safety catch on his MK48.

'The Taliban have been here?' O'Connor asked in Pashto, once the formal greetings had been exchanged and CPO Kennedy had joined him.

The village elders eyed O'Connor sullenly. Dressed in traditional baggy trousers, three-quarter tunics and turbans, their faces were lined by the harshness of their existence, their beards flecked with grey, their dark eyes full of suspicion.

'We can do this the easy way or the hard —' O'Connor stopped mid-sentence. A young man had burst from a house further down the side of the mountain and was running down the stony track that led to Laniyal.

'Fuck it,' Kennedy swore, taking a bead on the fleeing fugitive but knowing he couldn't shoot. O'Connor and Kennedy knew there was every chance he was Taliban, but the rules of engagement were very strict, even on a mission like this: if an Afghan was unarmed, the coalition forces couldn't fire.

'Keep two sentries on . . . the rest of us will have to search this place house by fucking house,' said O'Connor.

Two hours later, the search of the village had revealed nothing, and had only added to the resentment the fiercely independent Korengal Valley villagers already felt toward intruders in general, and the United States in particular.

'Stay off the track,' O'Connor ordered, as they prepared to move out toward Laniyal. 'The Taliban will be watching, so we'll stick to the high ground.' O'Connor shouldered his pack. His team had dispensed with heavy body armour, but with five days' rations, water and light sleeping gear, let alone the rest of their equipment and ammunition, the packs weighed in at a hefty 30 kilograms. It would be hard going up the ridge, so steep that at times, the patrol would be reduced to clawing their way over the broken rocks.

In the village of Laniyal, Jamal listened as his young Taliban warrior, breathless from his run, blurted out a warning. 'They are in Bibiyal, so they will be here soon!'

Jamal smiled, a slow, humourless smile. 'We are ready, my friend. The Infidel is going to regret he ever came back here.'

20

STOCKHOLM, SWEDEN

Rachel Bannister parked her hire car on Malmskillnadsgatan, not far from the Höterget metro station, in what had once been Stockholm's red light district. She checked the address Area 15 had provided, took the stairs to the third floor of a dilapidated building and knocked on the entrance to apartment nine.

The door was opened by a tall, well-endowed blonde woman, whom Rachel judged to be in her mid-thirties, but she looked much older. Beneath the make-up there was a hardness. 'Ingrid Andersson?'

'*Ja. Vad kan jag göra för dig*? Yes . . . what can I do for you?'

'In your professional world, you're known as Frida.'

Andersson suddenly looked anxious.

'You have an appointment this evening at nine-thirty. Your client has booked you in the name of Geoff. An in-call for two hours, including anal, 4000 krona.'

'Who are you?' Andersson asked nervously.

'Don't worry, I'm not from the police.'

'If you're his wife, I don't want any trouble . . .'

Rachel shook her head.

'Then who are you?' Andersson asked, more assertive now.

Rachel delved into her shoulder bag, and extracted a brown envelope bulging with green hundred-krona notes. 'Let's just say I have an interest in your client . . . and I need to record this evening's activities.'

Andersson glanced at the money, but shook her head.

'There's 30 000 krona in this envelope,' said Rachel, looking past the prostitute. The apartment was tidy enough, but the furniture was old and worn. Rachel thought the equivalent of nearly US $5000 would probably clinch the deal. She was wrong.

Andersson shook her head again. 'What's to stop you handing over the recording to the police?'

It was time to get heavy. 'You'll just have to take our word on that. Your client is very well known internationally, and is already in a lot of trouble.'

'Then I'll just cancel.'

'I wouldn't if I were you.' Rachel extracted copies of the booking emails from her bag and handed them to Andersson. 'If we'd wanted to go to the police, we could have set you up to be raided. The police would have caught you and your client red-handed.' In 1999, the Swedish government had introduced a law that criminalised men who paid for sex. 'And we could still pass this information to them, so I suggest you cooperate, and everyone will be happy. The recording won't see the light of day.'

Andersson hesitated. 'He's into kinky sex,' she said. 'He likes me to dress up as an older schoolgirl, and spank him for misbehaving.'

'Does he now.' Rachel resisted rolling her eyes. 'His fetishes are not our concern, and provided you cooperate, neither are you.'

Andersson put her hand out for the envelope.

Professor Marcus Ahlstrom brought his Nobel lecture to a close. Ever since 1901, when the first Nobel Prize for Physics had been awarded to the German physicist Wilhelm Röntgen for his discovery of X-rays, the Nobel Foundation had required recipients to give a public lecture on their field of study, and Ahlstrom was revelling in the occasion. Marie Curie had been awarded the Nobel Prize for Physics in 1903 for her research into radiation, and in 1911 she'd again been awarded a Nobel Prize for Chemistry for her discovery of the element radium; one of only four scientists to be awarded a Nobel twice. Einstein had won it in 1921, not for his work on relativity, but for a paper on the photoelectric effect in which he showed electrons were ejected from gases, liquids and solids when they absorbed energy from light; a discovery that had led to the fiendishly difficult field of quantum physics.

'I am grateful that my work on thermal energy particles has been recognised here tonight, but much more needs to be done. The possibility of the combination of both nuclear fusion and nuclear fission to produce clean energy is an exciting prospect, and the solution to this most vexing of problems in nuclear physics is especially important at a time when climate change is undoubtedly being influenced by human activity,' Ahlstrom concluded.

We're going to have to school you in a new script, Rachel mused, as she observed her target from three rows back in Stockholm's prestigious Karolinska Institutet. His most striking features were his curly white hair and a large roman nose.

'As I've demonstrated here tonight, if governments fund the research, we can make progress toward a fossil fuel–free future.'

Rachel felt compelled to rise with the audience as Ahlstrom received a standing ovation.

'Who's been a naughty little boy then?' 'Frida' was dressed as a schoolgirl. She wore a tartan skirt, so short that it only just covered the tops of her long legs. The first three buttons on her white blouse were undone, and her large firm breasts threatened to burst the remaining fasteners. Ahlstrom had dressed in short pants and a white shirt, and he was wearing an Eton schoolboy cap.

'Answer me now . . . who's been a naughty little boy!'

'Me, Miss, so you'll have to pull my trousers down and spank me!' Ahlstrom whispered breathlessly.

Frida slowly unzipped his fly and undid the buttons on Ahlstrom's shorts, letting them fall to the floor. She pulled down his underpants and leaned over his shoulder, pushing her cleavage into Ahlstrom's face as she spanked his saggy butt cheeks with her whip. With her other hand, she fondled his erection.

'There's more punishment. You're going to have to be my slave now, aren't you! I'm going to tie you up to the bedhead and ride you!' Ahlstrom nodded, pouting with his bottom lip, and Frida led him over to an old four-poster bed. She bound his wrists and ankles and secured them to the posts.

'Whip me,' Ahlstrom croaked, 'whip me!'

Frida sat astride him, straddling his small erection. 'You – mustn't – be – a – naughty – boy – again,' she whispered, moving up and down on his shaft and whipping Alhstrom's calves behind her in time to her admonishments.

Rachel watched Ahlstrom emerge from the same dingy building on Malmskillnadsgatan she had visited earlier. He hailed one of Stockholm's ubiquitous black taxis and Rachel waited until the taxi was out of sight before making her way up to apartment nine.

'I will need to check the recording,' Rachel said, after Andersson had let her in.

'It's on the table.'

Rachel pressed the play button and watched until she was satisfied they had captured Ahlstrom's fetishes. 'We won't trouble you again, and neither will your client,' she added.

Rachel drove the short distance to Ahlstrom's hotel, the Grand Hôtel in Södra Blasieholmshamnen, and she parked on the waterfront across from the hotel entrance.

Armed with Area 15's information on Ahlstrom's room number, there was no need to bribe the concierge. She made her way up to Ahlstrom's executive suite and knocked lightly on the door.

'What is it?'

Rachel detected a note of irritation in Ahlstrom's voice. 'I have an urgent message from the Nobel Laureate Committee, Professor Ahlstrom.'

'It's after midnight,' Ahlstrom complained, opening the door. 'What's the message?'

'My apologies, Professor Ahlstrom, but this is somewhat sensitive. Do you mind if I come in?'

'If you must,' he said, his voice softening a little as he eyed Rachel's cleavage.

'We have a proposal for you,' Rachel said, placing the video camera on the coffee table. 'But first, we'd like you to have a look at this.' She pressed the play button and watched Ahlstrom's countenance turn rapidly from intrigue to anger.

'Who the fuck are you!' he demanded.

'Let's just say we are a multinational, and we're about to make you an offer.'

'Well, you can go fuck yourselves, and you're not as clever as you think you are,' Ahlstrom stormed, 'because I now have your evidence,' he said, reaching for the video camera.

'We're not that stupid, Professor. That cassette's a copy. And we know more about you than you think,' Rachel replied icily. 'Two months ago, your wife Vivienne filed for divorce. We've spoken with her, and she's willing to settle for the house, plus half your earnings from the Nobel, which this year is set at eight million krona, which would put her share at about US $650 000.'

'So you're working for her. Well, you can tell her this from me . . . if she thinks she's getting her hands on any of this prize, she can go fuck herself!'

'I assure you, Professor Ahlstrom, the courts will take a very different view, and in any case, we're not working for your wife. But if your activities in Stockholm become public, the Nobel committee may well review their decision.'

'For spending time with a call girl? You're kidding yourselves. What did you say your name was?'

'My name doesn't matter, although you will get to meet me formally in due course. And in the case of the call girl, you may be right, although the committee would undoubtedly be displeased with the publicity, particularly on the eve of the presentation by the King . . . but I'm not talking about your sexual activities, Professor.' Rachel withdrew a copy of Ahlstrom's communications with one of Stockholm's drug dealers. 'Cocaine is quite another matter. The authorities take a very dim view of that here.'

'You bastards . . . Where did you get this?'

'That doesn't matter either. You're in a very precarious position, Professor,' Rachel said, pushing another document across the coffee table. 'That's a legal opinion on your divorce case, and your chances of keeping all of the Nobel Prize winnings. In two words, "very slim." '

'What do want from me?' Ahlstrom asked. Some of his anger had given way to resignation.

'It's very simple, Professor. I represent the wealthiest industrialist in the world, and he's making you a very generous offer. An appointment as a research consultant at one of our nuclear laboratories. We have two complexes, one in California, and a much smaller but highly classified complex in Idaho, which are the equal of any in the world. You will be assigned to our gated community in California, where fifty per cent of your time will be allocated to your own research, in fields of your choosing. Publication of results will be at our discretion. The rest of your time will be spent delivering lectures debunking climate change.'

'The hell I will . . . I've spent the last decade promoting clean energy,' Ahlstrom protested, suddenly re-energised.

'You wouldn't be the first scientist to change course on this issue, Professor, and in your case, you don't have any choice. Here's a list of your gambling and drug debts, including a list of the threats you've received.' Rachel watched the colour drain from Ahlstrom's face. 'Even if you managed to keep the entire Nobel, you still wouldn't be in the clear, and once your wife takes you to the cleaners, you won't have a house either.'

Ahlstrom slumped back into the lounge, his face pale, any fight extinguished.

'There are three copies of the agreement for signature . . . two for us and one for you. You are to resign your position at MIT, with effect immediately, and move to our nuclear complex outside of San Francisco in California, where you will be provided with an office and access to our laboratories. In return, we will organise the settlement of your divorce, and cover your drug and gambling debts. The divorce settlement terms will include the deeds of your house being signed over to your wife, along with half the proceeds of your Nobel Prize. Your share will be used as down payment on a two million dollar house on the laboratory estate. Provided you meet your part of the bargain, the debt will eventually be waived. The position attracts a salary of US $300 000 a year. Travel, accommodation and administrative expenses will be met by us.'

'Anything else?' Ahlstrom rasped.

'Yes. Before you take up your official duties, we will organise psychotherapy sessions to address your gambling and drug dependence. Your sexual peccadillos are entirely your affair, provided they are discreet. Wives of other scientists and staff are off-limits,' Rachel said matter-of-factly, proffering Ahlstrom a pen.

'Let me congratulate you on your award, Professor Ahlstrom. I will be in the audience to see you receive it. And welcome to EVRAN.'

21

KORENGAL VALLEY, AFGHANISTAN

O'Connor clawed his way over the broken granite and paused at the top of the ridge, breathing hard. He stayed behind cover, and focused his binoculars on the village of Laniyal below them. The stone houses were built on such steep slopes that the Afghans could step on to the roofs of those that were below the dirt track. O'Connor signalled for CPO Kennedy to join him and for the rest of the patrol to stay down and hidden.

CPO Kennedy crawled forward on his hands and knees. 'What've we got?'

'Not sure yet, but that little bastard will have alerted them that we're on the way. Wait . . . look, in among the trees in the orchard,' O'Connor warned.

'Got it . . . RPG . . . and there – in from the other side of the track . . . another RPG.'

O'Connor turned to Kennedy and grinned. 'Remember the Zulus?'

'Right on. The buffalo horns.' The Zulu tribe in southern Africa were perhaps the first to perfect it – an ambush in the shape of the horns of the buffalo. The 'horns' would not be the ones to open fire; instead they would allow the enemy to pass through. When the adversary collided with the head, the horns would close the trap and a quarry would be encircled.

'Well, we're not playing that game.' O'Connor turned and signalled for the combat air control team to come forward.

'This is going to get a bit sticky,' O'Connor said, after he'd pointed out the ambush to Ventura and Rayburn. 'What've we got in the air?'

'We've got a drone out of Creech above us, but if that's just the welcoming committee down there, we're gonna need a bit more than that,' Ventura replied, reaching for his radio.

Rayburn set up the SOFLAM laser tripod behind a gnarled cedar tree, took the cover off the lens and focused through the eyepiece. He held the tiny red dot, first on the RPG team in the orchard, and then on the team below the road.

Beside him, Ventura's radio crackled in response to his request for more assistance. 'This is Burglar One Three. We're inbound,' the co-pilot of the huge four-engined C-130 gunship radioed. 'Time over your location, ten minutes. What've you got down there, over?'

'This is Tailpipe Two Two,' Ventura replied. 'We're not sure yet, but we have two RPG teams on the approaches to Laniyal, grid 359753 and intel indicates a possible larger force. Our location 300 metres to the north-east on top of the ridgeline . . . not cleared to fire, repeat not cleared to fire without permission, over.'

'Burglar One Three, copied . . . not cleared to fire without permission.'

O'Connor pondered his next move. Clearly they were expected, and even more clearly, they were not welcome, and if the intel was anything to go by, they were well and truly outnumbered; but already, he could hear the familiar sounds of the four Rolls Royce turboprops of the C-130. High above, the Ghostrider was beginning to circle, and the crew were standing by, the images of the village on their screens. His mind made up, he turned to Ventura. 'Take out the RPGs, and we'll see how they react.'

'Bombs, missiles or cannon?'

O'Connor smiled grimly, observing the rocket grenade teams through his binoculars. 'Cannon should do it,' he said. 'We may need the heavy stuff for later.'

'Tailpipe Two Two, this is Burglar One Three, we've got you visual on the ridgeline.' Ghostrider's weapons fire controller was coming through loud and clear. 'Two targets locked on – 300 metres to your south-west, over.' The Taliban's body heat showed clearly on the sensor screens, and the laser point ensured that regardless of which weapon suite was used, the targets could be engaged.

'Burglar One Three, roger . . . you're cleared to engage. Request cannon, over.'

Rayburn continued to paint the team in the orchard with the tiny red dot of death, and the orchard erupted as the massive thirty-millimetre rounds ripped into trees and body parts. Seconds later, firing at 200 rounds a minute, a burst from the cannon on the world's deadliest aircraft dispatched the second RPG team.

'Movement,' CPO Kennedy hissed, indicating the trees further down the ridge. 'Fifteen, twenty . . . holy shit . . . that's just the first wave. There's gotta be another hundred of these camel jockeys behind 'em.'

'I see 'em,' O'Connor replied.

The Taliban and al Qaeda commanders might have been young, but Jamal and Yousef were already experienced veterans, fighting for a cause that they believed in just as passionately as the West believed in freedom. Once the RPG teams had been hit, Jamal knew that the Infidel had tumbled to his plan. Apart from an intimate knowledge of the mountains, the only advantage he had was an overwhelming superiority in numbers, and it was time to exercise that.

Jamal turned to Yousef. 'We'll attack them up the ridge-line . . . once we've got them engaged, hit them from the flank.'

'The Infidel's dead meat,' Yousef snarled.

O'Connor knew well what he was up against. The enemy were as brave as any on the world's battlefields, and he wasn't about to take them for granted. 'Spread the guys across the ridge,' he ordered the chief, 'but tell them not to fire until I give the word. Ventura, Rayburn . . . you stay here and stay down. This is going to be a busy morning.'

'Affirmative,' Ventura acknowledged, 'Burglar's got 'em on their screens. They're suggesting bombs before they get too close.'

'Hit 'em, but danger close,' O'Connor agreed. 'Bombs on the way, Chief . . . pass it on.' The 250-pound guided bombs came in at just under US $100 000 each, but cost was the last thing on O'Connor's mind. The shock waves and noise would be horrendous, and he had to let the SEAL team know what was about to arrive on their patch of dirt.

The pilot lined up the huge aircraft for the run, while the rest of the superbly trained crew supported those in trouble on the ground below them, doing what each did best: fire control officer, electronic warfare officer, flight engineer, loadmaster, low-light TV operator, infrared detection set operator and the five aerial gunners who did the heavy lifting. The IDS operator held the cross hairs on the white figures thousands of feet below, and the first of the sleek cylinders of whispering death descended toward the ridge.

The earth shook and red-hot shards of metal screamed through the air, shredding the foliage from the trees and ripping into the insurgents. Some of the shrapnel reached dangerously close to O'Connor and his men, and the blast echoed around the mountains. The screams of the wounded rent the mists. O'Connor ducked as a burst of machine-gun fire, and then another, kicked up dust, dirt and shards of granite around their position.

'That's coming from across the river!' Kennedy yelled.

'Fuck,' O'Connor muttered, as a bullet took a chunk out of his arm.

'Where are they? I don't see them,' Ventura yelled, moving to the other side of his tree.

'Across the river . . . clearing . . . halfway up the mountain.'

'I've got them!' O'Connor yelled, spotting the muzzle flashes as another 250-pound bomb exploded closer to his position. The air was now thick with bullets as the Taliban down the ridge pushed up toward them. 'Ventura – can you see those guys across the river yet?'

'No . . .' Ventura desperately searched for the enemy position.

'Clearing . . . right two knuckles, muzzle flashes in the orchard 50 metres down from the first of the houses on the left of the village. The bastards have put women and children on the rooftops.'

'I've got them now,' Ventura yelled as sustained bursts raked the SEALs' position.

'What else have we got in the air?'

'Drone . . . but Bagram's diverted two Vipers. They've only got forty minutes fuel though.' 'Viper' was the pilots' nickname for the F-16 Fighting Falcon, one of the most advanced fighters in the world.

'Use the F-16s first then, the drone can stay all day – and warn them about the kids – danger close. And keep the gunship on those bastards down the ridge . . . they're starting to spoil my day!' O'Connor yelled, picking off two more Taliban as they ran toward him. The flashes from the 30-millimetre high explosive rounds increased in volume as the huge C-130 gunship circled and the computers kept the 30-millimetre chain guns aimed at the Taliban ridgeline below O'Connor and his men.

Ventura pressed the transmit button on his handset and began to talk the fighters in. 'Bandit One Nine, this is Tailpipe Two Two . . . we're taking heavy machine-gun fire from the ridge across the river from our position. Enemy at grid 355752 below the houses . . . danger close . . . women and children on the rooftops, traffic is an AC-130, Burglar One Three at 8000 feet and a drone, Night Thruster Two, at flight level two four zero, over.'

'This is Night Thruster Two,' Captain Rogers broke in, 'am now at flight level two zero, and holding five miles to the north,' he warned. Far away in Nevada, Rogers was once again wishing with every fibre of his being that he was back in the cockpit of Bandit One Nine's F-16 fighter.

'Bandit One Nine, copied that, wait out.' Major Michael Brickley was on his third tour of the Middle East. He was one of the United States Air Force's most experienced fighter pilots, and he knew well the problems of identifying targets on the ground.

'Tailpipe, this is Bandit, I have you on the ridge to the *east* of the river . . . the target is among the trees next to the clearing below the village on the *west* side of the river, right?'

'Affirmative, Bandit, we're above the east bank of the river.'

'Do I have clearance?'

'Affirmative, over.'

'Roger . . . beginning my run.'

'Bandit Two Nine, copied out.' Brickley's wingman was holding five miles to the east, waiting his turn at the target. At 350 knots, Brickley rolled into the attack, and the sensors inside the LITEN-ING targeting pod below the fuselage acquired the flashes of the machine guns 200 metres below the rooftops where the women were trying to shield their terrified children from the deafening noise. He held the consent button down, allowing the onboard computers, fed by the aircraft's sensors, to take account of the aircraft's speed, now around 600 feet per second, the wind direction and velocity, and the aircraft's altitude and height above the target. The bomb left the starboard pod and whispered toward the al Qaeda force on the ground; Brickley began his pull out of the dive.

'Bandit One Nine . . . Bandit Two Nine, missile on your tail!'

They were the last words Major Brickley heard. His wingman had picked up the smoke trail of a Scorpion missile launched from Laniyal, but this latest generation of surface-to-air missiles could defeat anything in the air.

O'Connor watched the F-16 explode in a fiery ball, debris raining down on the valley. Above the crackle and thump of bullets and machine gun fire, O'Connor thought he heard a cheer from down the ridge. Across the river, the guided bomb found its mark, exploding with a deafening blast of fire and smoke in a direct hit on the al

Qaeda fighters in the tree line. Further up the ridgeline, the children were screaming in terror, two of them badly wounded from the shrapnel. The ridge erupted again as another 250-pound bomb found its mark, and the roar of the second F-16 echoed down the valley as the wingman pulled out of a screaming dive, fighting against a maelstrom of anger, shock and fear. It was every wingman's nightmare to see his leader die in a ball of fire, but an ice-cool calm had to override everything else. A fighter pilot couldn't afford his judgement to be clouded by emotion.

Another machine gun opened up below O'Connor's position. 'This one's in a bunker!' Kennedy yelled.

'And there are bunkers across the river as well!' Ventura shouted to be heard above the noise as he picked up yet another machine gun still firing from the opposite village.

O'Connor hugged the ground as chunks of wood flew off the battle-scarred tree he was sheltering behind.

'Medic! Rayburn's been hit!' Kennedy yelled, and he took over the SOFLAM laser tripod.

'Bastards,' O'Connor muttered. No wonder the firing was still sustained; it was coming from bunkers in both locations. Time to call in bigger guns. 'Turn up the heat on these assholes, Ventura!' O'Connor ordered, picking off a Taliban fighter less than a hundred metres in front of his position.

'Burglar One Three, this is Tailpipe Two Two, request missile strike on our ridge, enemy one hundred metres to the south, bunker system, danger close, over.'

'Burglar One Three, you got it . . . we see them, wait out.'

'Night Thruster Two, this is Tailpipe Two Two.' Ventura spoke determinedly into his handset above the fury of the battle, calling in everything he could lay his hands on. 'We're still taking fire from across the river. Women and children no longer on the rooftops, but there's a bunker system below the village. Request bomb strikes . . . do you have Burglar One Three's flight path?' The aerial battlefield had become almost as busy as a regular airport, and the last thing Ventura or anyone in the air wanted was a collision between a drone and a Hercules or a missile or bomb hitting the wrong target.

'This is Night Thruster. I have Burglar One Three visual.' Rogers and Brady, his sensor operator, had been following the battle on the screens in front of them, and although they didn't have the same sweep of vision that a normal pilot had, the cameras and infrared systems in the drone were so sophisticated they gave a detailed view of the ground, even from 20 000 feet.

'Burglar One Three is turning to the east,' Brady confirmed.

Well aware that the Taliban might have more surface-to-air missiles, the Hercules gunship pilots calmly circled, the computers holding the withering fire on the laser designator. Behind them, in the rear of the aircraft crowded with armaments, the aerial gunners sweated profusely, loading and reloading the huge guns.

Back at Creech, Brady held the crosshairs on the few figures still moving in the tree line across the river from O'Connor. 'Target locked on . . .'

'Confirm weapon configuration,' requested the intel analyst behind Rogers.

'Two Paveway IIs.' The massive 500-pound bombs, with their nose-mounted laser seekers, were capable of destroying all but the deepest reinforced bunkers. 'Holding on target.' The screens pixelated as the first of the bombs struck within one metre of the aiming point and the al Qaeda position fell silent.

O'Connor and his men had barely recovered from the shock waves of the drone attack when four Hellfire missiles struck the Taliban positions in front of them. O'Connor shook his head to clear the ringing in his ears.

'They're pulling out!' Kennedy fired a burst at the fleeing Taliban from his M14.

O'Connor doubled over to Kennedy's position. 'How bad's Rayburn?'

'Pretty bad . . . the medic's with him behind the next tree.'

'Ventura – get a Black Hawk in here, fast. And let Night Thruster and Burglar know the Taliban have pulled out, but I want them to hang around.'

Less than thirty minutes later, the C-130 gunship laid down a curtain of sustained 30-millimetre cannon fire, just in case the Taliban had any ideas of claiming another aircraft, and the Black Hawk medevac chopper came in low and hard, weaving from side to side. Under the Geneva Convention, the 'dustoff' choppers, as they'd been known since Vietnam, could not be armed, so the medics were often in for a wild ride as the pilots took evasive action against the possibility of taking fire from the ground. The landing zone was tight, but these were some of the best helo pilots in the world, and Captain Ella Nicholson put it down in a cloud of dust, the rotors almost brushing the tree foliage.

The crew doubled over with a litter, and moments later, they had Rayburn on board, frantically fitting him with a drip as the helo lifted off, banking sharply under full power.

'We'll have to search every one of those houses down there, and the villagers aren't going to be pleased to see us, so stay spread out,' said O'Connor, leading the team down the ridgeline.

They propped on the outskirts of the village, while O'Connor made contact with one of the village elders.

'Put a sentry up behind that high rock, Chief,' ordered O'Connor. 'Two men to search each house, while the rest of us cover them . . . one house at a time.'

'Got it. Ventura – up behind the rock. Cover the ridge we've just left, and the one to the south.'

Stone hut by stone hut they searched, doing their best to be as unintrusive as they could. The old men watched resentfully, the women and children fearfully; but after two hours, there was nothing.

'Apart from a complete absence of young men, fuck-all,' Kennedy observed at the end of two hours of fruitless searching. The sun had reached its zenith, and the team, O'Connor knew, were close to exhaustion. The mental tiredness associated with close-quarter fighting was often not well understood, especially by the politicians in Washington. O'Connor contemplated his next move. If the Taliban were waiting for them at the next village, another firefight like the one they'd just been through might be asking a bit much, even from these battle-hardened warriors, but the intel operator interrupted his thoughts.

'This is just in from JSOC,' Chico said. 'They've analysed some satellite photos, and there's an area of recently disturbed soil, not far from Ventura's sentry position.'

O'Connor scanned the photographs Chico had downloaded from the Joint Special Operations Centre. The disturbed soil was clearly visible. The thermal imaging, or infrared cameras on board the satellite had picked up the different signatures. O'Connor knew well that if earth was recently turned, the looser soil would radiate heat differently from the surrounding undisturbed soil.

'This operation must have some clout,' Kennedy observed. 'It's not every day they make a satellite available to us mere mortals.'

O'Connor grinned. Gaining support from the Hercules C-130 gunship and the drone still circling above them was hard enough, but with competing requests for surveillance over the spiralling number of trouble spots in Egypt, Libya, Tunisia, Israel, Iran, Iraq, Somalia and Yemen, satellite tasking was at a premium. O'Connor was in no doubt who had ordered the pass. The huge KeyHole spy satellites were the size of an American yellow school bus, and their orbit was measured in kilometres rather than feet – as high as 36 000 kilometres above the earth's surface and travelling at five kilometres a second. McNamara would have been rebuffed all along the way, and O'Connor could vividly imagine the conversations. McNamara didn't take no for an answer when his men were up against it in the field, and the final call to the White House would have cleared the obstacles – instantly.

'You've noticed. That request would have gone all the way to the top, Chief. Let's see what they're hiding here.'

Chico was, like the rest of the team, multiskilled and as handy with a shovel as he was with a laptop, and within minutes he and O'Connor struck something hard underneath the loose soil.

The khaki-green metal container, stamped 'reusable do not destroy', was just under two metres long, and together they levered it out of the pit.

Kennedy let out a low whistle. 'Holy shit . . . a Scorpion SAM. How the fuck did these towel-heads get hold of one of those?'

'They've got more than one, I suspect,' O'Connor muttered. 'I think it was a Scorpion that got the F-16.' O'Connor searched the box, which revealed nothing other than the accessories and instructions. He was about to close the lid when he spotted the corner of a piece of paper sticking out from behind the foam padding in the case.

'Okay,' he said, 'we've got what we came for. Chief – put the elders under the spotlight again, but I doubt they'll tell us anything. Ventura – keep the gunship and drone on station in case we need them, and whistle up a couple of Black Hawks. We're out of here.'

'The piece of paper . . . need to know?' Kennedy asked, as they made their way back to the village.

'For the moment. I'll make sure you and the rest of the team are in the loop before it becomes public. And when it does, the shit will hit the fan . . . big time.'

High among the cedar trees on the mountains across the river, Jamal put down his binoculars. 'The Infidel has found one of the missiles, but we still have the others, and he will pay for today,' he added bitterly.

'*Insha'Allah*,' Yousef agreed. 'I will return, but for now I have another mission. If it's successful it will go some way toward atoning for today. We're going to hit the Infidel where it hurts him most.'

22

CIA HEADQUARTERS, LANGLEY, VIRGINIA

'You can go straight in. Ms Murray from the NSA's already there,' said Chanelle.

O'Connor flashed his usual smile at McNamara's PA, and he strode into the inner office.

'Welcome back . . . this is Barbara Murray from the NSA.'

'I've heard quite a lot about you, Mr O'Connor. Do you mind if I call you Curtis?'

'Not at all,' said O'Connor, taking one of his boss's battered leather couches. The striking redhead from the NSA was very easy on the eye, he thought.

'He's been called a lot of other names, most of them uncomplimentary,' said McNamara.

'Usually by enemies of the state, some of whom I left behind in Afghanistan. Thank you for that little mission, sir . . . most enjoyable.' The only time O'Connor ever called McNamara 'sir' was in front of junior CIA employees or people outside the agency.

It was a game, and both men played it well.

'My pleasure, O'Connor,' said McNamara, a smile dancing at the corners of his mouth. O'Connor didn't know it, but McNamara had already received an after action-report from the commanding general in Afghanistan, with a recommendation that, for the second time, O'Connor receive the agency's highest award for valour, the Distinguished Intelligence Cross. It would be awarded very quietly, although his colleagues in the agency would know. None would be surprised.

Barbara Murray looked from one man to the other. Clearly there was a strong camaraderie between the two, and their light-hearted banter was a pleasant change from the humourless corridors of power at the NSA. Since the tapping of the phones of leaders around the world had become public, the NSA was an agency under siege. And the rumours had been correct – O'Connor was not only ruggedly good looking, but there was an air of confidence about him. Clearly his own man. Taken? she wondered.

'So . . . what've we got? Barbara's cleared into the compartment,' McNamara added.

'The Taliban and possibly al Qaeda have acquired at least one, and perhaps several more Scorpion missiles,' O'Connor began, and he briefly brought McNamara and Murray up to date with the actions in the Korengal Valley. 'Given that technology is as closely guarded as any in this country, the question is how, but whoever is supplying these missiles may have made their first mistake,' O'Connor said, producing the piece of paper he'd found in Laniyal.

'I found this inside one of the missile cases . . . it's a packing note, with the EVRAN logo.'

'And the significance of that? EVRAN manufactures these

missiles,' McNamara said, taking the packing note.

'Ordinarily, there might be no significance, but that packing note hasn't come from EVRAN's missile plant in California. It's in Spanish and it's a packing note for Ipé timber from EVRAN Timbers in Brazil.' Ipé, or Brazilian walnut, was some of the hardest wood on the planet, and as a result, there was a huge demand for it to construct outdoor decks. 'I suspect it fell into the missile case when they opened it, and they didn't sanitise the case before they buried it.'

'It's not a smoking gun . . . but you think there's a link between the missiles and EVRAN timbers?' Murray asked.

'Don't know yet,' admitted O'Connor, 'and I can't decipher the employee's signature, but when we do, I'm willing to bet we'll find him at one of EVRAN's timber mills on the banks of the Amazon.'

Murray looked pensive. 'There are a couple of possibilities here, the most basic of which is someone inside EVRAN is doing this for the money.'

'And there would be a lot of it. We're talking missiles, plural,' said O'Connor.

'I agree, and ever since 9/11, al Qaeda and the Taliban – in fact every terrorist organisation on the planet – has found it hard to launder money, but we're picking up intelligence that they still have their backers, especially out of Saudi Arabia . . . backers who are prepared to take risks.'

McNamara nodded. 'I'd agree with that assessment. Treasury, State, Justice, Defense – we've all managed to tighten the screws on the terrorists' money trails, but they're still managing to get around our systems.'

'They're wary though,' said Murray. 'We've seen warnings on extremist websites, and you probably have too – warnings from al Qaeda leaders like Mustafa Abu al Yazid that the West's intelligence agencies can identify al Qaeda members through banks, credit cards and money transfer services. They're now resorting to methods that are harder to trace. International trade is particularly vulnerable to manipulation because of its sheer size and the complexity of the payment system. And al Qaeda is also using the mosque network and Islamic charities.'

'But even if they did have the sort of money needed to buy these missiles,' McNamara argued, 'you can't just roll up and load them on to a truck . . . you would need some pretty sophisticated fraud systems to take care of the documentation, and cover from fairly high up in the food chain.'

'The high-level cover is the other possibility: someone has infiltrated EVRAN with a view to working their way up the ladder to get hi-tech equipment to the terrorists,' Murray suggested.

'A very long-range strategy . . . it might take years to get someone in the right place,' McNamara demurred.

'Perhaps it goes right to the top . . . to Crowley himself?' said Murray.

'You have anything to back that?' McNamara demanded, taken aback.

Murray shook her head, but she didn't take a backward step. 'Just working on gut feeling and a principle of trusting no one.'

O'Connor smiled to himself. Murray may not have been around when Nixon was lying about his knowledge of the Watergate break-in, or when Reagan was twisting the truth over the Iran Contra scandal, but like McNamara, she'd seen enough to know that many politicians and those with 'rolled gold' credentials were not what they seemed.

'We've been monitoring General Khan twenty-four seven. He's kept in contact with the Taliban, which for a Pakistani from the ISI is not unusual. The ISI's a law unto itself, and Khan's obviously still a key player, but what is unusual are intermittent contacts we've intercepted between Khan and another iPhone that is rarely used. So far, we've only been able to trace it to a shell company. Curiously, we also picked up a short text to the same mystery iPhone from the owner of Galleria d'Arte Rubinstein, which is located in the Cannaregio region of northern Venice: one Zachary Rubinstein. He's suspected of dealing in stolen artifacts and the FBI have a file on him, but they've never had enough evidence to get the Italian authorities to search his premises. Here's a printout,' she said, handing copies to McNamara and O'Connor. 'The texts are short, and don't give much away, but Khan and Rubinstein obviously know who owns the mystery iPhone.'

O'Connor noted the first one. 'No word on Euclid, yet.' Aleta was clearly not the only one to have an interest in the Euclid Papyrus. Rubinstein and whoever owned the mystery phone were on to it as well.

'What's this "Cargo arrived, plans in place, choke point first, will confirm in A at P meeting at Kashta"?' McNamara asked.

'We're not sure,' said Murray, 'but we've also been monitoring the websites Khan and his PA log on to, and two weeks ago, travel arrangements were made for Khan to travel, first class, to Alexandria, which I think is the A in that text. What the P is we're still none the wiser; Khan spent two nights in Alexandria.'

'Staying in a hotel?' McNamara asked.

'No . . . we checked and all the hotels all turned up blank. Kashta refers to the Kashta Palace in Alexandria, which is shrouded in secrecy. The only thing we've managed to find out about it is that it appears to be heavily guarded at roughly the same time each year for a group of people.'

'Group?'

'We sent one of our embassy staff from Cairo to try to find out, but the only people on the property were two security guards, both of whom were very nervous and refused to answer any questions,' said Murray.

'Well, if that's where Khan was two weeks ago, it sounds as if he had company,' McNamara mused, ignoring the fact that the NSA had started to encroach on the CIA's turf. Turf battles wasted an enormous amount of time and energy, and McNamara wasn't one to look for credit. It was more important to get the job done.

'If I'm right – although I accept that may be a big if – and Crowley, or someone close to the top of EVRAN has somehow given the okay for these missiles to be exported, particularly to dubious contacts like Khan, perhaps it's time we organised an audit of EVRAN's books?' Murray suggested.

'We'd take a *lot* of heat,' said McNamara. 'That son of a bitch Crowley's so far up the administration's ass you'd be hard pressed to see the soles of his shoes, so we'd need a lot more than a "maybe" before the White House would okay that one. Big donor, this bastard . . . to both sides.'

'We've noticed. I didn't include it in the printouts, but based on these missiles being manufactured by EVRAN, I broadened the taps. We've not yet been able to break EVRAN's main encryption, but we have got into the phone of Crowley's personal assistant, Rachel Bannister, and I discovered Bannister is setting up a meeting between Crowley and Carter Davis.'

'Jesus Christ . . . What for,' chuckled McNamara. 'That bone-head would make Idi Amin look like Mensa material.'

'How about a late entry in the Republican race for the next election?' said Murray.

'What! Why?' McNamara asked, genuinely incredulous.

'A text between Crowley and Bannister points in that direction.'

'I've worked for many presidents,' said McNamara, 'but you'd have to go back to Warren Harding to find someone dumber than Carter Davis.'

Murray smiled, a conspiratorial look on her face.

It suited her, that smile, O'Connor thought.

'I've seen a study on presidential IQs,' she said, 'and I think Harding *was* rated the dumbest . . . appointed his mates from "the Ohio gang" to the top jobs, and the embezzlement and bribery in the Harding Administration put the modern scandals like Water-gate in the shade.'

'Not to mention the parties at the White House,' said O'Connor, grinning at the delicious irony of a president who got stuck into the grog during Prohibition.

McNamara shook his head. '1920 was the first time women got the vote in this country, and the Republican powerbrokers tapped Harding on the shoulder because they thought his good looks would appeal to women voters. Good thing he isn't running now in a world of videos and iPhones . . . treating your wife as a waitress and hav-ing multiple affairs doesn't do a lot for your re-election chances if your key demographic is women. Which, assuming your analysis is on target, makes me wonder why Crowley would be backing Davis, and by how much? There's not a lot of votes in the "thick as two short planks" demographic.'

'No – but they obviously think they can present Davis as a candidate with broad appeal. There's been a proliferation of Political Action Committees recently, and those PACs are being set up at the state rather than the federal level; we've traced all of them back to the headquarters of EVRAN.'

'For more than one candidate?'

Murray shook her head. 'This is pretty tightly held in the NSA, but we don't think so . . . we think they're being set up for Davis.'

'I thought that was illegal – not that laws have ever bothered Crowley,' McNamara mused, a thoughtful look on his face.

'It is, but only at the federal level. As you're no doubt aware, labour unions and corporations have long been prevented from influencing presidential campaigns, or at least that was the intention of Congress when they enacted the various laws, and the prohibition on corporations goes back to the Tilman Act in 1907. Since then, it's become far more complex, but after campaign donations for the 1972 Nixon campaign were laundered through Mexican banks which don't allow the US to subpoena their records, the 1974 Federal Election Campaign Act was brought in to strengthen the prohibition on corporations and unions, and it limits individual donations to $5000.'

'So in theory, Crowley can't donate more than that to Davis,' said O'Connor, 'but if he's setting PACs up at the state level, that would allow him to donate to any number of them, and where the state laws are weak, there'll be no limit at all. What about the Super PACs?'

'Super PACs are not allowed to make donations to individual candidates, but they can accept and make unlimited donations to a cause. In the 2012 campaign you had Super PACS like Winning our

Future, which was generally pro-Newt Gingrich, and Restore our Future, which spent around US $40 million supporting Mitt Romney. It costs an enormous amount of money to run for the White House . . . I think the campaign in 2012 was north of US $700 million, but that's petty cash to Crowley, and we think he's already getting around the law with a large number of ordinary state-based PACs and with several Super PACs.'

'The question is *why*?' O'Connor wondered. 'Campaign war chests might be petty cash to Crowley, but assholes like him don't spend that sort of money without a good reason, and particularly not on a dipshit like Carter Davis. Have you got anything on the likely Democratic candidate – ex-Secretary of Energy Hailey Campbell, for example?'

Murray smiled. 'There's already a groundswell of support for her and one Super PAC is up and running. It hasn't been announced yet, but Professor Megan Becker, the president's science advisor, is resigning to advise Campbell on her campaign. And she's not the only one. You can expect Chuck Buchanan, President McGovern's current chief of staff, to run it . . . and that's with the president's blessing. McGovern wants another Democrat to succeed him, and Buchanan's as tough as nails, although his appointment may raise more problems than it solves and Hailey's none too pleased.'

O'Connor raised his eyebrows. He'd clashed more than once with the tall eagle-eyed political staffer from Springfield, Illinois. 'Trouble in paradise?'

Murray nodded, aware that the disclosure of this information was way outside the NSA's brief, but she trusted these two to protect their sources. 'You could say that. Campbell doesn't want a bar of Buchanan, but she's being leaned on from a high level . . . Adlai

K. Washburn, the Chair of the Democratic National Committee no less.'

'Tennessee Whiskey Washburn. I thought they'd put that old fart out to pasture. But at least the debates will be interesting,' said McNamara. 'A sharp-as-a-tack ex-secretary of energy with an approval rating through the roof, against a "what's his face" from Montana.'

'The debates on climate change will be especially interesting,' said O'Connor. 'One candidate who knows it's way past time to act, and the other who wouldn't know shit from clay. Assuming Davis makes it through the primaries, he'll be in the pocket of the world's biggest polluter.'

'And there's something else,' said Murray. 'The phone taps have also revealed that Bannister's been in Stockholm recruiting a Professor Ahlstrom to work for EVRAN.'

'The Nobel Laureate? Why would he want to work for Crowley? Ahlstrom's been trying to get politicians to do something about global warming for decades,' O'Connor said.

'I agree – but if Crowley can get someone like Ahlstrom on Davis's team to debunk climate change, that's going to carry a lot of weight in an election.'

'So how does he get him to jump ship?'

'Ahlstrom's in a bucket of financial and marital trouble, and I wouldn't put it past Crowley to use that as leverage. I'll do some more digging,' Murray said.

'I wonder if our friend Crowley has an even bigger agenda than the White House . . . there are a lot of things not adding up here.' O'Connor had been analysing the discussion with interest, and he was wary. Apart from Hailey Campbell being pissed over having

Buchanan foisted on her campaign, none of what he'd heard made much sense.

'Hmm . . .' McNamara stroked his chin. 'It would be useful, Barbara, in the broad envelope of keeping close tabs on our friend Khan, if you could keep an eye on this. It's a long bow, but there may be a connection we can't yet see.'

Murray nodded knowingly. 'I'll see what I can do.'

'You've been most helpful, and we'll stay in touch,' McNamara said, getting to his feet.

'That's my card,' Murray said to O'Connor, giving him a card with her personal mobile and email. 'Don't hesitate to call if you need me,' she added. Her smile lingered before she turned on her heel and strode out the door.

'I think she's got the hots for you,' said McNamara, chuckling to himself.

'Never mix business with pleasure,' O'Connor countered.

'Hasn't stopped you in the past . . . or do I have to remind you of your little peccadillo in Moscow?'

O'Connor feigned indifference.

'Now,' McNamara said, more seriously. 'This race for the White House only makes sense if Crowley's backing Davis because he thinks he can control him; but there are a few other things that are not adding up. Where the hell is this "choke point" Khan's focusing on, and what's the P in that text?'

23

VILLA JANNAT, ISLAMABAD

The servant set the tray of drinks on the stone table: lemon squash for Omar Yousef and Tayeb Jamal, and a gin and tonic for Khan.

'So . . . everything set for the Phase One attack, Yousef?' General Khan asked. Yousef nodded.

Khan pulled up a Google Earth map of the Middle East on his laptop, and homed in on the Persian Gulf and Ras Tanura, the massive Saudi Arabian oil refinery. The largest in the world, it was located on the western coast of the gulf, just to the north of Bahrain.

'It's big,' Khan said, bringing up an image of the vast refinery with its myriad tanks, pipes and pumping stations. 'They disgorge around seven million barrels of crude a day, and process another million barrels into refined products – 4000 tankers a year.'

'And a lot of that money goes on absurd excesses,' Yousef said contemptuously, his face clouding. 'They have as many princes on the Saudi public purse as there are tankers at Ras Tanura – luxury yachts, black American Express Cards. One of them has just ordered an Airbus 380 with fourteen staterooms, a conference room and a movie theatre. There are even stables for horses and a garage in the tail for two Rolls Royces, while my people can't get enough to eat. Islam does not allow this!' Yousef exclaimed. 'But everything is set,' he added, his contempt for the excesses of the Saudis giving way to an enthusiasm for hitting the West. 'The Taipan anti-ship missiles are hidden among timber on two lorries, which we have positioned just outside of Quetta,' he said. The provincial capital of the Baluchistan province of Pakistan was located at altitude, close to Pakistan's western border and Afghanistan's Kandahar province. The once tourist-friendly city, known for its bazaars and craftsmanship, was now better known for terrorism. Two bitter conflicts – the Sunni extremist attacks on the minority Hazara Shia community, and the Baluch Liberation Army's struggle for independence – meant there were regular attacks on mosques and markets, which the police appeared powerless to prevent. It was a situation that suited al Qaeda admirably.

'We will depart Quetta the day after tomorrow at dawn, and we'll follow the N40 along the southern border of Afghanistan until we reach the Iranian border at Taftan,' Yousef said. 'That's a distance of about 700 kilometres.' The Regional Cooperation for Development Highway, which connected Pakistan with Iran and Turkey, was well constructed, but it passed through some of the most barren country on the planet. 'From Taftan, *insha'Allah*, once we're across the border, we'll head north on Route 84 to Zahedan, where we'll pick up two Toyota four-wheel drives.'

'Too difficult to get them through the border?'

Yousef nodded. 'The Iranians may not suspect two trucks loaded with timber, but an additional two Toyotas might raise some questions,' he said. 'From Zahedan, we'll head west across the desert to Bam, before turning south toward Bandar Abbas on the coast.' The port city, and capital of the Iranian Hormozgān Province, was the main base for the Iranian Navy.

'And the border crossing?' Khan asked.

'We have a contact, and we're timing the crossing with his shift,' said Yousef. 'It's unlikely the Iranians will look too closely at a shipment of timber, but in case they do, we have collateral.' Yousef reached for his briefcase and opened it. Inside were 250 million Iranian rials in used 50 000-rial bank notes, each one of which was worth roughly two dollars. The total was less than US $10 000. Ever since Iran had embarked on a mission to construct nuclear weapons, the sanctions imposed by the West had ensured that the value of the Iranian currency had collapsed.

'Excellent,' said Khan, mixing himself another gin and tonic. 'And you'll give forty-eight hours warning before the start of that attack?'

'I haven't forgotten,' said Yousef, extracting a battered stamp album. 'We go to stampgeekcol.com and post an acquisition.'

'And the Phase Two attacks . . . what's the situation in the United States?'

'We have three cells trained,' Yousef confirmed, 'and they are ready to go. All they need are the targets, and the Cobalt 60.'

Khan smiled, sipping on his drink and picturing the panic in the streets of the Western capital cities. Once the Cobalt 60 was released into the atmosphere, the intense gamma rays would pass through glass, concrete and all but the thickest lead shielding. When the cancer-causing rays hit the human body, Cobalt 60 had the power to break up DNA, mutating and killing cells. In a short while, thousands would be suffering burns and vomiting blood from bleeding stomachs and intestines. Red and white blood cells would be destroyed, followed by intense headaches, diarrhoea, seizures and comas.

'Cobalt 60 is one of the Infidel's worst nightmares. How are we placed in the United Kingdom and Australia?'

'Great Britain has not been difficult,' said Yousef. 'We have strongholds in Somalia in Hayo, and on the island of Lamu, and strong links with the Islamic Courts regime, and despite the Infidel's attacks from his bases in Djibouti, we've been able to train twenty-five Britons in jihadi techniques. They've now returned to the United Kingdom, and as you requested, we've arranged for a small furniture importing business to be set up. They're waiting for the word.'

'And in Australia?'

'That's been a little more difficult, but we've managed to get a contact with Jemaah Islamiah, who have cells there.' Based mainly in Indonesia, in the nineties, JI's Abu Bakar Bashir had sent terrorists to Australia to train around one hundred jihadists. Set up by Abdul Ayub and his twin brother Abdul Rahman, who had trained in Afghanistan with the Mujahideen, the pair fled after the Bali bombing, but many remained.

'Do they know what they're about?'

Yousef nodded. 'JI is focused mainly on overthrowing the Indonesian state, but we have a common cause against the West, and we've formed one cell from JI and another cell with Australians who have returned from ISIS in Syria.' Over one hundred young Australian men had trained and fought with the terrorist Islamic State of Iraq and Syria, swearing allegiance to Abu Bakr al-Baghdadi, the new caliph determined to impose Sharia law on the world. Radicalised, many had now returned to terrorise Australia. 'We've set up a furniture importing business in Melbourne as well, and once the Cobalt 60 arrives, they're ready to go.'

'The Cobalt 60 is being sourced,' Khan reassured his young protégé, 'and it will be delivered through the port system.' Khan allowed himself a smile. 'Shipping containers are the one of the Infidel's Achilles heels. If we take the Australians, the latest figures I have show that authorities only manage to inspect three per cent of shipping imports . . . 100 000 containers out of three million a year. Great Britain is not much better, and as for the United States, Homeland Security is more concerned with what comes *into* the country —' Khan paused mid-sentence. It was not necessary for the cells to know the source of the Cobalt 60. 'Assuming phases one and two are successful,' Khan continued, 'we will move on to phase three.'

'They will be successful,' said Yousef. His dark eyes blazed with a mixture of hatred and anticipation.

Khan brought up a map of the United States. 'The locations of their key nuclear facilities are published on the internet, and they're marked here,' he said, pointing to the yellow international hazard circles imposed on cooling tower outlines.

'The Infidel is not very clever,' Khan sneered. 'He commissioned a report on the weaknesses in his system, and then published it on the internet.' He opened up another window and a report entitled 'Protecting US Nuclear Facilities from Terrorist Attack'. 'As you can see, there are 104 commercial nuclear reactors in the United States, over thirty research reactors in universities dotted around the country, and more still in the military. The research reactors tend to be less protected than the nuclear power plants, but the power plants have weaknesses too, particularly those close to large population areas, and close to the sea or on rivers, like this one here.' Khan pointed to the Indian Point nuclear power plant on the east bank of the Hudson River, 55 kilometres to the north of Central Park in New York.

'The Infidel's emergency response plan for Indian Point, which is also on the internet, details the agreed responses from the emergency agencies, including the New York State Police, the Department of Energy, the Buchanan Fire Engine Co, the Hudson and Phelps Hospitals and Westinghouse. This map here shows the layout of the plant, and especially the containment buildings.'

'Unit One is no longer operating?' Yousef asked.

'Unit One, in the centre here, was shut down in 1974, but Unit Two was brought on line the same year, and Unit Three two years later. The containment buildings are the main targets. If we can breach those and destroy the Infidel's ability to contain a core meltdown, the radiological release to his environment will be catastrophic.'

'Worse than Fukushima?' asked Jamal.

'Far worse. For a start, there are over eight million people in New York City, and of those, they would have to evacuate over five million. By comparison, the Japanese have evacuated only 100 000. If we can interrupt the reactor cooling system, the cores in Unit Two and Three will heat the metal sheath around the uranium fuel. Once we've destroyed the cooling system, the reactor core itself will melt into the bottom of the reactor's steel pressure vessel,' said Khan, pointing to the plans. 'Once that fails – and we've seen this at both Chernobyl and Fukushima – the molten radioactive debris is forced from the pressure vessel. That then melts through the final concrete casing, and it's out of control.'

'An aircraft would be the best weapon,' Jamal mused, thinking aloud.

'We don't need to revisit 9/11, and flight schools in the United

States have been tightened up,' said Khan, 'but other areas haven't. The nuclear industry depends on intelligence agencies for information on the overall threat, and in 2008, the CIA identified al Qaeda as their number one nuclear concern.'

Yousef and Jamal smiled broadly at each other, their teeth flashing white in the semi-darkness.

'Since 9/11, the nuclear industry in the United States has spent US $2 billion on improvements to the security of their reactors, so this isn't going to be what the Infidel would call a walk in the park, but if we concentrate on his weaknesses we can still succeed.' Khan turned to another section of the report. 'They haven't named their sources, but those in the know have revealed that requirements for the nuclear industry to protect their reactors from rocket-propelled grenades were dropped because the industry kicked up a fuss over the costs.'

'And this is the weather data?' asked Yousef, scrutinising the computer predictions for radiation release.

'Those are the predicted plumes for various times of the day, based on historic wind and weather patterns,' said Khan. 'The forced evacuation of over five million people will be accompanied by frenzied panic,' he added, breaking into a smile. 'They've also admitted that the bullet-resistant shield used at power reactors is inadequate against a 50-calibre rifle with armour-piercing rounds.

'Their National Rifle Association have done us a big favour,' Khan continued. 'In most states of the US, it's perfectly legal to own a 50-calibre sub-machine gun,' he said, opening another window on his laptop and bringing up the site for a well-known gun broker. 'Here it is.' Khan pointed to a photograph. 'The Barrett 50-calibre . . . the one used against us here in Afghanistan, and most favoured by the Infidel's Special Forces.'

'Something he will pay for dearly,' Yousef replied grimly, remembering his close colleagues that were no longer with him.

'You can purchase a top-of-the-range Barrett for less than US $13 000 online. There's a catch, but it's easy to get around because the NRA have done us another favour.' Khan had always followed American politics closely. 'Every year or so, the Infidel turns on himself, and there's a massacre in a schoolyard somewhere.' Both his young protégés were listening intently. 'President McGovern has been trying to tighten up gun laws and background checks on buyers, but each time he's blocked in the Senate.'

'The NRA again?' Yousef asked.

Khan nodded. 'They're one of the most powerful lobbies in the United States, and they keep track of who votes for legislation in Congress. If you vote against them, they'll come after you when you're up for re-election. But,' Khan warned, 'our people in the United States need to be very careful. The purchases will have to be done singly, and in different states, and at decent intervals. We have plenty of time for this, which brings me to the question of getting people on the inside of the nuclear plants. It doesn't matter what the job is – driver, storeman – as long as they have access and can confirm our intelligence. How many of your people are in the United States now?'

'It's hard to get an accurate figure,' said Yousef, 'because the membership is growing, but we can put together at least one hundred across the country, and ten of those I would trust with my life.'

Khan nodded approvingly. 'Good, but the Infidel is watching our every move. Mobile phones are out, unless they're clean, and used on a one-time basis. All planning communication is to be done by courier or through the stamp website.'

General Khan ran through the possible nuclear targets in the

United States, ruling out any reactors run by EVRAN, before turning to America's most trusted allies, and the targets in Britain and Australia.

'Australia's relatively easy, at least in our choice of targets,' Khan said. 'They only have one research reactor, at a place called Lucas Heights to the south-west of Sydney. It's been threatened before, but no one's managed to carry out an attack . . . yet,' he added, pulling up Google Earth and the overhead satellite images of the layout of the reactor. 'There's a military base at Holsworthy, here,' Khan said, pointing to an area a few kilometres to the north-west, 'and according to Wikipedia, that houses 2 Commando Regiment, as well as the 6th Aviation Regiment, 17 Signals Regiment and a major medical unit. None of those are likely to bother us, because by the time we've blown up the reactor, it will be too late for them to respond. And if the prevailing winds are from the west, the plume will drift across Sydney, their biggest city.'

'The Australians will be very sorry they ever teamed up with the United States, I can guarantee it,' Yousef said.

'And the British?' Jamal asked.

'There we have more choice,' said Khan, opening up another website. 'They have sixteen commercial reactors, and as you can see, they range from Dungeness and Hinkley Point on the south-east and west coasts, on up to Hunterston and Torness in the mid-north. Dungeness is the closest to London, although the prevailing winds in London are from the southwest, so Hinkley Point would provide a better plume across the most populated areas. How many people can you call on in the UK?'

'We have more operatives there than Australia . . . enough to attack two, possibly three of their reactors.'

24

EVRAN HEADQUARTERS, DALLAS, TEXAS

Sheldon Crowley piloted his Aston Martin One-77 down the long, tree-lined gravel drive of his estate in Preston Hollow, Dallas. Only seventy-seven of this particular Aston Martin had ever been made, hence the name, and at US $1.85 million, it was one of the world's most expensive cars. Crowley was irascible and impatient, and he always chose the fastest route, but even he wouldn't be able to find space for the massive V12 7.3 litre car to reach its top speed: 350 kilometres an hour was in the realm of Formula One. He owned this car because he could, and because it was the rarest Aston Martin on the road.

The massive iron gates of Ploutos Park opened silently, and then just as silently closed behind him, and Crowley turned into leafy Inwood Road and headed for the gleaming twin towers of EVRAN's headquarters in downtown Dallas, a bare five miles distant.

The security guard saluted and Crowley drove into EVRAN's underground executive car park, pulling up beside his personal lift.

He inserted the key and the lift rose silently to the eighty-second floor, where Rachel was already at her desk.

Crowley strode into his palatial corner office, which commanded sweeping views of the city through the two entire walls that were constructed out of toughened plate glass. The other walls were replete with several of the great masters, including Rembrandt, Michelangelo and da Vinci, all legally purchased at auction, and each with a price tag in the tens of millions. Crowley paused momentarily to take in the gridlock on the streets below, the cars, vans, trucks and buses all powered by derivatives of oil and gas. His thoughts turned momentarily to the Euclid Papyrus and the rumoured alternative energy system, and he made a mental note to check to see if Rubinstein had anything to report.

Crowley's gaze shifted to the Dallas skyline. It gave him a particular satisfaction to have an office that looked down on humanity stuck in the gridlock on Elm and Commerce, in a city that was the fifth most congested in the United States. A brass telescope on a stand near one of the huge windows emphasised the point. It gave him even greater satisfaction to look down on the roofs of Dallas skyscrapers like the Bank of America Plaza and the JP Morgan Chase Tower, and the extraordinary prism architecture of Fountain Place with its 172 dancing fountains, which from up here looked like tiny bubblers in a park. Crowley had designed EVRAN Towers with just such dominance in mind. At 396 metres high, it was not only the tallest building in Dallas, it was taller than the Empire State Building and the fourth highest building in the United States after the new One World Trade Center on the north-west corner of the 9/11 site, and the Willis and Trump Towers in Chicago. The entire top floor of EVRAN was taken up by Crowley's and Rachel's offices, en suite bathrooms, sauna and massage rooms, and the boardroom complex, which included a spacious dining room and kitchen.

'Good morning. I trust you slept well.' Rachel's greeting, as she stepped into Crowley's office, was cool. She hated being in Dallas, although not because of the city. Her two-storey house provided by EVRAN on Dallas' elite Strait Lane was at the top of the spectrum – it was more a matter of who else was here, and Rachel had never liked to share. Some time ago, she had promised herself she would force her boss to divorce his twinset-and-pearls wife, and the management of his Ploutos Park estate would be added to her suite of fiercely guarded responsibilities.

Crowley poured himself a cup of coffee from the percolator on the sideboard. 'What's the program look like today?'

'In a word, busy,' Rachel said, placing a printout from his electronic diary on the desk. 'As instructed, I've left you a gap between nine and ten a.m. Will you be in the office?' she probed.

'There are some things you don't need to be involved in.' Crowley's response was crisp. Any knowledge of Crowley's meetings with assassins like the tattooed felon Elias D. Ruger was on a strictly need-to-know basis. Other than the head of Area 15, Eugene Reid, no one in EVRAN, including Rachel, had access into the Ruger compartment.

'The board meeting's at eleven, with lunch at one,' Rachel replied, equally crisply.

'They're all here?

'All here,' Rachel confirmed. The last executive to turn up late for a board meeting had been fired on the spot. Not that the monthly EVRAN board meeting was anything more than a rubber stamp.

The sparse minutes were only there to meet the requirements of the regulatory authorities.

'Recording system?'

'Checked and working for the boardroom, and in case you want anything recorded in a one-on-one, your office system is set to go as well.' Unbeknown to his executives, Crowley's conversations with them were all recorded, and the digital records secured with compartment passwords to which only he and Rachel had access. Crowley was determined that neither he nor EVRAN would ever be confronted by a Watergate-style tape. The less salubrious deals and directions were always discussed one-on-one in Crowley's office, with Rachel the only other person in the room. If it ever went to court, it would be the word of two people against one, or at least, that was Crowley's plan.

'And you wanted to talk to Pastor Shipley about nailing down the evangelical vote. Do you want me to put that through now?'

'Don't bother. I spoke to that Bible-bashing asshole last night. He won't have a bar of Davis, and won't campaign for his nomination.'

'Well, I can't say I'm surprised . . . I guess our weekend in Cannes is off the agenda?' Rachel smiled and raised an eyebrow.

'Have we get any dirt on Shipley yet?' Crowley asked irritably, ignoring her look and doodling with his solid-gold pen – a Panthère de Cartier encrusted with over 400 diamonds and emeralds.

'Perhaps. There might be a hole in his taxes. His Hermit Road mega-church rakes in just over US $40 million a year, which is tax-exempt, but for the past five years he's only declared a salary of US $50 000. Yet as you're well aware, he has a private jet and drives a Maserati. Area 15's working on that little anomaly.'

'No point in paying taxes if you don't have to, and putting him

in to the Inland Revenue Service isn't going to get us anywhere.
Where are we at with Carter Davis?'

'I've spoken to his PA, and Davis will take your call when you're
ready. But before we get to that, Mr Reid wants to see you . . . he says
it's urgent.'

Rachel opened the door to allow Reid access, and then moved to one
of the occasional tables where she quietly switched on the recording
system, one of three points in the room from where it could be activated.

'That'll be all, Rachel.'

Surprised, Rachel maintained a neutral look and withdrew, closing the soundproofed door behind her. She was very rarely excluded
from Crowley's discussions, and it infuriated her when she was. She
made a mental note to check the recordings.

'There's been a development in Cairo,' Reid said. Like Ruger, the
tall, thin head of Area 15 sported tattoos, including a flaming skull
and crossbones on his neck. 'You asked we keep a watching brief on
papyri in Egypt. Well, one has just surfaced. The Horus Papyrus.'

Crowley was instantly focused. One of the greatest threats to the
dogma of Christianity had finally been found.

'Our man in the Cairo Museum has sent us the following.' Reid
handed over the decrypted message, along with a photograph of
the papyrus and a translation of the hieroglyphics. 'O'Connor and

Weizman met with Badawi, the director, and donated the papyrus to the museum's collection, but on condition that Badawi hold off on any announcement while they search for the Euclid Papyrus. We've kept both under surveillance. As we speak, O'Connor's back in Washington, which leaves Weizman vulnerable.'

Crowley shook his head. 'The Horus Papyrus is unique, and that makes it worthy of a place in any collection,' he said mentally making space for it, 'but for the moment, its value lies in the threat it poses to the Christians and their dogma. The Euclid Papyrus is far more important, and Weizman and O'Connor might just lead us to it.'

'That may be so, but as far as the Horus Papyrus is concerned, Aboud's put an asking price of US $50 million on it.'

'Where does that come from? It's not in this message?'

'We've been monitoring Aboud's communications. He's offered it to Rubinstein in Venice on the quiet, which is why I asked to see you urgently.'

Crowley coloured visibly. 'So he thinks he can knock it off, and we're going to be none the wiser. Double-crossing little turd. What's Rubinstein's response?'

'He said he'd get back to him.'

'And the Jew will add another ten million on top of that and offer it to me.'

'Or the Vatican?'

'Or the evangelicals,' Crowley mused, a plan forming in his mind. 'Leave it with me, and keep monitoring Weizman, O'Connor, Rubinstein and Aboud, twenty-four seven. In the meantime, I'm meeting with an old colleague of yours, Elias Ruger.'

Crowley scrutinised Reid's face for any reaction to his mention of Reid's one-time fellow inmate of the Illinois State Penitentiary, but there was none.

'I've cleared him into Area 15, but only for assignments that affect him. You're to provide him with intelligence on matters that I might authorise from time to time, beginning with the brief on O'Connor and Weizman's activities in Alexandria and Cairo.'

Once Reid had left, Crowley buzzed Rachel. 'I'll be back in an hour. If Shipley's in town, squeeze him in before the board meeting. If he balks, tell him I'd like to make another donation.'

'Welcome to Dallas,' Crowley said to Ruger, lighting a cigar. The concierge had shown them into one of the private rooms in The Leopard Club, just one of Dallas' many gentlemen's clubs that provided exclusive services, day and night. He waited while the young waitress, her attire leaving nothing to the imagination, delivered coffee.

'I trust the accommodation we've provided is of a better standard than that of the state of Illinois?'

'It makes a pleasant change.' Ruger was just on six three in his socks, a huge bear of a man who kept himself very fit. His short, dark hair was tinged with grey, and his face was pockmarked – a legacy of teenage acne – with his right cheek scarred from a bar room brawl.

'Well, I'm glad Judge O'Reilly has corrected things . . .' Crowley let his words hang, leaving Ruger in no doubt who'd been behind his acquittal. 'And now that's out of the way, we need to discuss your future employment.' Ruger had been briefed by the County Court bagman that the price of his freedom would be explained once he arrived in Dallas.

Ruger was a man of few words. His face expressionless, he nodded.

'Like all big companies, to a certain extent, we rely on commercial intelligence, and both espionage and counter-espionage surveillance is provided by a department of EVRAN known as Area 15. The existence of this is on a need-to-know basis. Within Area 15, there are compartments – every so often, we face threats that have to be eliminated, if you get my drift.'

'I don't come cheap, Mr Crowley.'

'And we don't employ amateurs, Ruger,' Crowley replied icily. 'Money's not the issue. It's getting the assignments out of the way cleanly, without any trails. You've been provided with an apartment here in Dallas, with a retainer of US $100 000 a year, on the understanding that you drop whatever you might be doing when we call. Provided it doesn't expose your arrangement with us, what you do in your spare time is up to you. As to assignments, that will depend on their nature, but if they involve high-value targets, they come in at around US $300 000. Any questions?'

'Are there any targets at present?'

'There may be some problems in Montana.' Crowley gave Ruger a broad outline of the Davis candidature. 'I'm confident that Davis will run, but we've had to buy off some of the governor's indiscretions.'

Ruger shrugged and listened again while Crowley gave him the bare details on O'Connor and Weizman, and the search for the Euclid Papyrus in Alexandria. If Ruger wondered why the CEO of the world's biggest energy multinational might have an interest in an ancient artifact, he didn't show it.

'At the moment,' Crowley continued, 'surveillance in Egypt is being provided through the Egyptian Museum of Antiquities, courtesy of one Doctor Omar Aboud, but we may need to eliminate him,' he said, as if he were talking about a sports competition. 'He's not to be trusted. He doesn't know it, but we've discovered he's providing intelligence to an art dealer in Venice.' Crowley left Ruger in no doubt that he too, could expect his activities to be monitored. 'We'll deal with Aboud in due course, but a more immediate task is the transfer of some highly sensitive cargo from our nuclear laboratories in California. You'll be briefed on the details a little later today.'

Rachel picked up the phone on Crowley's massive cedar desk and seconds later handed it to her boss. 'Nancy Callahan, Governor Davis's PA,' she said softly.

'Ms Callahan, good morning, Sheldon Crowley here. Thank you . . . Governor Davis, good to hear your voice. I trust you're well.'

'Never fitter, Sheldon. To what do I owe this unexpected pleasure?'

'I've been watching from a distance, Carter, and you're doing one helluva job up there, and as you've got an election coming up soon, there are a few people down here who would like to help. I realise that it's short notice, but there's a very big donation in the offing, so if you can organise your busy schedule the week after next, I'll send my private jet, and we'll put you up at Ploutos Park.'

'Well, that's mighty neighbourly of you, Sheldon, just wait one . . .'

Crowley quietly switched to speakerphone. Carter Davis's voice was muffled by his hand over the phone, but it came through clearly enough. 'Nancy – what've we got on the week after next?'

'Monday's pretty clear, but Tuesday you have a bunch of meetings, including Pastor Elias Satchelby.'

'Put them off.'

'You've put Pastor Satchelby off three times already.'

'Put him off again. Wednesday?'

'Chamber of Commerce in the morning, the Jewish Board of Deputies in the afternoon, followed by the young high achievers' awards.'

'Get the deputy governor to stand in.'

'And you've got the judging for Miss Montana in the evening. I'll get the deputy governor to stand in for that as well.'

'No, no, I'll do that one . . . are you there, Sheldon? How about I come down Monday week and leave early on the Wednesday. I've got an important meeting Wednesday night I can't afford to put off.'

'We'll be very pleased to see you, and I should have mentioned, Mrs Davis is most welcome to come down if she's free.'

'Mrs Davis doesn't travel all that well, Sheldon, but no problem at all for me this end, and I'll look forward to it.'

'Excellent. I'll get our secretaries to make the arrangements. Nice talking to you.' Crowley handed the phone to Rachel.

Rachel rolled her eyes. 'Nancy . . . I don't think we've met, but I hope we can remedy that very soon. Now, one of EVRAN's Gulfstream jets will be at Helena airport to pick up the governor at nine a.m. on Monday week, and I'll email all the details through to you this morning . . . nice talking to you too.'

'Hasn't changed his spots. First time I've heard the "Miss Montana" contest described as an important meeting,' said Rachel.

'It will be up to you to keep him under control,' Crowley said irritably, 'but getting him down here is just the half of it. Unless we get those fucking evangelicals off their Christian asses and down to the ballot box, the election is wide open. Is Shipley here yet?'

'Just arrived.'

'Show him in.'

'Pastor Matthias, thank you so much for coming,' said Crowley, shaking Shipley by the hand.

Rachel winced. She too had shaken the pastor's hand and it was like grasping a flabby, wet fish. Pale, and portly, Shipley was bordering on obese. The private jet and the Maserati were not the only tax-free perks available in the business of saving souls. The Hermit Road mega-church had a fully staffed commercial kitchen to respond to Pastor Shipley's not inconsiderable love of gourmet food.

'My pleasure,' said Shipley, taking one of the office couches, 'although I hope it's not about this Davis candidature. We went through that last night.'

'I'll come to that in a moment, but first, let's discuss your building fund. I was thinking of something along the lines of US $50 000?'

'That's a very generous donation, Sheldon, and one that the Lord will welcome, but only if there are no strings attached. We could not possibly consider any candidate for the White House who has divorced his wife. The Bible's very clear about divorce,' Shipley said, reaching into his soft attaché case and withdrawing a well-worn leather Bible.

Rachel groaned inwardly.

'"What therefore God has joined together, let no man separate..." Mark 10:2.' Shipley tapped the page for emphasis. 'Whoever divorces his wife and marries another woman commits adultery. We need to be very clear on that, Sheldon.' He sniffed loudly.

'I seem to remember Ronald Reagan was divorced, and you got behind him . . . Have you ever heard of the Horus Papyrus, Matthias?' Crowley asked.

Rachel thought Shipley looked even paler than usual.

'Errant nonsense.'

'But nevertheless a threat to your church. Your empire is built on the authenticity of Christianity.'

'The Egyptians were pagans.'

'Which is the point, is it not? If the Christian religion is a mirror image of an earlier pagan religion, that's going to raise some very serious questions among your generous followers. An Egyptian God, Horus, who was born of a virgin on 25 December with a "star in the east" with three kings heralding his arrival. Three thousand years before Christ was even heard of, this Egyptian God had twelve disciples, walked on water, raised people from the dead and turned water into wine.'

'It's not the first time academics have tried to draw a parallel,' Shipley said weakly.

'No, indeed,' Crowley agreed. 'But it's more than just a parallel, Matthias. The Egyptian Book of the Dead contained the Ten Commandments, well before Moses got hold of them. And the ancient Egyptians inscribed hieroglyphics on the walls of the Temple of Luxor that depict the Annunciation. Just as the Archangel Gabriel announces the virgin birth of Christ to Mary, centuries before, the

Egyptian god Thoth has already announced Horus's virgin birth to Isis.'

Rachel observed both men closely. Crowley, she knew, thought religion was a crock of nonsense, but he'd clearly done his homework. If religion could help get his puppet in the White House, then he was going to harness it. Shipley's pallor had turned to puce and he was struggling to control his rage. Was this pastor a man of real faith, she wondered, or was his rage generated by the threat to the foundations of his multi-million-dollar empire?

'Until now, you've been able to dismiss these similarities as the ramblings of atheist academics, but now there's proof. This is the first time an ancient document, recording the complete details of the Egyptian religion, has surfaced . . . an almost identical religion to Christianity that predates Christ by three millennia. Those Egyptian stories that finished up in your Bible were handed down by word of mouth through the mists of time,' Crowley continued, grinding Shipley into the mud. 'And if the Horus Papyrus is published, the whole world will also know the Egyptian god was crucified and rose from the dead after three days . . . More than a remarkable coincidence wouldn't you say?'

'Where is this papyrus?' Shipley croaked.

Crowley smiled. 'It's safely locked away in a vault, and provided you get firmly behind the Davis campaign, that's where it will stay.'

25

CIA HEADQUARTERS, LANGLEY, VIRGINIA

'Murray seems pretty keen on an audit of Crowley's books,' O'Connor observed, as he and McNamara struggled to make sense of the intelligence coming out of the NSA and what Crowley and Khan might be up to in Alexandria.

'Apart from being easy on the eye, Murray's a very fine analyst . . . one of the best in the NSA, but I doubt she's spent too much time on the Hill, or in the back corridors of the White House. If we move on Crowley without rock-solid evidence, and it all turns to custard, we'll be hung out to dry. On the other hand, if Crowley has some sort of hold over Davis, and Davis wins the White House, Crowley gets a hold over the country.'

'You think Murray's drawing a long bow on Crowley's involvement?'

'Well, let's look at what we've got.' McNamara hadn't survived as the country's chief spymaster without considering every angle. 'Point one, Crowley's an A-grade asshole, and he's been lobbying the

Hill furiously to try and get the ban on the export licenses for both the Scorpion surface-to-air and the Taipan anti-ship missiles over-turned. He'd sell his grandma if he thought he could make a buck out of the deal, but until now, I haven't seen anything to indicate he might be working with terrorists . . . I mean not even Crowley's going to run that sort of risk for the sale of a few missiles. On the other hand, Khan I can understand . . . did you ever meet him?'

'Once, but only briefly when I was in Islamabad a couple of years back. He struck me as shifty. Although you could say that about more than one Pakistani general.'

'And politician . . . but we need to know why Crowley is keeping company with someone like Khan, and if there were other people in Alexandria, who were they, and why were they there? Secondly, what's this choke point Khan's referring to?' McNamara flicked a switch on his desk and a large video screen came to life on the oppo-site wall. He keyed in a computer command and a top-secret map of the world appeared, showing the current deployments of CIA teams.

'Now, where would you say the major choke points are in the world right now?'

O'Connor picked up a small laser pointer from the table. 'Depends whether we're looking at it from a Taliban or al Qaeda point of view,' he said. 'From a purely Taliban point of view in Afghanistan, the Khyber Pass is key, but given the firepower we've got out of Bagram and Creech, they're not going to control that for more than short bursts. The best they can hope for is to ambush the re-supply convoys.'

'Agreed, so if we look further afield, what most affects the West?'
It was one of the reasons O'Connor so much enjoyed working with

McNamara. Not only did his boss protect everyone's back and take the heat from 1600 Pennsylvania Avenue and the Hill, but like O'Connor, McNamara had that rare ability to put himself on the other side of the fence and look at things from a terrorist's point of view.

'Despite the fracking boom,' said O'Connor, 'oil's still one of the chinks in our armour, so if you're a terrorist, and you want to affect oil supplies on land, you hit the pipelines and the oil refineries. There are any number of those, but without a doubt, Abqaiq and Ras Tanura are the biggest and the most vulnerable choke points,' he continued, using his laser to highlight the Saudi-owned Abqaiq oil processing facility in the eastern desert of Saudi Arabia and the associated oil port of Ras Tanura on the coast. 'Two thirds of Saudi Arabia's oil exports go through Abqaiq and Ras Tanura . . . about seven million barrels a day.'

'Hard to hit, though,' McNamara mused. 'Al Qaeda's had a couple of unsuccessful cracks at them, but they're huge targets and the security's impressive.'

'Which on land leaves us with the Druzhba Pipeline,' said O'Connor, highlighting the world's longest oil pipeline, which ran from the south-east of Russia all the way through Ukraine, Hungary, Poland and Germany. 'That carries over a million barrels of oil a day.'

'And it's relatively easy to hit – there's 4000 kilometres of it – but attacking the Druzhba wouldn't hurt us directly,' said McNamara.

O'Connor nodded. 'Ever since 9/11 and the invasions of Afghanistan and Iraq, al Qaeda's main focus has been the United States . . . I think this attack's more likely to be at sea, and there are four choke points that a determined terrorist might have a crack at, starting with the Suez Canal.' O'Connor focused his laser pointer on the 193-kilometre-long canal that connected the Mediterranean with the Red Sea, allowing oil and other cargoes to be transported from Europe to Asia without having to take the much longer route around Africa and the Cape of Good Hope. 'When it was closed in '56, we felt it at the gas pumps, but the Suez crisis wasn't started by some crackpot religious terrorist . . . that was Nasser boring it up Eisenhower's ass,' O'Connor said. In 1956, the charismatic Egyptian president had nationalised the canal after the United States and Britain withdrew funding for the Aswan Dam, bringing on a spike in oil prices and another full-blown crisis in the Middle East which went from bad to worse when the British, French and Israelis met in secret and launched an attack against Egypt without warning the United States. Eisenhower had been livid.

McNamara's piercing blue eyes twinkled. Fiercely patriotic, he nevertheless saw the humour whenever 1600 Pennsylvania Avenue experienced discomfort. It was a subliminal payback for the amount of discomfort he'd experienced over the years in the Situation Room below the Oval Office. 'It was worse after the '67 Six Day War. What did they call it? The Yellow Fleet. Sixteen cargo ships stuck in the canal for eight years.' When war had broken out between Israel and the Egyptians and other Arab countries in 1967, Nasser had scuttled cargo ships and dredges at either end of the canal, trapping for eight years the sixteen vessels that had been travelling north. Over time, they had become covered in the yellow sands of the desert, gaining the sobriquet of 'the Yellow Fleet'.

'It was one of the catalysts for the supertanker,' McNamara observed. The closure of the Suez in 1956, and again between 1967 and 1975, had highlighted the vulnerability of what was, at the time, the world's major choke point. If oil had to be transported all the way round the Cape of Good Hope, then the oil companies had to make that worthwhile, and it had led to the design of the super-tanker, massive ships that were far too big to get into any of the world's enclosed harbours. 'And I see that bastard Crowley's just commissioned two more,' said McNamara. 'The *EVRAN Cosmos* and the *EVRAN Universe*: both 510 000 tonnes, four football fields long and a draught of 80 feet. They're the biggest in the world, and too big to go through the English Channel, but they would be, wouldn't they . . . arrogant prick.'

'Which is why I don't think Khan's choke point is the Suez,' said O'Connor. 'In the age of the supertanker, another closure of the Suez isn't going to hit us nearly as hard.'

'Although it's intriguing that Khan and Crowley appear to have met in Alexandria,' McNamara mused. 'But if not the Suez, where's the strike?'

'The Straits of Malacca is another possibility.' O'Connor focused his laser on the 800-kilometre-long stretch of water that separated the Indonesian island of Sumatra and the Malay Peninsula, the major shipping channel for ships moving from the Indian to the Pacific Oceans. 'Narrows to about one and a half nautical miles, here,' said O'Connor, 'just south of Singapore, and carries a bit over a million barrels of oil a day . . . about the same as Suez, and although that's significant, I wouldn't put it at the top of a terrorist's list.'

'Yeah, I agree. Any others?'

'The Bosphorus is the world's narrowest, in fact it's downright dangerous,' said O'Connor, indicating the 17-nautical-mile strait that flowed past Istanbul, connecting the Black Sea to the Sea of Marmara, through which ships gained access to the Aegean and the Mediterranean. 'The current runs at seven to eight knots, and there's a 45-degree turn required here, near Kandilli Point.'

'So it's easy to attack, but that's going to impact mainly on Russia and the Ukraine.'

'Exactly, which leaves the Strait of Hormuz, and that would be my pick,' said O'Connor, moving his laser pointer to the stretch of water that connected the Gulf of Oman with the Persian Gulf. It was one of the most sensitive choke points in the world, and the Arab Spring uprisings against dictators like Egypt's Mubarak and Tunisia's Ben Ali and his wife Leila, wanted by Interpol for high treason and money laundering, had further destabilised an already volatile region.

'If I was a terrorist, and I wanted to hit the West hard, especially the US, I'd do it there,' O'Connor continued. 'With seventeen million barrels of oil a day passing through that choke point, and most of it destined for Western Europe, Japan and the US, the queues at the gas stations would be longer than they were after the Yom Kippur War in '73.' In 1973, on Yom Kippur, the Day of Atonement and the holiest day on the Jewish calendar, ordinary Israelis had been either praying in the synagogues or relaxing. In the lead-up to the war, Egypt's president Anwar Sadat had demanded that the Egyptian Sinai, lost in the '67 Six Day War with Israel, be returned. Syria's president Hafez al-Assad had been similarly rebuffed in his demands for the return of the Golan Heights. On 6 October 1973, Egyptian forces stormed across the Suez Canal, and the Syrians attacked the Golan Heights with five divisions, taking the Israelis by surprise.

'I remember that war,' McNamara said. 'I'd only just started out in the CIA, and I'd been posted to Tel Aviv. Israel damned near got pushed into the Mediterranean. "Tricky Dicky" Nixon was missing in action and didn't attend a single formal meeting of the National Security Council. Spent the war bunkered down in his Key Biscayne retreat, stalling Special Prosecutor Cox's demands for the Watergate tapes.' With Israel down to its last three days of ammunition, and in danger of being pushed into the sea, it had been left mainly up to Secretary of State Henry Kissinger to organise support for Israel. The Arab states were furious, and the OPEC nations, led by Saudi Arabia, had promptly cut exports of petroleum to the United States.

O'Connor grinned. 'Not to mention having to deal with the fall-out of the resignation of his vice president. Spiro Agnew – caught with his hands in the cookie jar.'

'The queues at the gas stations stretched for block after block . . . people waiting for hours to fill up and panicking that fuel would run out,' said McNamara. 'You think an attack on Hormuz would have the same effect?'

'We're better prepared these days,' said O'Connor, 'but it would still hit the West hard. In 1973 oil shot up from eighteen dollars a barrel to over a hundred, and today, a closure of the Strait of Hormuz would have the same effect. A quadrupling of prices at the pump really starts to damage the West and the rest of the world's economy.'

'Which these al Qaeda assholes couldn't give a shit about,' agreed McNamara. 'Problem is, the satellites are working overtime in Iraq and Afghanistan, and on Syria, but I'll see what can be done.'

'Should we be briefing Pennsylvania Avenue on this?'

McNamara shook his head. 'Not until we've got a little more to go on. McGovern's up to his armpits with Iran and their nuclear program, Netanyahu and Israel, al-Assad and Syria, Karzai in

Afghanistan . . . he needs this like a synagogue needs a pork chop. I'll let them know through the back door, and I'll have a word with the Secretary of State. In the meantime, you'd better get yourself across to Alexandria and unearth who the hell was at that meeting and what was on the agenda at the Kashta Palace. Take a couple of extra days in Alexandria, and give Aleta my best,' McNamara said with a grin, getting to his feet.

O'Connor walked back to his temporary office, turning Barbara Murray's card over in his hand. It didn't escape him that she'd given him her personal card. He turned his thoughts to Carter Davis as president. Surely the American people couldn't be that gullible? He shook his head. With someone like Crowley behind him, Hailey Campbell might need a little more than Chuck Buchanan, Megan Becker and a high approval rating.

26

EVRAN HEADQUARTERS, DALLAS, TEXAS

Crowley sat at the centre of the polished mahogany board table with Rachel on his right. The rest of the places were taken up by some of the most highly paid executives on the planet: 'Big Jack' Allard, the CEO of EVRAN Coal, a huge multinational with interests in nearly half the world's coal mines; Frank McFarland, the CEO of EVRAN Energy, a vast oil and gas multinational, dwarfing the likes of ExxonMobil, BP, and Royal Dutch Shell; Barclay Roberts, the lanky CEO of EVRAN Defense Industries, at the top of world rankings which included Lockheed Martin, BAE Systems, Boeing and Northrop Grumman; Marcelo Costa, the wily Brazilian CEO of EVRAN Timber; along with Professor Truman Stockton, the CEO of EVRAN Nuclear and Albin Martin Jr., EVRAN's shady general counsel. Professor Marcus Ahlstrom sat on a chair against the wall, nervously looking on. None of Crowley's CEOs received less than US $50 million a year.

'You've all read the briefing notes. They're to be returned before you leave the building,' Crowley warned. 'Since we last met, a number of threats to our operations have intensified, but the one that's gaining the most traction in Washington right now is this climate change crap.' Crowley turned toward Rachel. 'Let's have the video.'

Rachel switched on a recording of the previous night's *Late Night Live,* a talk show out of New York. Hosted by the stylish and hugely influential Merrill Stewart, the controversial program commanded a viewing audience of over ten million, the largest since the finale of *Cheers* in 1993.

'With the country suffering some of the worst snow storms in years,' Stewart intoned, 'many of President McGovern's critics are furious over the president's plans to deal with global warming, claiming it's a myth and that any attempt to put a price on carbon will damage an already fragile economy. Please welcome Professor Megan Becker who, until she joined the team supporting former secretary of energy Hailey Campbell, was President McGovern's scientific advisor.'

The left-leaning audience broke into enthusiastic applause as the red-haired, five-foot-ten, blue-eyed environmentalist strode on to the set.

'Before we get to the president's position on global warming, Megan, perhaps you can answer the question on everyone's lips – is Hailey Campbell going to run?' Stewart's smile was disarming.

'A curve ball right up front,' Becker responded, her smile equally disarming. 'You would have to ask Ms Campbell.'

'Given that President McGovern can't run for a third term, why have you joined Campbell's team as an advisor?' persisted Stewart.

'The bases are loaded tonight, aren't they?' said Becker, smiling at the audience.

'You can't blame me for trying,' replied Stewart. 'Let's move on to President McGovern's new position on global warming. Do you think people understand what is meant by climate change and global warming?'

'No, and that's partly our fault,' said Becker turning toward the studio audience again. 'We scientists are sometimes not very good at putting arguments in terms that people in other professions can understand, but we've known the planet has been heating for a very long time. In the 1820s, the French mathematician Joseph Fourier calculated that because of its distance from the sun, our planet should be a lot cooler, which led him to the possibility of our atmosphere acting as a trap for the sun's heat reflected off the earth: what we now call the greenhouse effect. And then in the 1860s, the Irish physicist, John Tyndall, carried out experiments with a number of gases to see which were the best at trapping heat, and he found that carbon dioxide had an interesting property: it allowed visible light to pass through unimpeded, but it was by far and away the best at trapping heat. The best analogy I can give you is your car. When you lock your car and leave it in the sun, the light goes through the windows and the car heats up, because the heat can't escape, and it's the same with the earth's atmosphere. The Swedish Nobel Laureate Svante Arrhenius linked the changes in global temperature to the amount of carbon dioxide in the atmosphere, and those amounts have steadily increased as we burn more and more of the fossil fuels – coal, oil and gas.'

'This fear about the burning of coal, oil and gas doesn't seem to be shared by a large number of Americans,' challenged Stewart. 'The latest surveys indicate that nearly 50 per cent of Americans think that global warming can be attributed to natural fluctuations in the climate?'

'Yes, and in Australia, there is strong support to abolish their carbon tax, but that's hardly the point. Ninety-seven per cent of climate scientists are convinced that the science is rock-solid. The planet is heating to dangerous levels. Americans, Australians, Europeans – many of them have fallen victim to unseen but powerful forces that are funding public relations programs to convince them that climate change is a myth. It's not unlike the tobacco industry's efforts in the eighties and nineties to convince people that smoking wasn't harmful.'

'I saw a report just recently that the Nobel Laureate and clean energy proponent, Professor Marcus Ahlstrom, may have been lured over to work for EVRAN?' Stewart asked.

'He wouldn't be the first scientist to be lured into the fold. I suspect Ahlstrom is going to be part of the EVRAN public relations campaign to derail the science, because EVRAN is one of the biggest polluters in the world. You only have to look at the scale of their coal operations in Wyoming.'

The shot cut to some footage of the rare beauty of the snow-capped eastern Rocky Mountains.

'Wyoming might be one of our least populous states, second only to Alaska, but it's also one of the richest mining states in the country,' continued Becker. 'Last year, out of the billion tonnes of coal dug up by the US alone, nearly 400 million tonnes came out of the cowboy state.'

Stewart picked up that some in the audience looked shocked, and she judged it was time to allow some audience participation. 'We're going to open things up for some Q and A . . . yes,' she said, pointing to a young woman in the front row.

'My name's Sarah Kable, and I'm in my first year of environmental science at the University of Wyoming in Laramie. I'm curious to know how our energy consumption compares to the rest of the world?'

'With 300 million people, we represent five per cent of the world's population,' said Becker, 'but we're also the most developed and we use 25 per cent of the world's energy, albeit that is changing. By 2028, India will have surpassed China as the most populous nation on the planet, and by 2050, Nigeria will have a larger population than the US. By that time there will be nearly ten billion people on planet earth, and unless we change our habits and our sources of energy, fossil fuels are predicted to supply 80 per cent of the world's energy.'

'And you were saying before we came on that this threatens, of all things, our fisheries?' said Stewart.

Becker nodded. 'That's the elephant in the room. EVRAN is mining high sulfur coal from states like Illinois. When that's burned in power stations, it gives off sulfur dioxide, which then combines with water vapour in the air, producing sulfuric acid. That returns as acid rain, destroying forests and the marine environment. Already, brook trout and other species in some of our rivers have been completely wiped out.'

'Yes . . .' said Stewart, pointing to an elderly man two rows back.

'Surely with the advent of fracking, we're now getting cleaner energy, not to mention the creation of thousands of jobs?'

'Which is horizontal drilling, for those at home,' said Stewart, turning to Becker.

'Yes. A lot of people don't understand what's involved with fracking, but hydraulic fracturing, or "fracking", is a process of drilling, at first vertically, often through a precious water table, and then horizontally into seams of shale or coal to release oil and natural gas. Millions of gallons of water are trucked in and mixed with chemicals and sand, which is injected under very high pressures into the ground to fracture the shale or coal and release the gas. These chemicals include dangerous levels of lead, mercury, uranium and hydrochloric acid, much of which is left in the ground adjacent to the water tables. If —'

Rachel flicked off the video and waited for the explosion. She wasn't disappointed.

Crowley glared around the room. 'So we have an EVRAN bottom line worth billions that's being threatened by Sarah Shagnasty from the University of Bumblefuck-nowheresville, and she's getting airtime,' Crowley growled, his mood darkening. 'It's time to ratchet up the heat on these dickheads.'

'I agree,' said 'Big Tom' Allard. 'The new fracking technologies are paying off handsomely, particularly in Colorado, Wyoming and Utah, and we're doing equally well with the large deposits in Nova Scotia and New Brunswick in Canada, where we've got a large number of teams in the field, getting the folks to sign up. But we still need to deal with the loonie Left, who have hit us with a barn full of lawsuits.'

'Fuck 'em,' Crowley growled. 'What's the prognosis?' he asked, turning to EVRAN's general counsel. Albin Martin Jr. had previously served as the attorney general of Texas, where he'd been caught up in insider trading and forced to resign. Crowley had been quick to bring him on board.

'They're wasting their time and money,' Martin replied in his gruff Texan drawl. 'They're trotting out the usual bullshit, claiming fossil fuels should be left in the ground, but they're pissing into the wind and the courts will throw that out. To back it up, they're

claiming God knows how many endangered species are threatened – anything from the double-breasted split-tailed mattress
thrasher to the horny-toed frog, and they get every fucking wilderness do-gooder to protest outside the courts, but that won't hold
things up for very long.'

Crowley turned to Rachel. 'Remind me to have a word with
Louis Walden about that. We'll see these motherfuckers off the
field, whatever it takes. Perhaps now's a good time for a summary of
our new PR approach.'

'You've all met Professor Ahlstrom,' said Rachel, nodding
toward the Nobel Laureate who was still looking decidedly uncomfortable.

'The professor will be making a number of media appearances
to promote your companies. Our research is showing there's an
enormous amount of confusion in the public's mind about climate
change, and we intend to capitalise on that. As you can see from
this graph,' Rachel said, flicking up a PowerPoint, 'a recent poll in
the UK showed that only 31 per cent thought that climate change
was definitely happening, and that's down from the 44 per cent who
were worried about it previously.'

'We'll need to keep the PR pressure right up their ass,' said Crowley. 'Australia's consigned climate change to the trashcan, and their
prime minister was here only the other day, talking up the benefits
of coal. The European Union's backing right off on rules for emissions, so if they can do it in Europe and Australia, which is a coal
bucket, we can do it here.'

'Our PR campaigns here are having a similar effect,' Rachel said,
backing her boss and flicking up a second slide. 'Over a quarter of
Americans think global temperatures aren't rising, and given the

recent record low temperatures and snowfalls, we'll ram that home. Our PR policy will not only build on the confusion in the public's mind, but we can push the idea that volcanoes produce far more CO^2 than human activity. Recent scientific data also shows the Antarctic ice is growing, rather than shrinking, and we have a leaked draft of a report from the UN's International Panel on Climate Change, which shows the planet's temperature is flat-lining. *All* media requests are to be sent to me,' Rachel said, a touch of steel in her voice, 'and unless otherwise approved, Professor Ahlstrom will be our spokesperson on climate change. And you will note we refer to this as climate change, not global warming. Global warming runs the risk of giving a subliminal message contrary to the one we want out there.'

At the end of the board meeting, Crowley leaned over and whispered in Rachel's ear. 'Ask that dopey Truman Stockton to step into my office, and get me that latest report on that little shit, Costa . . . I'll see him as soon as I've dealt with Stockton.'

'Have a seat, Truman,' Crowley said to Professor Stockton, nodding to Rachel to activate the recording system. As CEO of EVRAN Nuclear Laboratories in California, the nuclear physicist was out of his depth, but that was precisely why Crowley had appointed him. He'd wanted someone who would comply with the movement of controlled stores without questioning their destination too closely. The more classified research was done up in EVRAN Idaho, where Idaho's chief nuclear physicist reported directly to Crowley.

'How's the new reactor coming along?'

'Going very well, Mr Crowley.' The professor adjusted his thick black glasses, which had a habit of riding onto the end of his nose. 'We should be ready to start our experiments by the end of the year, which will be well in front of the international effort.' Those experiments, Crowley knew, would revolve around a doughnut-shaped reactor known as a Tokamak. The reactor was encased in superconducting magnets designed to squeeze and heat a plasma of hydrogen isotopes to a temperature of 150 million degrees, generating 500 megawatts of electricity in the process. The output of energy was ten times the input, something that had never been achieved before.

'That's good news, Truman, and you will have noted that Professor Ahlstrom has agreed to join our team at EVRAN.'

'That *was* a surprise, Mr Crowley,' said Stockton.

Crowley let the nuclear physicist squirm. It hadn't been a deliberate 'divide and conquer' manoeuvre, but it was obvious Stockton saw Ahlstrom as a threat to his own standing, which pleased Crowley immensely.

'Given Professor Ahlstrom's standing in the academic world, he will be reporting directly to me,' Crowley said, increasing the nuclear physicist's discomfort. 'In the meantime, I've approved a new research project that will require three kilograms of Cobalt 60 to be released from storage in California and transported to our laboratories in Idaho. Mr Ruger has also joined our team, and he'll be in charge of the transfer, and the approvals from the Department of Energy will be handled here.'

'I'd like to visit those laboratories at some stage, Mr Crowley.'

'There are some areas of EVRAN which, for security reasons, are compartmentalised, and they're off-limits, even to nuclear physicists like you, Truman.'

Stockton nodded.

'Hasn't got a fucking clue,' Crowley muttered to Rachel after the scientist had left. 'But he's a useful idiot. Have you got the report on Costa?'

'There's an executive summary on the inside cover,' said Rachel, handing over the confidential file. 'I've also included the Area 15 report on Costa's internet activity, emails and phone contacts.' The CEO of EVRAN Timber had long been under surveillance. Crowley trusted none of his executives, and least of all the wily Brazilian.

'Anything of interest?' he asked, scanning the executive summary.

'The usual stuff. He's still taking time out with prostitutes and strippers in Manaus.' The capital of Amazonas, Brazil's largest state, had all the usual attractions of a major river port.

Crowley shrugged. 'I don't care what he does with his dick, as long as he keeps the government and the greenies under control.'

'That's more problematic,' said Rachel. 'You can see from the summary that the environmentalists are becoming more active, particularly over logging the Amazon, to the point where the government has to be seen to be taking action.'

'I've seen the photos of the protestors,' Crowley grunted. 'And I've got screaming headlines for our man, Costa. That's going to stop. Let's see what his plan is. Show him in.'

'Good to see you again, Marcelo,' Crowley intoned urbanely. 'Have a seat,' he said, guiding Costa toward a suite of blue suede lounges on the far side of the office. Crowley had modelled the area on the Oval Office, and in place of the presidential seal, the carpet between the lounges bore EVRAN's erupting-volcano logo.

'So, you heard the boardroom discussion on the greenies this morning; what's the score in Brazil?' Crowley asked, cutting straight to the chase.

Stocky, with a deep tan and a scar across his cheek from his earlier days as a drug runner, Marcelo Costa sported a neatly trimmed black goatee beard and moustache. Costa flashed his ivory teeth, but his smile was humourless. 'We have them under control, Sheldon.'

'And how is that being done, Marcelo?' Crowley's demeanour was suddenly icy. 'How is it that these clowns are able to issue a fucking press release on EVRAN's front doorstep?' Crowley extracted a photograph of protestors taken next to the 'EVRAN Timbers' sign at EVRAN's Manaus mill on the banks of the Amazon. Their banner read 'Logging in the Amazon has destroyed an area twice the size of Spain! EVRAN Criminals!'

'That won't happen again,' Costa replied evenly. 'I've doubled the number of guards, and I now have two of my own men in IBAMA.' The Instituto Brasileiro do Meio Ambiente e dos Recursos Naturais Renováveis was the Brazilian environment agency charged with overseeing the vast expanses of the Amazon jungle. The Amazon was not only the world's largest rainforest in both size and diversity, it also absorbed and stored massive amounts of the world's carbon. IBAMA's resources were stretched and despite the government's best efforts, IBAMA was not immune from corruption.

'We not only have warning of any inspections, but we're able to steer them away from our operations in the north-west down to the Mato Grosso on the border with Bolivia. You will have read the news reports of arrests?'

Crowley nodded. A Greenpeace survey had showed 72 per cent of logging in the Amazon was illegal, and that deforestation was occurring at a staggering 26 000 square kilometres a year, or the equivalent of six football fields a minute. Brazilian federal police had launched a crackdown on illegal logging and arrested the members of the gangs responsible for removing more than 80 million cubic feet of timber, which would fill over a thousand Olympic swimming pools.

'I've put the word out. Any protestors who think they can approach our mills should be very careful. If they tangle with my guards, they're likely to come off badly. There's a huge demand for decking hardwood. Ipé will continue to flow to our markets, and the greenies better get used to it.'

'Speaking of which, these are the latest private orders for cedar and mahogany,' Crowley said, passing over a list of clients to whom he'd promised favours. 'Once the orders are filled, make sure the list is destroyed.'

Costa smiled. In 2001, the Brazilian government had banned the export of mahogany but he and Crowley were well aware that over a quarter of the world's timber trade was illegal and EVRAN's export of Brazilian big-leaf mahogany, disguised as other tropical species, hadn't missed a beat.

'The mahogany's not a problem, but the big cedar trees are getting harder to find. It may take a while.'

'As long as it gets here. More importantly, is the next shipment for Karachi secure?' Thirty-two of the gleaming missiles had arrived the week before and Costa had ensured that the appropriate palms had been greased to avoid any scrutiny.

'The cargo is in one of our warehouses at the timber mill, and it's heavily guarded. It will be loaded on to the *EVRAN I*, disguised in batches of ipé, as soon as she docks in Manaus.'

'To assist you with your PR problems,' Crowley said, getting to his feet, 'Rachel is arranging for Ahlstrom to address the top business leaders and government ministers in Brasília.'

As soon as I've organised some media training, Rachel thought.

'Always a pleasure to visit,' Costa said, taking his cue and heading for the door.

Crowley watched Costa leave, and then turned to Rachel. 'Make sure Area 15 has twenty-four-hour tabs on that little turd. He's slicker than a rat with a gold tooth.'

'And twice as dangerous,' Rachel agreed.

27

ALEXANDRIA

After Aleta had picked O'Connor up, she took the desert road from the Burg al-Arab airport back to Alexandria and the Hotel Cecil.

'So . . . who did you have to sleep with to get a leave pass back here?' Aleta's feathers were still more than a little ruffled over O'Connor's abrupt departure for Washington.

'Still angry?' O'Connor had long ago concluded it would not be good for his health to be on the wrong side of this lady. Perhaps that was part of the attraction.

'A little,' she said, 'but provided you take me out to dinner, buy me flowers and jewellery, and tell me how nice I look, in six months time I *may* forgive you.'

'That soon?' he said, placing his hand on Aleta's taut, brown thigh.

'And that's not going to do it,' she said, making no attempt to remove his hand.

'You're very attractive, particularly when you're mad,' said O'Connor, 'and don't get any madder than you are already, but Washington has sent me here for a reason, although Tom McNamara sends his best.'

'Screw Tom McNamara.'

They drove on in silence before Aleta finally spoke.

'And that reason is?'

'Let's talk about that when we get back to Alexandria.'

O'Connor chose an outside table at the Athineos Café in Saad Zaghlol Square, a short distance from the hotel.

'I don't think I'll ever get used to what you do. Encrypted emails, iPhones, laptops. I assume there's a reason we couldn't talk in the car or the hotel room?' said Aleta.

'There are quite a few things not adding up around here . . . or back in the States,' replied O'Connor. 'I haven't had time to check the hire car or the room in the hotel; for now, I'm assuming both are bugged, but it's much harder to pick up conversations out here in the open air.'

'So what's not adding up?'

'The less you know the better, just in case anyone is ever, God forbid, trying to get information from you.'

Aleta shook her head. 'Uh-uh. After all we've been through together, Curtis Seamus O'Connor, that's not going to wash, so out with it.'

O'Connor smiled. Aleta wasn't cleared into any of the CIA compartments, and he was breaking longstanding rules, but she was right. Having been illegally placed on the CIA's assassination list, and then pursued halfway around the world, she had a right to know.

'We're not sure why, but a couple of weeks ago, there was a

meeting here at the Kashta Palace, involving a sacked Pakistani general, and several others, the identities of whom we're not sure. Missiles manufactured in the United States by EVRAN, owned by Sheldon Crowley, the richest industrialist in the world, have been turning up in Afghanistan. These missiles are so advanced, they're not even provided to our closest allies. Coupled with that, the owner of Galleria d'Arte Rubinstein in Venice, Zachary Rubinstein, seems to be operating as a highly paid fence for Egyptian artifacts, and depending on his clients, that might put you in danger. It might be a good idea to put the search for this papyrus on ice for a while.'

Aleta shook her head. 'You're telling an archaeologist to shelve a search for an ancient document that might turn Egyptology on its head? This is right up there with the search for the tomb of Tutankhamun.'

O'Connor raised his eyebrows in resignation. 'Well, it was worth a try . . . but don't underestimate these assholes, they're playing for keeps.'

Aleta frowned. 'This Sheldon Crowley . . . I've never met him, but his name crops up from time to time. He's an amateur Egyptologist, quite a good one, apparently, and an avid collector.'

'Would he be interested in something like the Euclid Papyrus?'

'Possibly. Collectors can go to extraordinary lengths to obtain something in which the rest of the world could have an interest.'

'Granted, but we're dealing with the world's wealthiest man. He has the means to buy some of the world's most sought after icons. Why would he have an interest in a papyrus written by an ancient mathematician – one that's rumoured to reveal the purpose of the pyramids?'

'Scientists and archaeologists have puzzled over the pyramids for centuries, and we still haven't worked out how they were built, let alone what they were used for . . .'

'Tombs for the pharaohs works for me,' said O'Connor with a grin.

'Was that the sound of your mind closing, Curtis O'Connor? For a man with an intellect and scientific background like yours, you're very quick to judge. I won't get back onto the crop circles,' said Aleta, her brown eyes dancing, 'but we're very quick to dismiss things we don't understand.'

'So you have a favourite theory?' O'Connor asked.

'On how the pyramids were built, or their purpose?'

'Both, but let's deal with how they were built first.'

'The short answer is, we don't know. For decades, the theory with the most credibility has been the notion that around 2360 BC, a hundred thousand slaves laboured for more than twenty years, using wooden levers and rollers, stone tools and plaited rope made out of flax, to haul over two and a half million limestone blocks. A lot of those blocks came from Aswan, which is 500 miles down the Nile, and some of them weighed more than 50 tonnes. Somehow they were hauled up ramps to construct a building that is half the height of the Empire State Building and sits on over 13 acres – but that theory no longer stacks up. Someone did the math on how many wooden rollers would be required, and allowing for the destruction of ten rollers for every ten-tonne block, they would have needed over twenty-five million rollers and levers.'

O'Connor nodded. 'A lot of trees, and Egypt and the Levant are not renowned for forests. But I read somewhere that the blocks might have been secured between wooden discs and rolled to the site.'

'I've read that theory too, and it's a method described by a Roman engineer, Vitruvius, in his book *De Architectura*. But he wrote in the first century BC. The ancient Egyptians around the time of Pharoah Khufu, whose tomb the Great Pyramid is purported to be, had no knowledge of the wheel. That came much later in the sixteenth century BC when Egypt was invaded by the Hyksos from west Asia. They brought with them the horse and the chariot that Hollywood is so keen to associate with Egyptians.'

'So when compared to the Great Pyramid, the Pharos lighthouse pales by comparison?'

'The lighthouse is still worthy of being one of the seven wonders of the ancient world, but the Pharos lighthouse, the Hanging Gardens of Babylon, Artemis's temple at Ephesus, the statue of Zeus at Olympia, the mausoleum at Halicarnassus and the Colossus of Rhodes . . . they've all either disappeared or fallen into ruin. The Great Pyramid is the oldest and the only wonder to be still standing. Regardless of what theory we come up with to get the blocks to the site, and somehow allow for the miles of massive ramps that were needed, we still haven't found an answer for the extraordinary precision of construction.'

'Our old friend Fibonacci . . . we don't seem to be able to shake him,' O'Connor said with a grin, signalling the waiter for another two coffees. In 1202 AD, Fibonacci, arguably one of the most talented mathematicians the world had ever seen, wrote his *Liber Abaci,* in which he introduced an extraordinary sequence of numbers, one well known to the Maya, the Inca and the Egyptians. Each term in the sequence was obtained by adding the previous two terms:

1, 1, 2, 3, 5, 8, 13, 21, 34, 55, 89, 144, 233 . . .

But even more importantly, the extraordinary ratio of 1.618 or phi, designated by the Greek letter Φ, was obtained by dividing any number by its predecessor. The early divisions produced approximations, but as the numbers got larger, the divisions stabilised to become 1.6180339 . . . a ratio that had captured the attention of Einstein, Schrödinger, and other great Nobel Laureates. It was postulated that Φ could be the connecting thread of the cosmos and perhaps the basis of the elusive theory of unity. The golden ratio had been shown to be part of life itself.

Aleta nodded. 'As you and I discovered with the Maya and the Inca, the golden ratio determines everything from the spirals on a nautilus shell, through to the distances between leaves on the plants, right up to the spirals in the galaxies of the universe. It's unseen but everywhere, and the ancients knew this,' she said. 'It's embedded in the pyramids of the Maya and the Inca, and there is compelling evidence the Egyptians knew about it as well, because the Great Pyramid's ratio of the length of its side to its height is 1.618. Yet it's so perfectly built, it would push the limits of even today's technology. There's even evidence,' Aleta said, her enthusiasm growing, 'that the original limestone casing was polished to today's optical standards and the surfaces were precisely flat planed to within 2/10000ths of an inch. The pyramid is aligned with the earth's cardinal compass points, and it's sited at the *exact* apex of the angle drawn to the east and west sides of the Nile delta. And if that's not enough, Khufu's engineers used basic units of measurement that are exactly one ten-millionth of the mean radius between the centre of the earth and the poles.'

'We both agree it was built by superb mathematicians and engineers, and not some primitive culture using hardened stone tools, but the purpose?' O'Connor asked. 'Leaving aside Hollywood's slaves under the whip, it would have taken just about every resource the Egyptians had.'

'Precisely, and even the most demented of pharaohs wouldn't have got away with that, especially not for decades. The tomb theory is in just as much trouble as the primitive construction theory. The first people to break into the Great Pyramid were the Arabs under Caliph al-Mamun, in 820 AD. They miscalculated the location of the original entrance, which the builders disguised, and had to bore their way in. After months of work, they eventually reached the internal descending passage. They then tunnelled their way into the inner chambers, in search of gold and mummies. They found neither,' Aleta said. 'Nor did they find any soot on the ceilings of the chambers, which would have been left from torches used in any earlier break-in . . . they were the first to get inside since the pyramid was built.'

'So you don't think it was Khufu's tomb?'

'In a word, no. Or any other tomb. And the most telling evidence for that is the construction of air shafts, which run from the King's Chamber to the surface of the pyramid. That's something that this papyrus may shed some light on. Dead pharaohs don't need air, especially if they want their bodies preserved for the afterlife. There has been no civilisation more expert than the Egyptians in the art of embalming, and they knew well that air would lead to deterioration and decomposition. Furthermore, there was none of the splendour that Howard Carter found in the tomb of Tutankhamun. The King's Chamber is plain rock, yet its roof has an unbelievably complex design, something that I'm hoping that this Euclid Papyrus might also shine a light on . . . if we can find it.'

'So not only was it never used as a tomb, but it wasn't designed as one. I'll bet that prompts some interesting arguments in your world,' said O'Connor.

Aleta smiled. 'That's an understatement. The world of archaeology is a bitch, and you can multiply that by ten for Egyptology. There's a herd mentality and woe betide anyone who challenges the accepted wisdom. Some have put forward a theory that the Great Pyramid was built, at least partly, as an observatory, utilising the angle of the air shafts to the heavens. Some argue that not only is the geometry of the pyramids very precisely aligned with the earth's geography, but the Great Pyramid is aligned with the heavens as well.'

'I read up on that on the plane flight. There seems to be some disagreement between these scientists . . . Orion versus Cygnus?'

Aleta nodded. '*Some* disagreement? A lot. The Orion theory was put forward in 1994, postulating the Egyptians laid the pyramids out to mirror the belt stars in the Orion constellation. The Orion constellation is located on the celestial equator, so it can be seen from anywhere in the world, and it was known to many of the ancient civilisations. In Arabic, the main stars are named Mintaka, which means 'the belt', Alnitak, 'the girdle', and Alnilam, 'the string of pearls'. All three of those Orion stars are immensely hot. Mintaka is what we call a giant star, and Alnilam and Alnitak are supergiants, hundreds of times larger than our sun, so there's no doubt they were very visible to the ancient Egyptians.'

'But the belt doesn't quite fit?'

'You have been reading! Not quite: Alnitak and Alnilam fit precisely over the tops of Khufu's Great Pyramid and Khafre's middle pyramid, but Mintaka falls to the south-west edge of Menkaure's pyramid, the third and smallest of the three.'

'And Cygnus?'

'There's still a lot of argument as to whether the complex is aligned with Orion or Cygnus. Cygnus is one of the Milky Way's northern constellations, and it takes its name from the Greek for swan. It would have been visible to the ancient Egyptians in the northern hemisphere's summer and autumn and the papyrus we discovered with Euclid's notations supports the theory that Cygnus' Delta, Gamma and Epsilon stars fit precisely on to the apex of each pyramid. But it's the star that Euclid appears to have superimposed over the rock formation near the Sphinx that's had me intrigued, and there's an even fainter dot to the north of it.'

'Which might also support the idea the pyramids were built as observatories?'

'I think that theory's pretty far-fetched. There are much simpler ways to build observatories.'

'None of which answers why Crowley seems so keen to get his hands on the Euclid Papyrus,' said O'Connor.

'I think I might know why. There's one theory that hasn't had a lot of attention to date, and that theory links the pyramid to an ancient energy grid. If that theory turns out to be correct, Crowley will want to make sure this papyrus never sees the light of day. I want to discuss this further with Professor Badawi, but the poor man's been inundated ever since the theft of Tutankhamun's funerary mask and I may not get to see him for weeks, perhaps months. With that in mind, and not knowing what you're going to be up to . . .' Aleta paused to look at Curtis over the top of her sunglasses. 'I've arranged to spend some time at Abydos, not far from Luxor. An American team from the University of Pennsylvania have made a very exciting discovery – the tomb of a previously unknown king.

You're very welcome to come but that depends on your schedule, which you've said absolutely nothing about?'

'I have a small task tonight, and then I have a couple of days before McNamara wants me back.'

'A couple of days . . . is that all I get?' Aleta pouted, but her eyes were smiling.

O'Connor parked in a narrow laneway, a hundred metres from the perimeter fence of the Kashta Palace, put on his balaclava and leather gloves and scanned the area with his night vision goggles. The CIA station chief at the Cairo embassy had done well, O'Connor mused. Not only had Cairo organised a lengthy surveillance, showing the palace had remained unused ever since the mysterious meeting here, but the station chief had also organised for one of his agents to infiltrate the cleaning company. The intelligence reports indicated a detachment of two security guards was based on site, operating out of a large control room in the basement that would be at full capacity when meetings took place with a level of security not out of place at a gathering of G7 world leaders. The shifts changed at seven a.m. and seven p.m, with an external patrol of the building conducted at ten p.m. and another at two a.m.

It was just on ten p.m., and right on cue, a swarthy, thickset guard appeared through the front door, cigarette dangling from his mouth. O'Connor waited until the guard completed his inspection of the exterior of the buildings and disappeared back inside. He focused his night-vision goggles on the iron perimeter fence. Wireless CCTV cameras were in place, every 60 metres, but at the rear of the complex, two large sycamore trees overhung the fence. O'Connor stood behind one of the trees, fixed a small, powerful laser to the tree trunk and aimed it at the camera covering that section of the fence. The near-perfect monochromatic light source of the laser obliterated any image being transmitted by the camera, and in the control centre, if it was being monitored at all, it would look like a simple malfunction.

O'Connor checked the silencer on his 45-calibre Glock 21 and replaced it in his shoulder holster. The Austrian pistol had long been O'Connor's weapon of choice. He scaled the fence with ease and headed toward the main building, moving silently through the extensive gardens, past statues, ponds and palm trees, his tools of trade in a bag slung across his broad shoulders. The agent in the cleaning crew had provided a layout of the building, and more importantly, the location of the alarm box and a large safe in the basement. It was possible that with security guards on the premises, the alarm would not be activated, but O'Connor wasn't prepared to take that risk, and he made his final approach along the front of the building, keeping close to the stone façade. The heavy wooden door was set under a stone arch and the lock was as the agent had reported, a relatively common 'five-pin and tumbler' barrel lock, and O'Connor chose a small diamond-shaped pick. O'Connor had excelled on the courses at 'the farm', the CIA's top secret training area on the south bank of the York River in Virginia, where instruction on the dark arts had no peer.

He slipped a tension wrench into the barrel lock and applied a small amount of pressure on the plug. He then took his pick and began work on each of the pins. Two minutes later, the final pin was forced flush with the shear line. He quietly turned the cam and the door swung open.

O'Connor moved quickly across the black-and-white Italian tiles in the foyer to a wooden cupboard on the far side. The faint sound of Arab music drifted up from the basement. At least they've got good taste, O'Connor thought, recognising the sultry tones of Elissa Khoury. He opened the cupboard door, sprung the back from the alarm box, quickly disabled it and disconnected the phone line, just in case it was programmed to send an automatic warning to the control room. He was about to retrieve his pick and tension wrench and close the door when the music got louder and a shaft of light appeared from the stairwell below. O'Connor moved back into the gloom of the foyer and waited.

The guard reached the top of the stairs and immediately spotted the open door. 'What the —!' The guard quickly moved toward the entrance, but before he could reach it, O'Connor moved behind him and cracked him over the head with the butt of his Glock, using just enough force to knock him out. His quarrel was not with innocent security guards. He dragged the unconscious guard to the rear of the foyer, retrieved some gaffer tape from his bag and in less than a minute immobilised him.

Now for the second guard, O'Connor thought, closing the heavy entrance door. The music coming from the control room gave O'Connor some cover, but he descended the stone steps slowly, Glock drawn, and he cautiously approached the control room. The guard had his back to him, swaying to the sensual tones of the music. Above him, one of the screens was filled with a blurry reddish-orange glow from the CCTV camera O'Connor had disabled. Was that what the first guard had gone to investigate? O'Connor closed the gap quickly but at the last moment the guard turned. Wide-eyed, he reached for his pistol lying on the table. O'Connor fired twice, hitting the guard in the wrist and shoulder. The guard's pistol described a gentle arc, clattering onto the stone floor.

'*Ebn El Sharmoota!* Son of a bitch!' The guard launched himself forward but O'Connor smashed him with a left hook and followed up with a knee into the man's groin. The guard doubled over in pain and O'Connor whipped him around and bound his hands behind his back. He continued to scream obscenities, and O'Connor none-too-gently wound gaffer tape over his mouth and secured him in the corridor.

'So far, so good,' O'Connor muttered as he made his way to the heavy safe door, which the Cairo agent had located at the end of the subterranean corridor. O'Connor already knew it would be a tough one to crack. Although it was a slightly older design with a combination lock, the manufacturer had silenced the mechanism, making it resistant to the time-honoured method of using a stethoscope to listen to the sound of the tumblers. The manufacturer had also installed a cobalt plate, which made it very resistant to drilling from the front, and O'Connor knew that even if he could get through the cobalt with the special drills he had in his kit, there was a real danger of fracturing the last line of defence – a glass relocking plate, which, if broken, would trigger a secondary locking mechanism that would effectively close the safe down. Once that was broken, even if the combination was known, it could not be opened. O'Connor had considered blowing it, but that was noisy and a last resort, and he'd resolved to come at it from an angle above the cobalt and glass plates.

O'Connor measured off 20 centimetres above the dial and extracted from his satchel a small, powerful drill fitted with a titanium bit. Using a wooden brace angled at 40 degrees, O'Connor began to drill through the tough, reinforced steel. It took nearly thirty minutes, but finally he felt the drill bit break through, and he quickly extracted it and inserted a fibre-optic borescope in its place.

Bingo, he thought. The CIA didn't muck around when it came to borescopes, and the image of the lock mechanism was crystal-clear. O'Connor turned the combination dial and watched as first the lug on the drive cam engaged the first wheel, and then a lug on the first wheel engaged a lug on the second wheel, which in turn engaged the third, until finally the last wheel began to turn. O'Connor slowly turned the dial and watched until a recessed notch on the fourth wheel came into view. He stopped it at the very top of the turn, directly underneath a small metal bar or 'fence'; it was designed so the bar would not drop until all the notches on each wheel were perfectly aligned. He slowly spun the dial back the other way, lining up the third wheel, then the second wheel, and finally the front wheel notch came into line and the metal bar dropped with a quiet *thunk*. O'Connor turned the safe's big three-pronged metal wheel and with the fence out of the way, the bolts slid back into their recess.

The door swung silently, to reveal several shelves, each labelled with different years, and each containing identical leather folios. The first year was labelled 1992 and O'Connor noted that each year the number of folios seemed to increase, until it stabilised at sixteen for the past five meetings. He extracted a folio from the most recent meeting and thumbed through it, letting out a low whistle, but the revelations were cut short by the sounds of sirens in the distance.

O'Connor quickly put the folio in his bag and packed his tools of trade. He drew his pistol and made his way past the control room, where the second guard was struggling futilely against his bonds. He cautiously ascended the stairs, but the first guard was still equally immobilised. Perhaps the guard had been able to activate an alarm as he reached for his pistol?

The sirens were getting closer and O'Connor quickly pondered his options. The police might surround the fence, but they would also undoubtedly use the driveway at the front, so he made his way unerringly through the corridors he'd committed to memory, and out onto the rear balcony. O'Connor vaulted the balustrade and disappeared into the gardens just as the first police car arrived at the front patio. He scanned the road at the back of the estate, but there was no sign of any police. He climbed the fence at the same point he'd come across, retrieved the laser from the tree and disappeared down the lane to his car, reasonably confident there would be nothing to connect him with the break-in. On the other hand, O'Connor had no knowledge of Area 15 . . . yet.

28

'This is most irregular, Mr Ruger,' Professor Stockton complained as he led the way to the fortified compound where the Cobalt 60 was kept. 'I can't understand why we have to ship Cobalt 60 in three separate small containers when they're all going to the same destination . . . one large container would have sufficed.'

'Above my pay grade, Professor. How do you make this stuff?'

'Cobalt 60 is highly radioactive, but let's go over to the reactor and I'll show you.'

Stockton escorted Ruger through security, where they both were equipped with white coats and hard hats. A short while later, they stood on a gantry above a fuel bath, the water used to keep the spent fuel rods cool an eerie aquamarine blue.

'Cobalt is mined like any other mineral, and once we process it, we get a powder which is pure Cobalt 59. In other words, 59 neutrons in the nucleus of the cobalt atom,' Professor Stockton explained. 'We compress the Cobalt 59 into pellets, and among the

uranium in the reactor, we're substituting a small number of rods
made up of those pellets coated with nickel. When each Cobalt 59
atom absorbs another neutron from the reactor's fission reaction,
it changes into radioactive Cobalt 60, and that's what you will be
transferring up to Idaho.'

'So what's it used for?'

'A whole range of things. It's important for the sterilisation of
medical equipment, and as a radiation source in the treatment of
cancer. It's also used in industrial radiography, where engineers
can inspect flaws in materials, and of course, terrorists would love
to get their hands on it, because once cobalt is lifted to the sixty-
neutron level, it has too many neutrons to remain stable. I won't get
too technical, but it returns to a stable state by decaying to nickel
and emitting cancer-causing gamma rays in the process, which
would be catastrophic in a city like New York. With a half-life of
over five years, this stuff hangs around for a long time.'

Ruger watched as the three small blue steel containers of Cobalt 60
were loaded into the shipping container. 'They look pretty solid.'

'They have to be. That said, there are never any guarantees with
radioactive material, Mr Ruger, but we comply with the standards
set down by bodies like the Environmental Protection Agency and
the UN's International Atomic Energy Agency. The cobalt itself is
encased in 11 inches of lead sheeting, and that's surrounded by a
double-insulated steel cage. Those containers have to pass testing
which simulates anything from a train crash to a ship collision, so
you can be confident that your cargo is well protected.'

Ruger slowed the brand new FUSO ten-tonne truck and pulled into the nondescript EVRAN warehouse on the outskirts of San Francisco, where two more drivers were waiting with another two trucks. As soon as it was loaded the first truck took off, headed for a warehouse in Chicago. The two six-metre shipping containers destined for overseas were loaded with furniture, and Ruger hid the blue cobalt containers inside cavities in two large sideboards.

Ruger and the other driver pulled out of the warehouse complex, and they headed south along Route 5 toward Los Angeles, sticking to the speed limit. It would take five days and five states to cover the three and a half thousand kilometres to New Orleans and the Port of South Louisiana. From Los Angeles, they would head across the deserts of Arizona to Phoenix; through Las Cruces in New Mexico; on to San Antonio in Texas; and finally South Louisiana. And the Port of South Louisiana had not been chosen by accident. It was the ninth largest port in the world after those like Shanghai, Singapore and Rotterdam, and it was easily the biggest in the United States. Between them, the Ports of New Orleans, South Louisiana and Baton Rouge stretched for nearly 300 kilometres along the banks of the Mississippi, and that posed a particular challenge for the port authorities. Only a fraction of cargoes could be checked, and the authorities relied on intelligence. The containers of furniture destined for overseas were being consigned with that in mind. In the United Kingdom, the cargo would be picked up at Felixstowe in Suffolk, the United Kingdom's busiest container port, and in Australia, the cargo was destined for Melbourne. With fewer than one in a hundred containers being physically examined in either country, the chances of the shielded cargo getting through were high.

Sadiq Boulos and Gamal Nadar walked from the Blackfriars Underground and headed down to Fleet Street, where they turned right to walk the last few blocks to St Paul's Cathedral.

'The house of the Infidel's false god has possibilities,' Boulos whispered, as they approached one of the greatest churches in all of Christendom.

'Let's see,' Nadar said quietly, looking behind him to ensure no one was within hearing distance. 'Security is probably not as tight as the other buildings in the financial district, and if we can get up to the Golden Gallery, that would be perfect. Lunchtime would be best . . . a lot of people are out of their offices then, although that won't make much difference. Gamma rays go through everything.' Nadar smiled broadly at the thought of it.

The traffic was heavy, and the pair had to wait for several iconic London taxis to pass, along with the number fifteen bus to Black-well, and the number seventy six to Tottenham, before they could cross to the cathedral's west front with its wide, stone steps and paired Corinthian columns. After the original church had been gutted in 1666, in the Great Fire of London, Sir Christopher Wren, arguably England's finest architect, had been engaged to redesign it in a baroque style.

It was not the first time the great church had been deliberately targeted. Sitting on Ludgate Hill, the highest ground in the City of London, the great dome had survived several attacks during the blitz, including a huge Nazi time-delay bomb that hit the cathedral on 10 October 1940. Had it gone off, the cathedral would have been totally destroyed, but the bomb was defused by two soldiers from the Royal Engineers, Lieutenant Robert Davies and Sapper George Wylie, both of whom received the rarely awarded George Cross.

Boulos and Nader, tourist maps of London in hand, paid their entrance fee and once inside, barely paused to look at the stunning candelabra, the beautiful high ceilings and the breathtaking stonework and marble in the various chapels, naves and choir stalls. Instead they headed toward the first of a series of stone stairs that would take them to the top of the dome. Two hundred and fifty-seven steps later, they reached the Whispering Gallery which ran around the interior of the dome, and where a whisper against one wall was audible on the opposite side. A further 119 steps, and they were able to inspect the Stone Gallery.

'We can do better,' Nadar said quietly. 'It's only 50 metres to the ground from here.'

Boulous nodded and they climbed another 152 steps to the Golden Gallery, which gave them stunning views of London. But the vista of the River Thames, Shakespeare's Globe Theatre and Tate Modern in one of the world's great cities was the last thing on their mind. Instead, they walked around the outside of the dome with its near shoulder-high iron railing providing protection. On the northern side, they could look down on Paternoster Square.

'Even if the wind is not in our favour, the effect will still be devastating,' Boulos whispered, taking a picture of the London Stock Exchange building, which took up the whole of the northern side of the square.

To the west, across the Atlantic Ocean, and to the east, across the Indian Ocean two more teams were playing the role of tourists, calculating likely wind directions in key cities in the US and Australia, and how they might best spread one of the deadliest substances on the planet.

29

The EVRAN jet carrying Rachel Bannister and the governor of Montana, Carter Davis, came to a stop at the Business Jet Centre at Love Field. Bannister and Davis were whisked through arrivals and Crowley's driver was waiting with one of EVRAN's specially armoured DTS Cadillacs. Despite his media-shy profile, Crowley hadn't got to be the most powerful industrialist in the world without making a lot of enemies, and when Area 15 assessed the risks as being high, the 4.6 litre, three-tonne V8s were there to minimise them. The cars were protected with hardened ballistic steel that was impervious to both 7.62-millimetre and 5.56-millimetre high-powered rifles. The floor and roof provided anti-mine and grenade protection and the heavily tinted windows were made from multi-layered ballistic glass. The fuel tanks, computer modules and batteries were similarly armored and normal tyres had been replaced with high-grade 'run-flat' wheels. Crowley insisted the EVRAN armoured fleet be of identical design to that of the Beast, the specially armoured Cadillac used by the president.

It had taken a bare ten minutes from touchdown to Crowley's driver saluting and ushering the governor and Rachel into the spacious, finely crafted leather seats.

'So . . . what does a gorgeous looking woman like you do when you're not working for Crowley?' Governor Davis asked, placing his hand on Rachel's thigh.

Rachel sighed audibly. On the Gulfstream 550, Rachel had managed to keep the governor's wandering hands at bay by ensuring the seating configuration had them facing each other over a coffee table. She took his arm and firmly placed the governor's hand back on his own flabby thigh. He might have had a 'million dollar body' in the earlier days, but good living had turned his once toned muscles to fat. What looked suspiciously like a double chin was forming, and his reddish hair was greying at the temples. 'Working for Mr Crowley is a full-time occupation, Governor. Now, if you look to your right, we're coming in to the Mayflower Estates area of Preston Hollow . . . As you're probably aware, George W. Bush and his wife have moved here, and it's home to the likes of Ross Perot, along with any number of business tycoons.'

'The Crespi-Hicks estate is somewhere around here?' asked Davis, his hand once again creeping across the plush leather of the rear seat.

'Valued at US $135 million and it sits on 25 acres, but none of these mansions come even close to Ploutos Park,' Rachel said, once more removing Davis's hand. Named after the Greek god of wealth, Crowley's estate sat on a staggering 79 acres. The six-storey stone mansion included fifteen bedrooms, twenty bathrooms, a library, a ballroom where ten huge crystal chandeliers hung from a cavernous ceiling, a large art-deco bar, a main kitchen lined with eighteenth-century Delft tiles, and a separate indoor commercial catering kitchen. The home theatre took up half the third floor, with the other half allocated to a games room.

The driver slowed the big Cadillac and pressed the remote, and the big wrought iron gates swung silently on their hinges.

'Impressive driveway,' Davis observed, as they came to a halt under a stone portico supported by four immense Greek-style stone pillars. The driver opened the rear door and saluted. Sheldon Crowley waited beside the heavy double cedar doors of the main house.

'Welcome to Ploutos Park, Carter,' he said, extending his hand. 'My wife Lillian sends her apologies, but she will join us later. We've put you in one of the guesthouses. Hank will take your bags over, and in the meantime, Chef has prepared lunch which we'll have in the cellar.'

Crowley led the way across the expensive black-and-white Italian tiles of the entry foyer, where four of the great masters, acquired legitimately, took pride of place: a Renoir, a Monet, a Raphael and a Cézanne. He turned left into the library, which was panelled in Italian walnut, past a feature wall that had cost a cool US $1 million per square metre, tiled in diamond, mother of pearl, abalone shell and black onyx. Rachel and Davis followed Crowley past display cases of priceless Egyptian artifacts, including a full-size mummy, down heavy wooden steps to the underground cellar.

'I had it modelled on the barrel room of Château Margaux. Are you familiar with that château?' Crowley asked.

'Can't say I am,' said Davis, casting his eyes around the cavernous cellar.

No surprises there, Rachel thought. Davis, she suspected, would have difficulty distinguishing a chardonnay from a chablis. Stone pillars supported the roof, and soft lighting played on the arches of the ceiling. Chef stood ready to carve rare roast beef. Crowley's personal sommelier was on hand to serve the wine. The rest of the cellar lunch, including crabs and freshly shucked oysters, was laid out on a long rough-hewn table in the centre of the cavern, the walls of which were lined with stone recesses containing thousands of bottles of the world's rarest wines.

'So how are things up in Montana?' Crowley asked, after the first course of Chesapeake Bay chowder was served and the sommelier had poured a 2004 Tyrrell's Vat 1 semillon from one of the world's leading semillon *terroirs* in the Hunter Valley of Australia.

'We'd be doin' a whole better if it weren't for those latte-sippin' greenies tryin' to tell us what we can and can't mine,' said Davis, emptying half a glass of semillon in one gulp.

Rachel nodded surreptitiously toward the sommelier, who immediately refilled the governor's glass.

'There's enough shale oil in Montana to make American self-sufficient into the next century, but all those greenies do is whinge and whine about the water table this, and the toxic waste that, hazardous methane this, and contaminated drinking water that . . . they're like a broken record.'

Crowley smiled. The conversation was going in precisely the direction he wanted. 'Washington any help?'

'Washington? You've got to be kidding me, Sheldon. Washington's nothing but a contraceptive to the prick of progress. They can't even get their act together over gray wolves. I doubt half of 'em have ever been outside the beltway. Congress keeps wolves on the endangered species list, and in the meantime they're wreaking havoc on the herds. The ranchers have had a gut full of Washington, and so have I,' Davis grumbled, alternately gulping at his wine and attacking a full lobster and rare roast beef. 'Hunting wolves might not be legal in Pennsylvania and Constitution Avenues, but up where I come from, wolves are vermin, end of story.'

Crowley nodded to the sommelier. The sommelier had decided on an Australian theme, and Kellermeister's 2008 shiraz from the Barossa in the south of Australia had not only taken out 'Best Barossa Shiraz' and 'Best Australian Shiraz', it had been accorded the 'Best Shiraz in the World' by over 400 judges at the London Wine Show. That achievement, Crowley decided, would be lost on Davis, so he moved straight to the punch line. 'There's a way to fix all of this,' he said.

'And how's that?' asked Davis.

'You could call the shots from Washington.'

'And how do you suppose I might do that, Sheldon?'

'Simple. Run for president.'

'Yeah, right. Those assholes have got the game sewn up down there. Besides, if you want to compete, you've got to have some very big backers, Sheldon. I've seen the figures . . . the campaign in 2008 cost over US $750 million.'

'Have a look around you, Carter. What do you see?'

'Huh? . . . Wine.'

'Not just any wine, Carter. There are over 8000 bottles of the world's rarest wines in this cellar, including two cases of Henri Jayer Richebourg Grand Cru, which, if you can get hold of it, comes in at over $20 000 a bottle. The jet that picked you up would set you back around $70 million.'

'Meaning . . .'

Oh God, thought Rachel. He's thicker than I thought.

'After we've finished here, I'll get Rachel to show you around, Carter, but this is no ordinary estate. The backing is here, and we want you to run.'

Davis shook his head. 'I'm quite comfortable where I am, thanks. They don't call Montana "Big Sky Country" for nothing. I'm mountain born and bred.'

And doesn't it show, Rachel thought. *Surely* Sheldon can't be serious.

'We'd still like you to run.'

'Afraid not, Sheldon, but it's mighty nice of you to offer, just the same,' said Davis, draining his glass again.

Crowley dismissed the staff, and turned back to Governor Davis. 'It's not that simple, Carter. You see, Washington and the greenies are not only causing you problems in Montana . . . they're causing me big problems down here. Granted, there are a lot of attractions for you in Montana. Stunning mountains, beautiful four-legged wildlife, and then there are the two-legged locals . . . and some of them are *very* attractive, in and out of bed.'

Davis coloured visibly. 'What the hell are you talkin' about, Crowley? I'll have you know that I've run on a ticket of faith and family values for the last ten years, and I'm not about to —'

'Spare me the crap, Davis,' said Crowley, an icy edge to his voice. 'You might have run on that hogshit, but you've been screwing your ass off every chance you get.'

'How dare you . . . who the fuck do you think you are? I'm leaving!' Davis got up, unsteady on his feet, and the chair fell backwards behind him.

'Your bedroom's in Helena, in the governor's mansion at 2 North Carson Street, two blocks from the Montana State Capitol building. Yet you seem to have two more bedrooms in Billings, or at least Emma Cooper and Brooklyn Murphy do, and you spend quite of bit of time in theirs, which is interesting, because they're both on your staff, yet neither is aware of your involvement with the other.'

Davis steadied himself, gripping the edge of the heavy wooden table, and Rachel watched the colour drain from his face.

'And then of course there's Harper Scott in Bozeman, and Abigail Roxburgh in Missoula.'

'You've got no proof of this, Crowley. You're just picking out names of employees I mix with in the course of my duties.'

'"Duties" has a broad definition in your lexicon, Davis. Missoula's a nice spot for picnics – confluence of the Clark Fork and Bitterroot Rivers – and given your platform of faith and family, you were smart enough to park out of sight, or so you thought.' Crowley paused, and then came in for the kill.

'Sit down, Davis.'

Rachel picked up the chair, more out of practicality than sympathy. What a pathetic individual this politician was, she thought. One of the many who preached faith and morals the loudest, and ignored them most often. And Crowley wanted him in the White House, the most powerful position in the world? For a fleeting moment, Rachel wondered about her involvement with Crowley and his empire. In her darkest moments, she increasingly questioned this, but she had long planned to oust the cloying Lillian. Now was not the time to lose focus.

'We are well aware that neither your wife nor your three children have any idea of your infidelities, Carter, and you're very fortunate that your peccadillos haven't come to the attention of the media . . . but when they do, you'll be finished, not only as a politician, but as a husband and a father. Not because you've been found out – plenty of politicians in this country have survived sexual scandals, but I can't think of one of them who survived when he was running on a campaign of faith and family.'

'When they come to the attention of the media? Are you threatening me, Crowley?'

Crowley shrugged. 'You can take it any way you like. To be frank, up until now, I couldn't have given a shit whose bedrooms you've haunted.'

'What do you mean "up until now"?'

'It's quite simple, Carter, because now, I need someone in the White House who can ensure policies are favourable for big business. Policies that are not held hostage by objections to fracking, or coal seam gas, or any of the other rubbish that the Left comes up with. I need someone in the White House who is unequivocally pro-jobs and pro the economy, and none of the Republicans running at present would know if a San Francisco trolley car was up their ass until the people got off, and even then you'd have to ring the bell – so that *someone* is you. You *will* run for the White House, and EVRAN will fund your campaign. Rachel here is not overjoyed at the prospect of managing it, but you will do exactly as she says.'

'And if I don't?' Davis demanded truculently.

Rachel rolled her eyes. This guy just didn't get it. For her to manage Davis through the primaries and gain the Republican nomination would be a monumental achievement, but the White

House? That, Rachel mused, was miracle territory. General Dwight D. Eisenhower might have slept with his driver, Kay Summersby, during World War Two, and Kennedy may have slept with Marlene Dietrich and Marilyn Monroe, to name but two, but they were intelligent men. Still, if Warren Harding, arguably the dumbest candidate in the history of the Presidency, could win in 1920, and if Andrew Johnson, who had turned up drunk at Abraham Lincoln's inauguration and was later one of only two presidents to be impeached – if they could gain the White House, it was possible, and she turned her thoughts to how she might secure the million dollar bonus Crowley had offered.

Crowley had anticipated Davis's reaction and he nodded to Rachel. Area 15 had obtained the video using cutting-edge surveillance techniques. Better equipped than either the CIA or the Mossad, Area 15's results were invariably impressive. The video had been shot at a distance, but Area 15's laser technology captured the audio, and the facial expressions of both Davis and Abigail, the well-endowed blonde PR executive from Missoula, were very clear.

The vision showed Davis parking his big Chevrolet Tahoe in the bushes opposite Kelly Island and the Bitterroot River.

'I promise you, sweetheart, when the next election is over, I'll be in my second term, and a divorce won't matter, but you've got to stay with me on this. It's you I love, and we'll be together.'

'You promise, Carty?'

Rachel stifled a desire to vomit.

'I promise . . .' The audio was reduced to heavy breathing and the camera caught their embrace in all its steamy detail, Davis plunging his hand down Abigail's ample cleavage, then fumbling for her dress zipper and the catch on her bra.

'Have you seen enough, Davis?'

'You bastard!' Davis had gone white.

'Rachel will show you the way to your guesthouse. Dinner will be at eight,' said Crowley, 'where we'll be joined by my wife, Lillian, and Pastor Shipley.'

'You're staying in one of two guesthouses,' Rachel said, as she led the way across the patio at the rear of the house on to a sandstone pathway and across a beautifully manicured lawn.

'What's that in there,' Davis asked, pointing to a collection of buildings shaded by tall, gracious oak trees.

'That's the fitness centre . . . Olympic pool, sauna, Jacuzzi and a massage studio, along with a conference centre.' It was rarely used by Crowley, except to entertain.

'I can get a massage?'

Not your sort of massage, Rachel thought. 'Of course. Or if you prefer, beyond the fitness centre are two tennis courts and an eighteen-hole championship golf course, where the professional will fit you out for shoes and clubs.' A small army of gardeners and horticulturists kept the golf course, tennis courts, hedges, rose gardens, vegetable garden and greenhouses in immaculate condition.

'Crowley has his own professional?'

'Mr Crowley doesn't do things by halves, Governor Davis,' said Rachel, as they reached the first of two opulent guesthouses. The price tag for Crowley's estate had never been published, but Rachel knew it dwarfed Los Angeles' US $125 million Fleur de Lys estate, Miami's Casa Casuarina and New York's CitySpire Penthouse. Rachel opened the door and stepped back to allow Davis access.

'Care for a drink?' he said, placing his arm around her waist.

'Let's get one thing clear right from the start, Governor Davis,'

Rachel said, removing his arm. 'Between now and the first Tuesday in November, you and I are going to be spending a lot of time together, and that time will be purely – *purely* – on a professional basis.'

'Ah, Carter. I trust you found everything in your accommodation to your liking.' By dinner, any trace of the real Sheldon Crowley had disappeared, and he radiated hospitality and diplomacy. 'Let me introduce my wife Lillian,' he said. Lillian was dressed in an impeccable Aquascutum black silk twin set, and black Stuart Weitzman shoes studded with diamonds. Her ample neck was adorned with string of Paspaley pearls, harvested off the west coast of Australia from the rare *Pinctada maxima* oyster. Known for producing the world's finest pearls, the original baroque string was of such rare quality it had taken several years to compile. They were complemented by Paspaley pearl earrings set in twenty-one-carat rose gold.

'Delighted to meet you, ma'am,' said Davis, still not sober despite a two-hour nap.

'And this is Pastor Shipley,' continued Crowley. 'Matthias has been part of the family for years now.'

'Delighted, Pastor,' said Davis. Looking slightly uncomfortable, he took the pale-faced pastor's outstretched hand.

'Sheldon tells me you're planning on running for president,' Shipley said, as they repaired to the smaller, more intimate of Ploutos Park's two dining rooms. The Italian suite featured high-backed silver chairs finished in gold brocade. The large table was inlaid with silver and gold and supported by four cherubs carved out of stone. Two huge oval mirrors hung above matching sideboards.

'I haven't announced it yet,' said Davis, 'but Sheldon has been very generous with his suggestions and support.'

Rachel maintained a neutral expression, but she was surprised by Davis' sudden change of heart. Was it the threat of exposure, she wondered, or had Davis genuinely reconsidered? Whatever the reasons, Rachel had no doubt that the perks of office would feature prominently in Davis's acceptance.

'Where do you think your appeal to the voters will lie?' asked Lillian, keen to get to know a little more about the candidate her husband had so suddenly announced.

'For the last three years, as the governor of Montana, I've run on a platform of faith and family. Montanans don't wear their religion on their sleeves but leaving aside the natives, they're mainly Catholic and Protestant. A platform of faith has served me very well, both as a compass for my personal life, and for guidance in making the crucial decisions that affect everyday Montanans.'

Rachel observed her new charge with interest. Davis was now clearly back in political spin mode, and if he'd managed to pass the bullshit test in the rough and tumble world of Montana, perhaps he might be able to bamboozle the broader American public for long enough to gain the keys to 1600 Pennsylvania Avenue. But it would depend on him keeping his dick in his pants, and that might be a big ask.

'We're basing Governor Davis's campaign on jobs and the economy. The issues that matter most to ordinary Americans, but I'm under no illusions as to the importance of the evangelical Christian vote,' said Rachel, 'and to that end, any support you can provide will be greatly appreciated, Pastor.' Rachel was acutely aware of Karl Rove's strategy to mobilise the Christian Right behind George

W. Bush in the 2000 election. Without that evangelical support, Al Gore would have been president.

Pastor Shipley seemed deep in thought, and he didn't reply immediately. 'Yes . . . Sheldon has already raised this with me, and I am of course, very happy to help,' he said finally, turning to Davis. 'A campaign slogan of "Faith and Family" is fine for the average voter, but there are around forty million evangelical Christians in this country, and they're a little more discerning. If you are to gain their support, Carter, it will depend on your *personal* relationship with Christ our Saviour, and if you're elected as our president, they will expect you to have God at the centre of your administration. Your administration must define itself by its Christian morals and ethics.'

Rachel groaned inwardly. It was going to be a *very* hypocritical campaign. But in the face of the likely Democrat candidate, the impressive Hailey Campbell, she knew they needed Pastor Matthias B. Shipley on board.

'I will organise a meeting of a thousand pastors whose influence stretches across this entire country and beyond – pastors like Bobby Calhoun, who runs the American Christian Broadcast Foundation. He reaches over seventy million Americans through his television and radio programs, and he's a very powerful man to have on side in an election campaign.'

The same Bobby Calhoun who had described Islam as an evil religion, Rachel mused, and had declared Hurricane Katrina 'God's retribution on the wickedness of New Orleans, Mississippi and Alabama'. An already weird state of politics in America was about to get a whole lot weirder.

30

MIRJAVEH, PAKISTAN–IRAN BORDER

Yousef dozed in the front seat of the first of the two Bedford trucks, both loaded with Pakistani sheesham logs, a timber of the rosewood genus, known for its unique grains, and much prized by the furniture manufacturing industry. The convoy had left the outskirts of Quetta before dawn, following the long, straight desert highway west toward the border with Iran. To the north the rugged, bare granite of the snow-capped Chagai mountains marked the border between Baluchistan Province and Afghanistan. Every so often, a lonely blue sign would announce the distance to the next small town, with the inevitable mosque and flat-roofed stone houses in an otherwise featureless desert.

It wasn't until late afternoon before Yousef was suddenly alert. The truck slowed, and they entered Taftan, the last town before the border with Iran, a few hundred metres further on. The highway was littered with rubbish, and a goat herd was unhurriedly moving his animals from the highway toward the town square.

They skirted the truck park on the Pakistan side and joined thirty more semi-trailers, queued at the Iranian border town of Mirjaveh and the crossing of the rail line from Quetta to the first major Iranian town, Zahedan to the west.

Colourful portraits of the bearded Ayatollah Ali Hosseini Khamenei, the Supreme Leader of Iran, were painted on the sides of the buildings. Here the dirt streets were clean. Barbed wire stretched into the foothills of the mountains to the north. To the south, a heavily fortified three-metre-high wall was under construction, running from Mirjaveh across 700 kilometres of desert to the town of Mand. Coupled with berms, ditches, and forts, it was designed to deter illegal immigrants and to stop the flow of drugs.

Yousef smiled to himself. With over four million users out of a population of 73 million, Iran, he knew, had the highest rate of opiate addiction in the world, and if the Ayatollahs thought they were going to stop the import of drugs with a three-metre wall, they were kidding themselves. The narcotics came from an area referred to as the 'Golden Crescent', an area that overlapped Afghanistan, Pakistan and Iran, and despite the Infidel spending more than US $7 billion trying to eradicate it, production had steadily increased. The Infidel was not very clever, he thought. Poppy growers in Afghanistan could get up to US $200 for a kilogram of dry opium, compared to forty cents for a kilogram of wheat. Of the world's annual production of over 9000 tonnes of opium, over 75 per cent came across the border from Afghanistan to Pakistan, where it was processed into heroin and then exported back to Iran and on to Europe. Yousef, for one, applauded. Much to the chagrin of the Infidel, opium was one of the key sources of finance for both the Taliban and al Qaeda.

The truck queue inched forward, and it was over two hours before Yousef was asked for his papers by the Iranian security guards.

'Get out of the truck,' the guard ordered.

Captain Kazaz pulled up the computer file for the 300 000-tonne supertanker *Leila*, a Lebanese flagged tanker in the Port Control Centre at Saudi Arabia's Ras Tanura oil port. He logged into the Terminal Ship Information System and checked on *Leila*'s history. Unlike some others, the supertanker was well maintained, although he made a mental note to check whether a minor deficiency, a faulty auxiliary pump, had been repaired since her last visit. Arabia's massive sea-island oil terminal was located just to the north of Dammam, the capital of the Eastern Province, the largest of Saudi Arabia's provinces and the most oil-rich area in the world. Ras Tanura meant 'cape oven', and it was aptly named. A searing heat enveloped the peninsula that protruded into the Persian Gulf.

Kazaz paused to take in the mass of consoles and control screens, the heartbeat of the state-of-the-art Vessel Traffic Management System, which at any second provided the exact position, bearing and approach and departure speeds of the massive tankers. He checked the wind speeds, currents, tide and the weather. Of greatest concern was the wind, and today it was blowing at 25 knots from the north-west. All ships, especially large tankers, acted like a sail. The wind blowing at 90 degrees on the *Leila,* a tanker 320 metres long with a height of 25 metres, would create a force of some 85 tonnes, but the *Leila*'s bow thrusters were rated at 2000 kilowatts, which would provide 27 tonnes of thrust. Each of Ras Tanura's four tugs, equipped with precise Voith-Schneider propulsion units, provided an additional 50 tonnes of thrust, and Kazaz was confident he had plenty in reserve should there be any trouble.

The 60-metre-high control tower swayed in the wind, and Kazaz looked north, toward the maze of pipes, cracking towers and storage tanks that defined the vast oil refinery. To the east, long piers jutted into the turquoise waters of the gulf. The south pier consisted of four berths capable of handling smaller 45 000-tonne tankers. It was here that a mere 80 000 barrels were loaded on to a small oil tanker in May 1939, the very first Saudi crude from the world's largest reserves. A little further up the coast, the north pier extended nearly two kilometres into the gulf. It had a capacity to berth six tankers simultaneously, but was still limited to tankers under 135 000 tonnes. To accommodate the massive ultra large crude carriers, or ULCCs, of 500 000 tonnes, four sea islands had been built in the gulf. The supertankers had a draught of over twenty metres, and were over four football fields in length. Backed by massive pumps, huge four-foot-diameter submarine pipelines delivered up to three million barrels of crude oil to these giants of the sea.

Saudi Aramco had originally started life as a joint American–Saudi venture in 1933, when the first King of Saudi Arabia, ibn Saud, granted a prospecting concession to American oil concerns. When oil was discovered in 1938, the company became known as the Saudi Arabian American oil company, or ARAMCO. After a long and bitter fight over royalties, the largest oil company in the world was finally nationalised in 1980, and brought under the direct control of the House of Saud and myriad princes, the lavish lifestyles of whom were an anathema to the likes of Jamal and Yousef.

Kazaz made a final call to the *Leila*'s agent to ensure customs and clearances were in order. He took the lift down to the car park and drove the short distance to the north pier where the *el-Alat 9*, one of four pilot boats, was waiting to take him out to the *Leila*.

'*Abqaiq, Manifa, Najimah, Tanajib* – are you in position, over?'

The four tugs acknowledged in turn and Kazaz assigned them positions running alphabetically from fore through to aft. That made it easier for him to remember where each tug was attached.

'This is the pilot, estimate your location in ten minutes, over.'

'*Leila,* roger . . . rope ladder is in position on the starboard side.'

'Make a run along the hull,' Kazaz ordered when he reached the tanker, towering above him. He checked *Leila*'s draft. The hull markings were registering 20.5 metres, close to the maximum of 21 metres. The helmsman brought the pilot boat alongside and Kazaz swung on to the ropes in one practised movement.

'*Shukran* . . . thank you,' said Kazaz, and he climbed sure-footedly to the deck high above him, where Abdullah Hadid, the master of the *Leila*, was waiting.

'*Ahlan wa sahlan* . . . welcome on board,' the short, wiry master said, extending his hand, a look of relief on his face. Despite his twenty years experience as a ship's master, Hadid was never comfortable in the close confines of a port or terminal where he was unsure of the currents and where the shipping lanes were crowded. Together, they signed the ship's register and commenced the pre-unberthing safety check with a tour of the tanker's vast deck, checking on mooring lines and anchor cables. Kazaz ensured that the Chiksan arms, the marine loading arms that enabled the crude to be pumped into the huge tanks, were safely disconnected and stowed on the sea island. Satisfied, he stepped into the *Leila*'s elevator with the captain and rode up seven storeys to the bridge, above which flew a red and white flag, indicating the pilot was on board.

English was the international language of the sea, and having ascertained that Captain Hadid, along with the *Leila*'s chief engineer, could communicate well, Kazaz familiarised himself with the layout of the bridge: the chart table, radars and helmsman's position, and the repeater dials, and then he briefed Hadid on the plan for unberthing.

'The wind is from the north-west at 25 knots, and the current is running at one and a half knots, so we'll use that to help ease the stern away from the aft dolphin,' Kazaz explained, while he waited for the four tug captains to confirm they were secured.

'Standby engines, single up lines,' he ordered. Kazaz walked across to the port wing of the big bridge and watched the dolphin crews cast off all but the essential mooring hawsers at the bow and the stern.

'*Leila* stern . . . let go aft . . . port twenty . . . dead slow ahead.' Kazaz listened while his orders were repeated back to him. '*Manifa, Najimah, Tanajib,* half astern.' On the bridge of the stern tug, *Tanajib,* the meter registering the strain on the line touched 80 tonnes and the stern of the huge tanker slowly swung away from the aft dolphin.

'Bow, this is bridge, let go for'ard . . . midships . . . dead slow astern . . . *Manifa* . . . come around to port.'

The massive tanker eased out into the channel and the four tugs, like attentive sheep dogs, responded instantly to Kazaz's measured commands. When manoeuvring a behemoth like this, Kazaz knew well that slow was good, and degree by degree, the monstrous bow, nearly 300 metres for'ard of the bridge, came around onto a heading for the narrow and treacherous Strait of Hormuz.

'It is sheesham timber,' Yousef explained to the Iranian Mirjaveh border guard, who seemed to be having difficulty reading the invoice. 'Two truckloads destined for a furniture shop in Bandar Abbas.' Yousef knew that if the border guards checked, they would find that Sheesham Furniture Bandar Abbas was a registered business, but eventually they would discover it was a shell company. 'They make very good furniture there,' Yousef added with a smile. The guard relaxed a little, walked around both trucks and returned a short while later with the paperwork stamped and approved.

Yousef settled back into the front passenger seat of the Bedford and the convoy headed north-west on Highway 84, across the Kavir-e Loot desert, where the temperature of the sand could get as high as 70°C, and on toward Zahedan, an Iranian desert city of half a million people. The air temperature had climbed and a heat haze shimmered off the desert on either side of the road.

Yousef connected his laptop through a satellite link, opened up the stamp website and logged in under the username of 'Ledifni'.

'Have just acquired a US #231 1893 Columbian Commemorative stamp,' he posted, together with the image of the American Bank Note Company's two-cent stamp. 'A much-desired boost to my collection . . . it is giving me a great deal of happiness.'

An hour later, the Bedford trucks ground their way past flat-roofed houses toward the centre of the city, where a large crowd had gathered near the Ali Ibn Abi Talib Mosque, chanting *Allahu Akbar! Allahu Akbar!* Three bodies swung in the breeze beneath a makeshift gantry, suspended from thick ropes around their necks. Yousef could hear the governor shouting through loud speakers. Two days before, an explosion had rocked the centre of the city.

'Let this be a lesson! These terrorists have been corrupt on earth. They have waged war against God, and they have acted contrary to national security! They were agents of arrogance . . . agents of arrogance!' the governor warned. It was a term the clerics used to refer to the United States. 'There is no doubt they were hired by the Great Satan to disrupt our lives!'

Yousef directed the driver to take a side street that led to one of al Qaeda's safe houses, where the two Toyota four-wheel drives were fuelled and ready to go.

A short while later, the enlarged convoy, led by Yousef in one of the Toyotas, headed west across the desert for Bam, the site of an ancient citadel on the old Silk Road which dated back to the sixth century BC. But the citadel was now in ruins. On 26 December 2003, an earthquake registering 6.6 on the Richter Scale had struck, killing 26 000 people, and the old fortress had been destroyed.

From there, the convoy headed northwest again, before turning south on Highway 91, where the trucks were forced to engage low gear as they ground their way up into the barren rocks of the Jebal Barez mountains. At the top of the range, Yousef could see a vast plain stretching below them, and in the distance, the Halil River and the city of Jiroft, one of the hottest places in Iran. They pushed on to the south, past the suddenly green cultivated fields of Anbarābād, and on through Kahnooj and Dehbārez, until they reached Minab, 100 kilometres to the east of Bandar Abbas. Minab was famous for its prawns and date palms, but more importantly for Yousef, it provided a safe house close to the coast and the Strait of Hormuz.

Yousef led the way through the centre of the city, past the roadside portraits of the bearded Ayatollah Khamenei, dressed in his traditional black turban and robes. The traffic was surprisingly light, and Yousef guessed correctly that the city's occupants had gravitated to the famous Panjshambe Bazar or 'Thursday's Bazaar', where vendors were selling anything from *ghalyeh mahi*, a spicy fish stew, to Persian carpets. Here, the older women wore the full-length burqa. Younger women wore long dresses and the headscarf or hijab, and to protect their faces from the heat, many women wore colourful woven masks, unique to this part of Iran.

A short distance past the city centre, Yousef turned off into a dirt lane leading to a lone, adobe mud-brick house. For the past two years, it had been home to al Qaeda agents inside Iran. Yousef gave orders to unload the timber from the trucks and configure the missile tubes.

Over 2000 kilometres away, in his villa in the hills above Islamabad, it was seven-thirty p.m. General Khan received the alert on his laptop, and he reached for a mobile he used rarely. 'Columbus has landed,' he texted. A further 12 500 kilometres away in Dallas, it was eight-thirty in the morning and Sheldon Crowley was at his desk on the eighty-second floor of EVRAN Towers. He sent a short encrypted direction to René du Bois, in the headquarters of the Crédit Group in Paris. 'Buy oil and sell all other stocks'.

The World Federation of Exchanges based in Paris took in

fifty-two regulated stock market exchanges around the world. René du Bois smiled and he swivelled in his leather chair toward a bank of screens providing him with a dizzying array of up-to-the-minute financial charts. One screen showed the total value of world equities at US $54.57 trillion. The Dow Jones industrial average was up nearly half a per cent, Standard & Poors 500 Index was up a third of a per cent, and the Nasdaq Composite Index was also up by 0.98 per cent. The figures would have meant little to the average person in the street, but to Du Bois, they represented gains of hundreds of millions of dollars. He keyed in a code, and a string of classified assessments from highly paid market analysts in Crédit Group appeared on another of his screens. Oil had rallied, and more importantly, Crédit Group analysts had estimated that over the next twelve months, world demand for oil would increase by 850 000 barrels per day, taking global demand to over ninety million barrels a day. Growth in the Chinese economy, even though down 0.2 per cent, was still expected to be at a healthy 7.5 per cent.

Not for very much longer, Du Bois mused. With insider knowledge, Crédit Group had made billions getting out of equities before the devastating effects of the 2008 crash. The value of world stocks had plunged a staggering 47 per cent, but stock markets had largely recovered since then. Pharos was right, it was time to strike again.

Du Bois keyed in another code, and pulled up the top twenty-five oil stocks by capitalisation. Over the past few weeks, Crédit Group had quietly increased its holdings in companies like ExxonMobil, BP, Chevron, Royal Dutch Shell, the Brazilian behemoth Petrobras and its counterpart in Asia, Petro China. The sheer volume of stock had driven share prices up nearly two percentage points, but Du Bois knew the surge in oil stocks in twenty-four hours' time would be considerably more dramatic, and the impact on world stock markets would not stop there.

Abdullah Hadid, the master of the *Leila,* rubbed his eyes. He had been on deck for nearly twenty-four hours, right through the tricky berthing at Ras Tanura, and the loading of over two million barrels of crude, but he would not hand over to the officer of the watch until the massive tanker was clear of the Strait of Hormuz and well into the Gulf of Oman where they would head for the Arabian Sea.

Hadid checked the radar plot, noting the blips on the screen that represented other ships. The southern shipping lane was reserved for outbound vessels, and *Leila* was almost abeam of the fishing village of Khasab, located on Oman's Musandam cape at the northernmost tip of the Arabian Peninsula. Ahead was the *Gulf Lexicon*, a Liberian flagged tanker of just over 200 000 tonnes. Ten nautical miles behind, another Dutch flagged tanker of similar tonnage, the *Black Viking,* was maintaining a steady 12 knots, smashing through the heavy chop. Hadid knew it would soon be time to begin a series of changes of course that would take the *Leila* through 270 degrees around the notorious bend between the coast of Iran and Oman. Hadid also noted a line of radar blips in the northern inbound shipping lane. Even though there was a three-kilometre median separating the inbound and outbound lanes, when large ships were operating in close proximity, that was not a lot of distance.

Hadid walked outside on to the port wing of the *Leila*'s bridge and scanned the horizon through his binoculars. It was as he suspected.

Even though the sun was setting, the shape was unmistakable. The 100 000-tonne Nimitz-class nuclear aircraft carrier USS *Truman* was entering the Gulf to join the American Fifth Fleet based out of Manama in Bahrain, just to the south of the Saudi refinery. Although the massive carrier's top speed was classified, it was powered by two nuclear reactors generating over a quarter of a million horsepower. The carrier's four huge screws gave the ship a staggering speed of over 30 knots. Manned by over 3200 officers and men, and escorted by the guided missile cruiser *Gettysburg,* and an array of destroyers, she carried ninety aircraft, including F/A-18 fighters, F-14B Tomcats, EA-6B Prowlers, and E-2C Hawkeyes. Hadid smiled to himself. Navigation laws in the confined waters of the Gulf stipulated they be on the surface, but the US Navy didn't always comply with regulations. Lurking beneath the relatively calm evening waters would, he knew, be the USS *Hyman G. Rickover,* and the USS *Bergall*. American nuclear carriers never went *anywhere* without at least one, and usually two nuclear submarines for extra protection. Ten nautical miles astern of Carrier Group Ten, an even larger vessel was looming on the horizon, all 500 000 tonnes of her: the *Atlantic Giant*, a tanker so massive it was too big to fit through the new locks of the Panama Canal, and too big to manoeuvre in the English Channel.

Hadid checked his position. They were now abeam the small fishing village of Kumzar, the most northerly inhabited place in Oman and accessible only by boat. It was time to begin the long turn that would take them around the rocky islands at the tip of the Arabian Peninsula.

'Starboard ten,' Hadid ordered.

'Starboard ten,' the helmsman acknowledged. Even though the ship's powerful hydraulics had acted in an instant, turning *Leila*'s state-of-the art rudders, such was the momentum of a supertanker that Hadid knew it would be several hundred metres more before the bow started to turn. Even in an emergency, with the engines straining at full astern, he knew it would take more than three nautical miles to stop her.

He looked past the myriad pumps and pipelines running for hundreds of metres up to the *Leila*'s bow. The sun was setting, shedding an orange glow on the white, choppy surface of the sea.

Yousef led the small convoy back down the dirt lane into Minab, and then south along the coast on Route 91. The missile launchers were now fully assembled on the back trays of the Bedford trucks, and covered with tightly lashed tarpaulins. To the west, the sun was setting in a fiery ball, reflected in a purple-orange heat haze over the shipping lanes of the Hormuz Strait and the Persian Gulf. To the east, a line of bare rocky hills paralleled the Iranian coast.

Traffic was light, and Yousef drove steadily. They passed through the small towns of Talvar and Bemãni-ye-gachine, veering closer to the coast until they reached Bondãrãn. Here, Yousef took a minor road that led east into the hills, the desert broken here and there by small oases where palm trees flourished on water courses. Three kilometres further on, Yousef turned off the road.

'Those palm trees over there,' he commanded, directing the trucks. 'Get the tarpaulins off, quickly . . . Get them ready!' Yousef knew they might still be seen by the Infidel's drones, but the sun had now set, and at least they were hidden from view on the ground. He climbed a rocky outcrop and focused his powerful binoculars on the shipping lanes in the Strait. Yousef could not believe the images in the twin lens. It was beyond his wildest dreams. *'Alhamdulillah! Allah be praised!'* he cried.

'Starboard ten,' Hadid ordered.

'Starboard ten,' the helmsman acknowledged.

The *Atlantic Giant* was approaching from the east. As big a supertanker as the *Leila* was, Hadid never ceased to be in awe of the ULCCs, of which there were only three in the world. The *Atlantic Giant* was still riding relatively high in the water, and Hadid guessed that she had already loaded some crude prior to calling in to the Gulf. Powered by a massive 50 000-shaft horsepower engine, the turbulence from her single 30-foot diameter, 50-tonne propeller was clearly visible. Capable of fitting four St Paul's Cathedrals into her holds, and longer than the Empire State building was tall, the *Atlantic Giant* would take on another two million barrels of crude oil.

Captain Rogers, together with his crew, weapons controller Sergeant Michelle Brady, and CIA intelligence analyst Major Ryan Crowe, took their places in the Creech Air Force Base briefing room and waited for the commander of the 432nd Wing, Colonel Joe Stillwell, to begin.

'The president has ordered an increased presence in the Persian Gulf,' Stillwell began, 'and as a result, the Fifth Fleet is being reinforced with the Harry S. Truman Carrier Group Ten,' said

Stillwell, throwing up real-time classified satellite imagery on to the screen. 'Notwithstanding the progress being made on the Iranian nuclear issue, the second carrier is a response to the increasingly aggressive rhetoric coming out of Tehran, including their threats to close the Strait of Hormuz. The Iranians have a layered strategy,' Stillwell continued, 'and they base this on anti-ship cruise missiles, naval mines and the Islamic Revolutionary Guard's fleet of fast attack craft.' He flicked up a photograph of the small but deadly speedboats. 'They're armed with torpedoes and rocket launchers, and our ships are particularly vulnerable in this busy waterway. It's not only narrow, but movement is restricted by up to twenty supertankers a day transiting the area. As a result, we now have an additional task, protecting the Fifth Fleet.

'We'll be operating our aircraft out of Qatar, providing twenty-four hour coverage over the Persian Gulf,' Stillwell continued, pulling up a satellite overhead of the huge al-Udeid Air Base outside of Doha, the capital of Qatar. The Arab monarchy was located on a peninsula just to the south of Bahrain and the Ras Tanura oil refinery. With the third largest natural gas reserves in the world, the tiny country was the world's richest. 'Any questions?'

'What's the situation with the Iranians, sir?' Sergeant Brady asked.

'In terms of potential for a conflict to escalate out of control, the Persian Gulf is on a par with the Cuban missile crisis,' said Stillwell. 'The present standoff with Iran over nuclear weapons is only the latest in a long history of brinkmanship.' Stillwell flashed up an image of the Iranian minelayer, *Iran Ajr*, the mines clearly visible on her decks. 'Most of you guys are too young to remember, but in September 1987, we launched Operation Praying Mantis, tracking the *Iran Ajr* out of its home port in Iran into international waters where it started to lay mines in the shipping channels. Our Special Forces helicopters and a SEAL team attacked the ship and disabled it. Unfortunately, we were not able to recover all the mines and the guided missile frigate USS *Samuel B. Roberts* was holed the following year when it hit one. During Praying Mantis, we sank an Iranian frigate, a gunboat and six of their armed speedboats . . . so this area can blow out of control very quickly.

'As to operations in the region's airspace,' Stillwell continued, 'some of you who have joined us recently may not be aware that last year, Captain Rogers was conducting surveillance over international waters in the Persian Gulf, when his predator drone was engaged by two Iranian Su-25 fighters.' Stillwell allowed himself a smile. 'They're not very good shots,' he said, 'but nevertheless, the Revolutionary Guard are aggressive, and they may try again.' Stillwell paused, choosing his words carefully. 'But they are playing a very dangerous game. It goes without saying that we are not, repeat not, to engage Iranian aircraft unless specifically authorised to do so.'

'Ready to fire?' Yousef called. The trucks were parked side on to the Strait, the launcher tubes for the gleaming white Taipan missiles now exposed, small portable radars humming. Number One missile launcher had already acquired the *Leila* at the relatively short range of 15 nautical miles, well inside its maximum of 75; and the number two launcher had locked on to the *Atlantic Giant,* in the closer inbound channel.

'Ready One!'

'Ready Two!'

Yousef made a final sweep with his binoculars. Apart from a small wooden fishing vessel, the seas adjacent to the coast of Iran were clear.

'Fire One! Fire Two!'

The booster rockets on the state-of-the-art weapons propelled the missiles from the launch tubes in an explosion of fire and smoke, their guidance fins extending as they exited. A fraction of a second later, the booster rockets separated as the missile jet engines took over and the Taipans, each on a different course, quickly reached their cruising speeds, skimming across the sea at a staggering 900 kilometres an hour – 250 metres a second. With the active radar seekers locked on to their respective targets, the digital computers in the nose cones used a 'three-axis' attitude reference system and radar altimeter, sending signals to the four guidance fins to make minute adjustments to hold course. It took less than two minutes for the first missile to reach its target.

The specially designed penetrating warhead cut through the outer hull, blowing a massive hole in the side of the *Atlantic Giant*. In an instant, air from outside the hull combined with the inert gases in the tanks that were part-filled with light crude and the explosive mixture erupted in a massive firewall.

Over in the outgoing lane, there was nothing Hadid could have done to save his ship. Seconds later, the other Taipan found its deadly mark, just above the water line. The *Leila* shuddered as the mid-ship tanks erupted, spewing blazing crude into the sea and on to the decks above.

'What the fuck!' Captain Rogers stared in disbelief at the control screens and the carnage erupting 10 000 feet below the Predator drone he was flying above the Persian Gulf. 'I have one – two tankers on fire in the shipping lanes . . . one outbound, one inbound, and they're big mothers, both of them. That's not mines, that has to be an attack . . . get the boss in here!'

Sergeant Brady reached for one of the handsets on her console. 'Sir, there's been an attack on shipping in the Persian Gulf. Could you come down here immediately?' She put the handset down. 'I can't see any other vessels in the area, other than tankers to the west and south, all in the shipping lanes.'

'Carrier Group Ten?'

'Currently to the west, abeam Az-Zubārah on the Qatar peninsula and on course to dock in Bahrain.'

CIA analyst Major Ryan Crowe stared intently at the images being relayed through the drone's cameras. As darkness fell over the gulf, Brady had switched to infrared, but the images were still very clear. 'It might be mines, but I think you're right,' said Crowe, 'it's too much of a coincidence for both ships to hit mines at the same instant, and we've been watching those Iranian motherfuckers for months. If they'd laid fresh mines, we'd have picked up on it.'

'*Lone Warrior*'s launching,' said Brady, focusing a camera on the deck of the big Nimitz-class nuclear carrier. Truman had often been referred to as 'the lone warrior', so the carrier's callsign was a perfect match. 'CENTCOM and NAVCENT are on to this,' she said, monitoring the increasing traffic on the headquarters command net. 'CENTCOM's asking for an update . . . designated FLASH.' It was the highest precedence any report could be given, and was to be handled in front of all other traffic. Central Command or

CENTCOM was headquartered out of MacDill Air Force Base in Tampa, Florida, with a forward headquarters in Qatar, and it was the next superior headquarters to Navy's Central Command or NAV-CENT in Bahrain, taking in the Middle East, North Africa and Central Asia, including Iraq, Iran, Afghanistan and the Persian Gulf.

It took only seconds for the edge-deck elevators on the *Truman* to raise two aircraft from the ship's vast hangars to the 1.8-hectare deck, and each of the four steam-powered catapults were able to lock into a T-bar on the jets' nose gear, flinging the aircraft down the catapult's shuttle. The pilots found themselves catapulted from zero to 165 miles per hour in two seconds, and the heat plumes from the afterburners of the F/A-18 Super Hornets were clearly visible on Brady's screens. Brady had spent time on the carrier, and she could picture the flight deck crews, almost in the prone position on the deck, thumbs in the air, to indicate all clear as the aircraft roared past only metres from their positions.

'What've we got?' Colonel Stillwell demanded as he raced into the room. He listened quietly and attentively while Major Crowe brought him up to speed, leaving Rogers free to pilot the drone.

'But there are no Iranian vessels near these tankers, and we've ruled out mines,' Crowe concluded.

'Submarines?' Stillwell mused.

'The Iranians have three Kilo-class Russian submarines, but they're all in port,' said Crowe, pulling up the latest satellite imagery of the Iranian navy dispositions on a separate screen. 'They also have fifteen Ghadir-class midget submarines, but Carrier Group Ten and her own subs would almost certainly have picked them up. They make enough noise to drown out conversation in Tehran.'

'DEFCON 3!' Brady advised.

'Jesus Christ,' Stillwell muttered. 'That's come from the president himself.' Standing for 'Defense Readiness Condition', the alerts ranged from DEFCON 5, for normal readiness, up to DEFCON 1, which had never been used and was reserved for imminent nuclear war.

'The entire US Air Force is coming to fifteen minutes notice to move . . . that's only been used three times in history,' Stillwell said, 'the Cuban missile crisis, the Arab attacks on Israel in the 1973 Yom Kippur War, and 9/11.'

'Look, sir – on the coast.' Rogers and Brady had switched their attention to the Iranian coastline just to the east of the now furiously blazing tankers. The Taipan missile tubes showed up clearly on the infrared scan.

'Two trucks, and look at the heat signature – those missile launchers have just been fired!' said Rogers, circling over the Bedfords.

'Take them out, sir?' Brady asked.

'Not unless you want to start a nuclear war, Sergeant.' Stillwell turned to Crowe. 'Feed this into the system – FLASH precedence, and request instructions. In the meantime, stay focused on that area of the coastline. What's the traffic on the roads?'

'Not much,' Brady replied. 'A tanker moving south on Route 91, toward Sirik, three cars and two Toyota pickups moving north on 91 toward Bondārān.'

Suddenly all the screens went blank. 'We've lost control,' Rogers said. 'Nothing's responding.'

31

EVRAN HEADQUARTERS, DALLAS, TEXAS

Sheldon Crowley and Rachel Bannister sat in Crowley's penthouse office, glued to CNC's coverage of the unfolding events in the Persian Gulf. Rachel watched with mounting horror, puzzled by the almost detached interest on the part of Crowley.

The mellifluous, but serious tones of Walter Cronkwell filled the airwaves. 'The president is calling for calm until the facts of what has happened can be ascertained. Here's the president a few moments ago.'

The coverage cut to a grave-looking President McGovern in the press briefing room on the first floor of the West Wing of the White House. It had once been just a space over the White House indoor swimming pool, located around the corner from the cabinet room and the Oval Office, but in 1969, President Nixon had the pool covered and the space above it converted to accommodate an increased White House press corps. Today, flanked by the stars and stripes on one side and the blue flag embossed with the president's coat of arms on the other, the president addressed the packed room of journalists and photographers.

'Today at approximately six-thirty p.m. local time, two super-tankers were sunk in the shipping lanes of the Persian Gulf . . . the *Atlantic Giant,* an ultra large crude carrier, in the northern inbound lane, and the *Leila,* a very large crude carrier in the southern outbound shipping lane, effectively closing the Strait of Hormuz to the flow of oil. Neither the how nor the why of these sinkings is yet clear, and they pose a grave, but *manageable* threat to oil supplies in this country and the world,' the president emphasised. As he spoke, the shot switched to queues two and three kilometres long forming at gas stations across the country, where prices had soared to more than US $12 a gallon. Rachel stared in disbelief at the fights breaking out in the queues as demand quickly outstripped supply, and some stations ran dry. The shot switched to Berlin, and then to Paris where prices had crashed through the €6 a litre barrier. In the United Kingdom fuel had reached a staggering 552 pence per litre, and in Australia, at the end of a much longer supply chain, the vision showed similar queues of angry motorists, confronted with upwards of A $6 a litre. Hundreds of millions of families around the world were suddenly facing fuel prices that were well outside their budget.

'And,' the president continued, the shot cutting back to his press conference, 'it would be a mistake to jump to conclusions here. I've called for an urgent report, and I've scheduled a meeting of the National Security Council immediately after this media conference, but I want the American people to know we are taking this very, very seriously, and I will ensure they are kept fully informed of developments. Now . . . I have time for just a few questions.'

The president smiled grimly as a dozen voices shouted questions at him. 'One at a time. Michelle?' he said, pointing to the political correspondent for the *New York Times*.

'There are reports that either mines or missiles are responsible, but either way, the general consensus is that Iran is behind this. Your views on that, Mr President?'

'Those reports are pure speculation, so we should avoid jumping to conclusions here.'

'Mr President, some analysts are comparing this to the Yom Kippur War,' said another reporter. 'Given that 35 per cent of the world's oil flows through this strait, those same analysts are predicting a rise to US $400 a barrel, which would mean pump prices that would wreck the world's economy. Your —'

'That's precisely the sort of irrational analysis that I'm talking about.' The president struggled to keep his voice free of frustration. 'For a start, the Strait of Hormuz carries 35 per cent of the world's *seaborne* oil trade, which equates to just 18 per cent of the ninety million barrels the world uses each day. Now granted, that's still a sizeable amount, but there's no need for this panic buying. Here in the United States we hold a strategic petroleum reserve of some 700 million barrels as a buffer against exactly this sort of situation.'

The camera cut back to Cronkwell in the studio. 'That's a little of what the president had to say at the White House a few moments ago, and we cross now to our political correspondent, Susan Murkowski, at the New York Stock Exchange. Not only have gas prices soared on the back of news of this attack, Susan, but oil stocks have soared while the rest of the stock market has gone in the opposite direction.'

'That's right, Walter. The Dow Jones has crashed to a new low, not seen since the global financial crisis of 2008. Back then, the market fell 54 per cent, but today's panic selling has well and truly surpassed that, with the market falling a massive 62 per cent almost overnight.'

Crowley salivated. Across the Atlantic, the head of Crédit Group was moving on the decimated markets. René du Bois ordered his stock analysts into a furious series of massive 'buy' orders on the biggest of the world's stock exchanges in New York, London, Deutsche Börse, Tokyo, Sydney and Shanghai. He focused on the Fortune 500 companies, buying hundreds of millions of shares at a fraction of their worth.

On the floor of the New York Stock Exchange, specialist traders at their kiosks were looking aghast, as were the brokers in their distinctive blue overalls embossed with their number in white and the US flag. Many were glued to the sea of red on banks of screens with their electronic pullthroughs; others were on the phone, dealing with desperate clients, and making an electronic record of orders to sell. The camera cut back to Susan Murkowski.

'Here's what George Sallis told me earlier in the day.' The chairman of Sallis Fund Management, the internationally renowned and respected George Sallis appeared, speaking from his penthouse office in Chicago. 'Today's stock market crash is unprecedented,' Sallis began. 'We would have to go back to 1929 to find something comparable in its ferocity and suddenness ... but it might have been even worse were it not for some very big buyers that we're now seeing come into the market.'

'Do we know who those buyers are?' Murkowski asked.

Sallis let out a deep breath and his shoulders sagged, the strain of the past twenty-four hours clearly showing on his craggy face.

'There are unconfirmed reports that the big banks and financial houses of Crédit Group are buying billions of dollars of a wide range of equities that most are offloading in panic selling. Under the circumstances this might seem quite odd, but a huge percentage of stocks are drastically undervalued, so perhaps it makes sense to the analysts in Crédit Group.'

'So if Crédit Group are right, this financial crisis might be over relatively quickly,' Murkowski suggested.

'I'd like to share your optimism, but the closure of the Strait of Hormuz has wide-ranging ramifications. Japan, with the third largest economy in the world, imports 75 per cent of its oil through the Strait, and this will not only devastate the Japanese economy, but China too will be severely affected. That will have a flow-on impact on European economies that are already under stress, and it will affect economies like Australia, where large quantities of iron ore and other minerals are exported to the Chinese manufacturing sector. It's about as serious as it gets, and recovery is going to be slow and painful, and that will depend very much on how soon the Strait of Hormuz can be re-opened.'

'A very grim picture, Walter.'

'Indeed,' said Cronkwell. 'That was our political correspondent, Susan Murkowski. And now to other news. The crisis in the Persian Gulf has meant President McGovern has cancelled a scheduled visit to Islamabad, designed to rebuild relationships between the US and Pakistan, a White House spokesman said today . . .'

The power of Pharos surged through Crowley's veins as he flicked off the coverage. In 1776, the great economist, Adam Smith, wrote *The Wealth of Nations,* in which he introduced the concept of a 'hidden hand' in the market – the notion that the market would regulate itself as a result of competition between buyers and sellers. But Pharos had taken the 'hidden hand' concept to a far more sinister level, and under Pharos's massive manipulation of a contrived 'boom and bust', eventually all the banks and the big multinationals would be owned by Pharos as part of the New World Order.

'You don't seem overly concerned, Sheldon?' Rachel ventured.

'There are two types of investors in the stock market, Rachel. Those who follow the herd, and those who know what they're doing. Freud, Jung, Søren Kierkegaard, Friedrich Nietzsche, economists like Thorstien Veblen . . . they've all written extensively about the herd mentality, and we've seen that manifest itself in spades over the last twenty-four hours. These people are driven by emotion. When there's a bubble, they're driven by greed.'

Rachel maintained a straight face. She had never known anyone more driven by greed than Crowley. She enjoyed what his wealth could buy, but hers was not so much an attraction to wealth as an attraction to the extraordinary power that came with it. She'd watched Crowley make hundreds of millions – actions that, if they became public, would have attracted a lengthy gaol term for insider trading. And she had watched him make a lot of money during the global financial crisis, but this time it was different. It was almost as if he was privy to information that no one else had.

'Right now, the herd is driven by gut-wrenching fear, a frenzied "Sell! Sell!" mentality that feeds on itself, driving the market still lower.' Crowley stood up and looked down at the streets below, many of them choked with the queues at the gas stations. 'Like those idiots down there who are driving the price of gasoline still higher. Their counterparts in the stock market have forgotten the basic lesson of Wall Street . . . we strike contrary to the masses.' He turned to the bank of screens on a side desk, secured by Area 15's encryption system. His eyes narrowed and he nodded almost imperceptively. Crédit Group banks were executing a massive attack, buying up blue chip stocks across the top ten stock exchanges in the world. Billions of dollars were being poured into the market, but such was the panic that the attack was doing little more than arresting an even more catastrophic slide.

One of the cable television channels was screening an interview with a self-funded retiree couple who had just watched their life savings disappear. The wife was quietly sobbing and the man wiped away a tear.

'The further it falls the better,' said Crowley.

32

CIA HEADQUARTERS, LANGLEY, VIRGINIA

'How's Aleta?' McNamara asked with a look on his face that said he already knew the answer to the question.

'I think diplomatic relations between her and you are on a par with those between Israel and Iran, but she'll get over it,' O'Connor replied. 'She's organised a gig at the Temple of Osiris at a place called Abydos, about 70 miles north-west of the Valley of the Kings. That will keep her busy . . . for a while.'

McNamara grinned. 'Well, depending on how soon we can get to the bottom of who's supplying these missiles, we may – *may* – be able to find time for you to finish your leave, but given what's happened in the Strait of Hormuz, that's not going to be any time soon. Murray will be here shortly, but she's already told me she thinks there's another shipment of missiles, probably already in Manaus at EVRAN Timbers. I'm not holding out much hope that the Brazilian authorities will search the warehouses. Crowley seems to have the customs boys and girls on his payroll, so you'll need to come up with a Plan B.'

'Why do I get the feeling I'm about to be thrown another hospital pass here?'

'That's because —' McNamara was interrupted by a quiet knock on the door.

'Ms Murray's here.'

'Thanks, Chanelle, show her in. Barbara – O'Connor you know . . . have a seat.' Murray flashed O'Connor a willing smile.

'It won't surprise either of you that this attack on the supertankers is burning my ass,' said McNamara. 'The launch trucks were picked up by one of our drone crews out of Creech. We haven't been able to confirm the missile type because the Iranians got to them before we could get a SEAL team in or do a satellite pass on to the area. It's a small oasis east of Bondārān on the Iranian southern coast, directly opposite the narrowest point of the Strait. Publicly, the Iranians are blaming al Qaeda, which, given what we know, may turn out to be correct,' McNamara said, a thoughtful look on his face, 'but judging by the conversations up on the seventh floor – and the less said about the mood at 1600 Pennsylvania Avenue, the better – you'd think that a threat to our oil supplies was the only one we're facing. Leaving aside the panic at the gas pumps and on Wall Street, let's review what we've got.'

O'Connor stifled a grin. In McNamara's nearly 40 years of service, he'd worked for no fewer than eight presidents. McNamara had seen it all, and the sinking of two supertankers, no matter how grave for the world economy, was not about to rattle him unduly.

'You're not alone there,' said Murray. 'It's pretty well the only topic of conversation at Fort Meade as well, but the information you sent me from your investigation of the Kashta Palace may be linked to the attack in the Strait of Hormuz,' she continued, turning to O'Connor.

McNamara smiled. 'He's a man of many skills,' he said, picking up on Murray's nuanced admiration.

'We can come to the agenda of this group in Alexandria shortly,' said Murray. 'Clearly Crowley is part of it, and he, Du Bois and the media mogul Louis Walden have major roles in Pharos's over-all plan; but of more immediate concern is the intelligence we've gained from their communications. We've thrown everything we have at EVRAN, but we still haven't broken their codes and ciphers. Whoever is running Crowley's systems is good. That said, I've had a quiet look at the metadata on the guys we suspect he's dealing with and I've got a fix on every desktop computer, laptop and mobile phone that Khan uses, as well as the Jewish art dealer Rubinstein, and this Doctor Aboud in the Cairo Museum. He's interesting, to say the least, and I'll come to a text from Khan in a moment, but the meta data led me to a stamp collector website – stampgeekcol.com, and that has me intrigued. Khan has logged on to it, as has someone using a computer located in Dallas. That may be one of Crowley's, because he's logging on through a sophisticated encryption system.

'Any conclusions? We've had a look at it as well,' said McNa-mara. 'It's aptly named – filled with postings by stamp geeks that are as boring as batshit. Unless Crowley or Khan are avid stamp collec-tors, it doesn't make a lot of sense . . .'

'Exactly. Unless it's being used as a communication portal,' said Murray.

'Question is, by whom?' O'Connor pondered.

'I haven't discussed this with anyone at Fort Meade yet, because frankly, I'd rather we handle it here. Easier if the top floor's not involved,' she added, rolling her eyes. 'After our last conversation about Crowley, I've concluded you're right. Big donors like him seem to be a protected species. As to Du Bois, his systems are encrypted as well, but not as well as EVRAN's, and we're now deep inside Crédit Group's operations.'

'Lawful?' McNamara asked.

'We've had some discussions with the Securities and Exchange Commission, although very discreetly – I wouldn't put it past the Crowleys of this world to have a well-placed mole. Their view is that the sheer volume of recent trade is highly unusual, and may warrant investigation, but there's no cast-iron evidence. The law covers insider trading and Section 9 of the Securities Exchange Act of 1934 specifically refers to stock manipulation, but that's in regard to individual stocks. Back in 1934, I don't think the legislators could foresee the whole market being manipulated by acts of terrorism.'

'But today, they don't get any bigger than Crowley or Du Bois's Crédit Group, backed by the likes of the media's Louis Walden,' said O'Connor. 'The synergy of the Pharos Group is frightening, and all the more so because their operations are almost impenetrable. No one but we three seem to know anything about them. I wonder if Pharos could be engaged in exactly that type of manipulation?'

'Well what is interesting,' Murray continued, 'are the comments on the website by a member called Ledifni.'

'Ledifni?' McNamara asked.

'They're getting cocky,' said Murray. 'Infidel spelt backwards. The post itself was pretty innocuous . . . acquisition of a US two-cent Columbian Commemorative stamp, but I traced it to a satellite phone broadcasting from a place called Mirjaveh, at the Pakistan border with Iran.'

'So you think this could be some sort of code to warn Khan and Crowley of an attack?' McNamara looked thoughtful, as did O'Connor.

'It's not ironclad,' Murray admitted, 'but we shouldn't rule it out.'

McNamara shook his head. 'I'd thought I'd seen it all, but if you're correct, manipulation of the markets on this scale is almost unthinkable. The information we've gleaned from the Kashta Palace raises more questions than it answers.' He opened the leather folder O'Connor had retrieved from the palace. 'We've got a safe full of agenda notes for a meeting of something called the Pharos Group – fifteen men and one woman – who've met every year in secret since 1992. But for what purpose?'

Murray raised an eyebrow. 'Why am I not surprised at *that* ratio.'

McNamara and O'Connor grinned at one another. 'Leaving aside your bruised ego,' O'Connor said, 'the "P" in that earlier Khan text intercept likely stands for the Pharos Group, but the question remains, is there an actual person called Pharos? Each folder was labelled with a participant's name, and apart from very prominent diplomats and generals, the rest of them are in Oxfam's top eighty-five who own half the world's wealth, but the notes refer to a "chairman". Who that might be remains a mystery.'

'Well we can probably rule out the woman,' Murray suggested, 'and the likes of Sam Talbot, the former head of the World Bank, Guthrie, the former US secretary of state, and General Bradshaw, the former chairman of the US Joint Chiefs. Those guys are very well connected in Washington, which is undoubtedly why they're there, but they're not particularly wealthy.'

'I agree,' said McNamara. '. . . European royalty?'

'The background notes indicate the group is keeping close tabs on the world economy, and on the key political systems. Royalty have always manipulated the power levers, but I'm leaning toward the likes of Du Bois, Walden or Crowley,' said O'Connor.

'With Crowley at short odds,' said McNamara, 'although Du Bois is a grade A asshole. Just ask that Filipina maid.'

Murray nodded. 'In the process of digging out their communications, one of the most interesting was Du Bois,' she said. 'Apart from the fact that the prosecution would dearly love to get hold of the intercepts I've got on the Filipina maid case – Du Bois has paid off more than one woman threatening to sue him for rape – the taps confirm he's not only the most powerful banker in the world today, he's also the most corrupt. It will not surprise many people that Wall Street and the world banking system is corrupt, but they would be surprised to know that the Federal Reserve is not really controlled by the US Government . . . it's backed by the big banks and the mega-wealthy.'

McNamara nodded. 'Goes back to 1907,' he said. 'The New York Stock exchange crashed 50 per cent, partly because of a failed scheme to manipulate the price of United Copper. When the share price of United Copper dropped from US $60 to US $10, that triggered a loss of confidence and a run on the banks that had leant money for the scheme, including the Knickerbocker Trust Company which went into liquidation along with hundreds of small businesses and banks. Knickerbocker was New York's third largest trust, and considered too big to fail . . . the more things change, the more they remain the same,' McNamara observed, a wry smile on his face. Ever since then, the Reserve's been underpinned by the big banking houses and the mega-wealthy: the Rothschilds, the Lehman Brothers, the Rockefellers, but today, Du Bois dwarfs them all – past or present.'

'So there could be a link between Du Bois, Crowley, Khan and the closure of the Strait of Hormuz,' O'Connor suggested.

'I think so,' said Murray. 'Shortly after the Ledifni comment was sent, Khan texted our mystery iPhone with a message "Columbus has landed". If these are stamp alerts, and if that phone does belong to Crowley, he would have been none too pleased with Khan. The packing note left in the missile case might be their first mistake, Khan's text might be their second, because if I'm right, the original Ledifni comment would have been made by one of the terrorists responsible for the attack on the shipping lane.'

'But that's the only evidence we have?' McNamara asked, anticipating the White House chief of staff would want a lot more than a text before he went to the president with a 'Clear and Present Danger' brief on Crowley.

'Not entirely. We may not have been able to break EVRAN's encryption, but our monitoring of Khan, Aboud and Rubinstein is interesting. Doctor Aboud's not what he seems. For starters, he bought his doctorate online from a shonky website in China.'

O'Connor made a mental note to warn Aleta.

'Secondly, Khan and Aboud are both in contact with Rubinstein. Finally, I've discovered Crowley collects very expensive masters, and that he has a passion for Egyptology, as does Khan. A day after the break-in at the Egyptian Museum, Rubinstein sent a text to Khan which simply read "FP merchandise received". The only other icon to be stolen with the mask of Tutankhamun was the priceless falcon pendant, which prompts the question as to whether Khan's the buyer – although it may be some time before he can pick it up, because we've also learned he's been diagnosed with cancer, and the treatment may take several months.'

McNamara stroked his chin. 'FP . . . falcon pendant. We may have to have a look inside Signor Rubinstein's gallery,' he said with a grin, looking at O'Connor.

O'Connor resignedly raised his eyes to the ceiling. 'But leaving aside the possibility of Khan, and even Crowley being involved in stolen art,' he said, 'it's the Pharos Group that has the most to gain from a closure of the Strait of Hormuz – a spooked market, a massive spike in oil prices, and a crash in shares that we haven't seen since the Great Depression. It prompts the question as to whether there's more to this than just manipulating the stock market . . . something even deeper,' said O'Connor.

McNamara looked thoughtful. 'Meaning?'

'I know these guys are all driven by money and power, probably more than they are by sex or anything else, but I keep coming back to the purpose of this group in Alexandria,' O'Connor responded. 'Those folders in the vault are presumably not allowed off the premises, and the briefs in them not only focus on the world's major economies, but the political situation in our country and the other key players: China, Russia, Germany, India and Brazil. Maybe there's more to Crowley's backing of Davis than we think?'

'We'll still need a damn sight more concrete evidence before we can go to the president and tell him Crowley's somehow linked to what happened in the Strait of Hormuz,' said McNamara. 'And apart from the fact we're not meant to be investigating American citizens, let alone one as powerful as Crowley, there's no law that says you can't back a candidate for the White House.'

'But there are limits,' said O'Connor.

'Agreed, but even if we could get the president to approve an all-out assault on Crowley's activities, as a Democrat, he'd be put in a tough position. The Republicans are already in bed with that asshole Louis Walden and Omega Centauri . . . Centauri News would go ballistic, and to ordinary Americans it would look like a politically motivated move. Neither the president nor Hailey Campbell would thank us for that. As to the missiles, assuming Crowley *is* involved, we're not even sure if he's using his own ship to transport this stuff.'

'No,' Murray agreed, 'although the *EVRAN I* did berth in Karachi two weeks before the timber was tracked across the border into Afghanistan.'

'Where's the ship now?' asked O'Connor.

'Headed for Manaus, which is about a thousand miles up the Amazon River.'

'Has it called into any US ports?' McNamara probed.

'No. The intercepts point to there being another shipment of missiles, which is why I think they're probably in Manaus already, but I'd still be inclined to audit EVRAN's books,' Murray ventured.

McNamara shook his head. 'I'd love to know what's in them too, but even if we could get hold of them, I'd never get that through the White House, and we'd take a lot of skin off in the attempt.'

O'Connor nodded. His boss, he knew, was never one for taking a step back, but he drew the line at suicide missions.

'That said, if there's another shipment of missiles already in Manaus, I think it's time we investigated EVRAN's operations in Brazil. Rubinstein's art gallery can wait a little longer,' McNamara said, again looking at O'Connor. 'If we can confirm a link between EVRAN and the missiles in the Korengal Valley, and perhaps those used in the Strait of Hormuz, it doesn't give us Crowley, but it may be enough for us to request an audit of EVRAN's books, especially if it turns out terrorists used Taipans in their attack on the *Leila* and the *Atlantic Giant*.'

'And apropos your observations on Crowley's links to Davis,' Murray said, turning to O'Connor, 'Crowley and his executive assistant, Rachel Bannister, are leaving no stone unturned. The intercepts indicate Davis's White House campaign has the highest priority in EVRAN, and they're putting a lot of energy into the evangelical vote . . . the same votes that Karl Rove tapped into to get George W. Bush elected. I know I'm not supposed to be tapping into American citizens' phones and emails, but something's not right here, and I'm backing my instincts . . . not that the cell phones of evangelical pastors are anything other than child's play.'

'I think your instincts are right, and I'll cover you. I don't care how we get it – Crowley's iPhones, Du Bois's computers, a posting on stampgeekcol.com or Pastor What's-his-face's laptop, but we need a break on this, and fast.'

'Any closet homosexuals?' O'Connor asked, grinning broadly.

'You'd be surprised,' said Murray, a conspiratorial look on her face. 'Pastor Shipley may rail against homosexuals, but he may not be all he seems.'

McNamara looked at both of them over the top of his glasses.

'Crowley will make sure he's nowhere to be seen,' Murray continued more seriously, 'but they're about to announce the Davis candidacy at the church Crowley attends . . . Pastor Matthias B. Shipley's Hermit Road mega-church.'

'Crowley attends church?' McNamara looked genuinely surprised.

'Not if he can avoid it, but his wife Lillian's a staunch Christian, and as a result, Crowley's a big donor – US $30 million toward the church building fund alone. Pastor Shipley wouldn't expect his emails to be tapped, so he's been fairly open, and even though Davis is coming in to the race late, they're not worried. The rest of the Republican field is pretty lacklustre and they're banking on the evangelical vote in the Iowa caucuses giving them a head start.'

McNamara nodded. 'Well, there's no doubt Iowa's important, both as the first indication of a candidate's potential, and in the presidential election. The Democrats won there in 2008 and went on to the White House, although you'd have to say they're a mix of red, blue and undecided in the Hawkeye state.' The nickname for Iowa went back to the 1832 war between Americans and the Sauks, Meskwakis and Kickapoo tribes, led by the native leader Black Hawk.

'And the evangelicals are far from monolithic,' Murray said. 'Davis can't hope to win them all, but they made up sixty per cent of the vote in 2008, which probably explains why Shipley's invited a whole bunch of pastors to the announcement. When voting's not compulsory, if they can get several thousand pastors to thump the pulpit on the Sunday before the first Tuesday in November, and urge their congregations to get out and vote for their man, Davis and EVRAN might just pull this off.'

'Jesus Christ,' McNamara muttered.

33

HERMIT ROAD MEGA-CHURCH, DALLAS

Governor Davis wiped the sweat from his brow. The hubbub from the cavernous church was clearly audible in Matthias B. Shipley's palatial office. Shipley had delivered on his promise, and the front pews of the 10 000-capacity auditorium had been filled by over 1000 pastors. Courtesy of EVRAN, they'd been flown in from across the country. Behind them the comfortable church seats were crammed to capacity with ordinary worshippers, excited by the prospect of being able to question 'the next Christian president of the United States'. Two hours of coaching from Rachel had Governor Davis wishing for a Montana pure malt whiskey, but he forced himself to focus.

'Finally, what are you going to say if someone asks you how you're going to convince the Lord to allow you to get into heaven?' Rachel probed.

'They're not going to ask that!' Davis grumbled.

'Pastor Jerry Falwell was one of the most powerful televangelists this country's ever seen, and that was one of his favourite questions to any presidential candidate.'

'Well I guess I'll say that throughout my life I've followed the teachings of the Bible.'

Rachel kept a straight face. 'For evangelicals, that's not the right answer,' she said, handing him another page with a typed dot point for his folio. 'Take a leaf out of George W. Bush's re-election campaign – that's what he said in 2004.'

Rachel looked at her watch. 'Make-up's down the hall, then it's show time.'

'My friends, we are moving into dangerous territory!' Pastor Shipley thundered, warming up his audience for the introduction of the governor.

The director in the control room high above the rear seats called for a shift in coverage.

'Zoom in, camera six.'

Shipley had a standing order that whenever a close-up was required, it was to be on the left, his best side. The huge screens above the stage and around the walls of the auditorium were filled with Shipley's facial features, bloated by good living. But his blue eyes were energised by adrenalin. Many of the congregation were following the direct broadcast on their laptops through the Hermit Road secure wi-fi.

'We need a committed Christian in the White House, someone who is a true servant of the Lord, because we are truly living in the end times! Those of you who have consulted the Rapture Index this morning will see that it's now at 186 points. That's close to a record high. God is giving us very clear warnings, but even the patience of the Almighty has its limits.'

Rachel watched with interest from the wings. Whatever might be said about these Christians, their unswerving belief that their God was in control was palpable. The Rapture Index website provided a running commentary on the fulfilment of biblical prophecies, covering forty-five categories, including the world economy, climate, oil supplies, unemployment, moral standards, Russia and Iran, a coming world government, and, most importantly of all, the peace process and Israel. Rachel too, had checked the Rapture Index, but only to prep her charge on possible questions. For her, there was one category missing and that was the 'barking mad' one.

'You only have to look at what these crazed Muslims have done in the Strait of Hormuz,' Shipley thundered. 'The Bible warns us that the end times are approaching, and we will see in our lifetime a terrifying New World Order run by the rich and powerful. It's right here in Chapter 7 of the Book of Daniel.' Pastor Shipley held his well-thumbed leather Bible aloft. 'When Daniel asks an angel to interpret his dream, the angel explains there will be a fourth empire after the Babylonians, the Persians and the Greeks. That fourth empire was not just the ancient Roman Empire, but a revival of that empire which we see rising today.' In a portent of the terrible times ahead, Shipley lowered his voice. '"As for the fourth beast",' he said, reading from Daniel, '"there shall be a fourth kingdom on earth that shall be different from the other kingdoms; it shall devour the whole earth, and trample it down, and break it to pieces." And we can see that starting to happen now, my friends. Make no mistake, there are powerful forces at work behind the scenes; the increase in wild fires, tsunamis, volcanic eruptions and floods has very little to do with climate change, my friends. Scientists continually fail to address the prophecies in the Bible, because if they did, they would come to the same conclusion as you and me. These are simply God's warnings.' Many in the congregation nodded in agreement. 'Hurricane Katrina was sent by God because of the gambling and sodomy in New Orleans, where each year, the Southern Decadence Labor Day gala for gays, lesbians and transgenders is hosted. God *hates* gays! God *hates* lesbians and transgenders, and anyone who disputes that, only has to go to the first book of the Bible in Genesis 19 where "the Lord rained upon Sodom and Gomorrah brimstone and fire . . . and he overthrew those cities!" In Leviticus, God has told us "do not lie with a man as one lies with a woman, for that is detestable"! Homosexuals are an abomination, yet we take no notice.' Pastor Shipley strode across the vast stage. 'God sent the floods in Colorado to an area where pagan New Age religion thrives, and God timed those floods to coincide with attempts by Washington to divide Israel and Jerusalem, so the Muslims and Arabs can form a Palestinian state, with al Quds, East Jerusalem as its capital. We are messing with God's will here!' Rachel quietly shook her head.

'That's why we need a Christian in the White House, to get America back on track before it's too late. Many of you will have heard the rumours that Hailey Campbell is planning on running.' Shipley lowered his voice again to emphasise the danger. 'My friends, we can't afford to let that happen. When Campbell speaks out in favour of homosexual marriage, when she regrets she didn't oppose the war against the Muslims in Iraq, she is defying the will of God! So please welcome *God's candidate,* the next president of the United States of America, Governor Carter Davis!'

Pastor Shipley may have given Davis his endorsement, but his fellow pastors and the Hermit Road congregation were yet to be convinced, and Davis was greeted with polite but muted applause.

'Get me the live feed for the Hermit Road announcement.'

It took Crowley's new personal assistant nearly five minutes, but Crowley controlled his frustration. Miranda Vandenberg had other talents. Tall, with long, slender legs, blue eyes and long, blonde hair, what she lacked in intellect she more than made up for with rat cunning. She had sized up Crowley's needs early, and accurately.

'Pause it,' Crowley said, as the secure phone rang on his desk. 'In the fridge in the boardroom kitchen, you'll find some Louis Roederer champagne – the '82 vintage. Farid . . . what can I do for you?'

'The stock market is starting to rise again, Sheldon. When do you expect Phase Two to commence?'

Irritated, Crowley took a deep breath. Khan was speaking on a scrambler, but in Crowley's world, communications were kept to essentials. 'The teams are in place?'

'Yes . . . the materials have arrived,' Khan confirmed.

'And the teams for Phase Three?' Crowley asked.

'They are standing by as well, but we're still waiting on the missiles.'

'I will let you know in good time, once they've left Manaus,' said Crowley, his voice steely. 'Tell your people to be patient. This is a marathon, Farid, not a sprint.'

Crowley slammed down the phone but his mood softened as Miranda returned. 'Get Reid in here, and once I've dealt with him . . .'

Miranda set the Louis Roederer champagne on the polished cedar table, activated the feed from the Hermit Road church that was being broadcast live through the American Christian Broadcast Foundation, and settled back on the couch, letting her short skirt ride up her brown thighs.

Davis grasped the big lectern with both hands, and the director called for another shift. 'Zoom in camera five.'

'My fellow Americans,' Davis began, looking toward the sizeable press contingent gathered in an area to one side of the church. 'I've come here today, to announce my intention to run for the presidency of the United States, and to ask for your prayers. As governor of Montana, I've been privileged to run on a platform of "Faith and Family". Today, I've added "Jobs" to that manifesto, because if you entrust me with this great office, I will build on what has served me well, both in my public, and in my private life.'

Rachel had insisted on the addition, but as she listened to Davis in campaign mode, she reflected on the not-inconsiderable payoffs for Abigail and the rest of his paramours. If any of those came unstuck, Rachel knew Davis and Crowley's campaign would turn to custard in an instant.

Davis turned and waved toward the huge red and blue banner behind him emblazoned with:

DAVIS FOR PRESIDENT
Faith, Family and Jobs

'Zoom in on the banner, camera five.'

'This election will be about the economy and jobs,' Davis continued. 'In Montana, I've put the economy front and centre, and my record speaks for itself. Shale oil and gas drilling is reaching new heights in the Bakken formation, and you've only got to look at the thousands of new jobs . . . *new jobs* . . . that we've created in the Sweet Grass and Park counties. We're well on the way to making America self-sufficient in oil and gas, and if the American people entrust me with the White House, I will pledge till my last breath to rebuild what the Democrats have destroyed. Together, and with the help of Almighty God, we will make America great again!'

As Davis launched into the dot points Rachel had provided him, interspersed with regular mentions of the Almighty and the Lord Jesus Christ, she listened to the increased applause with grudging respect. She hadn't changed her mind on Davis's IQ, but as a snake oil salesman in campaign mode, he was without peer. She began to think they might just pull this off, reminding herself that stranger things had happened.

'Murderer!' shouted a clearly agitated man who had leapt to his feet in the middle of the auditorium. He took off his coat to reveal a black T-shirt emblazoned with a skull and crossbones. 'You're setting us up for an absolute disaster in Montana! There are now over 400 000 tanker cars moving across this country every year, and so far, there have already been three rail derailments of Bakken crude that have resulted in fifty people dead and millions of gallons of flaming oil creating walls of flame three hundred feet high. And in Lac Megantic in Quebec, the whole town went up. Bakken crude is dangerous! It's light, has more methane, and burns easily!'

Shipley had already given orders for the protester to be evicted, but the man had carefully selected his seat in the middle of the vast auditorium, and the security guards were having trouble getting to him. The protestor was making the most of it.

'And you, Governor Davis . . . you and EVRAN and the rest of Big Oil are liars! You maintain fracking has been around for decades, but it hasn't! Deep horizontal drilling and the use of toxic chemicals only began in Ohio in 2011 and contrary to what you say, we know nothing of the damage to the water table and our drinking water! EVRAN has teams of salespeople tricking old retired couples into signing away the family farm for a pittance. You're in bed with EVRAN and Big Oil up to your miserable neck!'

The security guards finally managed to reach the protestor, and much to the discomfort of those in his row, they forcibly propelled him toward the aisle.

'But they know in Poland!' he shouted over his shoulder. 'Ask the farmers on the border with Ukraine about using 40 000 gallons of chemicals every time the rocks are fractured. Ask them how much mercury and hydrochloric acid are going into the water table!'

The protestor's shouting faded as two burly security guards forcibly ejected him from the church.

Rachel made a note to get a copy of his photograph for identification. Whoever he was, he was extraordinarily well briefed.

'There will always be those who resist change,' Davis began with a calculated shrug. 'For the record, I am not in bed with EVRAN, or Big Oil, or anyone else other than my loving wife of twenty-seven years.' He paused and smiled as the gentle laughter echoed around the auditorium. 'It's our twenty-eighth anniversary next month, and I thank God every day for sending her to me.' Many in the audience nodded approvingly, and a stronger burst of applause echoed off the walls.

'For those who may not be aware, fracking is a simple process which has been around for a very long time.' Rachel scrutinised the congregation as Davis continued speaking. From the looks on their faces, it was clear that quite a number had little or no idea of what fracking involved, and they were following the explanation closely.

'But this is not some hillbilly operation. Drilling for oil and gas is closely regulated by environmental regulations.'

Rachel made yet another note. Davis might get away with that here, or in Montana, but a national debate would require a far more careful answer.

'As to our friend's allegations on methane, he's quite wrong there. This gas occurs naturally. It's found right across the country. What we need to focus on here are the benefits derived from God's bountiful gifts. We've created over 200 000 jobs already, and many of these are for God-fearing families across this great land.'

Rachel muttered quietly to herself. 'Jesus Christ, Davis, I said remember your audience, not lay it on with a bloody trowel.' The remainder of her prepared speech, which focused on jobs and the economy, passed without further incident. Faith-based initiatives that would allow religious organisations like the Hermit Road mega-church to better compete for government funds gained loud applause. Rachel made another note. But then she braced herself for the most dangerous part of the meeting. She'd schooled Davis in every question she could think of, but religion was not her long suit, and this element of the Davis pitch was unscripted.

'And now my friends,' Pastor Shipley said, offering Davis a seat at a fake fireside setting on the stage, 'Governor Davis will be pleased to take questions.'

The first question came from a well-dressed woman in the second row. 'Governor Davis, we've heard a lot about the way Muslims want to introduce Sharia law to the West. Can you explain how you feel about Islam?'

Rachel took a deep breath. This was a curve ball on steroids.

'I'm not the first to say this,' Davis began, 'but there is no doubt that Islam is an evil religion. When Muslims say they want to introduce Sharia law, they mean it. They want to abolish our court system and put camel courts in their place. They want to take over the world, but as your president, I will never ever let that happen. There is only one true religion, and one true God, and that's the Lord Jesus Christ incarnate as the Son of the Father.'

The applause was stronger now, but Rachel made a note to request research into the Muslim vote. She listened with interest to the rest of the questions and Davis's responses.

For the last question a portly gentleman in the front, dressed in an expensive suit, got to his feet. 'Governor Davis, I wonder if you could give us an indication of what you might say to our Lord Jesus Christ when you meet Him in the end times. How are you going to convince Him that you have earned a place in Heaven?'

'Yes!' Rachel whispered to herself. She had a track record of being able to predict awkward questions, but it always gave her a kick when she nailed one, particularly when it came to a group like this. For Rachel, these people might just as well have come from another planet.

'We're all sinners,' Davis began, 'but when you accept Jesus

Christ as your personal Saviour, as I have, and you have, then we know – we *know* – that because of His sacrifice, *we* are saved. We are *right with God.'*

Even Rachel was taken aback. The auditorium erupted and the congregation got to their feet, applauding and cheering wildly. 'Hallelujah! Hallelujah!' they chanted. 'Amen! Amen!'

Crowley drained his champagne, flicked off the broadcast, and leaned back in the comfortable office sofa.

'Your new house comfortable?'

'Very, Mr Crowley. I can't thank you enough,' said Miranda. She put her own glass on the table, nestled back on the couch and again allowed her skirt to ride to the top of her thighs.

'You and I are going to be spending a lot of time together . . . and when we're alone, it's Sheldon,' he said, letting his hand wander onto her exposed leg.

'Sheldon it is, then,' she whispered huskily, her own hand wandering to the inside of Crowley's thigh. 'Shall I pour some more champagne?'

'Oh . . . I think the champagne can wait, don't you?' He put his arm around her and explored inside her bra.

'Let me make that easier,' Miranda whispered, 'it undoes at the front.' She undid the catch, releasing her firm, perky breasts, and felt the inside of Crowley's thigh and his growing erection.

Crowley unbuckled his belt and unzipped his fly, releasing his cock. 'Suck me,' he said hoarsely, sliding his hand into Miranda's black lace knickers and fingering her moist, warm clit.

Over a thousand miles to the north, in Montana, Abigail had also been watching the live broadcast. Her disbelief turned to white-hot anger. 'You bastard! You hypocritical, lying bastard!' she swore at the television screen.

A month before, a knock on her door had come in the early evening. She had been reluctant at first, but $200 000 was a lot of money. Abigail had eventually accepted that the governor had powerful friends who simply wanted to ensure his reputation was safe, and she signed the agreement to keep silent. The governor's reputation would have been safe with her anyway – up until now. 'No one mentioned anything about you running for the White House, you bastard! What about *me*? Is that bitch of a wife of yours going to be First Lady now?' she fumed.

Back in Pastor Shipley's office, Rachel flicked on CNC's analysis of the announcement.

'In breaking news,' Walter Cronkwell intoned, 'Governor Carter Davis has announced his intention to run for the Republican nomination for president, and we cross to our political correspondent, Susan Murkowski, who joins us from outside the Hermit Road mega-church in Dallas. A dark horse, and a surprise late addition to the field, Susan?' The vision faded to Murkowski standing on the wide steps of the church.

'Indeed it is, Walter. Governor Davis had given no previous indication he might run, but he's certainly energised a flagging Republican campaign, and if the reception he's received here is anything to go by, Governor Davis might prove to be more than a dark horse. Here's what one couple, clearly ecstatic about the prospect of a God-fearing president, had to say.'

The vision changed again to a grey-haired white couple in their late sixties.

'And what did you think of Governor Davis's announcement?' Murkowski asked, moving her microphone toward the woman.

'I think God has finally intervened,' the woman replied in her deep southern drawl. 'Just as He intervened to ensure George W. Bush was elected, God is going to bless America with Governor Davis. To be honest, before Governor Davis entered this election, I was at a loss to know who to vote for, but God is giving America one last chance before the end times for us to repent of our sins, and I know Governor Davis will provide us with that moral compass.'

Murkowski turned to the woman's husband who was nodding vigorously. 'And you, sir? What did you think?'

'Ruby and I don't always agree,' the man said with a smile, 'but she's right. The race is now on in earnest, and we'll be urging Christians right across the United States to get behind Governor Carter Davis, because you can tell he's one of us.'

'Forgive me, but how can you tell that?'

'By the way he speaks.'

'It's that simple?'

'A non-Christian wouldn't understand,' the parishioner said, his smile vanishing, 'but Governor Davis has asked for our prayers, and he's going to get them in spades, because he's God's man in the White House, and through President Davis, God will direct America.'

'So far, so good,' said Rachel, flicking off the broadcast, 'but we've got a long way to run, so let's not get carried away. By and large, your answers were fine, Carter, but you have to stay on message. And when we get to the wider audiences, you'll need to go easy on the God stuff. And don't say you're *not* in bed with EVRAN. That might come back to bite us, so vague that up. Tell them you're your own man. That way, they can't accuse you of misleading anyone.'

Davis listened grudgingly.

'And don't insist that fracking's covered by environmental regulations. That might play well for conservative audiences in the primaries, but it's bullshit and when we come up against Hailey Campbell, she'll tear you apart if you try that one.'

'How?'

Oh Christ, Rachel thought. We're okay with dot points, but push it past what's on the page in front of him, and he's fucked. Stay calm, she reminded herself.

'We don't want to touch that argument with a barge pole, because that protestor and others like him know that Republicans have approved exemptions in the Clean Water Act, the Clean Air Act, and introduced a host of other legislation specifically designed to allow the oil industry exemptions, and Campbell will hit you over the head. We need to concentrate on the jobs and economy angle, because that's the one that will play well with Middle America.'

Davis looked at Rachel quizzically.

Up in Montana, Abigail switched off the direct broadcast, her tears fuelling her anger. 'You bastard! You absolute fucking bastard!'

On the second Tuesday of each month, Pastor Matthias Shipley made the three hundred mile trip from Dallas to Little Rock in

Arkansas. If anyone called the Hermit Road office, the staff would respond very politely as they'd been instructed: that Pastor Shipley was interstate, winning souls for Christ.

Far less well known in Arkansas than he was in Texas, Pastor Shipley nevertheless always ensured that he arrived at Christian's apartment after dark.

'Matty . . . come on in. Make yourself comfortable. Glass of wine? Tonight I have some chablis, or a cab sav?'

'Cab sav, thank you,' Pastor Shipley said, leaving $800 on the sideboard. It was the usual fee for an all-night stay. Matthias couldn't explain it, but even after six years, he was still nervous every time he visited, and that in itself was a turn-on. Christian was everything he wanted in a man. Young, fit and athletic. Tonight, Christian was wearing cargo shorts and topless. Matthias ran his eyes over Christian's brown, rippling torso and broad shoulders. Christian's fabulously fit body never failed to arouse him.

'I probably should have asked you this question years ago – cheers – but how did you find me?' Christian asked.

'Online. Didn't I ever tell you that? I wanted a site that allowed me to filter my preferences . . . bottom or top, cut or uncut.'

'Was I the first choice?' Christian asked, sitting beside Matthias and putting his hand on the pastor's bulging crotch.

Pastor Shipley's pale, flabby face coloured. 'Uh . . . no, but the first guy was far too rough, and wouldn't go top. I was always bottom, but when I found you – pitching, catching – we seem to alternate pretty well.'

'Yeah, the sex is always good with you, Matty,' Christian said. He took the pastor's hand and slid it down the front of his own cargo shorts.

'And of course,' Pastor Shipley said, starting to relax, 'I just *love* your gorgeous cock . . . *so* big . . . '

Pastor Shipley put his glass down and unzipped Christian's shorts, releasing the male escort's throbbing manhood, all seven and a half inches of it, and he took Christian in his mouth.

'Pitcher or catcher, Matty?' Christian asked after a minute.

'Catcher,' the pastor croaked. 'Give me that big cock, Christian, give me that cock.'

Christian disappeared into his bedroom and brought out two of the fur suits that he knew Matthias liked so much. 'Fox or wolf?'

'You be the fox. I'll be the wolf,' Pastor Shipley said, breathless with excitement.

34

THE AMAZON

'If my mission here gets out, Washington will have McNamara's head on a plate,' O'Connor said to Manuel Oliveira, the CIA's chief of station in Brasília. They were sitting in Oliveira's secure office in the shielded area of the United States embassy in Avenue das Nações in the embassy sector, just to the north of Lago Paranoá. When the capital of Brazil had been moved to Brasília from Rio de Janeiro in the late 1950s, the River Paranoá was dammed to form the artificial lake, around which were dotted embassies, consulates, up-market residences, the University of Brasília and the Palácio da Alvorada, or Palace of the Dawn, the residence for the President of Brazil.

'Crowley might be high on our suspect list, but he's also pretty high on the White House Christmas card list. He's backing that dopey Carter Davis to the hilt, and if the early polls are anything to go by, Davis might just get up. If that happens, America will be run by a shadowy elite, so if we're going to roll Crowley and his cronies, we need some hard evidence that these missiles are coming out of Brazil, and that Crowley is behind it.'

'Well,' the veteran diplomat demurred, 'given the sway that EVRAN Timber holds in official circles here, the ambassador's very reluctant to make any official representation, but he's made some discreet enquiries. The chances of a complete search of the EVRAN warehouses in Manaus lie somewhere between fuck all and zero, but he'll keep trying.'

'There's a protest at one of Crowley's timber mills in Manaus tomorrow,' O'Connor observed.

'Even if the missiles are hidden in the timber coming out of Manaus, it would be hard to believe that Crowley would have any knowledge of it,' Oliveira said, 'but it's possible, and I don't have to tell you, but we're dealing with ruthless white collar thugs here. I don't have any proof, but where you're going, the word on the street is that more than one protestor has disappeared. You don't cross Marcelo Costa and EVRAN timber.'

'And by extension, Sheldon Crowley,' O'Connor agreed. 'Fraud and deception are part of the furniture in Washington and New York, and there are plenty of high-profile businessmen like Bernie Madoff serving life. But there are none that I can think of who might have attempted things on this scale. If Crowley *is* involved in this, he'll face the death penalty for treason.'

'And I see he's recently brought a Professor Ahlstrom on to his team,' said Oliveira, consulting the file he had on EVRAN Brazil.

'The Nobel Laureate. We suspect he's there to influence the next election, lobbying Washington against any action on climate change.'

'Well he's hit the ground running, and he's not only lobbying

Washington. We approved a visa for Professor Ahlstrom to address a business conference of high-powered CEOs that was held here in Brasília last week, and the following day he had lunch with the president at the palace.'

'Crowley's obviously more than a little concerned that the Brazilian government might be about to impose harsher restrictions on logging in the Amazon. That would put a very big dent in EVRAN Timber.'

'Crowley's got reason to be concerned,' said Oliveira. 'The government's under immense pressure from environmentalists, because over 20 per cent of the Amazon's already gone, but the president's also under pressure from the thousands of small farmers who occupy the Amazon illegally, and Crowley's taking advantage of that. It's not every day a Nobel Laureate, who's spent his life warning that if we don't *stop* burning fossil fuels the planet has a use-by date, jumps ship and decides that he's *pro* fossil fuel. We recorded what he had to say at the lunch,' said Oliveira, plugging a thumb drive into his desktop, 'but it's his conclusions that are probably of most interest.'

The glittering luncheon at the five-star Meliá Brasil 21 Hotel was attended by a who's who of the business world in South America, along with ministers, heads of government departments and ambassadors.

'I have not changed my position on climate change without a great deal of thought,' Ahlstrom concluded, 'but I'm now convinced climate change is a hoax. Just this past week, New York and Washington, along with much of the rest of America, have experienced the most severe snowstorms in living memory. The temperatures out in the Midwest have, on average, been thirty degrees colder than normal. *Thirty degrees*! Firemen battling a blaze in Minneapolis watched the spray from their hoses turn to ice before it hit the building. They could do with a little global warming up there . . . it's so cold their beers are turning to ice in the glass!'

The audience burst into applause. O'Connor observed the Nobel Laureate with interest: a man revelling in the laughter and adulation of big business.

'And down in Australia, crackpot climate scientists, along with fifty or so climate tourists, set off to prove global warming is melting the Antarctic. As one writer put it, they should have obtained a second opinion, or at least consulted mother nature, because their Russian charter ship, *Akademik Shokalskiy*, became trapped in record volumes of ice. I have bad news for these climate crackpots. NASA have reported that the sea ice around Antarctica is *growing*, not shrinking, and the earth is *cooling*, not warming up.' Ahlstrom waited for the applause to subside.

'So in summary, ladies and gentlemen, as the governor of Montana and presidential candidate, Carter Davis, reminded Americans in his recent address, we've just come through one of the most testing global financial crises in one hundred years, and we need to be focusing on growth and jobs. It's time to consign this morally bankrupt green agenda to the trashcan and let companies like EVRAN Timber in Brazil do what they do best – raise the standard of living for many fine Brazilians in one of the great countries of the world. I have come to realise that controlled logging is the ultimate in conservation, and loggers are the ultimate conservationists.'

O'Connor shook his head as the applause reached a crescendo and Professor Ahlstrom, his face flushed, beamed at his audience.

'I take it you think global warming is real?' Oliveira asked.

'I'm a scientist. It's not only real, but if we don't take action soon, it will be too late. In the meantime, I'm going to see what Marcelo Costa and EVRAN Timber are really up to.'

O'Connor drove his hire car out of the hotel car park in Manaus and headed down toward the river. Located at the confluence of the massive Negro and Solimões rivers in the heart of the Amazon jungle, the sprawling capital of the Amazonas state was eclectic. In 1960, the Brazilian government had been determined to lift the Amazon out of economic isolation, and declared Manaus a 'free economic zone'. Attracted by generous tax exemptions, EVRAN and other major companies had invested heavily, and much to the dismay of those trying to protect the forest, the area had become a hive of activity. Journalists, artists and intellectuals congregated at the various bars around the plaza of the famous Opera House, while closer to the port, at squares like Praça da Matriz, one could find the usual mix of sleaze, sailors and prostitutes. In the nineteenth century, when the rubber barons held sway here, the rue Visconde de Mauá had been part of a stylish area of the city. Now the wrought iron balconies were rusted and broken, and gaudy blue and pink paint peeled from the two-storey facades.

O'Connor parked and made his way along the waterfront, past dozens of wooden double-decked ferries that would not have been out of place on the Mississippi. He chose a spot where he had a good view of the Chibatão and Super terminals in the industrial area on the river. The intelligence predicting the arrival of the EVRAN container ship had been correct, he mused, focusing his binoculars on the 20 000-tonne MV *EVRAN I*, berthed at the Super Terminal wharf.

Both the Super Terminal and Chibatão docks were subject to changes in river heights of up to fourteen metres, so they had been constructed as floating wharves, connected to the shore by massive ramps. The world's greatest river system was navigable for large, ocean-going vessels for 1600 kilometres, all the way to Manaus, from where smaller vessels could navigate for another 1900 kilometres. Unlike other great rivers such as the Nile and the Mississippi, the ocean currents in the Atlantic ensured the Amazon did not form a delta, meaning silting was minimal, and the river required little dredging. At Manaus, the Rio Negro and the Amazon's major stem, the Rio Solimões, came together to form the official head of the Amazon. The dark waters of the Rio Negro, which originated in low, tropical rainforest, and the muddy waters of the Rio Solimões, which originated high in the Andes of Peru and Ecuador, refused to mix. Because of differences in temperature and speed, they danced, with an invisible barrier separating them, and their embrace was not complete for another ten kilometres downstream.

O'Connor observed the ship with interest. She had not long berthed, and three 45-tonne cranes were hovering above the containers, delivering the first of them to the tractors waiting to haul them along the bridge to the shore. O'Connor pondered his options. If the missiles were already in Manaus, they would likely be kept in shipping containers in one of EVRAN's storage areas, and without any definitive intelligence, searching them all would be impossible. The only chance of a complete search rested in the hands of the ambassador, and neither McNamara nor Oliveira were holding out any hope there.

O'Connor checked his watch. Time to make his way over to where the protestors were gathering near the slipway to EVRAN timbers. A barge stacked with red cedar and big leaf mahogany had arrived from deep within the jungles, where EVRAN was logging one of the world's last great forests. O'Connor watched the helmsman manoeuvre it toward the shore where the logs would be loaded onto the rail trolleys and hauled up into the mill.

'No more logging! Kick EVRAN out! Save our forests! Kick EVRAN out!'

The protestors chanted ceaselessly, waving myriad placards, ranging from the mildly clever 'Barking Up The Wrong Tree', to the more serious 'Six Football Fields Logged Every Minute'.

An effigy of Marcelo Costa with a noose around his neck swung from a street lamp. O'Connor melded in with the crowd, when suddenly he noticed a tall, solidly built man dressed in black. The man had climbed on to a gantry behind an EVRAN fence topped with razor wire. He looked familiar, and O'Connor quietly photographed him.

'If you interfere with the unloading of lawful cargoes of timber, you will be arrested,' the man announced through a hand-held megaphone.

The protestors responded by blocking the slipway. The man in black gave a signal and scores of guards, all dressed in black and armed with heavy clubs, streamed out of the doors of the nearby sheds. Two more guards opened the heavy steel gates and the guards swarmed on to the slipway, swinging their clubs with ruthless abandon. O'Connor withdrew a short distance. His mission was not going to be aided by getting embroiled with a bunch of baton-wielding thugs, particularly when it seemed there would be no official response. It gets more curious, he thought. No police and no media. Protestors filming the attack found themselves stripped of their iPhones, lifted by their arms and legs and thrown into the river. Outnumbered and overwhelmed, the protestors were no match for Costa's guards and they withdrew, blood streaming down some of their faces, colleagues supporting those with broken legs.

Back in his hotel room, O'Connor was considering his next move when he received an encrypted message from McNamara on his laptop:

> Text from Khan to Jamal: 'Next shipment due to leave M
> in next 48 hours.' I've confirmed that Crowley clearly has
> influence over key players - no chance of official search of
> containers, but little doubt missiles are about to be loaded.
> Execute Plan B.

'Jesus Christ,' O'Connor muttered, hoping that the piraña wouldn't be too active tonight.

O'Connor waited until it was dark, and drove down the narrow roads to the waterfront. On either side, the stone fences around the container storage areas were topped with barbed wire, but O'Connor had already reconnoitred an area about 400 metres from the Super Terminal wharf, and he parked under a clump of trees that gave him enough cover. He pulled on his wetsuit and scuba gear, putting any thought of piraña out of his mind, reminding himself that although they were curious, piraña were not the biggest threat to swimming or diving in the Amazon. Notwithstanding Hollywood's best efforts, attacks by piraña were rare, and usually only in specific circumstances – if the swimmer was bleeding, wearing shiny jewellery, or swimming where there was very little food. The candiru catfish was a far bigger threat – a primitive species of catfish that literally ripped a hole in its prey, allowing the rest of its school to enter the body. O'Connor put that out of his mind as well, and concentrated on the task ahead. He did his final checks, crossed a strip of sand and slipped into the dark waters of the Rio Negro.

O'Connor checked his wrist compass and swam easily, heading toward the *EVRAN I*. Visibility was poor and after what he judged to be 200 metres, O'Connor quietly surfaced. Another 200 metres out into the river, the lights on board the *EVRAN I* were burning brightly, casting long pencil-like flickers across the water. He checked his compass bearing again and slipped beneath the surface. Swimming more slowly now, lest he crash into a wharf pier, he approached cautiously. Above him, the cranes had fallen silent, but there was still movement on the *EVRAN I*'s deck. O'Connor resisted any temptation to switch on his powerful torch. Instead he slowed as he felt his way past the first of the piers. Twenty metres further on, he reached the *EVRAN I*'s hull. He moved carefully down toward the stern and felt his way around the ship's massive propeller blades and the rudder, swimming to the exposed river side of the hull.

O'Connor released a small, fibreglass limpet mine from his belt, the same type used by the SEAL teams. He activated the magnet and positioned it on the hull. Satisfied it was secure, he worked his way back to the pier side and attached a second limpet mine to the starboard hull. The mines contained just one kilogram of high explosive, but they were in the form of a shaped charge, designed to concentrate the energy of the explosion so that it would punch a hole through the hull. O'Connor worked his way back to the propeller and spent the next fifteen minutes tamping plastic explosives around the shaft. He attached the detonator and preset timing device and quietly swam back along the hull. O'Connor surfaced under the pier, checked his bearing and headed back to the beach.

Three hours later, three muffled explosions rocked the waterfront.

35

EVRAN HEADQUARTERS, DALLAS, TEXAS

Crowley arrived on the eighty-second floor in a foul mood. 'Where's Reid at the moment,' Crowley demanded, his face flushed with fury.

'He's in Area 15,' Miranda replied, taken aback.

'Get him in here now and get Costa on the secure line!'

'What the fuck is going on down there?' he demanded of Costa moments later, as Reid took a seat in front of his desk. 'Who the fuck's responsible for this?'

'We're not sure, yet, Mr Crowley,' Costa replied, 'but the police are investigating and I'm leaning on them . . . hard.'

'What the fuck was Security doing, apart from sitting on their fat asses?'

'Security's tight, Mr Crowley, but as far as we can tell, explosives were planted below the waterline, so there's no doubt it was a professional job. We had a large protest here yesterday – the usual bunch of tree-huggers, but I doubt they were responsible.'

'What's the damage?' Crowley growled.

'I only have the initial divers' and engineers' reports, but the hull was breached on the port and starboard sides, flooding the aft shaft compartments, and the propeller's been badly damaged as well. We'll know a little more in another twenty-four hours or so, but this ship is not going anywhere for several months. We'll probably have to find a way to tow it to a much larger port with dry-dock facilities . . . which leads me to the question of the sensitive cargo. Do you want that shipped to Karachi separately?'

'No. That's too fucking dangerous. Karachi will have to wait. In the meantime, I want a full report on the damage, and I want the perpetrators of this outrage found and dealt with!'

'We're on it, Mr Crowley.' Costa was wasting his breath. Crowley had already slammed the phone into its cradle on the scrambler.

'Any ideas, Reid?'

The head of Area 15 shook his head. 'I've done some preliminary searching, but there's nothing on the radar.'

'Keep looking. In the meantime, what's happening with that bitch Campbell?'

'She and her campaign team are staying at the Carlyle hotel in New York. We've managed to bug the suite,' Reid said, glancing at Crowley's new PA. 'They're heading for the Iowa caucuses tomorrow, but they're scheduled to have a strategy meeting about now, if you want to listen in real time.'

Crowley took a seat at a desk surrounded by a dizzying array of powerful computers. The meeting at the Carlyle was just getting underway and the audio was coming through on the headphones as clearly as if they'd been in the room.

'In summary,' Chuck Buchanan concluded, 'for this campaign, we have to keep in mind what America and the world will look like in 2016.' The arrogant ex-White House chief of staff spoke in crisp tones, addressing the small group of powerful Democrats who had assembled in the Empire Suite of the Carlyle, one of New York's finest hotels. Along with their star candidate, Hailey Campbell, and the environmentalist Professor Megan Becker, ten of the Democratic Party's top political operatives had gathered for what would be the first of hundreds of meetings in Campbell's attempt to win the Democratic nomination, and ultimately, the White House. The campaign team was already in high gear.

'We need to focus on *our* strengths, and the Republicans' weaknesses,' said Buchanan. 'Last time round, they lost out big time with the Hispanics, so we have to continue with a moderate line on immigration. Right now, the Hispanics are onside, and we need to keep it that way. They're the fastest growing minority in the country. They make up 16 per cent of the population, and there are twenty-four million of them registered to vote. You only have to look at the '96 vote to see what a difference they can make – Bill Clinton garnered a whopping 72 per cent, trouncing Bob Dole's 21 per cent. They matter. Ditto gay marriage, for the simple reason that, regardless of what we might think, gay marriage is supported by the majority of Americans.'

'I support it,' Hailey Campbell interjected, well aware of Buchanan's homophobic views. 'Around nine million Americans are gay, lesbian or bisexual, and most of those are of voting age, and they deserve our support. If the GOP and the Evangelicals carry on about marriage being between a man and a woman, that's more power to us,' she reminded them.

'And finally, our trump card,' said Buchanan. 'The GOP lost out to women, and notwithstanding the appeal to women voters in Montana of their latest entrant, Carter Davis, unless the Republicans come up with a female candidate, we can capitalise on the female factor.'

'I'm not in this race because I'm a woman,' Hailey Campbell snapped, her piercing blue eyes defiantly cold. She had never liked the egotistical staffer, but had acceded to pressure from the Democratic National Committee to have him lead the campaign.

'Of course,' Buchanan replied unsmilingly, 'but it's a GOP weakness that we have to exploit at every opportunity.'

'You haven't mentioned global warming at all,' Campbell replied, just as unsmilingly.

Buchanan struggled to control his frustration. 'For very good reasons,' he said. 'Not only is it not a vote winner, but if you bring that up, it could cost you the White House. Last week's research might have indicated that 54 per cent of Americans think that global warming is due to human activity, but a sizeable number of those are Democrats. Undecided Republicans – those who might be swayed to vote for you for other reasons – will be put off in droves if you start putting a carbon tax front and centre. You've only got to look at what happened in Australia – it cost two prime ministers their office. This campaign has to be designed on what America is going to look like in the future, not today,' Buchanan insisted, 'and the whole thrust of the campaign has to be on the economy and jobs, jobs, jobs.'

'On the contrary, Chuck, the most recent research says 65 per cent of Americans *support* a price on carbon,' Professor Becker challenged, 'because they know it's the only way we're going to force the big emitters like EVRAN to put their house in order.' The environmental scientist angrily brushed her red curls from her forehead. She was more than a match for the ideological Buchanan, both in height and intellect. In return for joining the campaign team, Campbell had promised her that together, they could have a powerful impact on the world's intransigence toward global warming.

Buchanan glared at Becker. 'I've seen that tree-hugger research too,' he said, unable to hide the sneer in his voice, 'but you're leaving out the qualifier: they support putting a price on emissions that would help *create* jobs and *decrease* pollution, and if you believe a carbon tax will create jobs, you're on something illegal from the bottom of the garden. You can make statistics say anything if you phrase the question the right way. None other than the Nobel Laureate, Professor Marcus Ahlstrom, is now supporting Davis to the hilt. And when there's backing from someone of Ahlstrom's standing, even a moron like Davis is going to make mincemeat of any tax on carbon. By the time you're running for the White House, Hailey, if this economy doesn't pick up, fifty million Americans will be receiving food stamps, so any policy that remotely threatens jobs needs to be either ditched or kept under wraps.'

'I think Chuck's right, Hailey. You need to put climate change on ice until you get into the White House.' Adlai K. Washburn, the portly, red-faced chair of the Democratic National Committee, was as well known in Washington as any of the Kennedys, and notwithstanding his fondness for Tennessee whiskey, his authority was almost as powerful.

'Well, I think he's wrong,' Hailey countered defiantly. 'If the United States doesn't provide a lead on global warming, there aren't going to be any jobs . . . *period*.'

'It's at best a second-term issue, when you're no longer facing re-election,' said Washburn.

'And I don't have to remind you, Hailey,' Buchanan insisted, 'when it comes to jobs, the latest data from the Department of Commerce shows that multinationals like EVRAN and CEOs like that asshole Crowley – the companies that used to provide jobs for over twenty per cent of Americans – have cut the workforce here by over three million in the last decade on the basis of their so-called efficiency drives. In reality, those jobs have just been sent to low wage countries overseas, mostly to Asia – and while our economy's struggling and we're paying off trillions in debt, China's economy is rising fast. Guys like Crowley, who have a substantial interest in Chinese polluters, couldn't give a shit about global warming. The only time the big polluters in China clean up their act is when they've got the Olympics and the world is watching.'

'Don't talk to me about Crowley,' said Campbell, a steely edge to her voice. 'His latest venture is up in Alaska, where EVRAN's now prospecting for oil in one of the world's last pristine wildernesses, where the ice is melting so fast that by the middle of this century, the polar bears won't have any ice to hunt seals from.'

'Polar bears don't vote,' Buchanan griped.

Campbell gave her campaign manager a withering look, and she and Becker exchanged glances.

It had just gone nine p.m. when Crowley reclined on the couch and flicked on Walter Cronkwell and CNC's coverage of the Iowa caucus.

Miranda appeared, bra-less and dressed in a hip-hugging slinky black gown, the scanty neckline barely covering her breasts.

'You've changed,' Crowley said, admiring her cleavage.

'As you said, Sheldon, we're going to be spending a lot of time together, so I thought I might as well dress for the occasion.' Miranda bent over the low coffee table, exposing what little her dress had hidden, placing two glasses and an icebucket containing a bottle of Montrachet Grand Cru 1995, one of the world's great chardonnays.

Walter Cronkwell's voice filled the room.

'Some big surprises and not so big surprises in Iowa, Susan?'

'One very big surprise, Walter,' said Susan Murkowski, 'but in what was generally considered to be a lacklustre Republican field, the entry of the governor of Montana, Carter Davis, has electrified Republicans around the country. And even though he didn't feature in the straw poll or the debates last year, Davis has had a lot of exposure since he announced his decision to run, particularly in the powerful Centauri media.'

'Yes. Davis's critics would say the questions on Omega Centuari News interviews were nothing but meatball pitches, but the Iowans love him.'

'And that showed in the results,' said Murkowski. 'With all 1781 precincts in, Davis took an astounding 47.3 per cent of the vote.'

'So explain to our viewers why the Iowa caucus is so important. Why does a quiet, largely agricultural state have such an impact on the political process in Washington?'

'Perhaps the simplest way to understand the importance of Iowa in choosing the Republican and Democratic candidates, Walter, would be the notion that it's the first in the nation. It's a chance for candidates to get the party heavies in Washington to sit up and take notice, and that goes back to Senator George McGovern when he was running in the 1972 election. McGovern did a lot better than expected, which attracted the media's attention, and it's been that way ever since.'

'And what have the frontrunners been saying about Iran and the recent crisis in the Persian Gulf? I gather Carter Davis has been quite outspoken?'

Murkowski brushed at a wisp of dark hair and smiled. 'Outspoken would be one way to put it, Walter. Most of the Republican candidates have been guarded, but Carter Davis has condemned the theocratic state of Iran in no uncertain terms . . . here's a little of what he had to say.'

The image switched to an energised Carter Davis, standing in the back of a big red ZR5 Chevy pickup, surrounded by an equally energised crowd of Republican supporters, waving the stars and stripes, red-and-blue Republican Flags, and wearing large 'VOTE 1 DAVIS' lapel pins. Behind Davis, Rachel had strategically positioned the luxurious campaign bus for the television coverage, 'DAVIS for PRESIDENT' and 'FAITH and FREEDOM' emblazoned in blue and red on the sides.

'My fellow Americans, recently we've seen gas prices hike to a new record high of over twelve dollars a gallon – triple what they were before the sinking of the two supertankers, the *Leila* and the *Atlantic Giant*, and the closure of the Strait of Hormuz – followed by the biggest stock market crash since 1929. The finger is pointed firmly at Iran and the religious zealots who control their evil religion!' Davis thundered. 'This is a deliberate attempt to sabotage the jobs of hard-working American men and women – men and women *of the one true faith* who have made this great nation what it is today. When I become president, I'm not going to stand meekly by and just let this happen. As your president I will take decisive action to ensure this never happens again, and that means all options – *all* options – are on the table!'

The crowd cheered wildly, breaking into a chant: 'Carter Davis! Carter Davis! Carter Davis!'

Susan Murkowski reappeared. 'As you can see, Walter, Davis didn't mince his words. It's very early days, but he's now the Republican frontrunner, and if the results in Iowa are repeated in the upcoming primaries in other states, then come the presidential election, Davis will be the Republican candidate.'

'And the Department of Defense have still not confirmed that one of the USS *Truman*'s F/A-18s was shot down over the burning tankers in the Gulf, yet Carter Davis seems to be in no doubt – he thinks the Iranians shot it down. Do we know anything more about that?'

'There are other reports that indicate there may have been a collision with one of our drones. As you say the Department of Defense is remaining tight lipped, although they have confirmed the pilot was recovered from the sea.'

Cronkwell nodded. 'Well, it's to be hoped the pilot is okay. And turning to the Democrats, Hailey Campbell is well in front?' he asked, an avuncular smile creasing his craggy face.

Murkowski returned the smile. 'No surprises at all, Walter. The last poll in Iowa showed 65 per cent of voters would like to see her in the White House. Campbell's won the Iowa caucuses decisively, with 43 per cent of the vote, and her nearest rival, Vice President John Bilson, is a long way behind. He only managed 18.5 per cent of the vote . . . 11 per cent of Iowans were unable to name him.'

Walter Cronkwell maintained an inscrutable expression. 'Has Campbell had much to say about the crisis?'

'She's been very guarded, Walter, but here's what she had to say in answer to a question I put to her a little earlier today.'

The shot cut to a media conference on the steps of the Des Moines Capitol building.

'Ms Campbell,' Murkowski began, 'as far as the sinking of the supertankers in the Strait of Hormuz goes, Governor Davis is pointing the finger firmly at Iran . . . do you think he's right?'

'I've seen Governor Davis's response, and his rhetoric is bordering on reckless.' Dressed in a stylish white Chanel pantsuit, Hailey Campbell cut a striking and elegantly powerful figure. 'Firstly, let me extend my condolences to the families of those who have lost loved ones. The attack on these tankers and the closure of the Strait is an outrageous act of terrorism, but I note that Iran has been swift to deny any involvement. Before we start pointing fingers, let's wait to see the results of the investigations being carried out by the United Nations and our own Central Command, which has a forward headquarters nearby, at al-Udeid Air Base in Qatar. As I understand it, we've had SEAL team divers down on both wrecks attempting to ascertain the cause. In the meantime, can I add my voice to that of the president's appeal for calm. There is absolutely *no* need for continued panic-buying of fuel. Our reserves are in place to meet precisely this type of emergency, so I would urge my fellow Americans to remain calm . . .'

Crowley flicked off the broadcast. 'Our man is on track for the White House,' he said, sliding his hand up Miranda's thigh.

36

MENA HOUSE HOTEL, GIZA

The Cairo international airport might have only been 25 kilometres from the pyramids, but it took O'Connor and Aleta more than an hour to get through Cairo's chaotic traffic. O'Connor slowed at the entrance to the Mena House Hotel, built in the shadow of the Great Pyramid itself, but as he braked the car was stormed by a crowd of young men. The illegal guides were desperate for the rapidly diminishing tourist dollar, and they were aggressively proffering their services.

'These guys are getting more reckless the longer this Arab Spring goes on,' said Aleta, offering a sympathetic smile as she waved them away.

'For them, it's more like an Arab Winter.' O'Connor gently hit the brakes as one, more desperate than the rest, flung himself on to the bonnet. Hotel security cleared the way through to the entrance, and closed the boom gate behind their car.

'This place has so much history,' said Aleta, after they'd checked

in and settled into the Montgomery Suite, which had been decorated with many of the hotel's original masterpieces. The splendid door to the suite was inlaid with mother of pearl, and the living room was furnished with antique furniture. 'Trust you to get us a suite with furniture from a harem!'

O'Connor grinned. The furniture had indeed been sourced from the harem of a bygone sultan. The hotel itself had initially been built in 1869 as a hunting lodge for the Egyptian king Isma'il Pasha, and hadn't opened as a hotel until 1886. Over a hundred years later, it had retained all of its former glory. O'Connor detested ritzy five-star hotels, preferring those with a story to tell, and Mena House was no exception. While they hadn't added their own names to the guest book, there were some very distinguished entries, including Sir Arthur Conan Doyle, the future King George V and Queen Mary, Agatha Christie, Cecil B. DeMille, Frank Sinatra and Richard Nixon; and here too, in 1977, the Mena House Agreement had been thrashed out between President Sadat of Egypt and Prime Minister Menachem Begin of Israel, leading to the Camp David Accords and an historic peace treaty between the long-time enemies.

'Thank you for this,' Aleta said, as they stood out on the suite's private terrace, and she rested her head on O'Connor's shoulder. Beyond the sixteen hectares of gardens and palm trees, the Great Pyramid and the two smaller pyramids stood as sentinels to the ages, their secrets still intact. 'I'm still not accustomed to your standard of accommodation.'

'This isn't a dress rehearsal; this is life, and we're living it,' said O'Connor, putting his arm around Aleta's slender waist. 'When Accounts query it, I will argue persuasively that it was necessary to be close to the object of our investigation . . . and given what I found in the Kashta Palace, I suspect there's an element of truth to that. I'm still none the wiser as to why someone like Crowley would have an interest in this Euclid Papyrus. What time are we due with Professor Badawi?' His hand wandered on to the top of Aleta's taut thigh.

'In another hour . . . and no, as much as I might find that proposition attractive, it will take us that long to get through the traffic.'

'What proposition?' protested O'Connor, unable to stifle a grin.

'I know that look! Taxi or drive?'

'Taxi – this place is on a par with Lima and New Delhi. I'm over driving for one day.'

Professor Hassan Badawi was once again waiting to ensure there was no problem with security, and minutes later Aleta and O'Connor found themselves inside Badawi's musty, wood-panelled office, sharing tea with the professor.

'I'm so sorry to have read what you've been through, Hassan,' Aleta began. 'The mask of Tutankhamun was an unimaginable loss.'

Badawi smiled wanly. It seemed to Aleta that he had visibly aged. 'We can only hope the mask will be recovered soon. You can't put a price on it, and it's not only a loss to the museum, of course, it's a loss to the whole of society.' Badawi sipped his tea. *Shai,* or tea, was the national drink in Egypt, a position that coffee had never rivalled. It was so important that the Egyptian government ran tea plantations in Kenya to ensure a quality supply.

'Nearly two million people visit this museum every year . . . or used to,' Badawi continued. 'It seems we've been hit with a double whammy. The loss of the funerary mask has been devastating enough, but ever since the overthrow of Mubarak, the country's been in turmoil, and tourism has been decimated. We're really struggling.'

Aleta detected a tear in the old professor's eye and she placed her hand on his arm.

'I must apologise,' he said, reaching for his handkerchief, 'but this country has so much potential . . . so much! We used to provide leadership in the Arab world, and now we're in a shambles. Over twenty million Egyptians are living on US $1.50 a day, or less, and it's getting worse.'

'Egypt will rise again, and you have a lot of friends who will do everything they can to help,' Aleta offered reassuringly.

O'Connor watched the exchange between the two renowned archaeologists with interest. Two people who cared deeply, not only about the past, but about injustice and the future. Injustice in the world was something O'Connor had long struggled with himself. Given his assignments and the nature of his employment, he'd compartmentalised his anguish and banished those thoughts to the deeper recesses of his brain. But every once in a while a conversation like the one he'd just witnessed brought to the fore his frustration with the widening gap between the mega-wealthy and the poor, and, increasingly, a struggling middle class.

'Yes,' said Badawi. 'We can only hope that Egypt's military government will be temporary, and that democracy will rise again, otherwise corruption and nepotism will be worse than under Mubarak, and we had thirty long years of his dictatorship.' Badawi reached for a file on his desk. 'In between police investigations and media intrusion, I've been thinking about our last meeting. There's something really exciting about that photograph you showed me . . . and it's to do with the dots over the pyramids.'

Aleta felt a pang of remorse that she hadn't been entirely honest with her old friend, but she put her feelings to one side as O'Connor caught her eye. 'Yes . . . the superimposition of what looks to be a constellation over the top. But there's still argument over whether they're aligned with Orion, or Cygnus,' Aleta said, excited to find that an archaeologist of Professor Badawi's standing was thinking along the same lines. 'You think Euclid might have been trying to tell us something?' Aleta asked, after she'd outlined her theory on the two celestial bodies.

'He may have been. If the pyramids were not only aligned with the compass points but the movement of the stars as well, this is an exciting find. And I'm not one to delve into astronomy, but did you see that recent show on crop circles in the United Kingdom?'

Christ, O'Connor thought. Here we go again.

'No . . . I've been travelling. What show?' Aleta asked, her interest thoroughly aroused.

'Three more crop circles have appeared next to the Chilbolton Observatory in the UK – the Flower of Life, a detailed image of the Cygnus constellation, and a third which depicts the planets in our solar system,' Badawi explained, 'all of them extraordinarily intricate.'

'Appeared just after closing time at the Elephant and Castle,' said O'Connor, a wicked grin on his face.

'Just ignore him, Hassan. For a scientist, he has some peculiarly philistine views.'

'Then the scientist in our midst,' Badawi countered, 'might be interested to know that a chemical analysis of the flattened wheat showed the crop's molecular structure had been altered. They found rare radioactive isotopes which have never previously been found in a wheat crop.'

Aleta stared at O'Connor over the tops of her glasses with a 'what do you have to say to that' look.

'Hmm.' O'Connor didn't concede any ground, but his interest was suddenly piqued. It was the first time he'd heard about the chemical analysis of isotopes.

'Did the show throw any light on what the latest circles might mean?' asked Aleta.

Badawi smiled. 'Our friend the scientist over here might think this far-fetched,' he said, giving Aleta a conspiratorial wink, 'but there's speculation from quite reputable scientists that one may contain a warning. The solar system circle accurately depicts our planetary system, with one change. Earth is depicted with a jagged edge and a plume, which may be a representation of a planet rapidly warming – a ring of fire with a plume of smoke. As to the Flower of Life, the ancient representation of what we'd call radiant or free energy comes with a coded formula for a technology that produces energy without combustion, a technology that is based on the laws of nature, or the planet's vibrations – more than one scientist thinks that's worth looking at.'

'And the Cygnus constellation. I wonder if we should be looking at the significance of Cygnus instead of Orion?' Aleta asked.

'The Cygnus alpha star over the cemetery to the north-west of the middle pyramid has me intrigued,' said Badawi. 'Are you familiar with the northern night sky, Doctor O'Connor?'

'Only the major formations . . . I couldn't claim astronomy as a speciality,' replied O'Connor.

'One of the better maps was drawn by John Perring in 1837.' Badawi got up from behind his desk. 'I've laid it out over here on the chart table. You can see he's produced a detailed layout of the pyramids and the rest of the Giza plateau. Now, if we overlay Cygnus,' Badawi said, fitting a transparency of the constellation over the map, 'we can see the alpha, delta, gamma and epsilon stars, as well as the Cygnus beta star which falls over the Gebel Ghibli or 'southern hill' area east of the smallest pyramid on the boundary of an Islamic cemetery. But it's this small, unnamed star here that falls *inside* the Islamic cemetery that caught my attention.'

'I wondered about that,' said Aleta. 'It seems to fall over a well that Perring's marked on the map?'

'Exactly,' said Badawi, his dark eyes reflecting an enthusiasm for discovery and a possible solution to a long-standing puzzle. 'The well was known in ancient texts as Bir el-Samman.'

'And now?' asked O'Connor.

'It's still there, but an Islamic cemetery is out of bounds to non-Muslims, so before you can investigate the well, we'll need approval. The Muslim Brotherhood, or what's left of it, has its hands full right now. The military government is arresting its leaders left, right and centre, and its focus is elsewhere, although I still have contacts. But there's another problem. It's an artesian well, so it's connected to the water table beneath the Giza plateau, and that may mean an underwater maze.'

'We're trained to handle that,' O'Connor assured the Professor. 'If there's anything down there, it's probably been undisturbed for a very long time, so the visibility should be okay.'

'I hope so,' said Badawi. 'For a long time now, there's been speculation on what might lie beneath the pyramids, including predictions that one day, we will find the lost Hall of Records, although hard-headed archaeologists keep no more than an open mind on that.'

O'Connor grinned disarmingly. 'The Hall of Records? You will have to excuse my ignorance, but the more I hang around here, the less I seem to know.'

'The Hall of Records, like the lost Library of Alexandria, is said to contain papyri recording the history of ancient Egypt . . . although unlike the Library, we only have vague reports to go on,' Aleta explained. 'In the fifteenth century, al-Makrizi, a Cairo-born historian, wrote of subterranean passages that had been constructed in the vicinity of the pyramids for, as he put it, "depositories of the wisdom and acquirements in the different arts and sciences". And even before al-Makrizi, the fourth-century Greco-Roman historian Marcellinus wrote about winding subterranean passages near the Pyramids.'

'We've perhaps come close on a couple of occasions,' said Badawi. 'Henry Salt, who was the British consul general here in the early 1800s, discovered an entrance to some catacombs to the west of the Great Pyramid.'

'But no papyri?' O'Connor asked.

'No,' said Badawi. 'But in 1934, the tomb of Osiris, the Egyptian god of the afterlife, was found between the second pyramid and the Sphinx by Doctor Helim Hassan from the American University in Cairo. The chambers were explored in the nineties, and there are three tiers, one on top of the other, with access facilitated by vertical shafts. But again, no Hall of Records, and no papyri. And of course, the water table's risen since ancient times, so that may make things difficult.'

'Diving in confined spaces,' O'Connor mused aloud. 'That's not without its risks.'

The Muslim elders led the way into the cemetery to the south of the Sphinx, accompanied by Professor Badawi. O'Connor and Aleta followed with their gear. They passed through row after row of tombs, some dome-shaped, some with V-shaped roofs, some square, but all kept in white-washed condition, until finally they reached a grove of sycamore trees, including one that O'Connor judged to be over 200 years old.

O'Connor put his diving gear down near the paving stones around the well and extracted a lead from his pack.

'Professor Badawi, could you explain to the elders that I'm going to drop this weight into the well, to check its depth?' Better to have them understand each step than mistakenly take offence, he thought.

The translation into Arabic complete, O'Connor swung the lead line into the semi circular–shaped well and paid it out, watching the coloured knots that were ten metres apart. 'It's deep,' he said finally, 'about 15 metres to the surface of the water, and then another 35 metres to the bottom.'

'So we're looking at diving in about 30 metres of water,' said Aleta, 'and perhaps deeper if there are connecting passages through the water table.'

O'Connor nodded, unravelling a rope ladder and securing it

around the base of the nearest sycamore tree. The gear and safety checks took another twenty minutes, but finally, he and Aleta were ready.

'There's not going to be much room,' O'Connor said, 'so I'll do the exploratory dive, and we'll see where we go from there.' He attached his fins to his belt, and began the descent to the inky black surface below. He reached the surface of the water, put on his fins, switched on his head-mounted dive light and continued to use the rope to assist in the descent until he came to the last rung, some five metres below the surface. As black as the water appeared from above, down here it was clear and the powerful headlight beam picked out the ancient stone walls of the well. O'Connor checked his depth gauge and continued his descent. At nearly 25 metres, he saw it. The stone wall had given way to natural rock and an opening just below him that was about two metres across. O'Connor reached for his powerful hand light to supplement the one on his head. And just in case that failed, he had a third. It was a cardinal rule for diving in confined spaces and caves: always carry three sources of light. Despite the progress in technology, dive lights remained the least reliable of all diving equipment, and to be caught in a cave without any light source was a major cause of fatalities.

The natural tunnel ran at a right angle from the well toward the Pyramids themselves.

37

MISSOULA, MONTANA

Abigail Roxburgh sat in her office in Missoula. Unable to work, and with a tear rolling down her cheek, she absent-mindedly switched on the television. Not surprisingly, with the presidential election now less than a fortnight away, all the news channels were covering it. She settled for CNC and Walter Cronkwell.

'We're joined again by Susan Murkowski, this time from Alaska. So what's the feeling on the hustings up north, Susan?' Cronkwell asked.

'Very positive for Carter Davis, Walter.' The shot switched to Susan Murkowski, standing beside one of the marble pillars at the top of the steps of the Capitol Building on Fourth Street in Juneau.

'We're here in the capital of Alaska, where, despite the concerns of environmentalists over EVRAN's plans for oil drilling in the Arctic National Wildlife Reserve, Davis's promise of new jobs has him in front in the forty-ninth state of the union – a state that is perhaps lucky to be part of the United States at all.'

'Yes . . . we tend to forget,' Cronkwell intoned, 'that Alaska was actually purchased from the Russians in 1867 for two cents an acre. At today's prices, that only amounts to US $120 million, and even then, Alaska wasn't admitted to the union until very late, in January 1959. I guess since oil had yet to be discovered, the Russians would have had no idea of Alaska's value.'

'That's so, Walter, but those who love the pristine nature of this wilderness would argue that's worth way more than dirty black gold.' The camera panned across the stunning vista of Juneau harbour and the small city nestled at the base of snow-capped mountains that were thickly forested with pine trees.

'So with less than two weeks to go,' Cronkwell continued, 'someone who was virtually unknown outside of Montana a year ago is now looking like he could pull off a miracle . . . Davis might just be the next president of the United States?'

'Indeed he could. He was, as we all know, a surprise winner in the Iowa caucuses. It seems like only yesterday but that was nine months ago, and back then not too many political commentators, this journalist included, thought he would last the distance in the race for the Republican nomination. But in the intervening period, he's gone on to even more surprising wins in New Hampshire, Nevada, South Carolina, Colorado, Minnesota, Maine and Missouri.'

Abigail Roxburgh bit into her handkerchief. She'd watched every one of those wins, ballot by ballot, and even then, she'd thought she could remain quiet. It was still possible that her governor might return to Montana.

'But I think people really started to sit up and take notice when Davis swept the Republican field on Super Tuesday,' Murkowski said, 'when he took nine of the ten states on offer. And once he took

California, Texas, and Florida, it was all over. Those states alone gave him 116 electoral college votes and by then the Republican nomination was his.'

'And in the meantime, the wheels seem to be falling off Hailey Campbell's campaign?'

Murkowski nodded. 'Less than two weeks out from the election, she's sacked her campaign manager, Chuck Buchanan, who was chief of staff to President McGovern.'

'Do we know why?'

'My sources tell me there's been a rift between Buchanan and Hailey Campbell for some time, principally over policy on global warming. That's not at the centre of her campaign – like Davis, she's been concentrating on jobs and the economy, but when she's asked about it, Campbell leaves no doubt that she believes global warming is real, that a big factor is human activity, especially our burning of fossil fuels, and that we have to do something. For her part, she's been very clear that she won't allow the big emitters to continue as they have been. I'm told this all came to a head the other day when her team was discussing strategy for the last debate of the campaign, which goes to air tomorrow night. No doubt global warming will come up, because Davis is equally clear that, in his words, "global warming is a conspiracy theory from the loonie Left". The problem for Campbell is that the Nobel Laureate, Professor Marcus Ahlstrom, has been touring the country, supporting Davis, and if the polls are anything to go by, a lot of Americans are listening to him . . . especially when in spring, they were still shovelling snow off their driveways.'

'And the media, particularly Omega Centauri outlets, have been very pro-Davis?'

'And pro-Ahlstrom. In the early part of the race, Campbell was so well respected from her time as energy secretary that many analysts thought she would get to the White House in a canter, but the relentless pressure from the Omega Centauri corporation, coupled with saturation television advertising for Davis and a backing from Ahlstrom, has seen her lead virtually evaporate.'

'That was Susan Murkowski, reporting from Juneau in Alaska. Now in other news, President McGovern . . .'

Abigail's tears welled up again as she glanced at the front page of the *Montana Mercury*. The Omega Centauri tabloid boasted a huge headline:

BUCHANAN SACKED: CAMPBELL IN CLIMATE CHANGE CUCKOO LAND

The headline was accompanied by a cartoon of a big clump of mushrooms at the bottom of the garden. The biggest mushroom was capped with Hailey Campbell's head and the smaller ones with the heads of key advisors like Megan Becker. The subtitle read:

CAMPBELL AND THE DEMOCRATS: IN THE DARK, AND FED ON . . .

Abigail knew in her heart that her hopes of Davis divorcing his wife were gone forever, but she wasn't going to stand by and see that bitch on the front page of every paper and magazine, being interviewed as the new first lady. She flicked off the television and looked at her watch. Lunchtime. It was bitterly cold outside, but she needed some fresh air, and she took the lift down to the office foyer and walked the few blocks to the Higgins Avenue bridge across the Clark Fork River. Abigail stood in the middle of the bridge on the pedestrian walkway and pulled her parka hood tight. The wind was coming from the south-east and the pines on top of Mount Sentinel were heavy with snow. She looked toward Montana University, nestled at the base. In 1909, forestry students had erected a big white "M" on the side of the mountain. Since 1919, university freshmen hiked up the mountain each year to light the outline of the M with railroad lanterns to mark homecoming, the tradition of welcoming alumni back to the campus. Today the M was covered in snow, and Abigail's tears threatened to freeze before they reached the river flowing under the bridge. Her mind made up, she retraced her steps, determined to track down Susan Murkowski. Murkowski struck Abigail as a journalist who would listen.

38

EVRAN HEADQUARTERS, DALLAS, TEXAS

Crowley stood at the plate glass windows of his office and stared at the ant-like humanity on the streets of Dallas below. He felt a surge of exhilaration. It was all coming together. It had taken some months of complex planning, but the Cobalt 60 was finally in position and the plans for the attacks on the nuclear plants were well advanced.

The authorities in the gulf had dredged new channels around the hulks of the *Leila* and the *Atlantic Giant,* their burned-out super-structures protruding grotesquely above the waters. It would take many months to salvage them, and the oil had left greasy scars on the shoreline and all but wiped out the marine life. But the stock markets had recovered, and it was time to strike again. The long delays in the repair of the *EVRAN I* had irritated Crowley, but in less than two weeks, the Taipan and Scorpion missiles would be loaded and on their way from Manaus to Karachi, once again destined for the Hindu Kush and Iran. Best of all, despite Rachel's scepticism, Carter

Davis was now ahead of Hailey Campbell in the polls, albeit just. A lot would ride on their final debate, but the Campbell team, he knew, was in wild disarray over Campbell's stance on global warming, and with the help of Ahlstrom and Louis Walden, Crowley had a feeling Pharos would soon be in charge of the White House. From there, the path to the New World Order would become a reality.

He buzzed for Miranda.

'Ask Reid to step in.'

Crowley found himself savouring another evening with the tall, leggy blonde, and perhaps, he thought, it was time to give Rachel the flick; although, deep in the recesses of his mind, warning bells were sounding. Rachel might not have known about the extensive collection of stolen art held on the island of Corsica, but she still knew more than enough to damage him, perhaps irreparably.

Miranda flashed him a willing smile and departed, and Crowley dismissed the warning bells. The blonde was exciting, and Rachel had become passé.

'Have a seat, Reid,' said Crowley when the head of Area 15 arrived. 'Where are we at with O'Connor and Weizman?'

'Our source Aboud has reported only this morning that Weizman has not long returned from Abydos. And interestingly, O'Connor has joined her. They're preparing to descend into an ancient water table beneath the Pyramids.'

'Any clues to the Euclid Papyrus?'

'Not as yet, but Aboud is in no doubt that they're searching for it.'

'Keep me informed, and make sure Ruger is on standby.'

Ruger left and Crowley got up from his desk and stared out the window again, deep in thought. The path to the New World Order was on track, but the Euclid Papyrus threatened Pharos in general, and the EVRAN conglomerate in particular. Just as the discovery of oil in the early twentieth century had transformed the global energy sector, rendering coal-fired bunkers on ships obsolete and revolutionising the world's automobile and aircraft industry, any new form of energy hung like the sword of Damocles over Crowley and the other members of Pharos's sinister quest for ultimate power. Crowley returned to his desk, more determined than ever that the Euclid Papyrus would not see the light of day.

'Mr Reid to see you again, sir.'

'So soon? Show him in.'

'I thought you should see this intercept that just came in from Abigail Roxburgh's cell phone,' Reid said. 'It would appear she's considering exposing Davis. That's a text between her and that Susan Murkowski.'

Crowley stared at the printout, his anger rising.

> Have been watching your coverage of the presidential race
> with interest, but there is something you need to know about
> Carter Davis, and we should meet.

'Leave it with me.' Crowley waited for Reid to depart and buzzed Miranda. 'Get Ruger to come and see me . . . now,' he said, throwing caution to the winds.

39

MISSOULA, MONTANA

Ruger waited for Abigail Roxburgh to leave work, and then followed her at a discreet distance in his nondescript Chevrolet Cruze. He'd already reconnoitred her home – a hectare of Bitterroot River frontage in Lolo, south of Missoula. The mists were closing in as he followed his target out of the city on to Bitterroot Road. Fifteen minutes later, Abigail slowed at the lights and turned left into Glacier Drive, and then into River Drive.

Good, she's headed home, Ruger thought, as he followed her on to Red Fox Road. The house was set back, but better still from Ruger's point of view, it was on acreage, and the house was surrounded by aspen, old-growth cottonwood and ponderosa pines, offering a covered approach to the back deck, which overlooked the river and the hills to the east. He drove past as she turned into her driveway and pondered his options. One possibility was a shot from among the trees on the riverbank. He'd already ascertained that a dirt track near the river would give him a covered route to the back of the property, with a clear line of sight. He'd packed his Knights M110 7.62-millimetre sniper rifle in the trunk of the car, a rifle that had been used with impressive results in both the Iraq and Afghanistan wars. But Ruger knew a successful shot would depend on Roxburgh choosing to sit out on her deck to enjoy the misty evening, and as good as Area 15 was, they had no information on the habits of this target.

Failing that, he knew he could approach the house through the trees without being seen, and from his observations through binoculars, it didn't appear as if the house was alarmed. It would be a matter of defeating the locks.

The American Airlines Airbus A320 touched down in Missoula on time, and it took Susan Murkowski just fifteen minutes to clear the small red-brick international terminal, and another twenty minutes to book into the Hilton Garden Inn, by which time it was not yet six-thirty p.m. Her meeting with Roxburgh was not until eight at Roxburgh's house in Lolo. Unlike New York or Washington, at least everything was close here, Murkowski thought, and she headed down to the Blue Canyon Kitchen Tavern, the Garden Inn's rustic restaurant. She chose a table near the high windows. Outside, a misty evening was enveloping the distant, snow-capped hills.

It was odd that Roxburgh wanted the meeting at her home, Murkowski thought, as she ordered the honey and pecan encrusted baked brie, and the clams, sautéed in garlic, pesto and white wine. The braised pork belly and the grilled mountain buffalo, she would leave to the Montanans. Perhaps Roxburgh was afraid of being seen with a well-known journalist, although to date, no one had recognised her up here, for which she was grateful.

Ruger drove quietly down the dirt track beside the Bitterroot River with his lights extinguished, and he parked under a clump of ponderosa pines, 200 metres from the house. He scanned the rear of the property with his night vision goggles, but the back deck was vacant. Ruger looked at his watch. Coming on toward eight p.m. Time to move.

40

BIR EL-SAMMAN WELL, GIZA

O'Connor had no way of knowing how far the tunnel went, but a cardinal rule of diving forbade cave exploration on his own, and he set his dive computer and began the slow ascent to the surface. The deeper the dive, the more nitrogen would be absorbed into his bloodstream, exacerbated by the time spent at depth. Decompression sickness, commonly known as 'the bends', resulted from not making stops in an ascent to reduce the pressure of the nitrogen dissolved in the body.

He eventually reached the surface, removed his mouthpiece and called back up the shaft to Aleta. 'Okay, lower the tanks down, and then follow . . . but take it easy on the rope.'

Aleta lowered two foam-lined tanks that had been made to look like cylinders of air.

When Aleta reached him, he said quietly, 'I've found a linking tunnel at 25 metres. I'll lead.'

Aleta put her fins on and followed O'Connor into the depths of the well.

O'Connor reached the linking tunnel and hammered a steel peg into the rock, to which he fastened the end of a guideline from a dispenser on his belt. More than one diver had died swimming into what seemed like a single tunnel, only to turn around hundreds of metres later and be confronted with a maze of passageways, with no way of determining which one led to the exit.

O'Connor and Aleta exchanged the thumb and forefinger 'o-ring'. O'Connor checked his air pressure and made a mental note to leave at least two thirds of the remaining air for the exit. It was yet another rule for what was easily the most dangerous form of diving. They made their way along a passage that from time to time expanded into small flooded caverns formed out of the natural rock, but it wasn't until they were almost 500 metres in that they came to a much larger cave. O'Connor pointed upwards to where the torch light picked up empty recesses cut into the rocks just below the surface of the water. Aleta followed O'Connor and they broke the surface to find themselves in a large subterranean cavern.

'*Mon Dieu!*' Aleta exclaimed.

'The Hall of Records?'

'Very possibly, but any papyri that were not stored in waterproof urns would long since have deteriorated.' She gazed around in wonderment. 'Look! Up there!' she said excitedly. 'Someone's gone to the same trouble they went to in Alexandria.'

O'Connor followed Aleta's gaze to where a number of urns had been stored in the recesses above a ledge. O'Connor heaved himself up and helped Aleta out of the water.

'There are inscriptions here,' Aleta said, after they'd taken off their rebreathers, 'but they're in ancient Greek, not hieroglyphics.'

Aleta ran her eye over the carvings on the bottom of each recess. 'Every space has a different author, but it's the date that's interesting . . . they're all marked 31 BC.'

'What's the significance?' O'Connor asked.

'The battle of Actium,' said Aleta. 'In September of that year the Roman Senate declared war on Cleopatra because of the influence she wielded over Marc Antony. Antony had given her several of the eastern Roman territories, the so-called Donations of Alexandria, and a furious Senate threw its support behind his rival, Octavian,' she said. 'Octavian went on to defeat Antony and Cleopatra in a naval engagement on the Ionian Sea near the city of Actium in what is now Greece.'

'So what's the connection? I know that Octavian was the founder of the Roman Empire, but beyond that . . .'

'We'll make an historian out of you yet! But it's not the history of Rome that makes the inscription of the dates important, it's what was happening in *Alexandria* in 31 BC. After Octavian's victory, the librarians in Alexandria feared retribution from Octavian's advancing forces. In the end, Octavian's takeover of Alexandria was relatively peaceful, but they had no way of predicting that, so when Antony and Cleopatra committed suicide, the librarians smuggled the library's prize collections overland to Giza, probably by camel train.'

'Prize collections?'

'Look at the catalogue of names here,' she said, pointing to the markings on the recesses. 'Eratosthenes was the library's third librarian and is credited with calculating the circumference of the earth. He produced the first map of the world based on the knowledge of the day . . . wrote numerous treatises, and I suspect there are copies of them in that urn,' she said, staring at the ancient receptacle. 'Archimedes . . . probably one of the most famous of the ancient mathematicians, and the discoverer of *pi*. And look . . . Aristarchus, the first person to state the earth revolves around the sun, a full 1800 years before Copernicus. And here!' she said excitedly. 'Euclid!'

'Just two urns for him,' said O'Connor, 'and one a little larger than the other.'

Aleta's face was flushed with excitement. 'We have to take these back to the surface!'

O'Connor looked at his watch. 'I doubt Professor Badawi has too much of an idea of diving tables, but it's time we returned, in case he sounds an alarm. We don't want the eyes of the world on this just yet, and not a word about this, especially in front of Aboud.'

Aleta's disappointment showed clearly on her face. 'I suppose so,' she said, scanning the rest of the as-yet-unexplored recesses.

'We'll just tell them the passage was interesting, and we'll need to bring down a longer supply of air to explore it further.'

'We'll have to tell Badawi . . . we can't possibly not.'

'But not in front of his deputy. I've done some background checks on this guy . . . let's just say he's not what he seems.'

Aleta nodded resignedly. O'Connor's was a shadowy world, she knew, but she had long ago learned to trust this extraordinary man.

'We'll hide these urns in our satchels,' O'Connor said, 'and we can bring Badawi into the picture later.'

O'Connor carefully removed the urns, and placed them in the foam-lined tanks.

Back in the Montgomery suite, O'Connor pulled the curtains on the view of the Great Pyramid and on any prying eyes, and switched on the lights.

Not for the first time, Aleta's heart raced as she put on a pair of white gloves, ran her knife around the pitch seal on the larger urn and carefully prised open the lid. Just as carefully, she extracted the contents, two leather pouches, and opened the first of them.

'An original copy of *The Elements*! Or at least the first three books of it,' she exclaimed, quickly translating the Greek.

'And I'm betting that the other pouches contain the rest of it. Quite a find. A first edition, so to speak,' O'Connor said with a grin.

Aleta turned her attention to the smaller of the two urns, and after painstakingly removing the lid, she extracted the contents. 'Just a single leather pouch.' She slowly unravelled it, and laid the papyrus from within on the table.

41

LOLO, MONTANA

The mists drifted silently through the trees. Ruger checked the silencer on his M110 sniper rifle and crept toward the house, keeping to the shadows. Fifty metres from the back door, he laid the rifle behind a large cottonwood tree, checked the garotte in his pocket, and approached the back deck. He crept up the wooden steps, and moved toward the door. The sounds of country music were drifting from the living room. Through the curtains, he could see his well-endowed quarry. Abigail was in her kitchen, preparing supper. Ruger checked the lock on the French doors, only to find they were fitted with an old-style mortice lock. Prepared for any contingency, he selected a set of keys from his satchel. At least the music would shroud the sounds of the lock jigglers, he thought, as he tried first one, then another. It wasn't until the fourth jiggler that he felt the lock give.

Susan Murkowski paid the cab driver, and looked around. The mists among the cottonwoods were eerie, and she felt a sudden shiver down her spine. Murkowski felt for her iPhone, checked it had reception, and then switched it to silent. She walked up the long driveway and pressed the old-fashioned ceramic bell push.

Ruger swore softly as he heard the doorbell. He pulled the jiggler from the lock and withdrew into the shadows.

Abigail looked through the peephole. Recognising Murkowski, she opened the door.

'Susan? I'm Abigail Roxburgh. Come in, and thank you for coming all this way,' Roxburgh said nervously, leading the way in.

'Your text didn't say much, but if the polls for Davis are anything to go by, we might be talking about the next president of the United States, and that's important.'

'And it's that possibility that is worrying me sick. Davis is not all he seems. I've brewed some coffee, and we can have it in here,' Abigail said, turning the music down, 'but it's always nice to sit out on the back deck, even though it's misty.'

The voices carried clearly, and Ruger withdrew down the back stairs and quickly retraced his steps toward the trees, pondering his options. He knew Crowley would be none too pleased if the target spilled the beans before he got to her.

'Misty is good . . . although it's quite eerie,' said Murkowski, following Abigail out on to the deck. 'You don't get nervous out here? The neighbours seem a ways away?'

'Not really,' said Abigail, taking one of the padded wooden deck chairs while Murkowski took the other. 'At least not up until now. But let me start at the beginning. Governor Davis and I . . .'

Ruger braced the M110 sniper rifle against the big cottonwood

tree and adjusted the AN/PVS night sight, which gave him a mag-
nification of 8.5x. He held the crosshairs on Abigail's temple and
slowly squeezed the trigger.

Murkowski screamed as blood sprayed all over her and the deck.
About to vomit, she held her hand to her mouth and dropped to
the decking, suddenly realising she too might be in the sights of an
assassin. She groped for her iPhone, entered her code and dialled
911. Beyond the trees she heard a car start.

'Fuck,' Ruger swore, as he risked the lights and drove quickly
down the dirt track. Gaining River Drive, he could hear the sirens
in the distance. He turned into Glacier Drive and headed toward
the safety of the heavier traffic on Bitterroot Road.

Hours later, Murkowski composed herself as she prepared to go to
air for the late-night bulletin.

'You okay, Murk?' her producer asked.

'Bit shaken up, but I'll be fine.'

'And in five, four, three, two, one . . .'

'And we cross live to Susan Murkowski in Lolo, Montana, for
breaking news,' the evening announcer began. 'A shocking murder
tonight, Susan.'

Rachel Bannister was watching in San Francisco. She texted Crowley
and Davis to switch on CNC as she listened with increasing alarm.

'I gather Ms Roxburgh was on Governor Davis's staff,' the

announcer continued, 'and before she was killed, she texted you saying she had some information on the governor that you needed to hear . . . Was there anything in your discussion that might give an indication as to why she was shot?'

Rachel made a note of the three most damaging statements reported by Murkowski: 'worries me sick'; 'Governor Davis not all he seems'; and 'Governor Davis and I'. The last was not difficult – other than refuting what the tabloid media might make of it. She pondered her options. Far better to hold a media conference now, rather than let the media make up their own stories. Properly handled, this was a grass fire that could be put out. But who was behind it? Rachel had a terrible feeling she knew. Crowley was a ruthless businessman, but would that ruthlessness extend to this? Ever since she'd been excluded from the conversation with Ruger – a man with a record and a shady past – Rachel had felt the first pangs of fear in the pit of her stomach. Perhaps it was time to confront Crowley, but for the moment there was a more urgent task at hand.

The story had spread very quickly, and Rachel waited for the huge throng of journalists to settle at the press conference, before introducing Governor Davis.

As coached, Davis was on message. 'Firstly, my heart goes out to the family and friends of Abigail Roxburgh in what has been a tragedy for them, and for the state of Montana,' he began. 'Abigail was a loyal, hard-working employee,' he continued, reading from the dot points Rachel had prepared, 'and she will be sadly missed. She will be forever in our prayers.'

Rachel had deliberately kept the opening statement short, banking on the journalists asking the leading questions. She wasn't disappointed, as ten journalists shouted at once.

'One at a time, please,' said Davis, showing the results of Rachel's intensive training. 'Yes,' he said, indicating the attractive young journalist in the front row.

'Governor Davis, what do you think Ms Roxburgh meant when she said your probable win on Tuesday "worried her sick"?'

Davis nodded, maintaining the grave look Rachel made him rehearse. 'When I left Montana to announce my candidacy for this great office, Abigail – Ms Roxburgh – who was on my staff, asked to see me, and she was in tears in my office. Her exact words were, "Governor Davis, I am so worried. The greatest leaders in this country are so often assassinated . . . and I keep thinking about Kennedy. You've been —" and forgive me, but these were her exact words, "you've been the best governor Montana has ever had, and you would make a great president, but it worries me sick that an assassin's bullet has your name on it." I have no doubt that in contacting Ms Murkowski, Ms Roxburgh was trying to sound yet another warning to me. Let me say, I have the greatest faith in this country's Secret Service. They are the best in the world. Yes . . . over here,' Davis said, choosing an older male journalist, with a body that reflected hard living. At his first media conference, Rachel had been furious. The first ten questions had gone to attractive females.

'So what do you think she meant when she said, "Governor Davis is not all he seems"?'

Rachel had anticipated the question and she'd coached him, not only in the verbal response, but the equally important body language. Davis allowed himself a grim smile.

'That was something else that, on more than one occasion, Abigail – Ms Roxburgh – had said to me. If I remember her words correctly, they were along the lines of "Governor Davis, you're not at all what you seem. You give the impression to the public that you're a knock-about guy, and they love you for that" – and again, you will have to forgive me, because this is not a time for political statements, but she followed that up with something about me being as sharp as a tack, and that the people loved me because I *seemed* to be one of them. Her exact words were, "behind the scenes, you're always putting your intellect up against those who might be out to take advantage of ordinary, hard-working Montanans." I will miss her more than words can say,' Davis said, pulling a white handkerchief from his pocket. As coached, he dabbed at his eyes.

'So who do you think might have had a grudge against Ms Roxburgh, Governor?' Rachel had planted the question with one of the Omega Centauri hacks.

'As far as I know, Ms Roxburgh didn't have an enemy in the world. She was *always* willing to help those less fortunate than herself. That said, we have made some tough decisions in Montana, decisions that focus on jobs and the economy, and we've been tough on graft and corruption, and those on the wrong side of the law resent that. I only hope Ms Roxburgh has not paid the ultimate price for being a loyal member of my staff.'

Crowley flicked off the television and buzzed Miranda to summon Reid.

'I want round-the-clock surveillance on these three people,' he said, handing the head of Area 15 a list with three names on it: Emma Cooper, Brooklyn Murphy and Harper Scott. 'I want to know who they call, who they text, where they go, when they fart, and if there's even an inkling of them giving an interview on the Republican presidential candidate, Carter Davis, you're to call me . . . even if it's three a.m.'

42

THE GREAT PYRAMID, GIZA

'I'm beginning to understand why Crowley is so keen to get his hands on this,' Aleta said, breathless with excitement as she examined the papyrus. 'There are two documents here. The first is the original hieroglyphic record of the calculations done by Pharaoh Khufu's engineers when they built the Great Pyramid.' She pointed to the pintail ducks and scarab beetles, and the heading on the first papyrus leaf: *Pyramids – Construction*. 'But the second document is in Greek, in Euclid's hand, and I think it might explain the real purpose of the Pyramids of Giza . . .'

'So this *is* the Euclid Papyrus.'

'Without a doubt!'

O'Connor listened attentively as Aleta translated Euclid's Greek and his notes on the engineering calculations. 'We're going to have to check this out,' O'Connor said finally, 'and the only way to do that is to get inside the Great Pyramid.'

'Into areas that are well off limits to the public,' said Aleta.

'Which means bringing Badawi on board.'

'Well . . . we were going to do that anyway,' she reminded him.

'Yes, although I'd be a lot happier if Badawi kept his deputy out of the picture.'

'I'll ensure he sees us alone.'

The next day, Professor Badawi escorted O'Connor and Aleta into his office.

'We have a confession to make, Hassan, so I hope you won't be too cross with us,' Aleta began after Badawi had served tea.

'How could I possibly be cross with you, my dear?' the avuncular professor asked, his weathered face softened by his smile.

'I have reason to believe that your deputy may not be all he seems,' O'Connor explained.

'Do you have any evidence for that?' Badawi asked, his smile vanishing.

'He's been in contact with someone in Venice whom the authorities in Washington are watching closely. You'll have to trust me on this one. If anything is amiss, we'll try to deal with it quietly so that it doesn't damage the museum's reputation. In the meantime, we'd be grateful if you could keep our discussions to yourself.'

Professor Badawi looked at O'Connor long and hard. 'Doctor Aboud asked to attend this meeting . . . he was none too pleased when he was excluded.'

'Aboud is a graduate of the Australian National University in Canberra?'

'A very fine university,' said Badawi. 'It has a particularly good reputation for research, and Doctor Aboud gained his doctorate from ANU's School of Archaeology and Anthropology. He studied the Graeco-Roman period of Egypt and he's an expert on the works of Herodotus and Diodorus Siculus. Doctor Aboud is one of the few in the world who have studied the difficult works of Manetho, an Egyptian priest during the reign of Ptolemy I and Ptolemy II.'

O'Connor handed Badawi a sanitised version of the NSA report on Aboud. 'He bought his doctorate from the Degrees and Diplomas Order Centre, a Chinese website operating out of Shenzhen.'

Badawi shook his head in disbelief as he read the promo from the website:

> Buy a degree is more and more important for someone couldn't get a degree from his university. How to buy a degree and where to buy degree that means your choose. Our degree mill will service for you online everyday!
> We already have the high-end printing equipment, all kinds of import the original paper, mature processing technology and perfect service system. No matter from watermark, seal, or hot stamping or laser, we can do it 100% of similar! And you don't have to sit for endless examinations and do assignments.

'According to the Chinese Degrees and Diplomas Order Centre, and you can look their website up for yourself, ANU is a particularly fine university, and I'm sure ANU will be delighted to find it's being advertised as having over 200 books in their library. Since ANU actually has five libraries, that's forty books in each,' O'Connor said, unable to stifle a wry smile.

Badawi stared at the report, and the colour drained from his face. 'I'm shocked. But there have been occasions when I've wondered about some of his remarks. Where did you get this information?' he asked finally.

'My turn to come clean, Professor. Let's just say I'm not what I might seem either. I do have a doctorate in biochemistry and lethal viruses – won with a lot of blood, sweat and tears in the laboratories of Trinity College Dublin – but when I'm not with Aleta on her archaeological pursuits, I work for the United States government. I can't tell you much more than that, other than to say we're worried that Aboud may be about to drag the museum into an unholy international political row. I've always had my suspicions, which is one of the reasons we haven't been able to be totally honest with you. Now that we've isolated Aboud, I'll leave Aleta to bring you up to speed on our archaeological investigations.'

'I can only apologise, Hassan, but we truly are on your side.'

The old professor's smile returned, albeit wanly. 'If it were anyone else but you, Aleta, I might have difficulty believing anything any more. Some more tea?'

Aleta nodded and took a deep breath. 'Firstly, the photo we showed you of the original papyrus with Euclid's notations and the Flower of Life wasn't bought in Lima. It was a photograph of a very old papyrus we found in the Souk el-Attarine.' Badawi's eyes widened as Aleta recounted her discovery in the basement of the papyrus store in Alexandria and their subsequent dive on the ruins in Alexandria harbour.

'You've found the lost Library of Alexandria!'

'There's every possibility, but you can understand why we wanted to keep this quiet. If we'd announced this, the world's media would be all over you and the Department of Antiquities like a rash. But when we're ready, we would like *you* to make the announcement.'

'When you're ready?'

'We've also discovered a passage off the holy well at Bir el-Samman.' Aleta quickly brought Badawi up to date on the discovery of the subterranean cavern.

'The Hall of Records?' Badawi wondered excitedly.

'Quite possibly, but even more importantly, we were able to bring two urns out without Aboud or the Muslim elders being any the wiser.'

'Or me!'

'Again, we'd like you to make the announcement of this discovery, Hassan, but not yet. One of those urns contained an original copy of Euclid's *The Elements*, but the other,' said Aleta, opening her attaché case and withdrawing a rigid protective folder, 'is even more exciting.' She carefully laid the ancient papyri leaves on Badawi's desk.

Badawi reached for a magnifying glass and studied the documents. 'I think,' he said, after what seemed like an age, 'that you've found the Euclid Papyrus. What an incredible discovery.' He paused and took a deep breath. 'In all my years of Egyptology, I've never seen anything like this. It will turn on its head the widely accepted notion that the Great Pyramid was Khufu's tomb. If this papyrus is correct, Khufu's engineers were way more advanced than we've ever given them credit.'

'There's no doubt that the Egyptian engineers were amazingly successful in aligning the pyramids with the earth and the Cygnus constellation,' said Aleta. 'And as you and I both know, even today, the Great Pyramid is not only the most accurately aligned

construction on the planet but it's still by far the largest and most
precise as well. We'll have to find a way to explain this to the average person. Not only did the pharaoh's engineers incorporate the
Fibonacci sequence, but when you take the height of the Great
Pyramid compared to its base, it's precisely the same relationship as
a circle has to its circumference. The extremely concise side angle
of 51° 51' 14.3" means the mathematical value of *Pi* is contained
within the pyramid's shape.'

'Yes,' Badawi agreed. 'You may not be aware, Doctor O'Connor,
but in 1859, an Englishman, John Taylor, published some aston-
ishing findings on the Great Pyramid. The discovery that *Pi* was
embedded in its construction prompted Taylor to conclude that not
only was there a relationship between the height of the pyramid to
its base, but the height-to-base ratio was the same as the distance
between the centre of the earth to the poles. He found that the
"inch" Khufu's engineers had used was just .001 larger than today's
British inch. But more importantly, there are 25 pyramid inches in a
cubit, 365.24 cubits in the base of the Great Pyramid, and it's beyond
coincidence that 365.24 is the precise number of days in a calendar
year. The pyramid inch is one 500-millionth of the earth's axis of
rotation, so there's absolutely no doubt that Khufu's engineers were
not only aware of the geometry of our planet – their measurement
systems were based on that.'

'It is extraordinary,' O'Connor agreed, 'but the question is, how
much did Khufu's engineers know about frequency resonance and
the possibility that a pyramid could be built with a natural vibration
frequency? Euclid seems in no doubt, but if he's correct, there will
be evidence inside the pyramid and to check, we're going to need
your help, Hassan. Those areas are off-limits.'

Badawi nodded. 'That's not a problem. I'm not without influence in this town. You can start as early as tomorrow morning if you wish, or perhaps it would be better if we went into the pyramid after it's closed to the public?'

Aboud took his headphones off, locked them in the drawer in his office, opened his safe and extracted the mobile phone he'd been given by Area 15.

'He's pretty agile for his age,' O'Connor said softly, as he and Aleta followed Badawi into the ancient entrance of the Great Pyramid. The 'Robber's Tunnel' dug by Caliph al-Mamum's workers in 820 AD had now been used by millions of tourists, but Badawi was heading for areas within that were sealed off to the public.

From a distance, Aboud focused his binoculars and watched the trio disappear inside.

'Yes, he is agile, but he knows every block of limestone in here.'

O'Connor grinned mischievously. 'I wonder what the pyramid equivalent of the mile high club is? I'll bet it's been done,' he said, a wistful note in his voice.

'Stop it . . . we can save that activity for the Montgomery suite club,' she whispered.

'Now that would be an interesting list!'

'But only if you behave!'

They followed Badawi along the rough-walled passage and up some narrow stone steps that wound their way around the original granite portcullis blocks that the Egyptian engineers had set in place to seal access to the upper chambers.

'Have you been inside before, Doctor O'Connor?' Badawi asked as they climbed steeply toward the Grand Gallery.

'Once . . . but a long time ago, and there were a lot of tourists.'

Their voices echoed off some of the two million limestone blocks used in the pyramid's construction. At the start of the Grand Gallery, two ramps flanked the gallery's sides, but instead of climbing any further, Badawi led the way between them, down into a stone passageway that took them to the so-called Queen's Chamber. Most Egyptologists had agreed that it was highly unlikely any queen had ever been buried there.

'It's smaller than I expected,' O'Connor said, looking around the stone room with its pitched limestone ceiling and bare walls.

'Yes . . . about six metres square, and about five metres high,' Badawi said.

'And there's the residues on the walls,' O'Connor said, shining his powerful torch onto salt encrustations.

'There's been a lot of speculation about the salt,' said Badawi, 'and it's not only been found here, but along the entrance passage as well. Some, undoubtedly of the Christian persuasion, have put it down to the great flood in the Bible, but I think we can rule that one out, as there are no water marks on the exterior of the pyramid,' he said with a wry smile. 'No one has produced a plausible explanation but that might be about to change.'

O'Connor was suddenly energised. His in-depth knowledge of the chemistry involved gave him an even greater insight into the revelation. 'According to the Euclid Papyrus, the Queen's Chamber was used to produce hydrogen. The existence of the salt then makes sense.'

'I'm not following,' said Aleta.

'The easiest way to produce hydrogen, or H_2, is to displace it from an acid. Hydrochloric acid and a hydrated mixture of zinc chloride would work perfectly.' O'Connor pulled out a notebook and drew Aleta and Badawi the basic formula for the reaction.

$$Zn + 2HCl = H_2 + ZnCl^2$$
$$\textit{Zinc + Hydrochloric acid = Hydrogen + Zinc Chloride}$$

'The ancient Egyptians had access to both zinc and hydrochloric acid,' he continued.

'I'm not sure if it helps,' Badawi added, 'but I have seen an analysis of the salt on these walls. It was done back in 1978, when Doctor Patrick Flanagan sent a sample to the Arizona Bureau of Geology. It was a mixture of limestone, salt and gypsum.'

'Which in chemical terms is calcium carbonate, sodium chloride and calcium sulfate,' said O'Connor, 'which makes perfect sense. That's precisely the residue you would expect if hot hydrogen gas was reacting with the limestone in this chamber.'

'Good thing we have a chemist on this team,' said Aleta.

O'Connor grinned. 'Makes a change,' he said. 'Taking the lead next to you two.' He examined the openings of the two shafts that ran from either side of the chamber. Apart from a very small cleft, both were blocked at the bottom. 'These shafts would have been used to deliver the hydrated zinc chloride on one side and the dilute hydrochloric acid on the other, but they would have needed to be kept full to allow the weight of the fluids to force seepage through this small cleft.'

A sudden comprehension of a decades-old question appeared on Badawi's face. 'We've always been puzzled by these two small shafts . . . some have advocated they were a means of providing air, but they end sixteen metres before the outside of the pyramid, not far the King's Chamber. You might be right! They could have delivered liquids to create a reaction here.'

'And if the hydrogen needed cooling, then that might explain the niche in the wall here,' O'Connor said, pointing to an elongated cavity that resembled a fireplace. 'That could have housed a cooling chamber.'

'And there's something else. You remember the Gantenbrink door?' Aleta turned to Badawi looking pensive.

'What's the Gantenbrink door?' O'Connor asked.

'In 1992,' Badawi said, 'a German engineer, Rudolph Gantenbrink, explored one of these small Queen's Chamber shafts using a robot . . . this one here,' he said, pointing to the southern shaft. 'The robot came up against a limestone block at the top, and embedded in the block were what looked like protruding copper electrodes.'

'And over a hundred years earlier, in 1872,' Aleta added, 'Charles Smyth and his team found a small bronze grapnel hook, a portion of cedar, which may have been its handle, and a small granite ball.'

'I wonder . . .' O'Connor said, considering the possibilities. 'Did the grapnel hook look like this?' he asked, pulling out his notebook and quickly sketching a picture that looked like the hooks of two coathangers bound together.

Aleta nodded. 'Pretty much.'

'Then I think Euclid's on the money here. If the hooks – and there will be another one for the other shaft – had cedar handles, they would have floated on top of the fluids and been in touch with each electrode. As long as the shafts were nearly full, the circuit created would remain uninterrupted. But as soon as the level of fluid dropped, the circuit would be broken, signalling the need for more fluids to be pumped into the shafts.'

'That's supposing the Egyptian engineers had a knowledge of electrical circuits.' The old professor was still struggling to come to terms with a hypothesis that, if true, would disprove everything he'd ever learned about the Great Pyramid and its purpose.

'Given what's in the Euclid Papyrus, I don't think we have to suppose that . . . I think this is evidence they did. Remember the Baghdad battery?' Aleta said.

'Yes, it's quite extraordinary. Are you familiar with it, Doctor O'Connor?' Badawi asked.

'Not in any detail . . . only that it was displayed in the Baghdad National Museum, and when we invaded Iraq and we reached Baghdad, we went to great lengths to protect the Oil Ministry, while we did nothing to protect the National Museum, which was being looted just down the road.' O'Connor shook his head at the Coalition's ham-fisted approach.

Badawi nodded. 'It was found just outside Baghdad in 1936, and has been dated back to the time of the Library of Alexandria. Essentially, it consisted of a clay jar with a stopper made out of asphalt. The stopper had an iron rod surrounded by a copper cylinder and if filled with vinegar, or any other liquid that could carry an electric charge, it produced just over a volt.'

'And that battery was around centuries before Volta invented the modern version in 1800,' said Aleta, 'so it's more than possible Khufu's engineers had their own version of the Baghdad battery. We just haven't found it yet.'

'But even if we accept that the engineers produced hydrogen in this chamber, that's still short of Euclid's notations on the real purpose of the Great Pyramid,' said Badawi. 'Let's take the grand gallery up to the King's Chamber.'

Aleta and O'Connor followed the professor back along the connecting stone passage and together the trio ascended the grand gallery's wooden walkway.

'This is the antechamber,' Badawi explained. 'You can see the big grooves in the limestone that were used to secure the massive granite portcullis blocks, designed by the engineers to seal off the main chamber,' he said, leading the way into the King's Chamber itself. 'The first people to break into this chamber were the Muslims in 820 AD . . . Caliph al-Mamun's workers. Not only were the walls unmarked, but unlike the tombs of Tutankhamun, and other pharaohs, the chamber was almost empty, apart from this.' Badawi pointed to the huge, lidless, empty coffer damaged on one corner. The walls of the chamber, constructed from massive granite blocks, were also totally bare and devoid of the usual markings.

'Pretty much as it was built all those thousands of years ago,' said Badawi. 'The coffer has likely never held a mummy, and as it's wider than the ascending passage, it would have been placed here before the roof of the chamber above us was sealed with five rows of granite beams. They're called relieving beams,' he said, pointing to the stone beams above them. 'The traditional theory is they were put there to relieve pressure on the flat roof of the chamber, but in light of the Euclid Papyrus, I'm not so sure about the pressure relief theory. Added to that, there are many, many people who have reported strange energetic effects when they've visited this chamber.'

'I'm not surprised,' O'Connor agreed, a thoughtful look on his face. He stared at the roof above him, imagining the hundreds of thousands of tonnes pressing down on it. 'Why would Khufu's

engineers go to all the trouble of quarrying, dressing, and trans-
porting an extra 3000 tonnes of granite from Aswan, 500 miles up
the Nile, not to mention the difficulty of positioning them so high
up in the structure, when a simple inverted V would perform the
same function? It doesn't make any sense. And the two shafts that
connect this chamber with the outside of the pyramid clearly had
nothing to do with ventilation. You don't ventilate a mummy and
expose it to the atmosphere.'

O'Connor turned to Aleta and Badawi. The looks on the faces
of the two renowned archaeologists confirmed Egyptology had just
been turned on its head.

'I think Euclid was right . . . the Great Pyramid is not at all what
it seems.'

43

ISLAMABAD, LONDON, MELBOURNE, CHICAGO

It had taken many months of training, planning and positioning, but at last, the teams of terrorists in Great Britain, Australia and the United States were ready to attack the West.

General Khan felt a surge of adrenalin as he read the single word text from Crowley:

Execute.

At last, they could strike again at the Infidel he hated with such passion. Khan pulled up the stampgeekcol.com website and made a comment under his codename. 'I have just acquired a 1971 Republik Österreich two-schilling stamp commemorating twenty-five years of nationalised industry, featuring the Austrian nitrogen plant at Linz.' Khan added the image of the plant that depicted a plume of smoke issuing from a maze of towers and pipes.

Eleven thousand kilometres away, ensconced in her impenetrable office at NSA headquarters at Fort Meade, Barbara Murray struggled to make sense of General Khan's latest posting on the website. She put through an encrypted call to Tom McNamara.

'The attacks on the *Leila* and the *Atlantic Giant* were preceded by benign acquisition postings on stampgeek,' Murray said, 'but I'm not sure what this latest post from Khan means, other than we can expect another attack. I doubt it has anything to do with Austria.'

'I agree. But that doesn't give us much to go on, and it's a bit hard to put forces on alert on the basis of a probable attack in an unknown location. I'll brief the president and the National Security Council of course, but I suspect we'll need something more concrete . . . Any luck on breaking Crowley's encryptions?'

'Not yet, but I'm working on it.'

Murray was almost 100 per cent sure another attack was imminent, but she was sympathetic to McNamara's position. The system was too big and unwieldy to act on every possible alert, and if the post turned out to be a message about some other activity, albeit undoubtedly illegal, he would be pilloried for crying wolf. Her fingers flew across the keyboard as she fed a fresh set of criteria into the massive NSA computers in yet another attempt to break open EVRAN and Crowley's encryption codes.

Across the Atlantic, Sadiq Boulos and Gamal Nadar knelt on their prayer mats in their dilapidated two-bedroom flat in a housing estate in Peckham, less than five kilometres to the south of St

Paul's Cathedral. Nadar, who had been charged with detonating the bomb, took the lead. Both men believed this would be their last prayer before they were welcomed into heaven. Together, they assumed the *sujood* position, kneeling on their prayer mats. They had long since determined *Qibla* as being to the south-east. It differed, depending on what part of the world you were in, but when praying, *Qibla* was the direction a Muslim must face toward Mecca, the birthplace of the Prophet Muhammad, and the holiest site in all of Islam.

'*Allahu Akbar* . . . Allah is great . . .

'*Subhana rubbiyal a'ala* . . . How perfect is my Lord . . .

'*Assalamu alaikum wa rahmatullah* . . . peace and mercy of Allah be upon you.'

At the end of the prayers, Nadar and Boulos embraced. It was time to go.

'Soon we will join Muhammad, peace be upon him,' said Nadar, extracting the small blue Cobalt 60 container from where it had been hidden in the back of a wardrobe. He opened the prepared briefcase, which, save for an indentation for the cobalt, was filled with 20 kilograms of plastic explosive, and then turned toward Boulos, smiling as he opened the container and the lead shielding. The Cobalt 60 glowed a deep, eerie blue, and both men were immediately subjected to intense, cancer-causing gamma rays. In a few hours, they would become very ill, but the bomb was planned for detonation well before then.

'And the half-life . . . 5.27 years,' said Boulos. 'The Infidel's city will have to be evacuated.' He had read up on the deadly substance and had been delighted with his findings.

Nadar fitted the radioactive metal into the slot he'd prepared.

'It fits perfectly, Sadiq, *Alhamdulillah* . . . praise be to Allah!' He closed the briefcase and locked it.

'Paradise is not far away, Sadiq.' The pair had often discussed this paradise the Qu'ran so temptingly offered, and at last, they had their opportunity to go there.

'Yes, and not only that, Gamal, but the virgins . . . the houris will be so beautiful!' Boulos said, turning to his favourite *hadith,* or saying, the *Al-Itqan fi Ulum al-Qur'an* by Jalaluddin Suyuti. The celebrated fifteenth-century Egyptian religious scholar had held a chair in the mosque of Baybars in Cairo, and his interpretation of the Holy Qu'ran was one in which both Nadar and Boulos put great store. Boulos turned to page 351, and began to read.

> *Each time we sleep with a Houri we find her virgin.*
> *Besides, the penis of the Elected never softens. The*
> *erection is eternal; the sensation that you feel each time*
> *you make love is utterly delicious and out of this world*
> *and were you to experience it in this world you would*
> *faint. Each chosen one will marry seventy houris, besides*
> *the women he married on earth, and all will have*
> *appetising vaginas.*

Nadar and Boulos had both bought smart casual clothes for the occasion, warned that sloppy dress and backpacks might arouse suspicion, particularly for men of Middle Eastern appearance. No one took the slightest notice of either them or the briefcase and they climbed the 528 narrow steps, past the Whispering Gallery and the Stone Gallery, and on up to the Golden Gallery, almost at the top of the dome.

Nidal Basara and Jibral Maloof had rented a small two-bedroom flat on the Esplanade at Burnham-on-Sea, a small town in Somerset at the mouth of the River Parrett and Bridgewater Bay. More importantly, Burnham-on-Sea was very close to the massive Hinkley Point nuclear power station.

Basara piloted their small fishing tinny out of the mouth of the river, and headed west along the coast. The tinny attracted no more attention than the passing gulls, and they motored quietly into the Bristol Channel, keeping a distance from the shore.

'There it is, Jibral! That will be the Infidel's downfall,' Basara said, scanning the huge reactor through his binoculars. 'Once we've achieved a core meltdown, the winds will take the radioactive cloud right across his biggest city.'

'*Insha'Allah!*' Maloof replied enthusiastically.

Abdul Qureshi and Shadib Said were seasoned terrorists. They had both spent twelve months fighting on the side of the Sunni Muslim Brotherhood in the long and protracted Syrian civil war against President Bashar al-Assad's Alawite minority. The Alawites, a sect of Shia Islam, were allied with Iran and Hassan Nasrallah's Iranian-backed Shi'ite Hezbollah, based out of Lebanon. The Syrian conflict had only entrenched the view of both young men: that

Shi'ite Muslims were heretics, and the only true Muslims were Sunnis.

It was a split that went back to the death of the Prophet Muhammad himself. The Prophet was illiterate, and when he died in 632, he left no written directions as to who should be his successor. A bitter fight broke out between those who thought Muhammad's successor should be a blood relative, and those who thought the most theologically qualified should succeed him. The proponents of the blood relative argument were the *Shia-t-Ali,* the followers of Ali, who was both the Prophet's cousin and son-in-law, having married the Prophet's daughter Fatima. On the other side, the proponents of the best qualified candidate were the Sunni, which in Arabic meant 'one who follows the traditions of the Prophet'. They backed Muhammad's close friend and advisor, Abu Bakr, who eventually won, becoming the first in a long line of Caliphs, not extinguished until Mustapha Atatürk, the father of modern Turkey, abolished the office in 1924. Much like the Protestants and Catholics in Northern Ireland, the Sunni's and Shi'ites had been at each other's throats for centuries. But they did have a common enemy to which these two fanatical young Sunnis had now turned their attention: the West.

Just on three-thirty p.m., Qureshi and Said emerged from Melbourne's iconic Flinders Street Station.

'The wind is from the south, Shadib, so we'll use the Skydeck.' Even though the Skydeck's outside viewing platform faced South Melbourne, Qureshi had designed the bomb so the explosion would blow the cobalt outwards, and he was confident the wind would take the deadly cloud around the sides of the building and to the north, into the city centre. They took the walkway across the Yarra River, and made their way to the Eureka Skydeck, the southern hemisphere's highest viewing platform. They took the fast lift to the top, and immediately stepped through the air lock on to the terrace, an outside platform that was almost 300 metres above the city.

'Perfect,' Qureshi whispered as he took a last look at the view across South Melbourne and the magnificent Port Phillip Bay. 'The tennis is on at Rod Laver Arena, and those women exposing themselves are about to play their last matches,' he hissed, his voice laden with contempt. The sight of the scantily clad players, their knickers in plain view when they served, had more than once brought him to a point of apoplexy.

'That's why they need Sharia law in this country,' Said agreed. 'I would stone them to death.'

In Sydney, Iqbal Safar and Hazim Gerges were unaware of what their colleagues were up to in Melbourne. Al Qaeda, far from being the cohesive terrorist group that was sometimes portrayed in the media, consisted of disparate groups of young fanatics, increasingly beholden to no one but themselves.

Radicalised at an early age by a fiery Muslim preacher who had blamed Australian women for their own rapes, Safar and Gerges hated the West with a passion, and particularly Western women. Their Imam was right. Women who did not cover up and wear the veil were like meat left out on the footpath that would be eaten by cats. They were inviting assault. Like their Imam, they believed that women were used by Satan to control men. Now, both were looking forward to the pure virgins and appetising vaginas they knew they would find in heaven.

'The best approach will be along the Heathcote Road,' Safar suggested, as he spread the map out on the kitchen table of the flat they'd rented in Liverpool. 'If you look here,' he said, bringing up the Lucas Heights nuclear reactor on Google Earth, 'the shortest way in is through the thick bush to the south of the perimeter fence. That's the decommissioned HIFAR reactor there, and the new OPAL core is in this building here.'

'Yes, but why must we wait?' the fiery young Gerges complained. 'Fuck them. Let's hit them now!'

'We shall see, Hazim. If we don't hear anything soon, that might be our best approach.'

Nasib Touma picked the lock on the door to the stairway that led to the 110th floor of the Willis Tower in Chicago, although 110 didn't appear on any Willis Tower public elevator – for very good reasons. Formerly known as the Sears Tower, the 110th floor was the nickname electricians used for the 442-metre-high roof of what was now the second tallest building in the whole of the United States, just behind New York's new One World Trade Centre constructed on the site decimated by the September 11 attacks. Dressed in khaki electrician's overalls embossed with 'Willis Tower', Touma and his accomplice, Hassan Botros, made their way on to the roof of the building.

'We are lucky today, *Alhamdulillah* . . . praise be to Allah,' Touma said. 'The wind is coming from the north. This is going to spread right across his business district.'

'Allah is on our side, Nasib,' Botros agreed. He walked up to the chest-high ledge and looked down across the Chicago River and the massive city below. 'There are nearly three million of the Infidel down there,' he said, steadying himself against the wind.

'And you can add another 100 000 visitors who won't be going home, *Insha'Allah*. And look, over there,' Touma said, pointing to the south-east. 'There's LaSalle Street and his Federal Reserve building and the Chicago Stock Exchange.' Touma held on to the ledge. Already the deadly cobalt was starting to affect him. 'This is not only the Great Satan's second-largest business city . . . it's a world financial centre,' he said. 'There are sixty-six Fortune 1000 companies down there and this will send shock waves through their share market.' Touma had done his research, but he needn't have bothered. Crowley had personally chosen the densely populated city.

Kaliq Sarraf and Lutfi Ghanem motored quietly up the Hudson River in the small cruiser they'd rented for six months. They passed the memorial to the Battle for Stony Point on the west bank, where in 1779, during the American Revolution, a small group from George Washington's Continental Army, under the command of General 'Mad Anthony' Wayne, had defeated the British troops in a daring raid against the colonial outpost.

'Like the Infidel's General Wayne, we will defeat them at their own game,' he said, as the nuclear power plant came into view on the east bank of the river.

'Look at it, Kaliq,' said Ghanem, staring in awe at the huge Indian Point reactors.

44

THE RITZ-CARLTON HOTEL, DALLAS, TEXAS

Rachel watched from the wings of the stage in the ballroom of the fashionable five-star Ritz-Carlton in Dallas. She had done all she could, and provided Davis didn't put his foot in it, she was quietly confident they would not only win this fourth and final debate of the presidential election, but the election itself – particularly since a segment of the night's topic on foreign policy and global issues included climate change, Campbell's Achilles heel.

Her thoughts turned to Sheldon Crowley. In the long months apart, she'd been more than a little surprised at how much she'd missed being around him. Was it the power of power? she'd wondered. After all, Crowley was not particularly physically attractive. Rachel had read somewhere that men and women who had a high need for power had sex more often than those who did not. Not for the first time she wondered if Miranda had somehow managed to usurp her position in Crowley's inner circle, but she forced herself to concentrate on the task at hand.

'Good evening from the grand ballroom of the Ritz-Carlton

Hotel in Dallas,' Walter Cronkwell intoned from the centre of the stage. 'I'm Walter Cronkwell of CNC news. This is the fourth and last debate of the presidential campaign, which is brought to you by the Commission on Presidential Debates, and tonight's debate is on foreign policy and global issues. With President McGovern completing the eighth year of his presidency, we have two new candidates vying for election. The questions are mine, and I have not shared them with the candidates or their aides.'

Rachel smiled to herself. Davis didn't know it, but Area 15 had found hacking into Cronkwell's computer child's play.

'The audience has taken a vow of silence – no applause, no reaction of any kind, except right now when we welcome former secretary of energy Hailey Campbell and Governor Carter Davis of Montana.'

The audience applauded wildly, taking advantage of their opportunity. Rachel watched the reaction with interest. It was impossible to know who the wolf whistles were for, but even if the audience was supporting Campbell, it didn't matter; from now on the vow of silence would apply. The two candidates shook hands, and Rachel picked up on Campbell's reluctance as Davis got closer and kissed her on the cheek. Rachel had dressed Davis in a conservative and expensive dark-blue suit, white shirt and a soft red tie. But as distinguished as she'd made her candidate look, she had to admire Hailey Campbell. The woman was all style, and her dark blue Armani pantsuit and scarf reflected that in spades. In turn, both candidates shook hands with Cronkwell, and then took their places at the table, Cronkwell with his back to the audience, the candidates facing them.

'Both your campaigns have agreed to certain rules,' Cronkwell began, 'and the evening will be divided into segments for discussion, including one on global warming, which has been such a feature of this campaign, and one on the Middle East. Given the attacks on the two supertankers in the Strait of Hormuz, and the subsequent stock market crash, the Middle East remains a critical foreign policy challenge for the next occupant of the White House. You will each have three minutes to respond to the questions, then we'll move on to general discussion. Now, as Governor Davis has won the toss, the first question goes to you, Governor. The United States has now been involved in two very costly wars in Afghanistan and Iraq . . .'

Neither candidate was allowed briefing notes, and Rachel listened as Davis outlined the Republican policy on the Middle East as she'd coached him. Armed with the questions, she'd only needed to prep Davis on what would be asked, which cut the amount of information down immeasurably, whereas Campbell, she knew, would have spent days on hypotheticals, with her staff peppering her with 'What if Cronkwell asks this?'

'The United States cannot continue to be the world's policeman,' Davis concluded, 'and as your president, I will always be willing to facilitate a peaceful solution, but that does not include taking the lead. In the past, the young men and women of our defence forces have shed far too much blood on the battlefield, while other countries have sat back and allowed the United States to do the heavy lifting. We need to put our energy into jobs and the economy at home.'

EVRAN had spent millions and Rachel was armed with the best research money could buy; research that showed very clearly Americans were sick of foreign wars that cost trillions when the jobless rate was still high, with over four million in the long-term unemployed bracket. Davis's answers were designed to appeal exactly to what Americans hoped for.

Even so, as the debate came to the final topic, Rachel judged her candidate was behind. Davis had performed well in the set answers, but the super-intelligent Campbell was measured and balanced, and she consistently outdebated her candidate in the freestyle discussions. Rachel listened approvingly to Davis as the topic of climate change came up; and he concluded his response in the manner she'd painstakingly rehearsed him.

'In summary, I would say to the people of America, as you've shovelled snow off your driveways, you can rest assured, global warming is a figment of the Left's imagination. A few months ago, Professor Ahlstrom, one of the finest scientists alive today, summed it up when he said "We need to consign this morally bankrupt green agenda to the trashcan." '

Rachel scanned the audience. Many of them were nodding furiously.

Hailey Campbell's eyes flashed with determination and courage as she began her response.

'I've noted with interest Governor Davis's remarks on global warming, and indeed similar views put forward in the media, particularly Omega Centauri, who seem to think it is they, rather than the American public, who will decide this election.' She paused for a moment, looking around the room. 'But my position has not changed, and if it costs me the presidency, so be it. Let me tell you why. The snow-storms we've experienced are unprecedented, as is the increased frequency and ferocity of tsunamis like the one that destroyed the Fukishima nuclear plant in Japan, volcanic eruptions, wildfires in California and Australia, hurricanes like Katrina which devastated New Orleans, and typhoons like Haiyan which killed over 6000 people in the Philippines. And while we can't point to a single event like Katrina and say "Aha, that's because of climate change!", we *can* look at *trends*. The Intergovernmental Panel on Climate Change has warned that it is now 95 per cent certain that global temperatures are rising and that human activity is to blame. Indeed, the overwhelming majority of scientists agree that devastating weather trends are directly related to our warming of the planet. In the time available, let me deal with just one issue that is at the centre of this very hot debate,' Campbell said. When some in the audience smiled at her intentional pun, she smiled back, reaching out to them.

Rachel looked on in admiration. The woman had guts, and the audience was listening.

'According to NASA, the ten warmest years on record have occurred since 1997. In 2006, as a result of warmer winter temperatures, Lake Erie, the fourth largest in the Great Lakes and the tenth largest lake in the world, failed to freeze for the first time in recorded history. As a result, this caused *heavier* snowstorms. Why? Because more water was available for evaporation and precipitation.' Hailey Campbell paused, aware of the looks of surprise on some in the audience.

'And without getting too technical, many distinguished scientists point to global warming as being a major factor in the snow-storms we've had across America.' She and Megan Becker had spent many hours working on how to best communicate the science to the layperson. Both were aware that all Louis Walden and his gutter-dwelling tabloids in the Omega Centauri Corporation had to do was whistle up a 'Cloud Cuckoo Land' headline alongside frustrated Americans shovelling snow, and with the help of social media like Facebook and Twitter, the message would go viral.

'The recent snow-storms in the United States are related to something scientists refer to as the "polar vortex", which, as you'd expect, is a whirlwind of extremely cold air near the poles. Winds of around 100 miles per hour keep that cold air locked up unless something causes the winds to weaken. And what causes that? You will be relieved to know,' Campbell said with a smile, 'that there isn't time to go into Rossby waves that transport energy from the troposphere to the stratosphere, throwing the winds off balance.'

Some in the audience smiled back, others looked bemused, but Rachel detected a man in the front row nodding in furious agreement.

'Suffice to say, as the air in the arctic warms, the vortex can be split, and as one scientist put it, the vortex starts to "wobble like a drunk on his fourth martini". That powerful, icy blast escapes southward, creating the snowstorms the Republicans are using as "proof" that global warming is a myth. Global warming is actually *causing* the snowstorms. And it's not only snow – as the oceans warm, the air will contain more moisture, generating the monster storms we've seen here and in the United Kingdom, and the recent lethal mudslides in São Paulo, in Brazil. If we don't do something about this, get used to extreme weather, and get used to it becoming much worse.

'The big polluters are driven by just two things, profit and share price,' Campbell continued. 'They couldn't care less about the average Joe in the street, but I do! Along with poverty, and the activities of religious extremists, global warming is one of the greatest challenges facing the world today. If we are to have *any* hope of avoiding even greater catastrophic destruction, this is an area where the United States *does* need to do the heavy lifting, so that other big polluters like China and India will come on board.

We need a world leader to set the example, and as your president, I will do just that!'

Across town on the eighty-second floor of EVRAN Towers, Crowley looked at the message on his encrypted phone and muted the debate on the television. Miranda lifted her head from his shoulder.

'I've got to take a call, but I think we can open another Romanée Conti.' At over US $3500 a bottle, few people ever got to taste the legendary Grand Cru Pinot Noir from the Côte de Nuits subregion of Burgundy. It had been described as one of the greatest wines in the world.

'Should I put my bra back on?' Miranda asked, a mischievous smile on her face.

'We'll only have to take it off again when I fuck you on the couch,' Crowley said. Their relationship had progressed to the point where Crowley was spending more and more time with the leggy blonde.

Crowley listened intently while Aboud described the conversation he'd recorded in Professor Badawi's office. 'So where are they now?' he demanded when Aboud had finished.

'They're staying at the Mena House Hotel.'

'It's critical we recover that papyrus. I'll have someone there in the next twenty-four hours. In the meantime, keep the listening device on, and keep me informed.'

Crowley put a call through to Ruger. 'You're to leave immediately for Cairo,' he concluded. 'I'll have one of our jets made ready. I want them under twenty-four-seven surveillance, and at the very first chance you get, I want both the papyrus and the bitch . . . and the professor. I'll need them to decipher it. Borg El Arab in Alexandria is far easier than Cairo International, so you can operate in and out of there. Once we get them to the villa on Corsica and the document's deciphered, we'll get rid of them. As for O'Connor, eliminate him, but watch him . . . he won't be easy.'

Within minutes of the debate concluding, Omega's attack-dog editor in chief, Joe Humphrey, had masterminded the headlines and held discussions with his boss, Louis Walden.

'That's a pretty quick poll,' Walden said.

'There wasn't time to take a large sample, but come Tuesday that'll be lost in the noise. We've got the momentum, and it's building,' Humphrey said, neglecting to tell his boss the poll had been taken around the office. There were some things Louis didn't need to know.

CAMPBELL INSISTS ON CLIMATE TAX

An Omega Centauri poll taken just after the fourth presidential debate gave it to the Republican Party's candidate, Governor Carter Davis of Montana, by a decisive margin. After the Democratic candidate, former Energy Secretary Hailey Campbell, foreshadowed a tax on carbon emissions that will cost hundreds of thousands of jobs and stall an already fragile economy, some analysts are predicting Governor Davis will take the White House in a landslide. By next Tuesday, it's almost certain that Governor Davis will be the president-elect.

Rachel nodded in approval as she read Omega's internet coverage, which she knew would be replicated in all their news outlets the following morning.

It was five a.m. in Giza, but O'Connor and Aleta had risen early to watch the debate. Now they sat sipping coffee together, staring at the early poll that put Davis ahead.

'I can't believe the American people would vote for someone like Carter Davis,' Aleta said, looking at her laptop, 'but if this poll is right, he'll soon be in the White House.'

'And that asshole Walden's pushing it for all it's worth,' O'Connor said, 'although it wouldn't be the first time a major media organisation has sought to change a government.'

O'Connor's encrypted phone beeped.

'Oh no,' Aleta said, holding her hand to her mouth.

''Fraid so . . . A ship we've been tracking is getting ready to depart Manaus. I think you'd better come back with me to the States . . . I don't like the idea of you being here on your own. There are powerful forces at work here.'

Aleta shook her head. 'I'll be okay. Professor Badawi has plenty of room at his place. His wife died a few years back, and he said I was very welcome to stay. Plus, he has a safe.'

'I'd still be a lot happier if you came back with me.'

'So you can leave me to go off doing God knows what? I'm an archaeologist, Curtis, and the last time I looked, unless I can get a job in the Smithsonian, there's not much scope for my work in Washington. How long are you going to be gone this time?' she asked, her voice softening as she got up and stood behind him, sliding her hands down his shirt.

It was late in the evening as Rachel waited in the hotel lobby while Davis accepted the congratulations of well-wishers, his Secret Service detail ever watchful.

Crowley, she knew, would have watched the debate from his penthouse office, just across town. It was the closest she'd been to him for weeks, and once again, she found herself stifling thoughts of him with Miranda, but they continued to eat away at her. Her mind made up, she would ensure Davis was safely in his suite, and then try to spend an hour or two with Crowley . . . After tonight, she'd earned it, she told herself.

'The momentum is with us,' Rachel told Davis, as she escorted him to his suite. 'I have to go out for a while, but absolutely no more interviews. We're on the home straight here – there's less than forty-eight hours to go.'

She headed back to the lobby where she got the concierge to hail her a cab.

'EVRAN Towers,' she said, not bothering to provide the address. Rachel felt the excitement that came with her old position. There wasn't a cabby in Dallas who didn't know how to find the company's massive skyscrapers.

'I'm sorry to bother you, Governor Davis,' the woman on the hotel switchboard said, 'but I have one of your Secret Service men with me, and if you agree, he's okayed a call from Mr Cronkwell. Can I put him through?'

'Of course,' Davis said, downing his third double whiskey.

'Walter . . . great job at moderating tonight, I really appreciated it.'

'The pleasure was all mine, Governor.'

'What can I do for you?'

'I know this is a little irregular, Governor, but I've cleared it with your Secret Service detail and there's someone I'd like you to meet . . . Susan Murkowski from our network.'

'Delighted – send her on up,' Davis said, pouring himself another double. 'I'm in the Ritz-Carlton suite. I'll let the Secret Service people in the corridor know she's coming . . . And don't let me take up *your* time – you deserve a rest.'

'Thank you, Governor,' said Cronkwell, hanging up the phone. He winked at Murkowski. 'All set. Got your chastity belt on?'

'Susan – may I call you Susan?' said Davis, opening the door to Murkowski. 'Come on in.'

'Of course – thank you, Governor,' she said, following him in to the stylish lounge and dining room with soft lighting and elegant velvet couches. A large walnut sideboard took up one wall. 'What a wonderful view.' The best suite in the hotel commanded panoramic views of the city lights.

'What can I get you – a wine? Whiskey? Bourbon and soda?'

'Oh, I'm fine, Governor . . . I'm not a big drinker.'

'Nonsense. What'll it be?'

'Well, a red wine, if you have one.' Murkowski noticed the governor was already a little unsteady on his feet.

Davis disappeared into the kitchen area and returned with a Californian Broken Earth cabernet sauvignon.

'Come and join me on the couch,' Davis said, pouring Murkowski a large glass. 'What did you think of the debate?'

'I thought you did very well, Governor,' said Murkowski, refraining from adding she thought Hailey Campbell had done better.

'Yeah . . . I don't know what Hailey's smokin', but, if you'll pardon my French, she sure as hell doesn't get this climate change bullshit.' Davis rested his hand on Murkowski's knee.

'Can I get you another whiskey, Governor?'

'Why, that's mighty nice of you . . . don't mind if I do. Good drop, this Eagle Rare.'

'You've run a very successful campaign, Governor,' Murkowski said, pouring him another whiskey from the sideboard. 'And you have some very big backers.' She returned to the couch, handing Davis the crystal tumbler.

'Louis Walden's been right behind you,' she continued, 'but there's been an enormous amount of money spent on advertising . . . close to $800 million?'

'More than that,' the governor said, putting his hand back on Murkowski's knee. 'My backers have very deep pockets.' Murkowski kept a neutral expression, but the governor wasn't looking at her. His eyes were fixated on her cleavage. This, Murkowski thought, is going to require careful handling. On the one hand, avoiding his attempts to grope her, and on the other, getting him hammered enough to divulge all the information she wanted.

45

CIA HEADQUARTERS, LANGLEY, VIRGINIA

'Things are starting to move.' McNamara brought up the latest imagery on his wall screen. 'This satellite picture is less than two hours old and you can see the *EVRAN I* has entered the Amazon River again and is approaching Manaus. You must have done a pretty good job – they had to tow it to a dry dock in Rio de Janeiro, and it's taken them nearly nine months to repair her.' McNamara was delighted at the very thought of it. 'Crowley would've been apopleptic. We haven't managed to get anyone on the inside, but we've had EVRAN timber under constant observation the whole time. If the missiles are there, my guess is Crowley won't risk them on anything other than his own ship, but we'll see. They'll be loading her just as soon as they can. Oliveira down in Brasília's done a good job – the paperwork indicates she's destined for Karachi, and ten armed guards were observed boarding her.'

'Which adds strength to the hypothesis that she's carrying missiles,' said O'Connor. 'You don't need armed guards for cargoes of timber.'

'Precisely.' McNamara pulled up some detailed images of the ship. 'As container ships go, she's not particularly big – about 20 000 tonnes – but you can see the containers for'ard of the bridge are stacked three high, and aft of the bridge, she's capable of carrying forty large containers lengthwise, four containers high, ten to a row. Your task is to board her, overcome any resistance, and see what you can find.'

'Before or after breakfast?'

'I'll leave the timing to you,' said McNamara, grinning broadly, 'although perhaps during the early hours of the morning might be best. But if there's nothing on board, we're fucked and there'll be one hell of a stink from Crowley, but judging from the intercept Murray picked up between Khan and the Taliban we should hit paydirt.'

'What assets have we got?'

'I've briefed the chairman of the Joint Chiefs, the chief of Naval Operations, and the commandant of the Marine Corps, and we agreed not to rope the president into this until we're certain . . . as long as I carry the can if things go wrong.'

'Decent of them.'

'The guided-missile destroyer USS *Lassen* was due for some home porting maintenance at Station Norfolk, but the crew's been recalled from leave.' Located south of Washington in Norfolk, Virginia, the huge base was the largest naval station in the world, with seven miles of piers supporting over seventy warships and aircraft on the Sewells Point area of the Hampton Roads peninsula.

'I'll bet they're pleased about that.' It was a part of being in the military the public didn't see, and the sacrifices the young men and women made, along with their families, were often not well understood.

'No aircraft carrier or nuclear submarines?' Even after all the years of working with Tom McNamara, O'Connor never ceased to be surprised at his boss's contacts and his ability to pull the right strings.

'They're still busy in the gulf. Besides, if we need those, we're in a bigger pile of shit than we think. The *Lassen*'s due in Belém about now.' The capital of Brazil's northern state of Pará was the gate to the Amazon and the port was one of the nation's busiest. 'One of our jets is standing by at Andrews to fly you into Val de Cães international, and from there you can join the *Lassen*. She's carrying a replacement crew for the *EVRAN I* and you'll have the same team you had in the Korengal Valley.'

Here we go again, O'Connor thought.

'The *Lassen* will shadow the *EVRAN I* out of the Amazon, and as soon as she's clear of Brazil's territorial waters, you can implement a VBSS operation.' VBSS, or Vessel Board Search and Seizure was something the navy, marine corps and United States coast guard all trained for to varying degrees, but both O'Connor and McNamara knew this operation was at the high-risk end of the scale.

'Any thoughts?' McNamara asked.

O'Connor recognised his tone of voice, and it was time to get serious. 'I'll have to kick it around with the SEAL team, but we've got the usual options. I'm assuming the *Lassen* will have two Sea Hawk helos, but Crowley's thugs don't fuck about, and we'll take a lot of fire if we try to land or fast-rope onto either the for'ard or aft containers. I suspect the best option might be to go for a night boarding using rigid hull inflatables, and use the *Lassen* and the helos as a diversion. I mean, we'll ask the *EVRAN I* to heave to, but . . .'

'Yeah . . . I think you're going to have to fight your way on board.'
O'Connor had no way of knowing how true that would be.

The *EVRAN I* cleared the mouth of the Amazon River just before
midnight, on a south-easterly course across the South Atlantic
Ocean that would take her around the Cape of Good Hope, from
where she would turn north across the Indian Ocean and the Arabian Sea to dock in the teeming Pakistani port of Karachi. Wisal
Umrani, the master of the *EVRAN I*, checked the radar screen on
the bridge. The traffic entering and leaving the Amazon had been
heavy earlier, but now the number of blips on the screen had dimin-
ished. Apart from one contact about five miles astern, and three
more well to the north and south, the seas ahead looked relatively
clear, and Umrani began to relax. His crew had been augmented
by ten heavily armed guards. When he'd queried it, he'd been told
it was necessary for protection against pirates. Other than that, it
looked like it would be a normal voyage, and Umrani, a Pakistani
by birth, was looking forward to a few days R&R with his young
family in his home city of Karachi.

O'Connor finished introducing the members of SEAL team six to
the captain of the USS *Lassen,* Commander Tom Guivarra, and his
men went below decks to carry out a final check on their gear. There
wasn't a man among them who would rather be anywhere else,
including O'Connor's number two, the lanky Chief Petty Officer

Rudy Kennedy, Petty Officer Louis Estrada, and Alejandro 'Chico' Ramirez, the team's intelligence operator.

O'Connor stared at the dark ocean ahead. The 9000-tonne *Lassen* was armed with Harpoon, Tomahawk and surface-to-air missiles, vertical launching systems, 127-millimetre, 25-millimetre and 12.7-millimetre guns and 20-millimetre Phalanx close protection systems. Life for those on board the *EVRAN I* was about to get interesting, he thought.

An hour later, the captain swivelled in his chair on the bridge. 'She's just into international waters,' Guivarra said, 'so any time you like, we'll crank this baby up.'

'Let's go,' O'Connor said with a grin, his teeth showing white against a blackened face.

'Full ahead!'

'Full ahead, sir!' There was nothing Tommy Guivarra liked better than an excuse to put the pedal to the metal. Top speed was classified, but it was in excess of 30 knots, and the *Lassen*'s General Electric gas turbines transmitted an enormous burst of power. Almost immediately, a huge feather of foam shot out from the stern as the big twin screws reached their peak revolutions.

Three nautical miles astern of their quarry, Guivarra slowed the destroyer to allow the launch of the two 11-metre RHIBs carrying O'Connor and his men. The rigid hull inflatables, or RHIBs, were capable of a staggering 70 knots, twice the speed of the destroyer.

O'Connor crouched in the bow of the lead RHIB, along with four members of SEAL team six. The seas were around one metre, and the RHIB flew off the top of the swells, becoming airborne before crashing down with a bone-shattering thump, clouds of spray flying either side of the bow. Chief Petty Officer Kennedy was in the bow of the second RHIB, and O'Connor knew that he could not have asked for a better team.

'Captain . . . there's an unidentified ship approaching.' *EVRAN I*'s first officer had been watching the fast-closing blip on the radar. Normally he would hesitate to call the captain from his cabin, but this looked anything but normal.

Umrani rubbed his eyes as he came on to the bridge. 'What is it?'

'The radar, Captain,' the first officer said, pointing to the screen glowing with a soft green light. A single green line from the centre of the screen was circulating, and each time the radar signal was dead astern, the blip was highlighted. 'Whatever that is, it's got to be doing 30 knots, and it's coming up on the starboard side.'

'Hold your course.' Umrani picked up a set of binoculars and walked out on to the starboard wing. He adjusted the focus and picked up the *Lassen*'s slim bow profile and the high, arcing bow wave. Puzzled, he walked back in to the bridge.

'It's naval . . . looks like a destroyer or a frigate. We'll be on their radar, and the weather's reasonable, so they must have seen us .`. . Wait, they're signalling us to heave to,' he said, reading the flashes from the destroyer's bridge. 'Signal back *Why? We are the* EVRAN I, *a container ship bound for Karachi.*'

The reply was swift. *We know that. This is USS* Lassen. *Heave to.*

Umrani shrugged. 'Slow astern,' he ordered, not wishing to put too much strain on the newly repaired screw.

'What's going on!' Diego Sánchez demanded. Umrani had disliked Sánchez from the moment he'd come on board. The tall, solidly built commander, like the rest of his guards, was dressed in black.

'I'm heaving to . . . I'm not sure why, but there's a US Navy ship coming up behind us, and they've ordered us to stop.

'The hell they have . . . Keep going.'

'I'm the captain of this ship, Senor Sánchez, and what I say goes.'

Sánchez whipped out his pistol and put it to the head of the astonished captain. 'Full ahead, or you've just given your last order.'

The colour drained from Umrani's face. 'Full ahead,' he ordered the equally astonished officer of the watch.

'All guards on deck, López to the bridge,' Sánchez ordered over his two-way radio. A short while later, Sánchez's second-in-command appeared.

The officer of the watch on board the USS *Lassen* was on to the move in a flash. 'She's picking up speed again, sir.'

'They're going to do it the hard way,' Commander Guivarra acknowledged. 'Get the birds up.'

First one Sea Hawk, then another, took off from the stern of the destroyer and adopted a holding pattern at 3000 feet, ready to create a diversion. Guivarra, seated in his captain's chair, picked up his binoculars and grinned. They must be hurting big-time, he thought, as he focused on the RHIBs, smashing their way across the waves, well out to the port side of the *EVRAN I*.

'Slow down,' O'Connor ordered the coxswain on the RHIB, 'we're almost abeam of her now.' He flipped the safety catch on his M14. Over to the south-west, O'Connor could see the *Lassen* taking up station on the starboard side of the *EVRAN I*.

'*Lassen*, this is Hopi One Four, in position over.'

'*Lassen*, copied out.'

Suddenly, the night sky was lit up further to the south-west. Staying out of range of any small arms fire, the Sea Hawks were discharging flares, far enough away so as to not light up the sea around the container ship, but sufficiently abnormal to attract attention. As the flares lit up the sky, the guards on board the *EVRAN I* took up positions on the starboard gunwales.

'Go, go, go!' O'Connor ordered, and both coxswains gunned the RHIBs to over 40 knots, approaching the container ship from her port side.

The RHIBs made it to the side of the *EVRAN I* and one after another, the grappling ladders were fired from their compressed air launchers. O'Connor and Kennedy led the way, followed by the rest of the team.

On the bridge, Sánchez watched the flare display for some time, but then he smelled a rat. He dashed across to the portside wing, in time to see the last of the SEALs clambering over the side.

'*Merda!* Shit!' He fired at the disappearing figures and the bullets twanged off the steel superstructure. 'López! Portside! Repel boarders!' Sánchez screamed into his two-way.

O'Connor sent CPO Kennedy and three men to cover the port side, while he led Petty Officer Estrada and the rest of them, dodging around companionways, past sea cocks and hatches. The first two guards came running toward the stern, and O'Connor fired two quick bursts. Both fell, clutching at their chests, their AK-47 Kalashnikovs clattering to the deck. The three guards following them immediately took cover, and sparks flew as the air was suddenly thick with bullets ricocheting off the steel bulkheads.

'Man down!' One of the SEALs had been hit, but O'Connor and Estrada pressed on, taking out the three guards with short but deadly accurate bursts of fire. 'Five down . . . five to go!' Estrada yelled. O'Connor smiled to himself. In tight spots like this, the Estradas and the Kennedys of this world were irreplaceable. Firing broke out on the port side as CPO Kennedy and his team accounted for two more.

O'Connor moved forward, more cautiously now. He propped by the next bulkhead and signalled Estrada to freeze. There it was again. A movement about 20 metres down the companionway that ran under the containers. O'Connor ducked as his quarry opened up with another burst of AK-47 fire. The noise in the confined space was deafening. His quarry changed magazines, exposing his left shoulder and O'Connor fired again, taking him out. 'That's eight!' he called to a grinning Estrada, who had taken cover behind a heavy steel stanchion. After yet another sustained burst of fire on the port side, CPO Kennedy came up on the headsets. 'Another thug down.'

'By my count, that leaves just one, and I suspect he'll be on the bridge,' O'Connor replied. 'Cover the portside, we'll take the bridge . . . How's the casualty?'

'Stomach wound – not good, but he's stable.' Every member of the SEAL team was trained in first aid, but on this mission they'd brought along a hospital corpsman, who was working to stem the blood flow.

O'Connor and Estrada moved forward alongside the bridge superstructure and O'Connor cautiously opened a hatch, only to find a terrified crew member cowering in the companionway. O'Connor waved a calming open palm at him and moved on toward the ladder leading to the bridge. Sparks flew as Sánchez emptied his pistol from outside the bridge hatch. O'Connor ducked and waited till the firing stopped. He aimed instinctively and fired back, and Sánchez tumbled down the ladder landing at his feet, pistol still in hand.

O'Connor kicked the pistol away, recognising Sánchez as the same thickset thug who'd set the dogs on the protesters at the EVRAN timber yards in Manaus.

'He's still alive . . . truss him,' O'Connor said, taking the ladder to the bridge, where he found a white-faced captain and an equally white-faced first officer and helmsman.

It had taken nearly three hours of searching, but four containers on the aft deck eventually yielded their secrets: thirty-two gleaming Taipan and Scorpion missiles hidden among loads of EVRAN ipé timber.

'I appreciate you may not have known about this cargo,' O'Connor told a very frightened Umrani in fluent Portuguese, 'but that's for others to decide,' he said. 'You and your crew are confined to your cabins, and you are to obey the orders of the stand-in crew who will be taking this ship back to Norfolk . . . *Entendes*? Do you understand?' O'Connor indicated the marines who were already boarding to crew the ship.

Umrani nodded vigorously.

Four hours later the USS *Lassen* docked back in Belém, and O'Connor thanked his host.

'What a pity you couldn't stay. Belém is not without its night life,' Tommy Guivarra said, as he accompanied O'Connor to the gangplank.

'Next time,' O'Connor said with a grin, shaking the commander by the hand and saluting before he and the rest of his team headed off to board the waiting CIA jet.

46

RITZ-CARLTON HOTEL, DALLAS, TEXAS

Hugh Watson, the Washington bureau chief for CNC, and Walter Cronkwell listened. Over a few well-earned beverages of choice, Susan Murkowski, now returned to Cronkwell's room, related her late night session with Governor Davis.

'He's like a fucking octopus, Walter. Thanks very much for setting up that little soirée . . . not!'

'He wouldn't be the first one in the White House to have wandering hands, buddy,' Watson said. 'The question is what the fuck do we do with what you've got? It's fucking dynamite!'

'It's all of that,' the elder statesman of the journalist fraternity agreed. 'Never in all my years of covering Washington and presidential elections have I ever seen anything like this.'

The three veterans of the inner beltway were old friends. In the hard-bitten world of journalism, it was the survival of the fittest, and this team had seen it all, at least until now.

'I mean you'd have to go back to 1988 and fucking Gary Hart and the Donna Rice affair to rival this,' Watson said. 'You're probably too young and gorgeous to remember . . . can I stroke your inner thigh?'

'Fuck off!'

It was some time before they all stopped laughing. A release from the tensions of an extraordinarily tough campaign. It was a tough gig, and there was nowhere tougher than inside the Washington beltway.

'I remember the Hart affair well,' the elder statesman said. 'What was the dare to the Press Corps? "Follow me around. I don't care. I'm serious. If anyone wants to put a tail on me, go ahead. They'll be very bored." But they weren't!' There was more laughter as Cronkwell poured himself another bourbon. 'The *Miami Herald* had been on to Hart for weeks before he came out with that shocker . . . they'd actually identified Donna Rice as the woman seen leaving Hart's Washington apartment.'

'Yeah . . . and what was Hart's defence . . . they hadn't watched both entrances?' Watson chuckled.

'And the usual shit . . . the wife came out and stood by her man.' Murkowski shook her head.

Watson, who played a pretty mean guitar in his spare time, in the West Texas Crude band, broke into song. 'Stand by your man . . .'

'Don't give up your day job,' Murkowski said, pouring herself another chardonnay. 'Jesus . . . have I drunk the whole bottle?'

'There's another in the fridge,' Watson said, getting up to retrieve it. 'What is it that young women see in powerful men?'

'I read an article on that once,' said Murkowski. 'They've done a lot of research, and men and women who need power also have a greater need for sex. They're apparently linked, because they both cause an increase in hormone testosterone, and that ramps up the dopamine, a chemical messenger in the brain, activating a reward network.'

'Bloody hell . . . at least it might explain why fat, ugly, rich men attract beautiful women, but to be serious . . . I'm not sure we can run this. Two days before the election? All hell will break loose, and you're going to be in the spotlight, not only from the media here, but the world's media.'

'I can handle that, Hugh. It's not just that this guy's an asshole, or even a creep. There's been plenty of those . . . look at Nixon, or if you want to go back, Harding. All sorts of assholes have occupied the most powerful office in the world, but it's different this time. When Davis, albeit legless, told me that Sheldon Crowley was backing him up to his boot straps, my immediate thought was it's illegal. But more importantly, if Davis wins, and he almost certainly will, EVRAN is in control of the White House.'

'Woudn't be the first time a president has been beholden to the big end of town,' Cronkwell observed. 'Look at Woodrow Wilson . . . obscure professor at Princeton who had an affair, and the likes of the Rothschilds and Rockefellers had him over a barrel.'

'But if we publish this, and Davis still wins, he might then be impeached, or at the very least, he'll be a lame duck president,' Watson said, 'and with China on the rise, I don't think the country can afford that. I wonder if this is one of those times we remain silent.'

'I can't help wondering about the assassination of Abigail Roxburgh, though. She might have been about to spill the beans on Davis,' said Murkowski. 'The question is, who bumped her off, and on whose orders?'

'Has an election ever been delayed?' Watson mused.

Cronkwell shook his head. 'Never. Some of Abraham Lincoln's aides urged him to suspend the 1864 election because of the civil war, although that probably had as much to do with his aides believing

Lincoln was going to lose. Lincoln was having none of it. He believed the election was a necessity. From memory, he said "We cannot have a free government without elections; and if the rebellion could force us to forgo, or postpone, a national election, it might fairly claim to have already conquered us." And there's no authority for it,' Cronkwell added. 'Congress commissioned some research when there were fears that the November 2004 elections might be threatened by terrorism, and that report found the president has no authority to postpone an election, so McGovern couldn't do it . . .'

'And wouldn't want to,' said Watson. 'It would look like the Democrats were trying to manipulate the result.'

'So any postponement would require Congress to pass a law,' Cronkwell concluded, 'and at the moment, that mob on the Hill are flat out agreeing how they're going to govern themselves. Perhaps we should sit on this and hope Hailey gets across the line.'

Murkowski took another sip of wine, but the euphoria of the first few glasses was fading. 'I don't think she's got a snowball's chance in hell. No one can try to do something about global warming in this country without earning the wrath of the rich and powerful, who have most to lose. If we don't expose this, and it later comes out we knew all about it, we're going to be crucified. I think I should at least put a call through to his bitch-face campaign manager and let her know what we've got.'

Crowley and Watson both pondered the suggestion.

'I mean, she's hardly likely to spill the beans. She'll just deny it, but at least we can say we put it to them?'

Crowley nodded in agreement.

'Give it a shot,' Watson said.

47

MELBOURNE AND DALLAS

Qureshi and Said stood together, looking across Melbourne's iconic Port Phillip Bay. The second most populous city in Australia, Melbourne was known as the sporting and cultural capital of the nation, where the largest network of trams in the world had rattled around the bay and inner suburbs since the late 1800s.

Qureshi glanced around him. The terrace on the Eureka Skydeck viewing platform was open and windy, and only four other tourists were out here, all of them focused on the bayside suburbs of Brighton and St Kilda to the south-east. But even the tourists crowded on the other side of the airlock were being bombarded with deadly doses of radiation, as were the occupants of the building itself. He whispered to Said, 'Now we will join the Prophet Muhammad, peace be upon him.'

Qureshi quietly inserted the detonator cord into the slot in the briefcase, and held it up against the wire mesh with the backing plate against his chest.

An alert security guard inside the viewing platform had watched the odd behaviour, and he rushed for the airlock.

'Hey you!' he yelled, running toward the two young men.

Qureshi turned, smiled, and pressed the detonator.

The massive explosion engulfed the terrace, killing him, Said, and the security guard instantly.

The wind caught the fine particles of Cobalt 60, taking them around the sides of the skyscraper and back across the Yarra River toward the city. The greatest concentration of radioactivity was around Flinders Street and the lower ends of Queen and Elizabeth streets, but the winds took some of it further afield, where it settled on the footpaths around office buildings as far north as Lonsdale Street, east to Exhibition Street, and west as far as William Street.

Sirens filled Melbourne's graceful streets as emergency workers rushed to the Eureka Skydeck building, unaware of the stream of gamma rays emanating from the lookout. But it was not long before word on the radioactive blast got out, and spread like a fire in high winds. Chaos enveloped the city, and those who couldn't get on the crowded trams were fleeing on foot. Parents pushing strollers had tears rolling down their cheeks and the streets were in gridlock as office workers scrambled to get their cars out of the underground car parks. Unable to get free of the traffic, some motorists abandoned their cars where they were, bringing the city to a standstill.

Crowley hung up on Aboud, and took another encrypted call from Khan.

'The first part of Phase Two has been successful, Sheldon.'

'You've done well, Farid.'

'There is still a little matter of your part of the bargain, Sheldon. I'm ready to pick up the Van Gogh.'

Crowley's lips tightened. Compared to Vermeer's *The Concert* and Rembrandt's *Storm on the Sea of Galilee,* Vincent van Gogh's *Poppy Flowers* was a minor acquisition, but he still hated to part with it. That said, Khan might be needed in the future.

'I'll probably be in Corsica very shortly. Quite possibly before the election. I'll let you know when you can pick it up.'

Crowley put down the receiver just as Miranda returned with the Grand Cru.

'Should I dim the lights, Sheldon?'

'Let's leave them on,' he said, not yet tired of admiring her trim body and her perky breasts. Crowley repaired to the couch and poured two more glasses of Romanée Conti. 'To us,' he said, clinking the fine crystal with Miranda's. She sipped her wine and put her glass down, her breasts swinging freely under her loose silk dress.

'Where were we . . .' she whispered huskily, running her hand through Crowley's fine grey hair.

Eighty-two floors below, Rachel keyed in her code just as her phone rang.

Rachel hung up from Murkowski's call and shook her head in disbelief. On the Sunday before the election, Davis gets maggoted, puts the hard word on one of the best-known journalists in the country, and spills the beans on EVRAN. She keyed in another code and took Crowley's private lift to the eighty-second floor, wondering how long her denial would hold up.

Rachel got out of the lift and stifled a gasp. The sounds emanating from Crowley's office were unmistakeable.

'Fuck me, Sheldon! Fuck me hard!'

'I'm going to come,' Crowley grunted.

'I'm coming too, Sheldon . . . oh *fuck*!'

'So. This is what you get up to when I'm not around.'

Crowley got off Miranda and turned to find a furious Rachel glaring at him.

'What I get up to when you're not around is none of your business, Bannister,' Crowley growled, recovering and quickly reverting to type. But his mind was racing. Rachel knew far too much. He finished putting his trousers on and Miranda, delighted that Rachel was now on the outer, retreated down the carpeted corridor to what had once been Rachel's office.

Crowley walked over to his desk and unlocked the drawer where he kept his pistol.

'As you won't be needing me any more, I resign,' Rachel said through clenched teeth, struggling to control her fury. 'You arrogant, deceitful bastard! After all I did for you, and this is the way you repay me!'

Crowley shrugged.

'And as your latest squeeze seems to have taken my position, she can run the rest of the Davis campaign. Her first problem is going to be a big one. Before I came over here, I escorted that creep you want to put in the White House to his suite. He's got himself so pissed he wouldn't know where he was, and the Secret Service has somehow allowed that journalist, Murkowski, in to see him. Until now, I've managed to force Davis to keep his dick in his pants, but as soon as I was out of sight, he's put the hard word on Murkowski, and in the process, spilled his guts on you and EVRAN. I suspect the authorities are going to be all over you like a rash in the morning, and I hope it costs you and Davis the election. You bastard!

I hope you rot in hell!' Rachel turned on her heel.

'Hold it right there!'

Rachel turned back to find Crowley pointing his gun at her, and in an instant she realised her mistake. Her knowledge of EVRAN would be her downfall, and a wrenching fear tore at her guts.

'Sit down!'

Crowley picked up the phone. It was time to get out, at least until the election was over. By the time the FBI found out he'd fled to Corsica, the election would be done and dusted. With his hold over Davis, he had no doubt that his return could be orchestrated. In the meantime, Miranda would have to step in and handle the next forty-eight hours.

48

LONDON AND CHICAGO

Nadar and Boulos squeezed past the other tourists on the narrow landing of St Paul's Golden Gallery at the top of the great dome. They waited until there were two vacant spots on the northern side, which overlooked Paternoster Square and the London Stock Exchange. Nadar placed his briefcase on top of the metal guardrail, and surreptitiously connected the detonator cord. He needn't have worried. The other tourists, oblivious to the deadly gamma rays, were all absorbed in the sweeping views of London.

Nadar turned to his young companion and smiled.

'*Allahu Akbar!*' he shouted. Tourists turned in alarm. Nadar screamed again, uncontrollably now. '*Allahu Akbar!*' The briefcase exploded in a horrific blast of fire and smoke. Millions of fine particles of radioactive Cobalt 60 drifted across the stock exchange and the financial district, the wind carrying residues as far as New Oxford Street to the west, Pentonville Road to the north, and the Moorfields Eye Hospital to the east.

Within minutes, London's streets were filled with sirens.

The northerly wind was blowing strongly across the roof of the Willis Tower in downtown Chicago. Touma and Botros took a last look across Lake Michigan.

'This will bring the Great Satan to his knees,' Touma said, extracting the detonator cord and plugging it into the socket in the briefcase. They walked around the rooftop to the southernmost area which overlooked the crucial financial district. Hundreds of metres below them, thousands of workers sat glued in front of their screens, watching for fluctuations in the markets around the world. The Dwight D. Eisenhower Expressway was packed with cars and buses, and on West Jackson Boulevard, the coffee shops and pizza bars were doing a brisk business.

'Let's do this together, said Nasib and he and Botros grasped the detonator.

'*Allahu Akbar!*' they shouted in unison. The explosion bent the antennae off their footings and the wind quickly spread the Cobalt 60. Within minutes, deadly gamma rays enveloped the busy, thriving city.

49

CAIRO

'Have you heard from your man?' Badawi asked Aleta as they descended the front steps of the Cairo Museum and headed toward his carpark.

'I wish,' Aleta said. 'I've come to accept that there are things he does that I can't know about . . . and to be honest, I think I'd rather not know. I'd die worrying about him.'

The hot, velvet Cairo night was closing in, and Ruger observed the pair from a distance as they got into Badawi's Volvo.

'Are you in love with him?' Badawi asked.

'I'm not sure that "love" in the normal sense of the word is a good descriptor,' she said, as they headed south along the Nile Corniche. Badawi's villa was in Maadi, a fashionable suburb on the banks of the river to the south of Cairo in the older area of El Sarayat.

'I care deeply about him, and we share a lot of interests . . . and, dare I say it, there is a sense of adventure about him that I'm crazy for, but I take it one day at a time.'

Ruger followed at a distance. He knew where they were going – Area 15 had already provided the address. Having cased the villa earlier, he'd confirmed that Badawi was the only occupant – no servants, not even a gardener. His plan was simple, and sometimes the simple plans were the best.

Rather than having names, most of the streets in Maadi had numbers, and Ruger closed up on the Volvo as they drove along Street Thirteen and turned off into Street Eighty-Six. Ruger slowed as the gates on the villa swung open and he followed Badawi up his short drive.

Ruger leapt from the car and wrenched open the door of the Volvo.

'Get out of the car, both of you, now!' he ordered. 'Do exactly as you're told and no one is going to get hurt. Inside the house. Move it!'

Shocked, Aleta and the professor did as they were told.

'Empty your pockets, slowly, and no false moves. You first, Professor Badawi.'

Aleta glanced at her mentor. At first she thought they had fallen victim to one of the increased numbers of robberies taking place since the tourist dollar had dried up. Now she wasn't so sure. If their assailant knew their names . . .

Ruger pocketed Badawi's mobile phone. 'Now yours, Doctor Weizman,' he said, pointing his gun at her.

'Into the study, both of you,' Ruger ordered

Once in the room, he turned to the professor. 'Open the safe.'

Aleta's heart sank. It was becoming clear what the purpose of the robbery was, but she had no way of knowing what was to follow. She and the professor would soon be bound and gagged, and headed for Corsica.

50

LUCAS HEIGHTS NUCLEAR REACTOR, SYDNEY

'Look what they've done for Allah in Melbourne, Iqbal!' Hazim Gerges, the younger and more fiery of the two jihadis, almost spat the words at his fellow terrorist, Iqbal Safar. 'Why are we waiting?'

'There's been nothing posted on the stamp website. We were told to wait.'

'We don't even know who we're waiting for, Iqbal. He's probably dead by now. Look at the carnage in Melbourne, *Alhamdulillah* . . . thanks be to Allah!' Gerges pointed to the television. The coverage of the chaos had been non-stop since the attack.

'We have the explosives, wire cutters, and thanks to our contact on the inside, we know where to put them. We need to move, Iqbal! Are we soldiers for Allah? Are we *Mujahideen* or not?' The term literally meant struggle.

'We *are* Mujahideen,' Safar agreed. 'We'll go tonight.'

Safar kept to the speed limit as they drove out of Liverpool and south along Heathcote Road. It was after midnight and the traffic was light and Safar drove steadily around a long sweeping bend.

'That's the intersection,' Gerges said excitedly, as the New Illawarra Road, which would have taken them to the entrance to the nuclear reactor, loomed up on the left.

Safar slowed and extinguished the lights as he pulled off the shoulder into a spot they'd reconnoitred earlier. It was partially hidden from the highway. They quickly extracted from the boot their big backpacks filled with explosive, AK-47 Kalashnikovs and wire cutters, and together they headed into the bush toward the reactor, Safar leading.

Safar checked his compass. 'It's a little over 200 metres to the fence, Hazim,' he said. Ten minutes later, they reached the fence at a point near Einstein Avenue, and Safar went to work with his heavy wire cutters.

Back on the highway, a police patrol car picked up the terrorists' parked car in their headlights.

'What do you reckon that is, Sarge? Abandoned?' Constable Murphy mused as he slowed.

'Dunno . . . pull in behind it and we'll run a rego check.' New South Wales patrol cars were equipped with the most sophisticated image-recognition cameras available, and hundreds of thousands of registration plates were fed into the police central computers every day, identifying stolen cars – and a surprising number that were not registered.

'Registered to an Iqbal Safar at an address in Liverpool, so he's local,' Constable Murphy said.

'Run a check on him,' Sergeant Willis replied, shining his torch into the vehicle.

'Nothing unusual inside the car,' he said.

'And no criminal convictions, Sarge, but he's on ASIO's radar . . . spent time in Syria, but they couldn't pin anything on him.'

'Ordinarily I'd say he might have broken down,' the alert sergeant remarked, 'but he's parked as far into the bushes as he could get it, and the bloody reactor's only about 200 metres in through there. Put a call through to Security. Tell them we don't want to be alarmist, but just in case.'

'Move it, Iqbal,' an agitated Gerges urged his partner. 'There are cameras on this fence.'

The phone rang in the central security guardhouse.

'Okay,' Bill Sullivan said, 'thanks for the warning.' The duty guard checked the screens. 'Jesus Christ!' he swore. His colleague looked up from his paperwork. 'What's up?'

'The southern border fence near Einstein Avenue,' Sullivan said, pointing to the screen. 'Sound the alarm, and grab your weapon.'

'They're on to us!' Gerges said nervously as a siren began to wail. They climbed through the fence and raced toward the new OPAL reactor on the western side of the complex.

The security car, lights flashing, came flying along Rutherford Avenue and down Fermi Street, catching the terrorists in the headlights.

'You – hold it right there!' Sullivan yelled. He and his partner both leapt from the car, pistols drawn.

Safar had spent many months in Syria, training for just such a moment. He calmly fired two bursts from his AK-47, killing the guards instantly.

'Security's four-wheel drive . . . we'll go in that,' Safar yelled. He gunned the Toyota down Mendeleeff Avenue, lined up the entrance to the reactor and floored the accelerator. The vehicle bounced up the steps and the bull bar hit the doors in an explosion of glass, setting off more alarms.

Armed with the layout of the reactor, Safar blasted his way through several more doors, Gerges urging him on from behind. They reached the reactor's pool. Glowing an eerie blue and contained by reinforced concrete, it was precisely this design that would work in their favour. The concrete block would direct the force of the explosion into the core of the reactor, spilling the highly radioactive coolant, and exposing the core.

The sirens were growing in the distance. Safar quickly connected the detonators to the 50-kilogram ammonium nitrate bombs in each backpack.

'*Allahu Akbar! Allahu Akbar!*' the pair screamed together as Sergeant Willis' patrol car and a second and then a third patrol car screeched to a halt and the police ran into the building, guns drawn.

For Sergeant Willis and his young constable, it was their last day on the job. The massive explosion ripped the heart out of the reactor, and the reinforced concrete block concentrated the explosion against the core. Freed of its coolant, the core began to heat dangerously toward a meltdown, as thousands of litres of radioactive coolant escaped.

51

CIA HEADQUARTERS, LANGLEY, VIRGINIA

Barbara Murray was shown into McNamara's office where he was following the financial carnage on Wall Street on the TV screen. They could see the despair on the faces of the brokers and traders amid the chaos on the floor of the New York stock exchange.

'The Melbourne bombing sent a shudder through the markets,' CNC's finance correspondent observed, 'and the London and Chicago bombings started a wholesale sell-off, but when the Australian nuclear reactor was bombed, raising the prospect of attacks on other nuclear facilities, the markets went into free-fall.' Her face white, the normally calm and well-respected correspondent was clearly rattled. The shot cut first to the streets of a deserted Chicago, then Melbourne, and then to London, where vast areas of the city north of the River Thames had been evacuated, including the financial district. Then there were images of Sydney, the harbourside city eerily deserted, the streets jammed with cars and vans, left when their owners fled on foot. Smoke was still billowing from the reactor at Lucas Heights, with the authorities desperately trying to contain the meltdown. Outside the hospitals, patients – both the seriously ill and the 'worried well' – had spilled on to the footpaths. The situation had only been made worse by the numbers of doctors and nurses who had also fallen ill.

'No analyst has been brave enough to predict where this might end, but the Dow Jones has suffered its biggest one-day fall since records began,' she said. 'After the closure of the Strait of Hormuz, the markets fell 62 per cent, but already we're in unthinkable territory, and a short while ago, the Dow had fallen a staggering 71 per cent. It would have fallen even further were it not for some aggressive buying that once again is thought to be coming from the Crédit Group banks.'

McNamara turned to Murray. 'If that were the only problem we had, we could probably get by,' he said, a grim look on his face. 'I've just been advised that Doctor Weizman and Professor Badawi have been taken hostage,' and he brought Murray up to date on the seizure of the missiles aboard *EVRAN I*.

'Do we know who's responsible for the kidnap?'

'There's been no announcement as to who might have done it . . . although obviously we have our suspicions.'

'Pharos?' Murray asked.

'Or Crowley . . . or Crowley acting on behalf of Pharos. Crowley's not in Dallas, and his office is saying they can't comment on the chairman's whereabouts for security reasons. The president's called an emergency meeting of the National Security Council, but as soon as that breaks up, I'll clear the way for a warrant to search EVRAN's headquarters on the basis of the missile discovery. But it's still not a smoking gun – for all we know, Crowley may not be involved, so we'll need some top cover.'

'Where's O'Connor at the moment?'

'On his way back from Belém in the Amazon. Why?'

'Because you may want to redirect him to Venice, or at least alert the Italian *polizia*,' she said, passing over a top-secret summary of her latest intercepts. 'After some months in hospital, Khan has recovered, and is now in Venice picking up what we suspect is the Tutankhamun falcon pendant from Rubinstein. He obviously still has a lot of pull in the Pakistani military, because he's travelling on a Pakistani Air Force Gulfstream IV executive jet, and interestingly, its return flight plan is via Figari Sud-Corse.'

'Corsica?'

Murray nodded. 'We're still working on it, but one of those intercepts seems to indicate that he has something else to pick up . . . I can't be sure, but it seems very odd that a Pakistani Air Force jet would be using an airport other than Corsica's main international one.'

McNamara read the transcript, and for a while said nothing, weighing up the risks. 'If we alert the Italian *polizia,* they'll want to bring in the Guardia di Finanza, their financial police, and that will make the media. If there's a connection with Crowley, that may tip his hand, and put Weizman and Badawi at even greater risk . . . if they're still alive,' he added chillingly. 'It's risky, but I think we'd better get O'Connor to have a look inside Galleria d'Arte Rubinstein.'

52

VENICE

Three a.m. O'Connor put Aleta out of his mind as he crossed the Calle Ghetto Vecchio bridge. The Campo del Ghetto Nuovo square was deserted, and he made his way silently toward the narrow cobblestoned alley, and to Galleria d'Arte Rubinstein's entrance, a wooden door at the far end.

O'Connor smiled grimly to himself. The entrance was unmarked and there was no sign of a burglar alarm. Perhaps the last thing Rubinstein wanted was the Italian *polizia* poking around his gallery and he relied on anonymity for security. If you had business with the dark side of the art world you would know where to go. The door was heavy and old, and the lock was almost as old – a 'five-pin and tumbler' barrel lock. He delved into his shoulder bag and extracted a small tension wrench and a selection of picks. Two minutes later, the old door swung easily on its heavily oiled hinges and O'Connor closed it gently behind him and listened. Nothing. He switched on his torch and made his way through a strangely sparse display room, down a stone passage and into a back room. O'Connor closed the door, and confident it would not be seen from the passage or square outside, he switched on the light and looked around.

Neatness was not one of Rubinstein's long suits, he thought, as he was confronted with two heavy desks, piled high with papers, art magazines and other paraphernalia. Set in the stone wall on the far side of what appeared to be Rubinstein's office was the heavy steel door of an old combination safe with a single dial.

O'Connor extracted a stethoscope from his bag, spun the dial to clear the tumblers and placed the stethoscope diaphragm on the gradations. He turned the dial very slowly to the right until the cam and lever mechanism engaged with a click. Standard 25 as the last number, he thought.

Working slowly, as he'd been taught on his course by an old master safecracker recruited from the dark side, O'Connor rocked the dial back and forth until he picked up a soft *nikt* on 68. A while later, he picked up another *nikt* on 52 and he allowed himself another grim smile as the final *nikt* in his earpiece fell on 33. He quickly cleared the tumblers, and dialed in the combination. The rusty handle turned with a clunk and he swung the vault door open.

O'Connor let out a low whistle as he recognised a Picasso, a Monet, a Gauguin and a Matisse, the proceeds of a break-in to the Kunsthal art gallery in Rotterdam in the Netherlands; but it was the old locked trunk in the corner of the vault that caught his eye.

He had it open in an instant, and he extracted the first of several leather journals and thumbed through what was clearly one of Rubinstein's *real* books of account, arranged by client, in alphabetical order. It took less than a minute to find the transactions attributable to Crowley, and O'Connor let out another whistle. He ran his eye over a voluminous list of priceless stolen art: a Rembrandt and a Vermeer from the Isabella Stewart Gardner Museum in Boston, Turner's 1813 *Landscape in Devonshire*, and Vincent van Gogh's *Poppy Flowers*. The criminal world no longer surprised O'Connor, but the sheer audacity of the last entry was extraordinary: 'Funerary mask of Tutankhamun €110 million'. Perhaps even more importantly, a very minor stolen Egyptian artifact had, three years earlier, been consigned by courier, to a villa in the mountains north of Sartène on the island of Corsica.

O'Connor photographed the pages relevant to Crowley and turned his attention to the Khan entries. The list was not as extensive, but again, it was the last entry that caught his attention: 'Tutakhamun falcon pendant €60 million'.

He photographed the Khan entries and relocked the old trunk.

As the CIA Gulfstream jet levelled off at 30 000 feet, O'Connor eased into one of the secure communications stations and put on the headphones for an encrypted call back to Langley. He briefed McNamara on what he'd discovered in Rubinstein's art gallery, and then listened as McNamara brought him up to speed on the FBI raid on EVRAN.

'The FBI have uncovered a commercial intelligence operation in EVRAN headquarters that would rival what we've got here,' said McNamara. 'While that's not illegal in itself, it would appear that Davis was in possession of Walter Cronkwell's script before the debate. That will send the media into a tailspin and call the whole Davis candidacy into question, but that's not our problem. The question is, where is Crowley? Because I'm hoping Crowley will also lead us to the whereabouts of Badawi and Aleta, over.'

'Hopi One Four, roger . . . the address I gave you for Crowley's Corsican villa puts it in the hills above Sartène, and if Khan's aircraft is headed for Figari Sud-Corse, there's a strong chance that he's headed for the villa as well. If Crowley can't be found in Dallas it may be that he's in Corsica too. Let's hope so, over.'

'Roger . . . I've been in touch with my contacts in Paris. They've agreed we should search the villa, but they've also told me it's heavily guarded, so they're readying a detachment from their Groupe d'Intervention de la Gendarmerie Nationale.'

O'Connor nodded as he listened. He'd worked with the group before and it was one of the best. A special forces unit of the French military, they were specifically trained to deal with counter-terrorist and hostage rescue missions.

'Given the circumstances, and what we have riding on this, the French have agreed to a joint mission, which will be launched from Figari Sud-Corse, and I put that about 50 kilometres from Crowley's villa. I didn't want you to feel lonely, and since they've been with you from the start, your Korengal team is inbound to Corsica as we speak. As to the Pharos Group, the trading on the stock market by the Crédit Group of banks has come to the attention of the Securities and Exchange Commission and the Commodity Futures Trading Commission, and we've sent them across a top-secret brief. Apparently it's raised more than a few eyebrows, and our chief of station in Cairo is liaising with his counterparts to organise a raid on the Kashta Palace in Alexandria.'

O'Connor moved back to one of the big, comfortable leather chairs in the cabin, and as the pilots changed course for Corsica, he once again had to detach himself from his feelings for Aleta.

53

CHÂTEAU CORNUCOPIA, CORSICA

Crowley pushed the button under his desk in the stone-walled study of his château, and the huge 80-inch screen rose silently from the sideboard. He flicked on CNC to get an update on the election, but he first had to sit through images of the continuing panic on the streets of London, Chicago, Sydney and Melbourne. When the anchor finally got to the election, Crowley listened intently for any mention of what might have happened in Dallas.

'So in summary, Susan,' Cronkwell concluded, 'when Americans go to the polls on Tuesday, it looks as if a sizeable majority will be voting for Carter Davis.'

'That's right, Walter. Even in normally solid Democrat states like Illinois and Delaware, people are worried about their jobs. People have a lot of respect for Campbell, though here's what one woman in Delaware had to say.' A woman in her late fifties appeared on screen, outside a store in West Loockerman Street.

'Don't get me wrong. I have a lot of respect for Hailey . . . a lot of respect. And I admire her determination to tackle global warming, but I work for a big chemical and pharmaceutical company. I've still got a mortgage and I'm worried about my job, so I'll have to vote for Carter Davis – not so much because he's a committed Christian and an upright man, although I think we need that in a president, but because I think he'll do the best for the economy.'

'If the polls are right, Walter, come inauguration day, it will no longer be Governor Davis, but *President* Davis.'

'That was Susan Murkowski, reporting from Governor Davis's home state of Montana, where the governor is spending the last day of the campaign.'

Crowley flicked off the broadcast. Despite the Dallas incident, the journalist hadn't reported it. Perhaps it wasn't nearly as serious as Bannister had made out. Oblivious to the FBI raid on his head-quarters and his estate, Crowley's spirits rose. Things were getting untidy, and although the Egyptian media and some international media were carrying the story, he was confident no connection had been made between him and the disappearance of Badawi and Weizman. As soon as they had deciphered the Euclid Papyrus, Ruger could eliminate both them and Bannister in the one hit.

'We need to delay on this as long as possible, Hassan,' Aleta said. Since their arrival in Corsica, they'd been locked in a stone-walled section of the middle floor of the villa. 'I've got a feeling that Crow-ley's need to have this translated without letting anyone else know what's in it is the only thing keeping us alive.'

Professor Badawi nodded. 'I agree. And it's easy to see why.

I think Euclid's interpretation of the drawings of Khufu's engineers is very accurate. When you think about it, there's a lot of energy tied up in the planet, and I'm not talking about fossil fuels – there's magnetic, thermal, electrical . . . a whole range of sources, including what Khufu's engineers discovered about vibrations and frequency resonance. We can hear the hum of an aircraft engine, but if you slow those revolutions down to the earth's rate of once in every twenty-four hours, we can't.'

Aleta nodded, looking at the notes on the papyrus. 'Exactly. The earth's pulse would be huge, but inaudible. From what I'm reading here, Khufu's engineers managed to tap into the earth's vibrations and use them as a source of unlimited energy.'

'We've always gone with the herd's tomb theory,' said Badawi, 'but the Euclid Papyrus blows that out of the water.'

Aleta nodded, staring at the hieroglyphics. 'It's all here. The Egyptians built this massive pyramid, designing it as a precise mathematical correlation of the dimensions of the earth . . . that much we've known for some time. But this is proof they found a way to convert the earth's vibrational energy into what we know as microwave energy – with the pyramid's very precise dimensions enabling it to vibrate in harmony with the earth. That energy was channeled through a series of resonators in the grand gallery and converted into airborne sound which passed through an acoustic filter in the antechamber, and on in to the King's Chamber.'

'And that explains why the chamber was devoid of the usual hieroglyphics and why, instead of being made from limestone blocks, the walls were made out of specially quarried granite,' said Badawi. Despite their grave predicament, the old professor was excited. The mystery had puzzled him for decades.

'And if you look here,' Aleta continued, pointing to another papyrus leaf, 'the King's Chamber was constructed with dimensions that created a resonance that was in harmony with the incoming sound. The specially quarried granite then vibrated in sympathy, stressing the quartz in the granite, which started a flow of electrons.'

'What today we call the piezoelectric effect,' Badawi agreed. 'It's quite extraordinary – so complex, yet so simple.'

'Curtis would be proud of me,' Aleta said, smiling wistfully, 'even though I'm only reading Euclid's notes. By this point the Egyptians had generated enormous and unlimited acoustic and electron or electromagnetic energy. The hydrogen which was produced down in the Queen's Chamber, resonating at the same frequency, absorbed the energy from the King's Chamber, and the single electron in the hydrogen atom was pumped up to a higher energy state.'

'In other words, the hydrogen now has energy stored in trillions upon trillions of atoms. We know the northern shaft to the Kings chamber was originally lined with metal. Khufu's engineers would have used those to focus a low-energy beam . . . the same cosmic microwave background beams that are constantly bombarding the earth today. This would have then reacted with the highly ener-gised hydrogen atoms, forcing the electrons back to their original state and releasing the stored energy, generating an immensely powerful beam that could then be channelled out through the metal-lined southern shaft. The Egyptians would have then har-nessed that power, which explains why many of their constructions have been planed to within thousandths of an inch.' Badawi let out a low whistle. 'The existence of this papyrus has been rumoured around the souks for decades, and I suspect Crowley must have had some inkling of just how explosive this technology is . . . it could consign his precious fossil fuel industry to the past.'

Aleta's eyes lit up. 'We may have found a way to leave the oil in the ground!' And then just as quickly her spirits sagged as the door opened and Crowley entered.

54

FIGARI SUD-CORSE AIRFIELD, CORSICA

'This is Sheldon Crowley,' O'Connor said, flicking up an image of the silver-haired industrialist. The French Groupe d'Intervention de la Gendarmerie Nationale, or GIGN team, had commandeered one of the small office complexes away from the main terminal of the small provincial airfield. It had not escaped O'Connor's attention that the airport was also favoured by Crowley. Two of EVRAN's Gulfstream G550s, their stylised volcano logos prominent on their fuselage, were parked well away from any other aircraft.

'He's wanted in the United States on suspicion of high treason, and if possible, we want to take him alive. He may have up to three hostages with him,' O'Connor said, flashing up photos of Aleta, Professor Badawi and Rachel Bannister, in turn, before switching to a photograph of Khan.

'This is Lieutenant General Farid Khan, ex-head of the Pakistani Inter Service Intelligence agency, whom we suspect of coordinating the recent attacks on Chicago, London, Sydney and Melbourne, and on the Strait of Hormuz. We suspect he is also in the villa, and we have evidence that both he and Crowley are involved in dealing in stolen art and ancient artifacts.' O'Connor didn't elaborate. The Tutankhamun mask and the falcon pendant were, for the moment, in a need-to-know compartment. The press would soon enough cover this operation, without turning it into a media circus.

'The villa is located in the mountains above the town of Sartène,' O'Connor continued. 'The only entrance by road is well guarded, and there may be guards in the surrounds. For that reason, we're opting for combined air assault on to the top-storey balcony, here,' he said, flicking up the latest satellite imagery. The stone fortress-like villa was perched high on a rocky outcrop, with each corner reinforced with an external stone turret. The only thing that appeared to remove it from the fifteenth century was the mass of aerials and dishes on the highest portion of the moss-covered roof.

'GIGN, call sign Hopi One Three, will be in the lead helicopter, and the US SEAL team, call sign Hopi One Four, will follow in the second chopper. GIGN will clear the top floor, and once that's secure, we will clear the lower floors, but that may change, depending on what we find. You can leave that to Capitaine Durand and me. Should the opposition get tiresome, we'll be supported by a Eurocopter Tigre attack helicopter which will keep the guards on the gate pinned down until we can deal with them, and we'll use the captured villa as a base. H hour is 1830 hours. Any questions?

Two of the Korengal team exchanged glances and raised their eyebrows. Things were never dull around O'Connor.

The two AS 532 Cougars lifted off just before dusk, the GIGN team in the lead helo, followed by the Tigre. O'Connor looked around his crew, and he felt a surge of pride to once again be with the old team. CPO Kennedy, PO Estrada and the rest, their faces blackened, were sitting calmly on the floor. The best of the best, O'Connor mused.

They climbed quickly toward the rugged mountains to the north, the pilots' visors reflecting the soft glow of the instrument panels. Down on the Mediterranean coast to the south, the lights of communes like Bonifacio flickered in the night.

55

CHÂTEAU CORNUCOPIA, CORSICA

General Khan's driver slowed at the heavily fortified entrance to Crowley's villa in the mountains above Sartène.

The guard, dressed in black, with an earpiece in his ear and armed with an Uzi submachine gun of the type favoured by the Israelis, peered into the black Mercedes.

'Could I see your passport?'

The guard handed back Khan's passport and stepped back. 'Mr Crowley is expecting you,' he said, opening the heavy wrought iron gates.

From his seat in the second chopper, O'Connor's gaze was fixed on the lead Cougar as it approached the top-floor patio. Suddenly there was a burst of gunfire from the guardhouse. The four-bladed twin-engined Tigre attack helicopter immediately dived from its station above the assaulting Cougars. The gunner fired four withering bursts of 30-millimetre cannon fire, temporarily silencing the guardhouse, but the damage was done. Smoke was pouring from one engine and the lead Cougar lurched offline, the pilot forced to put it down hard on the lawns in front of the château. The French counter-terrorist forces fanned out, and were immediately engaged by guards further down the drive.

Crowley, his own weapon drawn, withdrew from the patio, just before the Tigre attack helicopter raked it with fire in preparation for O'Connor and his SEAL team's assault. His mind racing, Crowley made for the rooms where Badawi and Aleta were being held.

'Get moving!' he ordered, forcing the pair out into the stone passage and across to his office. With one eye on his hostages, he punched in the codes to the subterranean vault.

'Put your hands on top of your heads! Down the stairs!' He locked the door behind him and followed, still trying to form a plan.

'Hold it there!' Crowley walked past them, waving his gun menacingly. He punched in the final code, flicked the override switch for the computers and turned on the lights. 'In there!'

'*Mon Dieu!*' Aleta held her hand to her mouth. There, among the priceless artwork, in a case of its own, was the mask of Tutankhamun.

'Sit at that desk over there, both of you, and if you so much as move a muscle, you'll get a bullet through the head!'

Crowley sat at another desk as a plan began to form in his mind.

The rappelling ropes fell like long black snakes on to the patio, and O'Connor and CPO Kennedy, followed by the rest of the team, dropped to the cobblestones.

'We'll clear it room by room,' O'Connor ordered.

'Christ . . . that might take a while. Look at the size of this fucking place,' Estrada muttered.

A burst of fire came from inside the villa and O'Connor returned the compliment. Ruger, badly wounded, tumbled from the position he'd taken up in the ceiling on some heavy wooden beams. The team found Khan, cowering in a corner, and he was immediately handcuffed and arrested.

Down by the guardhouse, Capitaine Durand was putting in a final assault.

The SEALs did what they'd so often done when clearing houses in hostile towns and villages in Iraq and Afghanistan. Room by room, floor by floor, they cleared Crowley's stronghold, finding nothing other than terrified catering staff. It wasn't until they cleared the north tower that they found Rachel Bannister, tied and bound in a stone-walled room.

'So where's Crowley likely to be holed up?' O'Connor asked Rachel, after he'd listened impatiently to her story. O'Connor was desperate to find Aleta, but he maintained an outward calm.

'There's a vault,' Rachel said, eyes wide, and she led O'Connor and Kennedy to Crowley's office.

'Stand back . . . fire on!' O'Connor shouted.

He and his team took cover as they blew the locks on the heavy vault door. When the smoke cleared, they cautiously descended the stone steps, only to be confronted by a second steel door.

'Fire on!' O'Connor and Kennedy retreated back along the

stone passage. M14s at the ready, they waited for the smoke to clear. O'Connor steadied himself. Crowley was standing at the door with a gun to Aleta's head.

'Back up the corridor, or the bitch gets it!' Crowley growled.

O'Connor and Kennedy retreated back to Crowley's office. Crowley and Aleta emerged, the archaeologist white as a sheet with Crowley's gun to her head.

'Now here's how we're going to play it,' Crowley snarled. 'Your helicopter is going to take me and the bitch back to Figari Sud-Corse. The pilots are to land beside the EVRAN Gulfstreams. One false move by the French police or anyone else, and she gets it.'

Crowley had failed to notice Rachel, who'd been standing in his office, behind the vault door. With her life in ruins, she had nothing to lose. She picked up a massive iron paperweight and brought it down with all the force of a woman scorned, fracturing Crowley's skull.

56

O'Connor and Aleta watched President McGovern make his announcement on television, watched by hundreds of millions around the world.

The president left out the gruesome details – there was enough chaos on the markets without disclosing that counter-terrorist forces in New York had foiled an attempted attack on the Indian Point nuclear reactor, and that British forces had been similarly successful in preventing an attack on the Hinckley Point reactor in Somerset. Nor did he mention that the police in Montana had matched the tyre tracks near Abigail Roxburgh's Lolo homestead to a hire car from Missoula. Ruger had made the cardinal mistake of not wearing gloves throughout. His prints had not been hard to match. Instead, President McGovern stuck to his core message.

'As you all know, Governor Davis has resigned his presidential candidacy, just twenty-four hours before the people of this great nation are due to go to the polls. That has no precedent in our history, and many people have been calling for me to postpone the election. Even if I had the power to do that, I wouldn't. Abraham Lincoln was one of the greatest presidents ever to grace this White House, and when he was faced with a similar situation, albeit as a result of the Civil War, he had this to say: "We cannot have a free government without elections; and if the rebellion could force us to forgo, or postpone, a national election, it might fairly claim to have already conquered us."

'Although the circumstances are different, the message of the great statesman is just as pertinent today. We will never let terrorists and traitors conquer the very foundations on which this nation has been built.'

O'Connor and Aleta stood at the balustrade of Crowley's villa, looking down on the lights of Sartène, twinkling through the mists.

'So Crowley *was* Pharos,' Aleta mused.

'He was always at short odds,' said O'Connor, 'but with a powerful group like that, you could never be sure. They were all power mad. But none of them could have succeeded without the rest . . . I shudder to think what might have happened if they had.'

'Will they arrest them all?'

'Hard to say, but Crowley and Khan are going to spend the rest of their lives in gaol. I heard from McNamara that we got the terrorist ringleaders in Afghanistan with a drone strike out of Creech on a little village called Laniyal.' O'Connor allowed himself a grim smile at the memory of the blazing firefight in the Korengal Valley.

'And how about Hailey . . . what a landslide! But what a job in front of her.'

'I suspect now that the panic is subsiding, the clean-up of the Cobalt 60 in London, Chicago and Melbourne won't take as long as the media thinks. The stock markets are already starting to climb, although the reactor spill in Sydney's on a par with Fukishima . . . it will be quite a while before that city returns to anything like normal.'

'I think Hailey will do a great job,' said Aleta. 'Now we can actually *do* something about getting this global warming under control. To President Campbell,' she said, raising her glass to O'Connor's.

'Crowley has quite a good cellar,' O'Connor said, savouring the Clos des Goisses, 1988.

'Had,' Aleta said, moulding her body into his.

AUTHOR'S NOTE AND ACKNOWLEDGEMENTS

Until Daniel Estulin published his bestselling *The Bilderberg Group*, little was known about the secretive annual meetings of the world's wealthiest CEOs, royalty and political elite. The participants are household names: David Rockefeller, Henry Kissinger, Queen Beatrix, Tony Blair, to name but a few who, over the years, have attended the heavily guarded meetings. The group gets its name from the first meeting, promoted by Prince Bernhard of the Netherlands, and held at the luxurious Hotel De Bilderberg in the small Dutch village of Oosterbeek. Since then, the Bilderberg Group has met every year in a luxury hotel somewhere in the world – like the five-star Marriott in Copenhagen, the site of the 2014 meeting.

The secrecy surrounding political leaders meeting with the world's wealthiest industrialists has spawned myriad conspiracy theories, ranging from a downright evil cabal run by neo-Nazis, to the US Republican Party being run by Bilderbergers behind the scenes. This author makes no such accusation, but he keeps an open mind. That said, as the reader will have gathered, there is no doubt as to the aims of the Pharos Group. According to Oxfam, eighty-five people in the world share a combined wealth of $1.7 trillion – equal to that of the poorest half of the world population – 3.5 billion people. Oxfam argues that a growing inequality is being driven by a power grab by the small number of wealthy elites who co-opt the political process to rig the rules of the economic system in their favour. Manipulation of the world's stock markets is a distinct possibility, and the obscene wealth of the Crowleys of this world continues to be generated unabated, in the face of 80 per cent of the world's population living on less than $10 a day, with 22 000 children dying each day, because of poverty. We are a screwed-up species.

And manipulation is not confined to the stock market. Big Tobacco spent millions trying to manipulate public opinion, employing scientists and consultants to create doubt over the harmful effects of smoking, and to this day, Big Tobacco will not publicly admit that smoking causes lung cancer – notwithstanding it has understood the carcinogenic nature of its product for decades. When it comes to global warming, people like the fictional character of Professor Ahlstrom exist in real life, handsomely paid by the big emitters to promote the idea that global warming is a myth. Ahlstrom draws our attention to the snowstorms in the United States in 2013–14 as proof there is no such thing as global warming – yet scientists are well aware those snowstorms were caused by global warming fracturing the polar vortex and releasing very cold winds from the Arctic. The big emitters, those with most to lose, are taking the same approach as Big Tobacco. The more carbon taxes that are repealed, the better their bottom line – for the moment. Granted, no one country can tackle climate change on its own – we have to do it in concert – but as a species, we lack the leadership to achieve that, so we can expect ever increasingly destructive wildfires, snowstorms, hurricanes and cyclones – planet earth's reaction to what we're spewing into the atmosphere. Our grandchildren had better get used to it, for it is they who will pay, after it's too late.

As to religion and politics, religion has long been at the root of many of our tragically destructive wars, going back well before the Crusades. Many fundamentalists – Muslims, Christians, Orthodox Jews, Hindus, Buddhists, Calathumpians – all firmly believe they tread the one true path – yet if that's so, only one group can be right, and the other gods are entitled to be confused. The three great monotheistic religions all have their roots in Abraham, and Muhammad reportedly advised his early converts, 'Treat well the people of the Book', meaning the Christians and the Jews. 'Only argue with the People of the Book in the kindest way – except in the case of those of them who do wrong – saying, "We believe in what has been sent down to us and what has been sent down to you. *Our God and your God are one and we submit to him* [my italics]." ' (*Qur'an*, 29:46). Not much sign of that, as the barking mad brigade in ISIS seeks to impose a worldwide Caliphate and Sharia law from Syria and Iraq; Sunnis and Shi'ites continue at each others' throats, blowing up each other's mosques; fundamentalist Christians campaign to ensure not one square centimetre of the Holy Land is allowed into Palestinian hands; and some of the Orthodox Jews plot to destroy the al-Aqsa Mosque on Jerusalem's Temple Mount – the third holiest site in Islam – so the Third Temple can be built in its place. The most 'intelligent' species on the planet spends trillions developing ever more powerful weapons of mass destruction, and as they fall into the hands of religious terrorists taught by barely literate imams, our grandchildren had better get used to ever increasing levels of violence.

As I pen this note, hundreds of Palestinians, including four innocent boys playing football on a Gaza beach, have been killed by Israeli air and artillery strikes; and on the other side, Hamas keeps firing rockets on innocent Israelis. We could find a way to achieve peace – grant the Palestinians statehood as we said we would when the United Nations voted to partition Palestine on 29 November 1947. Resolution 181 recommended the creation of independent Jewish and Arab states, but decades later, only one state – that of Israel – has been achieved. We could grant the Palestinians East Jerusalem – al Quds as their capital. We could leave the largest Jewish settlements in the Occupied Territories in exchange for Israeli land, and remove the smaller ones back to greater Israel. It's complex, but the choice is stark – either settle for peace, or, as a screwed-up species does, keep bombing the living daylights out of one another, destroying innocent lives and families on both sides, in the forlorn and absurd hope that one side will give up.

Some who read this book will undoubtedly criticise me for giving terrorists ideas; they will not be the first. But my military background nothwithstanding, if these people think it takes an author like me to publish blueprints for terrorists, then we are in more trouble than we realise. Although privy to top-secret material in my past profession, I never publish anything that has not already been published on the internet – I simply put myself in the position of a terrorist with a laptop and a satellite link. It took me just minutes, for example, to find papers, published on the internet, on the weaknesses in the defences of the world's nuclear reactors, including the efforts of the nuclear industry to water down recommended improvements on the basis of cost. I am an optimist, but the longer I watch the collective performance of our species, I can only conclude that 'God' was having a bad hair day when she designed us (and that especially goes for her design of teeth, and root canal therapy).

I am indebted, as usual, to a great many people who have made this novel possible. Understandably, some do not want to be named, but you know who you are. The work of academics and Egyptologists like Graham Hancock, Robert Bauval, Christopher Dunn (*Lost Technologies of Ancient Egypt*) and many other researchers too numerous to mention has been invaluable. I am also grateful to my publisher Ben Ball, and the extraordinarily hardworking team at Penguin Random House. I am blessed to have two very fine editors in Belinda Byrne and Arwen Summers, and the proofreading by Sarah JH Fletcher was meticulous; any mistakes are mine and mine alone. Adam Laszczuk has once again excelled in the production of the cover. I am indebted to the PR team, headed by Sally Bateman and Alysha Farry; and to Peg McColl and Kate McCormack from the rights department who work so hard on my behalf at the world book fairs. Clare Forster, my agent at Curtis Brown has, as always, provided invaluable advice and support.

My thanks to Caroline Ladewig, who kindly read the early drafts and provided insightful feedback. To Antoinette and friends – I'm in your debt. To my two boys, David and Mark, and their partners Tammy and Catherine, I greatly value your humour and camaraderie. Finally, Robyn, as always, has been an invaluable ally, not least for her impeccable research.

The characters and organisations in this novel, such as Crédit Group, are entirely fictional.